Love Object

Love Object

a novel

Sally Cooper

THE DUNDURN GROUP
TORONTO · OXFORD

Editor: Barry Jowett
Copy-editor: Lloyd Davis
Design: Jennifer Scott
Printer: Transcontinental

Canadian Cataloguing in Publication Data

Cooper, Sally (Sally Elizabeth)
    Love Object

ISBN 1-55002-387-X

I. Title.

PS8555.O59228L69 2002   C813'.6   C2002-901067-5   PR9199.4.C665L69 2002

1   2   3   4   5   06   05   04   03   02

Canada

THE CANADA COUNCIL | LE CONSEIL DES ARTS
FOR THE ARTS | DU CANADA
SINCE 1957 | DEPUIS 1957

ONTARIO ARTS COUNCIL
CONSEIL DES ARTS DE L'ONTARIO

We acknowledge the support of the **Canada Council for the Arts** and the **Ontario Arts Council** for our publishing program. We also acknowledge the financial support of the **Government of Canada** through the **Book Publishing Industry Development Program, The Association for the Export of Canadian Books**, and the **Government of Ontario** through the **Ontario Book Publishers Tax Credit** program.

Care has been taken to trace the ownership of copyright material used in this book. The author and the publisher welcome any information enabling them to rectify any references or credit in subsequent editions.

J. Kirk Howard, President

Portions of *Love Object* in an earlier form appeared in *The Coastal Forest Review*.

Printed and bound in Canada.
Printed on recycled paper.

Dundurn Press
8 Market Street
Suite 200
Toronto, Ontario, Canada
M5E 1M6

Dundurn Press
73 Lime Walk
Headington, Oxford,
England
OX3 7AD

Dundurn Press
2250 Military Road
Tonawanda NY
U.S.A. 14150

For my family

1

You Are Somewhere

My Uncle Larry Brewer has meek snores: a mew followed by a sigh or a gasp, nothing like the riotous carols I'm used to hearing from my father Sam or from Grandma Vi. The effort of straining to catch Larry's snores is what wakes me up inside those first two dreams of Mother.

It's the Saturday of Canada Day weekend, July 2, 1983, and Larry's down to help Sam insulate the addition before returning up north to Drag County to wait for his next job. Our place in Apple Ford is one of Larry's stopovers on the Sudbury-Windsor route he's been running four times a year since my mother Sylvia left in 1978. He parks his rig at the arena and snort-laughs when Nicky and I beg to sleep there. Vi has just moved in with us but she makes a point of staying at a friend's after she sees Larry and Sam playing euchre at the kitchen table with Nicky and me.

When he plays euchre, Larry says he likes to imagine a real court, an upside-down court where the knaves, the jacks, the everyday guys have authority over the king. In most games the jack is the lowest face card but not euchre. In the euchre court, Larry points out, the queen is down near the bottom where she belongs. The order of the game appeals to Larry, the reversal of fortunes that comes when he least expects. He relishes the terminology too. Trump. Trick. Bower, which comes from the German *bauer*, meaning peasant or knave.

"Euchre is about the triumph of the *KNAY-vuh*," Larry says, drawling out the word as if he is afraid he sounds too smart. "I'm a perfect example. A jack-of-all-trades. I've driven bus, sharpened saws, cut hair, laid pipe, chopped trees, cleaned ditches, plowed snow." Hauling steel is the most gainfully employed Larry has ever been.

Vi says, "As far as I'm concerned a jack is a scoundrel. Just look up knave in the dictionary, Mercy," she says and I do and she is right.

"Not just *scoundrel*," I read, "but *rogue* and *rascal* too."

Larry flutters his eyelids then squints and talks in a flat Clint Eastwood voice until Vi leaves pulling her suitcase across the plywood floor of the addition.

Sam plays cards with indifference but we know better; Sam has memorized every possible combination of cards in a given game. He can quote Hoyle and he lays cards without looking at his hand. To add flair, he has devised several precise gestures and difficult manoeuvres: shuffling the deck away from his body, using one hand to deal, turning up cards with the flick of a finger. He wins every game then acts as if he has no idea why he bothered to play in the first place. The romance of the court and the beauty of inverted power delineation do nothing for Sam. To him, cards are a math problem and he plays with the confidence of one who understands the true nature of numbers and can manipulate them to lie for him and only him. A notion that each deal might bring something new and never been before is what causes his brother Larry to lose most times he plays. This same sense of mystery is also what spurs Larry to play again and again.

Saturday I wake up before my alarm with the sheets wound in knots around my legs. My skin, sticky with sweat, holds a pickled brine smell. Sylvia's crocheted afghan lies in a heap on the floor. Before doing anything else, I pick up the afghan and straighten it on the bed, Sylvia's instructions still ringing clear after five years. I'm less than a month away from my seventeenth birthday but I still have the same little girl's room Sylvia did up for me as a grade-six graduation gift: the white ruffled curtains, bed skirt and pillow shams, the blue fleur-de-lis wallpaper, the oval hooked rug with cardinal and jays on a leafy branch, the furniture painted white with gilt trim. True, posters of David Bowie in his suit and fedora do hang next to Sylvia's framed 3-D collages of humming-birds and finches and Stephen King has joined Lewis Carroll and the Brothers Grimm, but the rest is the same as it was before Sylvia left.

With a lamp on, I stand in front of the round dresser mirror that cuts me off at the shoulders. I am proud of my body this summer. Last summer, filing claim adjustment forms for Sam's insurance office, I gained ten pounds from sitting all day dipping into a bag of Licorice Allsorts in my desk. This summer I cycle to and from the Trout Club and spend my evenings in the back yard painting planks for the addition's board-and-batten siding. My legs and arms reflect my efforts. A hard muscle curves out on the back of each thigh and my arm pops a bulge when I flex.

11

My summer job is bussing tables and washing dishes at the Tecumseth Trout Club, an exclusive resort for fishermen. Members stay in the main lodge, coming for a weekend or a week.

The Club backs onto the Tecumseth River and sits away from the road, protected from local eyes by thick bunchy cedar. The Tecumseth River courses down from the escarpment and through the Trout Club ponds, swings around Apple Ford, then hustles back west to hie itself across a golf course and head south. In April the province dumps trout into the river and fishermen with rubber boots stretching over their trunks cluster along the road and railway bridges that cross the Tecumseth east, west, north and south of Apple Ford. The Trout Club stocks its man-made ponds at the same time.

The Trout Club kitchen has three deep sinks, for soap, bleach and rinse, banked on each side with grooved porcelain counters. If I leave early enough, I will be first at the sinks — before Duncan Matheson, my drying partner, arrives for the morning shift. I pull on shorts, tank top and sweatshirt, slip into my moccasins and catch my hair in a red plastic headband. At the Club, I will change into the requisite gabardine A-line skirt and white blouse.

Larry's plaintive murmurs drift up from the pullout sofa, Sam's joyous croaks chiming in from his summer bed on the front porch. I keep to the edge of the stairs to silence the creak, my ear cocked after each step for any variation in the snores' timbre and pitch but I hear none. I tiptoe through the living room though I needn't bother. Larry lies in a fetal clench with a rust velour seat cushion, the blankets low enough on his hips to reveal pale blue boxers under his white T-shirt. In the kitchen, my head hits Sylvia's macramé lampshade as I reach across the table to snatch my K-way from a chair. I tuck a strawberry Pop-Tart into my pouch and enter the addition. The room, with its newly dug cinder-block basement and west-facing window, is cool and smells of sawdust. Pillows of pink fibreglass insulation in white plastic bags are stacked against the far wall studs. A neat pile of dust, scrap wood and nails sits in the middle. Sam's tool belt hangs over a rod in the closet. I cross the plywood floor, open the new red door and jump onto the clumpy dirt. The sky is shifting from grey to pink.

The addition is Sam's idea, announced to Nicky and me as a family project at Christmas. With Vi here it makes some sense but in two years Nicky and I will likely be off to university or college and Sam won't need more space.

"Makes for a better house. More proportionate," Sam says to silence anyone who asks.

What is more important is that Nicky and I help so that we'll learn how and because the house is ours too or might some-day be. Nicky pitched in from the beginning, his bent neck patterned with knotted jute shadows as he and Sam pored over the blueprints. Sam accepted each excuse I gave when he suggested tasks, but once the walls went up he got adamant so I've agreed to paint the boards he is using to cover the outside. Painting is easy and I can do it away from interference — or so I thought.

Last Saturday, Sam and Nicky took the Dodge to pick up the planks from a lumberyard and piled them under an orange plastic tarp beside the small barn we call the garage. When I came home from the Trout Club, Sam showed me the paint and a red milk crate full of supplies. I waited until my next day off while Sam was at work before I wrestled the sawhorses out behind the garage where Sylvia's vegetable garden used to be and laid a long board across them. I flipped the milk crate on top of spread newspapers for a table. I placed a brush, a coffee can full of Varsol, some rags, a screwdriver, a hammer and a stir stick in a semicircle around the open paint can, stood back to admire the arrangement, then got to work.

The boards took longer than I thought and I got to counting the strokes and measuring the paint, saturating the brush to make each dip last. I propped each plank against the garage wall when I finished one side.

I wiped at my brow with my forearm, careful to hold the paintbrush away from my body. A slow blue drop lengthened from the tip of the brush. Before it could detach and aim for my bare leg, I flicked my wrist and flung the paint onto the grass.

An ache developed between my shoulder blades as I bent over the sawhorses and stroked the sopping brush up and down. Some paint bubbled but the grain absorbed almost all. I plunged the brush back into the can, wiping the drips on the rim. Blue splashed on the crisp brown grass.

When Sam's hand dropped on my shoulder I jerked the brush toward myself and a splotch hit my thigh. I hadn't heard the truck. I dipped a rag in Varsol and scrubbed a burn into my skin as the paint dissolved.

Sam bent and plucked a blue hank of lawn. The top of his head gleamed a burnished kidney. He'd combed pomade through what was left of his wavy hair and it shone. Around his jean shorts he'd slung his cowhide belt, heavy with tools.

"Your brush is too wet and your paint is sloppy."

"What's the big deal? They're painted and they look fine."

"They don't look fine. We'll see brush marks and drips and the knots need to be treated so sap doesn't bleed through. I should have showed you. It's my own fault."

I tossed the rag onto the newspapers. Watery blue liquid spread across the print.

"Your set-up is sloppy too. Don't just use the coffee cans for thinner; pour the paint in, one-third full. Then you can press the brush against the side to remove the excess, instead of against the brim of the can and spilling everywhere. But before that, you should sand each board and treat the knots. This isn't easy."

I didn't want him to say what he was going to say next.

"If you do something right the first time, you won't have to do it again. And besides," he added by way of a joke, "my way, you'll get more paint on the boards than yourself."

I've only worked one evening since then and my production speed was considerably slower. I followed Sam's every instruction to the letter — shaking then stirring the paint until it had the consistency of heavy sweet cream, adding citronella to make it bugproof, gluing a paper plate to the bottom of the can — before I remembered that I was supposed to prep the wood. I sanded the surface and shellacked the blemishes and knots of one board then had time to apply only one coat before it got too dark. Sam didn't say anything about quantity or the quality of the job so I took it I had done okay.

A thick morning mist coats the back of the yard and goose bumps rise on my legs. Long grass shot through with purple-whiskered thistles crowds the edges of the lawn. Split-rail fencing and four maple trees separate our property from a hilly field to the north. Beyond that are farmhouses, ranch bungalows and some mansions. Apple orchards and more fields. Our closest neighbours are middle-aged couples like the childless Fat and Terese Palmer, who have the town's only functioning outhouse, and Kipper and Shirl

McDonald, none of whose five kids, including the one who is a former convicted pyromaniac, lives at home.

What would Sylvia think of the addition? Is an extra room enough? Would Sylvia recognize our green-shingled house sheathed with blue board-and-batten?

The dreams of Mother catch in my throat. Without swallowing, I stride across the yard to where a narrow path cuts through the long grass. I stamp to provoke the grasshoppers into the scattershot flight I love but they cling in torpor to the swaying blades and my moccasins end up drenched in dew.

I skirt around Fat Palmer's outhouse through an empty lot then down the dirt hill that leads into Middle Street. Apple Ford has five streets: Front, Middle and Back run north-south while Victoria and Elizabeth go east-west. Front, Middle and Back have official names but nobody uses them and there are no signs.

Above a rise of lilacs on my right, a fence sags. Beyond that lies a shorn field, its hay gathered into rolls that loom in the vapour. There is only the clap of my feet in the quiet of no cars. I walk by blank-windowed red-brick houses until I reach the culvert over old Mrs. Brant's stream. The water flows from a pipe I remember not from the times I drank as a child when shortcutting between Front and Middle Street but from kneeling on the sodden grass after leaving Rick's that first night, when I mashed my lips against the cold lead and water shot over the ends of my hair, down my neck, into my blouse. I haven't drunk here since, but this morning I'm not coming for the pipe.

I hop off the culvert to the far side of the path and walk across ground mushy under dead leaves and needles to a maple as tall as the one outside my bedroom window. I press my belly against its trunk and stretch, my fingertips straining to stroke the tip of the seam I can't see. This scar from a lightning-severed branch is as mine as if I wear it on my own skin. With the dreams of Mother skittering over me I need even a moment of my hands on this old electric wound. As I charge the dreams, fixing them clear in my mind, I hear the urgent ring of the railroad-crossing signal south on Front Street. I lean harder into the bark, wishing to be crouched on the embankment beside the tracks when the train passes, its sweating oil movement shaking through me, embracing me in calm.

With a jolt, I let my arms fall free and head back down Mrs. Brant's driveway and north on Front Street to home. I don't linger or even look at Rick's storefront when I go by. In the three months since I saw Rick last I haven't passed this way once. Though he often works until four in the morning, by now Rick will have crawled into his loft bed and fallen asleep. I've never been up there with him, in his bed. I've never seen him sleep and don't know if he likes to lie on his stomach or his back or to clasp a pillow in a curl like Larry or if he snores and if so, what kind. I have only even seen him with his eyes closed once and he was standing up awake that time.

I trot past the church and the manse and up the hill to our place where I grab my bike from the garage. Yesterday's skirt and blouse are stuffed in a grocery bag on the rear wheel rack. I put my right foot on the pedal and push, then swing my left leg over. I am pumping before I hit asphalt. My neck aches, my throat is raw and my ears plugged at the damp cold on the first hill. By the time I reach the Ford Road it's like sailing with the rosy-gold sun on the back of my head, but it isn't enough. The dreams swarm over me and I let them.

1

I am on a train in a compartment with six
others who are speaking French. I try out my
voice. Softly, to myself, when the others are
asleep. The commotion of machinery is loud
but consistent. If I could find its rhythm, I
might sleep. I do not fit the seat, and pain
stabs my shoulders. The man beside me
speaks another language than French, maybe
German. He has made it clear he wants nothing to do with me.

2

Mid-morning. By myself. Blue seats. A new
train. The backsides of factories pass, breaking up long stretches of yellow-green fields.
The leaves are polished browns, not the
thrusting reds and oranges of home. I am in
France. Mother sits five rows ahead. From
the beginning Mother has refused to sit
beside me. The possibility of her arm jostling
mine or her bare knee grazing my unshaven
one disturbs her, arousing Mother to the
point of fear. I watch the back of Mother's
head, content.

The cook is the only one in the main lodge before me. I
turn on the hot tap, swishing the water around each stainless-steel sink. I like to hold the spout so the water hits the
side of the basin and spreads into one flat stream. At this
hour, the water takes at least five minutes to come out hot

so I let it run, and squat to get bleach, J-Cloths and SOS pads from the cupboard under the sink. I have my own set of yellow rubber gloves with M.B. written inside the cuffs in black magic marker.

When the water is steaming, I plug the centre drain and add three capfuls of Javex.

My body vibrates as if I have just stepped off a train. The Mother in my dream preoccupies me. That Mother is odd, nothing like Sylvia, but she is mine. My heartbeat is relentless in my ears, neck, chest. The dreams fill me with a strange happiness, maybe because they are set in France. French is my favourite and best subject in school. My last teacher gave slide shows on Fridays, serving croissants and cocoa. I feel closer to Sylvia than ever before.

When the middle sink is full, I swing the tap over the third sink and fill it with plain water. Then I turn on the cold. When I am able to hold my hand in the water, I squirt a circle of Sunlight into the first sink and fill it.

Sam writes messages to Sylvia on lined paper torn from pocket notepads bought at filling stations. He leaves these notes wherever they occur to him: his work table, the toaster oven, his dashboard. Every so often he collects the scraps in a handful and stuffs them into a Black Cat cigar box on his dresser.

Sam's messages to his wife turn up between lists of chores and sundries jotted down in spidery capital letters:

> CLEAN OUT EAVESTROUGH
> 3 BAG MILK
> YOU ARE MINE SWEETHEART
> CARTON EGGS

SIGN REPORT CARDS
26 RYE

MON — FILL TANK GAS ($13)
STAPLER BACK TO WORK
YOU ARE SOMEWHERE. I AM
SEARCHING. WHEREVER YOU ARE.
SHARPEN KNIVES

MINUTES LAST CLUB MEET
CLEAN GOOD SHOES
LET ME CALL YOU BABY. I'M THE ONE
FOR YOU. WAITING.
ROTO-TILL

After nearly five years with Sylvia gone, Sam's box is full of these absent-minded notes. I found them years ago and read them often, savouring the odd lines to my mother:

I WILL MAKE YOU MINE WHEN YOU
RETURN TO ME LOVE.
YOU ARE THE MOST AND DON'T I
KNOW IT.
HANG IN THERE DARLIN I'M RIGHT
HERE YOURS.

They are like Hallmark cards but not as poetic though Sam's words do hold a sombre hopefulness more appropriate to true love. I read these lines as if they were written to me, as if I am the one who left a lover yearning in our empty bed-room. I've believed that when I am a lover, the desperation and utter faith behind these lines will be my right. After Rick, I am no longer so sure.

This evidence of Sam's unfaltering belief in my mother's return comforts me. I've never thought about my parents loving each other. They've been apart since I was twelve and I've spent more time thinking about my mother's love for me than her love for my father. That Sam's love is obvious is good. I sit cross-legged on his pine bedroom floor, my toes falling asleep under the weight of my knees, my head dizzy from bending my neck, and let myself trust in the Sylvia of my father's urgent lines, a Sylvia certain she is loved but busy with important work.

For long moments, I can forget my body and believe in a distracted and vital Sylvia who writes intense, soothing, unsent replies to Sam. That Sylvia is on her way home.

Then the truth hits again, seething through me like acid released by a dam. Sam is wrong. Lovers are supposed to be together and if Sylvia reciprocated his love she would have made her way to him by now. It is easier to believe the romance: Sylvia in the clutches of another more possessive lover, unable to return to where she is loved the most. Sylvia is crazy; she could have wandered off and been picked up on the road by dangerous people.

I keep a folded newspaper clipping behind my bulletin board:

> **SAN FRANCISCO** —Kidnapper caught. Linda Smith, 15, was kidnapped after a Nasty Matters concert Feb.12 at the Filmore East. Smith claims the kidnapper used cigarettes and candle wax, among other things, to torture her. "We went for drives

and walks all the time but I was too scared to escape. When he went into the washroom at a Texaco I knew I had to run." Mark Weiss of Palo Alto will appear in court Tuesday.

Sylvia could be with a man like that, or a husband and wife, or even a biker gang. Maybe she is too crazy to get away.

My mother's clothes still hang in her closet; Sam has never remarried or even dated. Sylvia must have made a life away from her husband and children. A life important enough to run to. I tuck in my chin at the thought. Maybe that other life is my mother's due but I can't help but feel I deserve it too.

The only dishes at this time of morning are coffee cups and dessert plates stained with strawberry juice and dried cream. I put my gloves on and drop each dish into the soap sink.

In her new life my mother could be speeding around France on a moped, eyes goggled, hair and neck swathed in chiffon, a dusky Grace Kelly. Anything is possible. What is also possible, if Sylvia has escaped, if she is alive and free to choose, is that she might return to Apple Ford. Sam is ready, Nicky too. Me, I'm not so sure.

Walking Like an Indian

The summer I turned twelve Sylvia gave up. She was through being a mother and a wife, had done it well over the years but no more. She spent her days on the couch, moving to the kitchen to smoke when we came in from school. She tapped her nails on the table and stared out the window, waiting for Sam. When he got home, she rolled her eyes at him and went back to the couch. Often a few tears leaked out as she flopped onto her stomach and pushed her head under a throw pillow, punching the sides down with her fists.

Sylvia was young, nineteen, when she'd had me, then Nicky, one after the other. We were only ten months apart, twins in some ways. "I got what I wanted," she often told us with a tight smile. "A boy and a girl. That's why I stopped."

When I was little, looking into Sylvia's face was like looking into a sun: hot and blinding and full of joy. She was forever folding Nicky and me into her long arms, squeezing us between her knees, our hands buried deep in hers.

We played a game where Sylvia lay on her belly, her face buried in her arms, and Nicky and I ran around her, jumping across her hips, skipping between her legs — swiftly at first, keeping our distance, then daring more as she stayed still as a rock. We flopped on her back, feathered her neck with finger-tips, scratched her scalp, wet-willied her ears until she shot a hand out around one of each of our ankles and took us down in a shrieking, giggling mass. She flipped us on our backs and straddled us, covering our faces with her hands, tumbling our bodies around until we all three lay in a pile, exhausted, exhil-arated and panting. We begged Sam to join us, tugged his pant cuffs and pulled down his socks, but he rattled his newspaper, shook his head and stretched his legs up onto the couch. At odd moments next to my writhing brother, my chest trapped under Sylvia's knee, I'd look over at Sam and my laughter caught for one breath then came out flat the next.

Sylvia took us on walks along the side of the road to look for beer bottles in the ditch and into the woods by the river to collect driftwood from uprooted trees for her crafts. She put Nicky and I in charge of bagging pine cones and milkweed pods while she scoped out debris from decaying logs — the more gnarls, loops and twists the better.

When Sam came, he taught us survival techniques like how to make a toothbrush by removing the downy head of a cat-tail and where to find the tasty larva of the fish fly and how to listen for frogs to find water. He told of an Indian brave who saved himself from thirst by imitating a mouse he'd seen lick-ing dew off a rock.

More than anything, Sam said, he wanted to be an Indian when he was growing up. He used to spend hours in the bush behind their place in Drag County, snuck out there after his father had left for the hotel — when his mother didn't care what he did as long as he stayed out of her way. In a library book, he'd read that Indians could walk through the woods without making a sound — quieter than wolves even. They didn't snap twigs, crackle leaves, crunch gravel. When he went hunting he practised Indian-walking in the bush. Nicky and I weren't very good at it but Sylvia was excellent. She could be talking to us one minute, loosening bark or sawing a piece of wood free, and slip off soundless into the trees the next, gone no matter where we searched, then back, just as swift: silent and grinning.

When Sam wasn't around and we were alone with Sylvia, Nicky sometimes danced. He didn't need music, said he heard rhythms in his head, and when Sylvia was looking, his feet performed intricate steps — ball, toe, heel — that sent him whirling through two or three rooms, one after the other. Often Sylvia laughed, the clapping of her hands like heavy boots with taps on a wooden floor.

We'd seen Sam and Sylvia dance in our living room when my uncles came down for a fish fry at the arena. Larry and Sam were drinking rye and gingers with Reese and his fiancée Shanelle. Reese was watching his mouth then with his wedding date not set. Sylvia was getting dressed in the bedroom while Nadette cleaned up Larry Jr. who had yet to successfully toilet-train. Nicky and I kneeled on the floor in our pyjamas playing Snap. Sam stood as Sylvia strode out in a white halter top and pleated black palazzo pants. In her gold sandals she was as tall as Sam who hugged her in tight at the waist and danced her forward with his thighs. He sang along with the kitchen radio — *Roo-oo-bee, don't take your love to town* — then Reese pulled Shanelle up too and I watched from the floor and hoped.

Sylvia reached over Sam's shoulder and snagged her Peter Jacksons from the top of the buffet. As Sam sang into her hair, she rummaged for a cigarette and pushed it between her lips. Larry jumped up to light it then stayed standing in the middle of the room while his brothers two-stepped their wives around him. Sylvia gestured toward the table and Larry handed her a tumbler. Sam's palms held Sylvia's hips while she rested her wrists on his shoulders, taking alternate drags and sips. Her red lips glistened through the shroud of smoke. Larry looked about to tap Sylvia's bare shoulder before Sam steered her away. When Nadette came in, Larry gulped his drink.

"You two look more alike than twins," Nadette said. "It's not normal."

I nudged Nicky as if it was us she was talking about but it was my parents and Nadette was right. Sylvia puckered her lips and blew a smoke ring at Larry and everybody laughed. With a twist, Sylvia freed her hips from Sam's hands and sat on the couch, the black crepe spreading like a cape as she crossed one long thigh over the other.

Sometimes when Nicky danced, Sylvia took him by the hands, slid her bare feet under his toes and, counting out the steps, calibrated him in precise squares around the room.

With me it was different. The light around Sylvia was safe and warm, true, but structure was what I needed. Sylvia had rules — was full of them in fact, more than Sam, who hid behind newspapers and seemed not to care which rules Sylvia made and whether we followed them, as long as they were there and he was disturbed as little as possible about settling disputes.

Dinner was on the table at six, fifteen minutes after Sam got home from work, and Sylvia served our plates from the stove. Sam preferred the staples: pork chops, venison steak or chicken drumsticks with mashed potatoes and buttered white bread on the side. Sylvia added canned peas or creamed corn so we'd have a vegetable and insisted we all three ate everything on our plates. When she was feeling creative she made casseroles from her magazines: macaroni with peas and cream of mushroom soup, spiced with paprika and topped with a crust of crushed potato chips, or turkey pot pie with frozen carrot medallions and happy faces cut in the Tenderflake crust. Dessert was butter-scotch ice cream with corn syrup, or bananas cut up in brown sugar and evaporated milk.

We said "please" when we asked for a condiment and "thank you" when it was passed. We sat with paper serviettes unfolded on our laps and rested our forearms — and never our elbows — on the edge of the table. Our mouths were closed while we chewed and no part of my body was allowed to touch any part of my brother's or vice versa. No kicking the chair or drinking while eating or slurping or playing with food or inter-rupting. Sam talked about his clients and Sylvia talked about how she'd made the meal and, if it was new, where she'd got the recipe and what changes she'd made. She told about what-ever project she was working on too, the teak beads she'd found for the macramé owl hanging, the scratching technique she'd learned in pottery class, the lamp base she'd wired out of shellacked driftwood.

There were math games with Sam asking Sylvia for an equation then competing with us to find the answer fastest without writing anything down. Sylvia smiled close-mouthed while the three of us clamoured to shout the right answer first, the numbers often tripping over our tongues and coming out incomplete or backward in our haste. Sam loved the language of geometry — hypotenuse, vertex, congruent, isosceles — and had a particular fondness for the Pythagorean Theorem. He started us off — "The square of the hypotenuse…" — and we raced to see who could finish reciting it first: "…of a right-angled triangle equals the sum of the squares of the other two sides!" Cards roused a similar fierceness: cribbage or rummy with Sam was a madcap contest to add points for runs and pairs and sets and fifteens. It was rare that Nicky or I was swifter than Sam but we were neck and neck with each other. Sylvia always claimed she'd figured the answer before us but didn't need to bother with shouting it out.

On Sundays Sylvia walked Nicky and I down the hill to the United Church. She dressed me in homemade jumpers fastened with wooden buttons over white blouses and white leotards with two-toned brown shoes we'd found at the Salvation Army store. I tied my hair in braids with matching yarn ribbons. Nicky wore an orange shirt tucked into stretchy plaid pants with a paisley clip-on tie and desert boots. We stayed for the first part of the service, through two hymns from the choir and announcements, until Reverend Green called all the children forth to sit at his feet for a Jesus story then sent us down to the basement for Sunday school.

There were three others in my Sunday school class: Susan Baker from up on the highway near Vi, Jenny Taylor from the bottom of the hill and a boy named Duncan Matheson, who lived on Back Street and wanted a different one of us to marry him each week. Susan Baker was his favourite. I told Duncan I wouldn't marry him unless it was upstairs in the proper church. Our teacher was Lucy Stevens, a teenager from a church family who lived next to the ballpark where we sat on bleachers for Friday night regular games and at weekend tournaments to watch Sam catch pop flies in centre field.

Duncan's family was a church family too because his father came to service and his grandfather was an elder who carried a wooden plate around to collect the offering. Sam sang in the choir at Christmas but only because they needed deep men's voices not because he belonged. We weren't really United, Sylvia told us, we weren't anything, but one church was as good as another and this church was so close and worship was important.

Sylvia was most rigid about swearing, offended when as much as a *damn* or a *shit* came out of Nicky or me. Sam coached us on the alternatives — *darn, shoot, heck* — but I got caught saying the F-word and had to be dragged then shoved, into the bathroom where Sylvia held a pink bar of Dove under warm water until it was sudsy then rubbed it on my tongue. She let me spit after and rinse with Listerine but my mouth smarted and swallowing was hard, even with water. Nicky swore too but managed to avoid getting his mouth washed out.

For me the rules were stricter than for Nicky, but I never complained. The more exact the rules, the more able I was to perform them to the letter. My appearance had to be precise: T-shirt tucked in, pants belted, socks pulled up, not a hair out of place. Each morning I came to Sylvia with a hairbrush and a jar full of barrettes, ribbons, bobby pins and toggles. I leaned into her thighs as she brushed my tatted hair up into bunches which she fingered into two long ringlets and sprayed with Final Net. My room was spotless too: floor swept, rag rug lined up with the floorboards, all surfaces dusted, windows clear, socks rolled in pairs, sweaters folded with the arms crossed, panties in balls. It wasn't that I liked cleaning; I loathed it and spent hours hanging my head off my bed agonizing over whether to do it in the first place: how much was plenty and how much was too much and had I gone overboard enough? The rules themselves concerned me, not the cleaning. Sylvia's love depended on me not only obeying but excelling at those rules. It was unclear whether the rules were Sylvia's or my own.

That spring, when Sylvia took to the couch, Nicky and I forgot to bathe. It was Sam who noticed the grimy cuffs on our necks, wrists and ankles. He grabbed a hank of my sticky hair as I sat down for dinner and held it as if weighing it or testing it for ripeness. A close, feral scent rose up and I glanced at Nicky. Our eyes met. After a few seconds, Sam let the hair drop, and searched for somewhere to wipe his palm.

Sam pulled a pressback chair from the kitchen to the bottom of the stairs. He sat with the newspaper folded open to the crossword puzzle and pointed up.

"March," he said, and we did.

At ten and eleven, Nicky and I hadn't taken a bath together for a long time. Usually Sylvia stood over us one at a time, arms crossed, big hands cupping hipbones, ensuring that every crack and crevice was sufficiently scrubbed. This time Sylvia was in bed already and Nicky let the water run until it covered the drainage holes. In our bedrooms, we stripped down to the long white undervests that made us indistinguishable. Then we met in the hallway.

"You're not marching right. Raise your knees higher," I commanded.

Nicky tried, but his feet were so dirty they stuck to the floor.

We took turns sliding down the sloped end of the claw foot tub and splashing water onto the mirror. It became a contest to make the most noise so Sam would know we were taking a bath.

When I slid, my bum stuck to the porcelain and squeaked. It felt like a pinch and I squealed, causing Nicky to let out a loud fake laugh.

It was a long time before I realized that contrary to what Sylvia had told me, everything between my legs wasn't called my bum.

My bum held great interest — a place where I put marbles and pushed them around with my fingertips, savouring their glassy coolness, imagining an eye staring inside me. I'd take the marble out and hold it under my nose, compelled by the salty, slightly sour odour. Sometimes I tasted it. When I was eight, Jenny Watson had held out her finger and said, "Smell this." I had wrinkled my nose, but even then I was attracted. The between-my-legs smell. The smell of my underpants before bed.

After drying off, we fought over the square white container of baby powder, shaking it wildly, some of the powder sprinkling our bodies, the rest scattering across the bathroom, leaving spots on the mirror. Giggling, we whacked each other's bottoms and backs with flat hands, marking the sheer powdered skin. Then we tripped down the hall.

I broke free of Nicky's slapping hands and tramped white barefoot prints across my wooden floor and rag rug. I grabbed my red nightie from under my pillow and pulled it on, kicking my legs and arms out in a crazy dance so Nicky couldn't touch me.

He stopped.

Our eyes met for an instant. I turned and pulled the gilt scoop handles on the top drawer of my white dresser. I selected another nightgown, a seersucker baby doll with green and purple flowers, and turned to Nicky.

"Come here."

He did.

"Lift your arms up."

My tone of voice promised adventure and threatened menace if it wasn't obeyed. So Nicky obeyed.

"Lift them higher."

He lifted his arms higher. I slipped the cap-sleeved nightie over his up-stretched hands and wriggled it down until his head stuck out. I pinched and straightened with the attention and expertise I usually reserved for Barbie.

He stood still while I brushed his wet hair straight back and tied a purple ribbon around his head. He lifted his face while I rubbed berry lipgloss into his lips and wrapped a length of beads around his neck. Finally, I painted his nails red.

"I christen you Nina," I said, turning the corners of my mouth down and curtsying.

Nicky made a face. "I don't want to play with that name."

I considered. "Nicole. How about that? It's close to Nicholas. Or Nicola. What about Nicola? It's pretty."

"Okay," he said. His face shone.

The crinkly fabric looked bright and crisp on his dusted skin. His winter skin was a hard beige, like the rinds of certain melons. Streaks of missed dirt showed through the white powder and his body looked strange compared to mine. I stood in front of the mirror. Nicky fixed his eyes on me and would not look at his reflection.

I patted his shoulders and hips and twirled him around. No matter where I moved him, his eyes gripped mine.

I looked in the mirror, hoping he would do the same, and saw two girls: me and the one I had named Nicola. I stared at Nicola in her flouncy crinkled dress and brazen purple ribbon over dark wet hair, and finally Nicola's eyes darted off my face.

She glanced back at me then slowly turned to absorb her full reflection. Her chest expanded.

With one hand on my waist, Nicola took my hand and two-stepped me across the wooden floor. Her feet were unfettered, expressing complex rhythms with natural confidence. The powder was like silk under our toes. I let my own feet go, and threw my head back in long, toothy laughter. As the room spun past and Nicola's purple and green image cut across the mirror in the golden taffy evening light, Nicky didn't seem to care one bit. Who could care? In that moment he was Nicola. It was enough.

In the evenings I lay in bed and listened for the crunch of Sam's car in the driveway. Every night he went to committee meetings for the town or to play ball or to umpire or referee. When I heard the gravel, I pushed my chin into my chest and pulled my shoulders up around my ears. Some nights I called downstairs for my mother, but Sylvia no longer responded. Nicky called for her, too, but it was like yelling into a vacuum. She was in the bedroom below or sprawled on the couch. Maybe she was ignoring us. Neither of us had the courage to get up and check if she was there. What if she had left, crawled out the window and left us behind?

Nicky's bed shared a wall with mine. With my lips against the blue fleur-de-lis wallpaper, I whispered of mutations: "Sylvia's nose has grown into a long dirty parsnip. Her eyes are little piggy beads. Her teeth are black smelly Doberman's balls and her mouth oozes green poo. She is getting fatter and fatter and has developed a taste for plump juicy boy-flesh. My flesh is too stringy. But I am sure a witch like her would appreciate a meal of a boy like you, Nicky."

Nicky grew silent. I pictured him in emptiness, his mind sucked into the witch's void.

"I know you sleep curled in a ball near the bottom of your bed so the witch-mother can't find you."

The possibility of frightening my brother until he cracked spurred me on. I stopped the story only when I had convinced myself the witch-mother's eyes were glowing red outside my own door as she stood, drawn by her daughter's words, head tilted, waiting for me to get the story wrong.

In the quiet after my stories, I saw cobwebs forming in the night sky where the ceiling should have been. Spiders crawled over the webs, some hanging from threads. The longer I looked, the more the spiders multiplied and soon I saw them dropping on my covers, felt them creeping on my skin and pricking me. I scratched, leaving long red ridges on my cheeks and neck and arms.

In the morning the witch-mother was gone and Sylvia sat smoking at the kitchen table. The welts escaped her detection but Jenny Taylor pointed them out on the bus. Eventually I turned the bedroom light on when I went to sleep. No one seemed to mind.

That spring, Sylvia's eyes assumed a new position: up and to the left. Over and over, I was fooled, turning to look where they pointed only to find she was staring at a clay mask on the wall or the painted rung of a chair.

I avoided any space Sylvia's eyes might rest, in case my mother saw something she didn't want to and that something was me.

Nicky couldn't tolerate Sylvia's eyes not resting on him. Nicky wanted to be noticed.

He experimented. When he wore his tiny red stretch bathing suit to school, Sylvia didn't bat an eye. He wore Sam's boxers or his own pajama bottoms with a belt looped around his waist. He wore the same T-shirt for days on end. He went shirtless. He didn't comb his hair so it become a matted helmet. Each morning, Sylvia sat looking at a potted baby's tears on the windowsill, sucking on her cigarette and letting the smoke trail out her nostrils.

One day Nicky came downstairs with his nails, his knuckles and part of his neck painted with pink polish. The time I had painted his nails was already fading from my memory. I had removed the polish right away then so no one had seen it. This time Nicky had made sure that no one would miss it.

I was in the kitchen when Nicky came in. These days, if we wanted breakfast we had to get it ourselves. Nicky made toast, covering it with chunks of peanut butter, then tossing the knife into the sink with a clatter.

"Shit," said Nicky, louder than he needed to. Sylvia didn't flinch. Nicky sat and tapped his fingers on the table but Sylvia stayed facing the window, the heater on her cigarette burning until it was over an inch long, then dropping. I glared at Nicky. He wasn't supposed to wear polish on his own. I stood beside Sylvia at the edge of her vision and pushed the ashtray so the ashes would fall into it.

At school I was dying to say something, to use those freakish pink nails as a way of getting Nicky back for using my polish in the first place. Nicky walked around with his chin out and a big grin and somehow it was okay. I didn't know how he did it. He didn't have a good memory like mine and his grades were average but there was something about my brother — maybe something he'd said — that made the other boys want his approval. Maybe he'd blamed it on me. Making fun of him would make things worse.

Sam didn't see the nails until dinner time. Though more and more Sylvia's dinners came from a can, that night she served up a meatloaf, loosely-packed ground beef swimming in a yellow sauce. The table was set with no tablecloth or napkins, and the forks and knives were on the same side of the plate. Sam got out the milk and ketchup.

Despite the liquid, my first bite crunched.

"What's in it?" I asked.

Sylvia looked around with a smile, not meeting anyone's eyes.

"Soup. Tomato soup and mushroom."

"Are there onions?"

"Onions. Corn flakes. Mustard. Whatever was around. Maybe even some peanut butter."

My throat rose but I kept my mouth closed. Sylvia had slumped and didn't notice. The meat separated into a golden slosh.

"It's delicious. Right, kids?" Sam said, exaggerating his chewing and nodding toward Nicky and me.

"Right, Dad," I said, taking a big swallow of milk. I calculated how long I had to wait before I could safely get up and take a mouthful to the bathroom to deposit in the toilet.

Nicky nodded but didn't answer.

"Thank you," Sylvia said into her plate.

Nicky kept his hands on his lap, curling his fingers around his fork when he had to use it but when Nicky lifted his milk, Sam saw the nails.

Sam laid his utensils down, first the knife and then the fork, and stared, his face growing red. I counted my chews, four per mouthful, so as not to attract his attention.

The stares had the reverse effect on Nicky; soon he had both hands up on the table, fingertips outstretched, preening and fussing, admiring the job he'd done. By now some of the polish had chipped off, so the nails were more of a mess. He waved them under my nose until I had to hold chunks of lip and cheek skin between my teeth to stop the giggles. Nicky curled his fingers inward and blew.

Sam watched, eyes narrowing, then reached across the table, grabbed Nicky's fingers and squeezed. He gripped harder and harder, his eyes on the nails as if he expected them to fly off and parts of Nicky — the bad parts — to stream out. Nicky squinted at Sam and refused to budge or make a noise, even as his fingers turned pink, then a lurid blue-red, then white, the way my fingers did at school when I tried to make them fall off by wrapping elastic bands around them. They never did but I wasn't certain Nicky's wouldn't now.

"You!"

Sam slammed Nicky's hand down onto his plate, spraying me with meatloaf juice. I held back a yelp. Sylvia pulled out a cigarette and lit up, eyes directed at the fridge radio, waiting. Nicky smirked, only his red ears betraying his fear.

Sam stood.

"You're grounded until I say so. And your sister," he jerked his head in my direction, "can clean you up. I never want to see those nails again. You look like a fairy."

Sam's neck throbbed. His lips moved but no words came out. He walked into the mud room, pulled on his jacket and yanked open the back door.

Five minutes later, Nicky got up and left, too.

I snuck away to my room. Later that night, Nicky sat on the toilet seat while I dipped toilet paper into nail polish remover and scrubbed his fingernails until the skin around them was raw. We didn't speak; like Sylvia, he could barely look at me.

3

Storms

The last week of June, the week after school let out, was a week of thunderstorms. In the beginning the rain came first, the lightning stretching across the sky then snaking in on itself. By the end of the week, the clouds were stopped up, the water brewing inside, their countenances so dark, I imagined they contained more than water: bits of fur and roadkill; cat paws, raccoon tails, rabbit teeth, even whole groundhogs; birds' legs and beaks; human fingernails, earlobes, wrists and kneecaps; fragments of half-digested carrion: proof of the consuming powers of the storm, or perhaps the ingredients of the malice forthcoming. The brawling clouds had powers, I believed — the yellow veins of electricity and the ear-splitting cracks evidence of some great rage waiting to be spat out at the unsuspecting and the unprepared.

The mornings descended like a wall. At first daylight, I awoke in a frustrated panic, sheets tangled, old sweat collecting around my hairline, dreams of sirens lingering: ambulance, police, fire, all mingled together.

I lined up Mason jars behind the garage. Each day I unscrewed another lid to collect that day's rain. Each day I discovered the clouds brooded longer, and each day the water level was substantially higher — even though, as the week wore on, the rain fell with more and more force, splashing out of the jars and catching on the surrounding grass.

At the first low rumble, my forearms prickled. I kept time records and loudness records in the orange pocket notepads Sam brought home from gas stations. In the early evening's hush after the storm subsided, I walked around Apple Ford, assessing the damage, looking for ugliness, for evidence of that great wrath: fragments of bone and animal ears and bits of cloth, tangible proof that the storm's fury was real. I sought out trees struck by lightning and cut the wood free with Sam's hunting knife, smuggled out of the house because of its forbidden sharpness. I laid my hands on the shining burnt crevices where the limbs had been severed. Energy, perhaps electrical, perhaps more than that, surged into my hands and maybe into my veins. At home, I stored the bits of lightning wood in a box in my bedroom closet, checking them with the lights out to see if they glowed. Underneath, I was driven, certain as I was of my own flesh that something magical was to be gained from this knowledge, this accumulation, this seeing. I stayed quiet and paid attention. If I waited long enough, the secret of the storms' temper would be my own.

Now that we were home from school, Sylvia sat in our kitchen all day and smoked. Her hair was limp with humidity but her stretchy headband matched her blouse. She stared at the yard, green now, the grass long and unmanageable. Mowing it was Sylvia's job, but she no longer went outside and Sam wasn't home long enough. Sylvia stacked her butts in a hefty black and green ceramic ashtray. I emptied it before Sam came home. The summer before, Sylvia had smoked a little, one or two a day, and usually only in the evenings if Sam was there. She had worn lipstick then, painted her lips a solid flat red that left filmy kiss marks on the cigarette. Sometimes she'd handed a butt to me, lighted, and let me smoke it. She got out her compact to show me the smear of red that remained on my lips and I walked around pushing my lips out, wishing for someone to kiss. This summer, Sylvia wasn't wearing lipstick, her lips paler than her skin. This summer she was smoking the butts down until the white part was no longer visible. The kitchen was hazy with smoke and Nicky pretended to have choking fits whenever he came in.

Sometimes Sylvia spoke, her voice hoarse now, her words garbled. I winced, pretending to ignore it. Sylvia's voice used to be the first thing I heard when I got in from school, calling from the kitchen and asking how my day had gone. She would beam when she saw me, hand me a plate of Ritz crackers spread with peanut butter and granny apple slices with a few drops of lemon squeezed on them so they wouldn't brown, and sit down, eyebrows raised. I would pour everything into my mother who would smile and nod, seemingly overjoyed at her daughter's very existence. Now I had my doubts.

I had to pass through the kitchen to get from my bedroom to outside. I ran in and out, grabbing Mason jars from the top of the basement stairs, rummaging around in the junk drawer for labels, glue and magic markers. I tried to be fast; keeping records was messy business. It didn't fit any known rules. But the rules were starting to give, their seams weakened. There were ways of slipping through that went unnoticed.

The house with its dull brown rooms and green linoleum floors existed as a container for me, an endless source of supplies. I moved through it as I moved through the compartments of my night dreams, slowly but with purpose, sliding around the edges, wary of disturbing anyone.

On the third day, the rain caught me out in the carrots and weeds behind the garage, causing the round pen lines of my notes and charts to bleed into each other. That night by my window, greedily absorbing each breath of breeze that rustled the maple leaves, I traced the ridge marks my Bic pen had made on the pages underneath. Since I couldn't copy the figures correctly, the tone was set for the next day's collections. As the storms wore on, my figures became more and more fabulous; one day the water level was a foot high, the next it was three. I had no way to tell for sure.

The day after getting caught in the rain, I slipped into the kitchen to look through the drawers for a Baggie to carry my notebook in. I stood with my head cowed, my body angled away from Sylvia.

It didn't work.

"Come here, Mercy."

Sylvia's monotone voice had a weary quality that threatened to swallow me. I shuddered.

"I said over here. In front of me. Where I can see you."

I stood my ground.

"I'm in a hurry." I almost called Sylvia "Mommy" but this name didn't seem right anymore. I didn't want to stay, but leaving would make me somehow responsible for her sitting by the window smoking.

Sylvia's eyes moved. They lit on me for a second then flitted up to the cupboard where they rested.

"I want that hair cut. Come here."

I pushed the drawer shut with the heel of my hand. The drawer was loose and jammed partway. I moved over to the table, standing out of habit to Sylvia's left.

She raked her fingers through the tangles. She hadn't combed my hair into ponytails for months and now my thick hair hung in snarls.

It felt good to have my hair pulled. I liked to have my mother's hands in my hair, near my scalp. The pulls made my scalp tingle. I leaned into my mother. Sylvia tugged harder and the familiar sharp smell arose. I tilted my nose up. I liked to hold the hair to my nostrils and inhale. When it was wet I sucked on the ends. I hadn't washed it since before the storms, when I'd skidded a bar of soap over my head and dunked it under the tub water. I glanced at my mother. The corners of her eyes looked pinched.

With ragged nails, Sylvia tugged and twisted, the pulls getting keener.

I breathed through my mouth, my eyes on her taut aqua headband. Sylvia moved her long hands down. She tweaked my collar, brushed my shoulders, licked a finger and rubbed my knee. Her eyes stayed fixed on the floor beyond my feet. I pressed even closer, my side against Sylvia's, my knees against her thighs.

I stared at her, willing her to return the gaze. The hair tucked under Sylvia's headband lay in lank, oily clumps, the ends resting on her collar. Her wrists were so skinny the bones dug out of her skin. Her smell was one of smoke and underarms and hair — much like my own, only with a sourness I couldn't place. She no longer baked, read magazines, made clothes or talked on the phone. She didn't go to pottery or rug hooking, had abandoned knotting macramé and crafting driftwood. She just sat in her chair, knees and elbows crossed, and smoked. There were no more rules for knowing her. Even broken rules didn't alert her.

Sylvia grabbed a handful of hair and jerked it back.

"It should be off your face." Her voice was low and clear. Her breath smelled like a dirty dishrag and I turned my head away.

Sylvia yanked harder. I forgot all about staying out of trouble.

"It's my hair!" I yelled. "If you can keep your hair like that, I can do what I want with mine."

Sylvia rose out of her seat, her head veiled by swirls of sun-lit smoke, and cracked her hand across my jaw.

In that moment my mind formatted a new type of moth-er touch. Sylvia hadn't touched me in I didn't know how long. It was a trap: Sylvia's fingers in my hair, Sylvia letting me lean up against her, luring me. My mother's hands, the ones that used to be large safe places for me to hide my own fearful hands, now sprouted mean fingers out to destroy me. This mother made no sense. My mother's palm against my cheek broke the rules. The ringing slap had set me free. There were no rules now for loving Sylvia. I shook, unable to open my eyes.

Sylvia sat back down and waved her long fingers.

"Leave me alone."

Her hand fell back to her lap. She put a cigarette in her mouth and didn't bother to light it.

I backed out of the room. Sounds of whimpers and sniffing followed me. I quickened my step and went straight to the bathroom where I stared in the mirror at the welt that had been Sylvia's hand. I hoped it would stay, a badge I could wear before the world to prove something was wrong with my mother, and that I, Mercy Brewer, stood victorious in the face of it. Already though, the mark was fading.

I wanted to tell Nicky but he wasn't around. He wouldn't believe it. Even if he did, he wouldn't see it as a sign that Sylvia was different now. I didn't know why. All I knew was that the very sight of me disturbed Sylvia now, as if she was thinking about something important and couldn't be interrupted. Whenever I managed to catch her eyes, they were deserted. I was used to looking at my mother and seeing a gleaming, perfect, well-loved version of myself shine back. Now it seemed as if nothing of me was left in my mother's eyes and that scared me. If my mother couldn't see me, who could? I would almost rather have the witch-mother who sat outside our bedrooms with her glowing red eyes. At least that mother cared about what we were thinking, even if it was only to prove we were thinking bad thoughts about her. This mother, the one in the kitchen with the mean hands, was worse than any witch I could imagine. I vowed to study Sylvia and see how much she had changed. Maybe it wasn't even her sitting in the kitchen, the sunbeams crisscrossing her hair. Maybe she'd been transported or her soul had died but her body lived. Whatever it was, I wanted to stay as far away as possible.

On the fifth day of storms I started up the closet game. The sight of Nicky's hair capped over his brown neck as he bent over a stack of Lego blocks spurred me to action.

I entered the room on the balls of my feet, resisting the urge to dance. Behind my back I held his slingshot. For Nicky the temptation of an item taken away before he had thought to use it was too much, particularly if that item was a weapon.

I leapt in front of him and his head snapped up. I dangled the elastic of the slingshot before his eyes, holding it just out of reach as I would for a cat.

Nicky forgot about the Lego.

"Give me that. It's mine."

He made clumsy grabs at my wrists, stumbling to his feet. His ears reddened and his grabs turned into slaps.

He repeated himself: "You don't need that. Give it to me."

To taunt him further I wrinkled my forehead without smiling. I didn't say a word.

Nicky attempted a few short kicks. I danced into the hallway, the slingshot high above my head, Nicky jumping and smacking my arms and back. With one foot, I neatly flipped open the closet door and tossed the slingshot into the darkness. Nicky scrambled after it. I kicked his feet in and slammed the door, dropping the hook snugly into the eye.

We were used to this game. Usually Nicky stood close to the door, taking light breaths that I couldn't hear, until guilt or curiosity overcame me and I unhooked the lock. Then Nicky would bolt past me beneath my arm, glad to be small and hard and fast. I was fast too so he didn't waste any time.

This week was different. The heat in the open air was unbearable enough. Inside the closet Nicky might feel like he was suffocating. I'd hidden in my own adjacent closet to escape Larry Jr. on his visits and I remembered the sweat. It stung my open eyes. I'd sniffed it into my nostrils and tasted it on the corners of my mouth. It poured down my cheeks and dripped from my chin. The back walls of our closets had removable boards that led into a crawlspace blanketed by fuzzy slabs of pink insulation. Nicky and I had ventured in there together once but he'd backed out right away, fearful of the pink blocks turning into parasites and attaching themselves to him. He said that if so much as a finger touched the pink insulation, our whole bodies would itch for weeks, maybe months.

Nicky gave in.

"Let me out!" he yelled, pounding the door.

In the hall, I stood back, unsmiling, my eyes on the door-knob, ready to spring for safety or seize Nicky at the slightest indication the catch wouldn't hold.

"Lemme out. Lemme out. Lemme out."

His voice got higher and quieter, almost singsong.

I pretended I wasn't there, willing my ears to concentrate on the whir of a lawnmower next door. I considered tiptoeing down the stairs then sneaking back. Or just staying away. I had never gone that far. He might die if I did that. I was about to dare myself when a wail came from the closet, followed by a roar. My ears tingled. Maybe I should let him out. As I reached for the doorknob, I heard a thud. The shrill noise continued, sounding like a wheeze or a nasal guffaw.

I hit the door.

"Stop laughing, you idiot. I know it's fake."

Inside I wasn't so sure. Where was my mom? Nicky's laugh-ing was loud. Usually Sylvia interrupted any loud games, telling us to pipe down.

Regular thumps began. I rested my palms on the clock wallpaper, my breath coming in pants. I knew exactly where my mom was: in the kitchen smoking or more likely, asleep on the couch.

I quietly lifted the hook and was halfway to the stairs when both the keening and thumping stopped. I listened for a few moments longer then stole back. When Nicky was through playing dead and rattled the doorknob, he would burst into the hall and I could stand with my arms crossed and say, "What's your problem? It wasn't even locked."

I hung back, smirk in place, shaking from my shoulders down. Outside the lawnmower stopped; the air was motionless. From the closet came silence.

Maybe he really was dead. I curled my hand around the doorknob, ready to attack if need be. If he were dead, I'd be mad.

When I opened the door a few inches, Nicky flopped into the hall, arms raised over his head, armpits stained with sweat, his weight flipping the door all the way open. It swung back against Nicky's shoulder. His eyes had rolled back so I could only see the whites and the pink line of his inner eyelid. A froth lined his lips. It was white and frilled with yellow and purple and smelled curdled, like Pablum.

I refused to believe it. Wishing something couldn't make it come true. Besides, I hadn't really wished it. Not deep down. I wanted only to see what would happen. I pushed at Nicky's knee with my toes.

"Get up, Nicky. Stop faking."

No response. I willed his eyes to open. Fear clutched my shoulder blades.

A few seconds later, Nicky's eyes did open. He gazed

straight up at me with hatred and non-recognition. Then he closed his eyes and his body twitched. The twitches turned to shudders and soon his legs and arms were thrashing against the walls of the narrow hallway. A thin stream of liquid spilled from the corner of his mouth and his head thumped against the floor. I screamed and ran downstairs. It didn't matter any more about my mother. By locking Nicky into the closet I had made him a monster.

Sylvia was in the kitchen.

"Mama, there's something wrong with Nicky, he's on the floor hitting the wall. With his head. He's out of control." It was hard to get the words out for sobs. "I didn't mean to do anything," I said after a minute.

Sylvia's face seemed to click back into focus. She dropped her cigarette and charged out of the room, her legs taking impossibly long strides. I was right behind her.

When we got to the top of the stairs, Nicky was sitting up straight, his hands on his knees.

Sylvia lurched down beside him, folding him in long arms like prehistoric bird wings.

"He's okay, right?" I said, standing back at the top of the stairs.

She sat back and held Nicky's face in both hands. "Get a cloth!" she yelled, not taking her eyes off Nicky's.

I grabbed a facecloth and held it under lukewarm water, then wrung it out. Sylvia reached her hand out and I dropped the cloth into it. She swiped Nicky's mouth a few times. Using the corner of the cloth, she patted the foam off his lips and dabbed at his shirt.

Nicky croaked. Slowly he recognized me. He didn't seem to notice Sylvia.

"What?" he said.

"Did you call emergency? You have to call the volunteer fire department out here. The ambulance is too far," Sylvia said, clutching Nicky to her chest again.

"Not yet," I said. "I didn't think he was sick. It just happened." I didn't say I'd thought he was faking. It was wrong not to tell what had happened but it sounded stupid to say it; I was a horrible person for making him play the closet game.

"Don't bother calling anyone. He looks fine now." Sylvia rocked Nicky, her movements solid, her grip tight.

"But you didn't see him. He was rolling on the floor. He was out of control."

"What happened? Why was he doing that? Was it a game?" Sylvia's smile was the kind that made me feel like I had no idea what I was talking about. I doubted what I'd seen and felt worse for having caused it. If something was wrong with Nicky, we wouldn't know because Sylvia didn't think he needed to go to the hospital. My chest got all hard as if I'd swallowed a big piece of meat. I had put Nicky's life in danger. Then I'd laughed at him. What was wrong with me that I could do such things to my brother? I'd locked him in the closet because I thought it was fun. It was fun when he didn't get sick. In the dim hallway my mother's eyes were vacant hollows boring into me with full knowledge of my games, of my evil ways, and the scary thing was that those eyes didn't care one bit.

Nicky blinked as if he was coming out of a long, much-needed afternoon nap. Later he said he remembered nothing about the closet and was conscious only of a light bruise on the crown of his head. Nothing similar ever happened to him again. He shook his head and seemed surprised to be in our mother's arms. His eyes held a hatred so clean I could mistake it for love. Nothing I did would taint it; he could survive anything.

Sylvia released him. He sat back against the closet door, mouth closed. Sylvia stood up, arms trembling.

"I don't know what to do with you two," she said. "You are wild. I wouldn't be shocked if you killed each other one day, if you don't kill me first." She walked past me and went back downstairs.

I couldn't look at Nicky or even speak. But I didn't want to leave him. What if he had another fit? Then for sure I would call the fire department even if Sylvia told me not to. I would run down the street myself and pull the alarm. Nobody would get in the way now of me protecting my brother even though I was as aware as he was that the opportunity to protect him was over. He had grown past me and was strong in a way I had never expected, a way that magnified my own weakness: my meanness.

I asked him if he wanted to sit in the garage loft to watch the storm. The sky was near black so it was time.

Nicky didn't resist. Normally he avoided the storms, huddling in his room with his Lego bricks or a stack of comic books while the sky cracked open. Now, as low rumbles came across the fields, Nicky jumped up as if he craved the storm. I craved it too. Nothing was more important now than to be outside with Nicky, our faces against the air while the storm whirled around us.

On the final day of the thunderstorms, I woke early, my skin cool. Outside was silent. I got up and moved as if through heavy air, my hands relying on the walls and furniture edges, all of my senses cottoned up. I walked down the stairs, fingertips on the clock wallpaper, instinctively stepping as close to the inside as possible to avoid creaks. At the bottom I paused, my hand on the newel post, and listened to my father's snores warble through the half-open bedroom door. I checked the living room couch out of habit and was glad to see Sylvia not there. A few more steps, through the kitchen and the mud room, and I was in the back yard.

Outside, I folded myself into a chaise longue under the pear tree, the morning heat already enough to warm me, and gazed past the house. The slightest curve of sun was rising. Behind a pink film of clouds peered the concrete sky I'd grown used to all week, but the sun was there now and that was all I needed to know.

I fell asleep and dreamed and woke with my mouth hanging open, a clear stream of drool joining my lip to my red nightie. I was unsure where I was.

The chaise longue creaked as I got up, and an earwig skittered across the canvas. I walked through the long grass in the back yard and down the hill into the town in the sunshine, past all the familiar houses, cutting through the fallen branches along Mrs. Brant's stream, over the tracks, past Hoppy's Wrecking Yard and across the road to the ballpark. The park was full of activity: a fair with livestock and rides by the river and a baseball tournament. Sam was playing and so was Sylvia, who stood in right field wearing an oversized catcher's mitt. I wanted to be in the game but I couldn't make myself go over.

Instead, I headed toward the Stevens' house. Their front door was open, so I entered, passing through Mrs. Stevens' dining room with its rows of plates along the tops of the walls, into the long, skinny kitchen and out through the back yard where the Stevens were having a family party. They glanced up without acknowledging me. I continued until their voices and the umpire's shouts and the Ferris wheel music had faded into a low insect hum and I was in the grass alone. The field grass was much shorter now. It gleamed deep emerald. All sound disappeared. I heard only a roar like the inner folds of a conch shell pressed to my ear.

When I looked up, I was in a graveyard. I could see no houses or people in any direction, even though the Stevens' house wasn't that far behind me and the river was somewhere up ahead.

I looked around again. The field had filled with intricate bushes: lilacs, wild rose, sumac, honeysuckle, peony — and wilder things too: nettles, thistles, milkweed, golden rod, burdock. The field invited me to explore, to crawl between the branches on the dirt and grass floor. The bushes parted and receded as I made my way between the slim gravestones, many of which had upheaved themselves, exposing raw earth. The ground was spongy, lumpy. Water seeped into the edges of my footprints. The gravestones wore such mottled faces that even when I wet my fingers and rubbed the surface of the engraved letters I couldn't read the names of the buried. A secret wanted to reveal itself but no matter how deeply I went into the graveyard, I was unable to expose it.

I squatted and discovered pieces of blue and green glass and washed white china, the edges rubbed smooth as though by water. I folded my fingers over them, their sleekness calming me, flowing into my body. I had never heard of this cemetery before: to the best of my knowledge, Apple Ford had no burial sites for its citizens. I must have been the only one who knew about it. I couldn't believe I hadn't noticed a graveyard before.

Seconds later I was awake, really awake in the chaise longue, my skin gummy. I knew now what to do with the lightning wood. I would fashion a man from it and when the storms were over I would walk through town, find the graveyard and bury him there. This man would be my charm against Sylvia. Only his burial would protect me.

It happened in the kitchen the day after the storms broke, the sky a blue so bright it ached to look at it.

I woke to the crunch of gravel. Through the maple leaves outside my window, I saw the corner of the green Impala as Sam turned south out of the driveway. The house was silent. Outside was a cacophony: birds, squirrels, shrieks of children, cars, chainsaws, lawnmowers, hoses. It wouldn't thunder that day. Sylvia was sitting in the kitchen. I could tell it in my bones. I could almost smell the smoke sidling under my door, coming for me.

The storms had been a buffer against Sylvia all week. Now the skies were clear and there was nothing to protect me from my mother's rawness. Sylvia's presence, the force of her will, urged me to come downstairs to see for myself that all was clear, that the storms had made my mother fine if only I would see for myself. If I went down though it wouldn't be alright; it would be worse than ever. There was nothing I could say to my mother. The words sank into me, building on the mountain of hurt. The more Sylvia tried to make things look alright, the more obvious it became that they weren't.

Instead I sat on my bed. Sylvia no longer cared when I woke up — or if she even saw me all day. I'd swiped Sam's Swiss Army knife and I whittled and shaped the wood I'd collected with the spear blade and nail file. I glued white circles with numbers inside them on the sides, the brown mucilage coming from a bottle with a red rubber top. The end result would be a man. It would be big and it would have some charm. If I worked hard and fast enough, it might alter what was fermenting downstairs.

By the time the sky had darkened down to navy and June bugs were battering my screens, I was only half-finished, if that. The smell of burning meat, barbecue sauce and charcoal briquettes drifted in and made my stomach growl. I cut the numbers faster, no longer varying the sizes, just getting the job done. My fingers were gummed and I had to peel glue off my skin with my fingernails. Wood shavings and scraps of paper stuck in the holes of my afghan. I'd added pale yellow cocoon husks and praying mantis carcasses and maple keys and a Centennial penny flattened by the steam train. An old Latin textbook of Sam's formed the base.

Downstairs a door slammed. I heard Nicky's familiar stomp. Sylvia's voice rose sharply: "Where have you been?"

I picked at the crust of glue on the red rubber bottle top.

Sylvia spoke again, her voice quavering: "You can't just do what you want to. You have rules."

Something metal crashed and Sylvia pleaded: "Nicky, why can't you be nice? Why don't you say something? Answer me. Please answer me."

I picked up the scissors and nipped at the skin around my fingernails. Lately I hadn't heard much more than a guttural command from my mother.

Sylvia's pleas continued, picking up momentum, slicing through the thick, smoky evening air and pressing my fingers to move faster, the glue clotting on my skin.

"You're such a good-looking boy. You could make yourself look so good. I bet girls really like you. You have my dark hair and skin. You're going to be a beautiful man someday."

I imagined Sylvia drawing Nicky to her, twining her fingers through his hair, the way she did when she used to comb mine in the mornings. Nicky's hair was smooth with no knots to catch her fingers. My hair was frizzy and light brown, my skin pale. How strange to have a brother more beautiful than you. I strained to hear Nicky's voice, but Sylvia's loud singsong blotted everything out. Nicky must be standing still, leaning into her, lulled. She would pull his hair enough to make his scalp feel good. Nicky could never see what was really going on.

Then Nicky exploded.

"Fucking bitch!" he screeched, his voice higher than a girl's.

His feet thudded through the living room and down the hall. He ran up the stairs two at a time, hurling swear words behind him.

Goddamnbitchbastardfuckincunt! He screamed it like a single word, like the words he and I made up and said as fast as we could so no one would know we were swearing. I bent the glue cap back and wedged the scissor tip inside the slit. I pushed it around making the hole bigger and bigger until the cap gaped open.

Nicky slammed past my room, kicking my door a few times before stomping into his own room. Once there he was quiet, but downstairs Sylvia's voice was still going, the same up-and-down pleading and insisting and demanding and probing. She wasn't loud anymore; I could no longer understand any words. It was eerie. She continued as if she wasn't alone, as if Nicky's outburst had never happened and he stood, head bowed, in front of her as she combed his hair.

Soon the ranting ceased and Sylvia called us for dinner. Her voice was sweet, inviting.

"Hurry up," she added. "We're having barbecue. Your father is finishing up the hot dogs."

I put my paper, scissors, glue and wood back into the box and opened my door. Nicky stood outside, his cheeks flushed and his eyebrows forked over his nose. I couldn't condone his kicking my door and wasn't ready to be friends yet, so I shrugged and pushed past him into the bathroom.

He was close behind. He brushed my arm as he stretched his grime-streaked hands under the running water. Usually when we touched it was by accident and it was a contest to see who would be the first to recoil and brush away the germs. This contact was no accident. I didn't move away. Nicky squeezed closer and we stayed that way for a long time, leaning over the sink, hands under the hot tap that always ran lukewarm. We used our thumbs to rub away glue and dirt, but when we were done we kept our hands under the water, to feel its warmth on our skin, to listen to it rumble up through the pipes and splash out of the tap over our hands and down the drain. Right then, standing arm to arm and washing hands was the best thing in the world.

Soon, the hot water kicked in; I yelped and jumped back. Nicky's forehead was smooth and brown and he looked small. I reached past him to turn off the tap then sat on the side of the bathtub to wait. I didn't want to look at him anymore so I inspected my fingers, rubbing and peeling off the remaining glue.

"I'm not even hungry," Nicky said, his hand on the doorknob. He wanted me to laugh.

I met his eyes. "Why did you have to call her a bitch?" It was words like *bitch* that made my mom act strange. It scared me that my mom did whatever she could to make people say the words she hated so much. If she could make even Nicky say those words — Nicky who never got mad, Nicky who let me do anything I wanted to him — then maybe she was strange all on her own. But Nicky had yelled at her and I too had yelled at her three days ago. Nicky and I must just be bad. But Nicky was worse. He swore.

Nicky put his hands on his stomach and seemed to pull himself inward. He bit his bottom lip and his ears reddened.

"That just shows what you know," he said. "You're the one I should call the bitch!"

He looked ready to spit. He opened the door, pushed his fist hard against my shoulder and clomped down the stairs. It wasn't even a punch, and it certainly didn't hurt, but the meaning was there. I stood limp, aware of the throbbing shoulder but unwilling to feel anything. I listened for the commotion I was sure Nicky would arouse downstairs but it didn't come. The longer I heard nothing, the weirder it seemed.

The only light on in the kitchen was the one above the stove. Nicky sat at the table, his lips pinched white, a dirty triangle of burnt meat on a plate in front of him. The table was bare, without tablecloth, place mats, serviettes. There were no hot dogs, no barbecue. Our father was nowhere to be seen.

Sylvia stood at the stove, a cigarette dangling from her lips. She wore lipstick spread in thick uneven streaks. It was a ghastly colour, like brown bruised plums.

"I thought you said we were having hot dogs," I said.

Sylvia didn't answer. She clutched a variety of kitchen tools: a spatula, a straining spoon, a ladle, some wooden spoons and a bread knife. She banged them on the stove, against the frying pan that held three more blackened chops amid globs of white grease, on the stove overhang, on her own wrists.

Her eyes were like pennies — lighter, coppery, but flat and turned inside, not out.

"Sit down, Mercy," Nicky hissed. His hands clutched the edge of his seat, his eyes never leaving Sylvia.

"Yes, dear. Sit down. Let's have a nice family dinner."

Sylvia let the utensils fall as though she'd forgotten them and lifted a chop from the frying pan using the fingertips of both hands. She dropped the meat on the table in front of my seat. She waited there, posed, foot, ankle, knee, thigh, hip all turned out perfectly, like a housewife in a magazine ad for Crisco or Betty Crocker. Her hair was still oily but she had teased it back into place. It resembled the empty carapace of a beetle, wings slightly outstretched, poised for potential motion. Her eyes clouded over, giving her away. Around them hung shadowy sacs of skin, making her face look both bloated and drained.

"I won't sit. Nicky was right. No. Maybe he wasn't right. He said you were a bitch. I say—"

I couldn't finish the sentence. I'd said *bitch*! And not by accident. I was as bad as Nicky. Worse! I knew better. Those words made my mom act funny and here I was saying them. But I couldn't take them back. What little was left of my mom, the part that wanted a nice family dinner, was receding from those sunken eyes. What could I do to bring her back? Getting angry wouldn't help. I ducked my head and slid into my seat, trying not to gag as I picked up my fork and knife and sawed at the chop.

"I'm not finished with you, young lady," Sylvia said, her words congealed with tears. Still, I detected the steel underneath.

"I'm sorry."

"This is not good enough. I wish your father were here to see this. Darn it." Sylvia ground the heels of her hands into her cheekbones.

Nicky and I cut into the meat, pushing the blunted edges of our knives against the bone to sever the charred flesh. Maybe if we ate the way she wanted she would be happy. I glanced at Nicky but he just glared into his meat.

Eating didn't work. Sylvia sniffed in hard. She whirled around to the stove, seized a wooden spoon and brandished it like a sword, eventually turning it on herself, beating it against her bony forearms. Nicky slid off his seat and crouched under the table. I raised a piece of burnt pork to my lips. Sylvia ran from the room. She slammed two doors, one after the other, and wailed.

The portion of meat perched on the end of my fork was black on the outside, inside a pinkish grey. I hated meat, always had. I would sit at the table through Sam and Sylvia's dinner conversations, chewing on a single piece until my jaw felt like thick rubber bands and ached when I tried to separate my teeth. Given the chance, I would slip away to the washroom and let the chewed flesh fall from my lips into the toilet bowl while I ran water and pretended to wash my hands. I wasn't sure whether Sylvia ever found out, but lately, except for tonight, it hadn't mattered when I didn't put meat on my plate, those nights it was even served.

I popped the triangle of pork into my mouth and held it there, letting the grease seep into my palate. I wondered how long it would take me to melt the meat with my juices, how long I could sit there, squeezing the meat against the roof of my mouth with my tongue before it would dissolve and the pork flesh would become part of me without the aid of my teeth.

I picked up the knife and lapsed into the game Sylvia had slapped my hands for playing when I was younger: mommy fork and daddy knife. I danced them lightly along the edge of the table, thinking of how suave they both were, how debonair, and how they both helped each other. I didn't notice Sam was home until the bedroom door slammed. Nicky was gone. So was his chop.

With my tongue, I nudged the chewed pork through my teeth. It plopped on the table. I went to the hall doorway. High animal yelps and chokes came from my parents' bedroom. The fat from the meat made my tongue stick to the roof of my mouth. My whole body was arid, porous. I wanted to see inside the room. I couldn't hear Sam's voice. Was he going crazy too?

I tucked in my chin. This was the first time I'd said that word, even if it was only inside my mind. *Crazy*. I shook my head and widened my eyes. If my mom was crazy I wanted to see everything, to witness all the qualities about Sylvia that put her in this category, to understand what about Sylvia defined her as crazy and took her away from being the mother I had known and turned her into a beast who'd beat herself less than an hour before.

The sounds stopped so I snuck closer, wrapping myself around the hallway's French door. The bedroom door opened and Sam filled the frame. He was wearing the tight green pants — with the yellow stripe down each leg — of his Tecumseth Chiefs ball uniform and a white T-shirt, his neck and arms a golden red from his first summer burn. He pushed the heels of both his hands against the crosspiece under his gun rack, then jostled past me, reaching back to yank the door shut. For a split second I was able to see inside.

The bedside lamp was on and a thin crack of buttery light illuminated the hallway. A noise like whales keening started up, surrounding me as I glimpsed a white pile on the bed. The noises came from here. The white heap thrashed and moaned but no matter how hard I tried to figure out the angles and limbs and monstrous lumpy middle, it didn't look human.

Just as Sam pulled the door closed, I caught sight of something more. Beneath the ragged bear hair, the face was red and black and much bigger than a person's but I knew it was my mother. And knew in that brief wedge-of-light moment before my father's sun-reddened hand pulled the wrought iron handle and latched the door on my mother, that the face held a secret. A secret I did not want. A secret only I would understand.

4

Deliverance

After Sam shut the bedroom door on Sylvia, I retreated upstairs where I pulled on an old pair of terry-cloth sleepers and lay on my bed peering through my afghan's loops at the maple's shadow limbs crawling and heaving across the stippled ceiling. Downstairs, doors opened and closed and a car left the driveway then soon after another one arrived, but I didn't get up to see which. Ten minutes later Grandma Vi called up to tell me to pack some T-shirts, I was coming to sleep over. I put my running shoes over the sleeper feet and went out to her car. Nicky came too but Sam picked him up in the middle of the night so when I woke up in Vi's spare bed, Nicky was gone.

Vi's house was on the highway, not far away at all, though we hadn't seen her much in recent months. After a couple of days I could separate the smells: budgie shavings, urine, cigarette smoke, burnt meat and lavender perfume. Some mornings a sweet vermouth scent from the living room where Vi had left the bottle open the night before.

The one-storey house was dark with the damp feeling of a basement. The lamps were stout, able to spare only weak circles that were difficult to read by. Each room except the kitchen had one whole mirrored wall. In the living room, an autumn forest scene that covered a second wall embarrassed me because it was obvious that such a forest would fool no one.

I slept in the spare room at the back of the house, where the buzz and rumble of Vi's snores and the early morning truck traffic woke me before dawn. A set of *Reader's Digest* Condensed Books lined the shelf of the double bed. I pulled them down one by one and read abbreviated versions of books like *Valley of the Dolls* and *Up the Down Staircase*, a flashlight held under my chin. Vi had other books too, paperbacks with glossy black covers and raised red lettering and titles like *The Exorcist* and *Rosemary's Baby* and *Helter Skelter* that I read when Vi wasn't around.

The back yard was short, wide and treeless. A waist-high chain-link fence separated it from acres of flat field whose openness induced a dizziness in me that the rolling hills near our house had not prepared me for. A sliding door led from the living room to a patio made of concrete squares etched between with dandelion leaves. The grass looked bitten and brown. While Vi slept in the mornings I lounged under a canvas umbrella, my bum on one nylon-weave lawn chair, my feet on the other, my skin slathered in baby oil and *Alice in Wonderland* on my lap. Vi's pinched back yard looked unlikely to offer up a rabbit hole for me to fall into. Groundhog maybe.

Grandma Vi was the only person I knew who wore wigs, alternating between a frosty blond shag and a curly chestnut. She shuffled around her house in cracked gold lamé mules and pantsuits in her favourite colours: turquoise, purple and orange. Each afternoon she spent a good forty-five minutes building up

her face, starting with a solid layer of Caramel Creme foundation. A pair of black horn-rims with a rhinestone insert on each
tip gave her the look of a great horned owl on the attack. She
talked from the minute she got up — about her operations, how
her husband Earl had run around and how her sons never visited her when she was in the hospital. How Sylvia was in the hospital now and it was a good thing Sam went. At least he said he
did. I didn't know the word uterus until I moved into Vi's. Now
I was hearing on a daily basis about Vi's hysterectomy, when
they removed her source of life. Vi never forgot to emphasize
how if it weren't for her uterus, I wouldn't be here.

The first night with Nicky sleeping on the couch, I lay
awake beneath the curved vinyl spines of the Condensed Books
and took account of all I'd done to cause my mother to go crazy.
I'd broken the rules of love and imagined my mother was a
witch. I was cruel to Nicky. I'd yelled at my mother, sworn at
her, called her names. My mother had howled like a beast and
struck herself with utensils because I was too much to handle.

That night I refused to go to sleep. If craziness was catching, I wanted to be aware the minute it happened so I could
stop it. Maybe that was my mother's flaw: she hadn't paid
attention and the craziness had taken her over. I resolved from
then on to pay attention.

I was no stranger to staying up nights with my thoughts.
Some nights I cried for hours with the fierce love I felt for the
baby Jesus and the grown-up Jesus.

God was a different matter.

In the waiting room at the doctor's office there was a large
book with a picture of the grown-up Jesus surrounded by children on its blue cover. The same book was in the dentist's
office and the skin doctor's office where I'd gone once a week

over the winter to have my plantar's wart scraped. The stories of impossibly good children who became terminally ill then died and went to Heaven both fascinated and horrified me. One particular story drew me and I savoured every word. Whenever I visited a doctor, I went straight for the blue book and flipped through the pages with it on my lap, my cheeks hot as I searched for the story of The Boy with the Arm.

The Boy with the Arm was a good gentle boy with a biblical name like Davey or Johnny. Everyone liked him. He had thick, straight blond hair and wire-framed glasses. When he found out he was sick and had to stay in bed because he probably wouldn't live, his only worry was whether God would be able to find the soul of a boy so small and take him to Heaven. This troubled The Boy so much that it was all he talked about, and his sweet-hearted mother too became fretful. Finally, when he was close to dying and unable to breathe well or speak loudly, he came upon a solution: if he raised his arm every night before he went to sleep, God would be able to see him and know that this little boy's soul needed to be taken to Heaven. With the help of his mother, he propped up his arm and fell asleep with a smile on his face. That night, The Boy with the Arm died and went peacefully to Heaven. Beside the story was a picture of The Boy sleeping with his arm bolstered by striped pillows while his soul floated toward the ceiling.

I was hooked. In the waiting room, I devoured the story, anxious to feel the thrill of The Boy with the Arm's death before the nurse called my name.

Each night after a doctor's appointment and the inevitable encounter with the story of The Boy with the Arm, I lay in bed debating whether the story was true. Did God know the little boy was dead and that his soul was ready for Heaven, or was it the arm in the air that signalled Him? If it was the arm, what would have happened if the little boy hadn't propped up his? Would the Devil take him? I didn't think so.

My concept of the Devil was more vague than my concepts of Jesus and God. The Sunday school taught by Lucy Stevens in the United Church basement never mentioned the Devil, and it didn't provide me with stories like The Boy with the Arm. The bad characters in Sunday school were people: evil kings and disciples like Judas-Who-Betrayed-Jesus. The closest I'd come to the Devil was the red costume with tail, horns and pitchfork Duncan Matheson had worn last Hallowe'en over his mother's protests. If The Boy hadn't signalled with his arm, maybe he would have ended up in space, his body stretching then breaking apart as he got sucked into a black hole, his chance at Heaven missed.

Part of me believed it was impossible for God not to know the boy was dead — after all, He'd created everything. Surely He was aware of each person who died and needed to come to Heaven. On the other hand, what if like Santa Claus, He was fallible, sometimes so busy He needed human help to do His job?

There was one way to test God: go to sleep with my arm raised. If God did know everything, as Lucy Stevens said and I preferred to believe, He'd realize I was just a little kid with a plantar's wart who wasn't dying or ready to go to Heaven. Yet, there was the thrilling possibility that maybe God did respond to signals from down below, that there was a code between God and good children wherein they helped Him with the little tasks He might not notice in his grandness. But I'd found the story of The Boy with the Arm by accident. If such a code did exist, no one had told me. The thought of God using children as helpers firmed my belief that I was not a good child which led to the third and perhaps most exciting prospect: if I slept with my arm raised and I wasn't a good enough child to go to Heaven, the Devil in his red suit might come and take my soul; in fact, God might even be the one to point me out.

Most nights when I tried this experiment, I raised and lowered my arm several times before I gave in and hid it under the sheets, fearful of success. Only then was I able to fall asleep.

Thus it was that God had the same status that Santa Claus used to have in my mind: an energy beyond my understanding, bigger than I was and potentially out of control.

I needed a way to signal this God-energy; to let God know I wasn't crazy, no matter what He might think about my mother; to tell God to leave me alone. I lay in the centre of the double bed in Vi's spare bedroom and spread my body so my fingers touched the edge. With my eyes closed, I tried to sink into the mattress. In this position, I thought long and hard about normal and crazy. If I concentrated on what I was not, maybe God would get the message, a prayer that told Him what I did not want to be. One thing was sure. Crazy was not what I wanted to be.

In the evenings, I sat at Vi's counter at Effie's Diner, two houses down at the BP station. I filled in crossword puzzles and read *Alice* and ate grilled cheese with salted fries and ketchup while Vi talked about her varicose veins and flirted with the men who'd stopped by for a burger before going home to their wives. People said hi to me and I smiled with the corners of my mouth but mostly I kept my head down and my eyes on the page.

Some nights Sam dropped in on his way home from work and handed me a pocket notebook or a rubber oval change

purse or a black comb in a sleeve that he'd purchased out front
where people paid for gas. He stayed long enough for a coffee
and to tell Vi and me about his day. Nicky, he said, was helping on a farm. Farm work was good for a boy.

When Vi was out of earshot, I asked why I couldn't help
on the farm, too. Wasn't farm work good for a girl?

Sam explained that Nicky was going to the Sousas' and
Jack and Betty had two daughters and didn't need another girl.

"Your grandma likes having you around too. You're good
for her," he said, pecking me on the temple and standing to go.

Though I kept my head down, I could tell through my
bangs that Vi had her eye on me. Every twenty minutes or so,
she made a point of lifting my plate, bleach-soaked J-Cloth in
hand, and swiping the counter beneath it. I'd twirl on my
stool, knees together and up, folded crossword book in hand,
my pencil steadily filling in words while she swooped past. Her
jokes, definitions, soap opera gossip and stories about her sons
were part of the restaurant din.

Then she told the story of how Sylvia had come to
Apple Ford.

"It was in the middle of an electrical storm, the rain lung-
ing down so sudden men were wringing out their pant legs
afterward. For five minutes, the clouds spat crystal green hail-
stones. Then they were gone. Nothing was damaged. Later
they found out Apple Ford was the only town hit."

For the first time in the weeks since I'd come to Vi's, I looked
up. Her eyes, already magnified by the horn-rims, widened.

"The storm left only one memento: Sylvia.

"No one ever found out where she came from, and it was
your daddy she decided to marry."

I sat unblinking.

"Sylvia chose Sam," Vi said, squeezing the J-Cloth in her fist, then shaking it out over the floor. "Not the other way around. He couldn't have said no if he'd tried."

The Sam in Vi's stories was always helpless. He was her oldest by five years and hadn't done a thing right since those nights at the logging camp when Earl stayed out. Those nights, Vi would hold Sam tight between her legs in the dark, her Oxford dictionary open on his lap. He'd fix his sharp blue eyes on the door and listen for bears while she fingered the tissue-like pages. Her shoulders shook, but even at six years his were rigid as a man's, the hard blades jutting into her breasts.

After the story, Vi stuck a lit menthol into her sideways grin and tossed the J-Cloth into the sink.

When she went into the back to get a fresh canister of butterscotch ice cream, I left my crossword puzzle book and *Alice in Wonderland* on the counter and went outside. From the corner of Number 8 highway, I walked along the sideroad on the dirt shoulders of the irregularly-edged asphalt. There were some houses, high up on hills, and a stretch of pine and marsh. I turned north onto County Line 3 and walked another stretch by the river cottages where Sylvia took pottery, then across the bridge and past the park and the Stevens', willing myself not to glance toward the graveyard I'd dreamed. Uphill into town I remembered Front Street from when I'd started school when there were no sidewalks, only dirt paths worn into the lilac bushes that separated lawns from road. Front Street had more stores then: pool hall, hardware, shoe and watch repair, tack shop. We had a general store still but most of the others were empty storefronts that I peered into, imagining what a person could sell there.

The air was warm and I felt no chill in my jeans and Drag County Fall Fair T shirt. At my house I wedged behind the tangled peonies, tiger lilies and bleeding hearts in Sylvia's flower garden and looked in at the violet shadows Sam and Nicky made on the living room wall as they watched TV. Nicky got to come home in the evenings. Vi and Sam both said it was at my grandmother's insistence, not my father's, but I wondered if I had been sent to live with Vi because Sam was a man and fathers weren't supposed to raise girls.

Already I had forgotten my mother's face. I relied on the Sylvia of Vi's story, dark-eyed and -haired, rising up in the midst of the elements, commanding them to retreat once they'd served her purpose and calling them back when she was ready to leave.

This I remembered: each day the week before my mother went away there'd been a thunderstorm. The same weather that had delivered my mother had taken her away.

I continued north in the opposite direction from Vi's. I needed to walk, was all. To walk and think about how I was connected to Sylvia's craziness. Was I crazy too? Maybe I was too young to be sent to the crazy ward of the hospital so Vi was looking after me instead. Maybe they thought I would catch what Sylvia had because I was a girl.

Beyond our place, the houses were farther apart and the driveways longer. The road was lined with maples and beyond them stretched apple orchards and fields of corn, clover, sod and potatoes. I liked the sod best: acres and acres of shiny green lawn that made me want to run off the road, lie down and roll the entire length of it, folding the sod around me like a thick green blanket. The corn was good too; it reached past my waist. Endless inviting rows of stalk after stalk, a place I could wander into and walk and walk and never leave. I sniffed in deep, letting the corn smell fill my nostrils. Everything was growing; nothing had been cut down.

Two or three cars slowed down, then passed. I was almost at the next sideroad when a truck stopped, pulling onto the soft shoulder. A man leaned out, removed his cap and said, "You must be Sam Brewer's kid." He pushed his hand through hair greased back like Fonzie's. His skin was the hard red of some coats.

I said, "Yes," my voice clear.

The man was quiet then, scratching his head. He was familiar. I had seen him somewhere, with Sam, but I couldn't remember where.

"C'mon, then," he said. "I'll give you a ride as far as my place."

His offer confused me. It assumed my journey had a destination. If he drove me to his farm, I would have a longer distance to walk back. Then again, maybe I wouldn't go back. Vi's house smelled like the budgies that sat three to a cage and screamed in her kitchen.

I nodded and walked around the front of the truck, one arm outstretched to protect myself in case the vehicle rolled forward. The door was open, and on the third try, I lifted myself onto Jack Sousa's oily front seat.

I'd been in trucks like this before. It was the truck of a farmer, the floor cluttered with stained work gloves and bits of hay clumped with manure. The truck was old and had a comforting outdoor smell, like Sam's suede jacket when he came home from hunting.

Mr. Sousa didn't talk for a while. His farm was a couple of lines over. In the summers he had a honey stand painted with a big cartoon bee by the side of the road. I had been there once with Sam. Mr. Sousa had joked about his daughters being out at confirmation class. He seemed to think I'd be bored without other girls to talk to. It turned out I was, but I didn't want him to know, so I spent the time petting a bony, bowlegged rust hound that had teats as long as my fingers. The dog's ears were silky. I explored further and found bites which I rubbed with my finger pads. When I'd asked if I could let the hound off her chain, both men had laughed and Sam told me to get away from the dog and find something else to do, his voice suddenly harsh like Jack Sousa's. Sam believed dogs were for hunting or farms and wouldn't let us keep one as a pet.

"You're the one with the crazy mother, aren't you?"

I stiffened, my eyes on the passing headlights.

"That is correct."

"What's your name again? Mary? Martyr? I remember something odd and churchy about it. Nobody said anything to Sylvia at the time — she wouldn't stand for it — but I know it was a doozy."

"Mercy. My name is Mercy."

Mr. Sousa picked his hat up from the seat and put it back on.

"Sorry if I offended you. I've known Sylvia a long time. You know how gossip travels. Don't think anyone was surprised. You?"

I opened the window. I turned my face toward the fresh air, letting the watery corn smell wash over me.

"I keep forgetting she's your mama. I tend to let my tongue run away with itself. You'll have to forgive me. My wife says I'm a worse gossip than the church ladies. I 'spect you see her all the time."

Mr. Sousa looked over at me and grinned.

"Who?" I hadn't seen my mother for weeks, since she went away. I edged closer to the door.

"My wife. Mrs. Sousa. She comes practically every day now to your place to do what all needs doing. Your brother's at our place every day. Your father says he's a bit girly, that one, but I'm putting him to work. Seems alright to me. Who's taking care of you? Not Vi, is it?" He looked at me again, his smile forgotten.

I folded my fingers around the door handle. What if I opened it, hurled myself onto the road and rolled into the ditch? If I curled into a ball, maybe it wouldn't hurt so much. As long as it didn't kill me.

Mr. Sousa glanced at the road, then back at me.

"Seems like you take after Sam. Sensible and practical. He always was that. He and me went to school together after Vi and her husband split and she moved down here. I was pretty good-looking in them days, believe it or not, an old farmer like me."

He laughed, filling the cab with a wet tobacco smell similar to the stink of feet.

"I swear, I don't know what we thought when Sam announced he was marrying her. 'Course, we were all pretty taken by her when she came to town like that. Good thing Sam's brothers was too young, or there might have been some competition. But Larry was thirteen, not yet in high school and Reese younger'n that. Besides, them two went back up to live with Earl after that one year. Least I'm pretty sure that's where they went because it wasn't Vi what raised them. Probably what killed Earl in the end, those two boys. Sam was the best of them and he stayed though not with Vi. He and Sylvia were hitched by then. Anyways, Sylvia was too unpredictable. Sam should of stuck with what he knew."

I wasn't sure what he meant. I straightened and stared right at Mr. Sousa. Maybe if I was nice to him, he would take me back to his farm and I could see Nicky tomorrow. Mr. Sousa's two daughters, Tory and Elizabeth, were a year apart like Nicky and I, but older. Like Lucy Stevens. Elizabeth taught Sunday school. Though it seemed as if Nicky was happier without me. Maybe he thought the Sousas were his new family.

"I don't think you know my mother very well."

Mr. Sousa snorted.

"Perhaps you misunderstood me there. I'm talking about events that happened a long time ago. Before your time."

I shifted so my hip was pressed against the armrest on the door. I put both hands on the handle.

"I would like you to let me out now, please," I said, my eyes on the dirt shoulder.

"That wouldn't be very neighbourly. We're almost at the farm. You can get out there and call your father to come and get you."

I pictured Nicky playing with the Sousas' hound.

"I'll jump," I said, my voice level. I was almost as surprised as he by the threat.

Jack Sousa glanced at me a couple of times then sighed.

"It wouldn't be right if I just let you off. Tell you what. I'll turn right here and take you up to the pancake place on the highway. I'll give you some coffee money. You can use the phone there and call your dad."

I nodded. I kept my hand on the door. Coffee money. I wasn't allowed to drink coffee. Not even at Vi's.

At Wheel of Pancakes, Jack Sousa smiled as I fumbled with the door handle, my shoulders tight. I hoped he wouldn't decide to reach over and open the door for me. That's what Sam would do. I might bite him if he did. He didn't.

I jumped down and held the door open. I had no money at all and I wanted him to make good on his offer. We stared at each other for a long time, he with his grin, me working up the courage to ask for the money. Then he laughed his moist tobacco laugh and reached into his back pocket. I remembered the thick square bulge with the oily outline his wallet made when I'd visited his farm. Sam had said, "You wouldn't think it, but there's a rich man." If I asked for more money, if I told Jack Sousa I was running away from home — or didn't tell him anything, just that I needed it — he would give it to me. I saw myself reaching over to the open wallet, plucking out a handful of bills and dancing off into the bushes with a quick wave. Mr. Sousa wouldn't follow, wouldn't even say anything to Sam. But who knew what he might say to others? I had to resist the urge to put my hand out as I did with my father on allowance day.

Mr. Sousa leaned across the seat and pressed two one-dollar bills into my palm. One bill was crisp, new, unfolded. The other was dirty, tattered, with a corner missing and numbers written on it in blue pen. I mumbled "thank you" and was glad to leave. I didn't want to spend a minute longer with Jack Sousa. The bills made him suspect.

I had been walking up the highway for almost half an hour when Vi pulled up in her black Duster and ordered me into the car. By that time, my calves hurt and my arms were chilly so I obliged.

I slunk down. Vi faced straight ahead, holding her back away from the seat, occasionally adjusting her horn-rims or poking a finger under her wig. Vi wasn't fussy about wearing seatbelts so I pulled both my feet up on the seat and leaned my head against the door. I listened to the wheels on the road and tried to let the sounds of the car carry me to sleep.

Vi pushed the lighter in.

"I want you to get me my cigarettes, up there on the visor."
Vi held her shoulders as if they were resting on a shelf.

I struggled up and removed a cigarette as the lighter popped.

"Light it for me, please."

I yanked the lighter out, mesmerized by the glowing red circle of its tip. Vi clamped the cigarette in the side of her lips and leaned over, both hands still on the wheel, left eye on the road. The cigarette tip flared orange and she pulled away, twin smoke streams flowing from her nostrils.

"I don't think much of people who run away from their problems," she said.

It took me a moment. At first I thought Vi was referring to Sylvia. Then I realized she was talking about *me*. But I wasn't running away, only walking to sort out my thoughts. There was a difference. I turned to the window and pretended I had a chainsaw or a medieval hatchet that sliced through each pole as it raced past.

Vi loosened the grip of her fingers on the steering wheel, allowing one hand to drop down and hang from the bottom.

"Before I give you back to your father, I'm going to tell you about the first time Sam met Sylvia."

I didn't blink. Vi must have thought that if I knew more about Sylvia before she was married, I might not be bothered so much by her craziness. The opposite was true. I turned to face her, my body still. The more I knew, the more the craziness obsessed me and the more I saw myself as crazy. Crazy was the easiest thing to believe in. To believe in it, I needed to know the truth.

"It starts with Sam. He was always good in school and he was the top athlete. It was the same back in Drag. We moved down before his senior year and he picked right up where he left off. He was very popular, though to look at him now, you might not think so. He always had a girl. One after the other. I couldn't keep them straight. That was nothing compared to his brothers. Or so I hear. I suppose that was to be expected if teenage boys don't have their mother around. After Earl left, that's when I moved down here. Larry and Reese went back north to Earl so he raised them through high school. I always said that's what killed him, not the heart attack. Served him right, wild as those boys were. Sam was the best of them. It's no wonder they ended up after the women the way they were at that age, their father's nature being what it was. But Sam was no slouch, let me tell you."

Vi took a long pull on her cigarette, letting the smoke filter out the corner of her mouth.

I had a hard time picturing Sam as popular. My father had a wide easy smile, but he hid his face behind glasses bigger and blacker than Vi's own, and the front and top of his head were almost bare.

"On the day Sylvia came to town," Vi continued, "things changed. She was dark-haired and dark-skinned with those sloe-eyes that the boys liked so much."

"She had slow eyes?" My mother's eyes weren't slow. If anything they were quick as whips, able to spot the slightest imperfection and bring it to the attention of her sharp tongue.

"Sloe eyes? Well they certainly aren't like yours. Do you know what a sloe is?"

"Isn't it a kind of animal that hangs from a tree? The lazy one?"

I didn't like to admit I didn't know. Being wrong was better than not knowing.

"That's a sloth. A sloe is a plum, a dark velvety plum. Your mother's eyes have that same quality. Men love it. Your eyes are blue like Sam's."

There was nothing Vi relished more than handing out definitions.

"Anything else?"

"No."

My grandmother talked about men a lot. Maybe she would fall in love and find a new husband.

"Alright, then. No one knew exactly where this new girl lived or even how old she was. She showed up at the high school and the kids could talk of nothing else, boys or girls. The girls all wanted to be her friend and when they couldn't get close to her, they turned on her. The boys — well that was another story.

"It wasn't that she was beautiful, exactly, because she wasn't. Not if you ask me. Sure, her hair was dark and shiny and her eyes big with long lashes. But her face was pointy and she had a crooked nose. Besides, she was so tall and skinny. No curves on her. She wore her hair short, in a ducktail and the girls said she would stride into the washroom at school, take a handful of grease from a tin in her purse and slick it through her hair. No one knew whose class she was in, or if she was even in the school, but she was always there. And it didn't take long for her to find Sam."

Vi stopped to finish off her cigarette. She pushed in the lighter for the next one. Vi had never told me stories before. I didn't know where she got them. Perhaps they'd always been out there, hovering, waiting for Vi to pull them in.

"I was running a laundry and a dry clean then. I had Sam in there most evenings after his track and field practice helping me load up the machines, then sorting and folding the sheets and shirts and whatnot. It was so hot we both wore elastics around our heads to hold our glasses in place.

"One day, Sam was out front, loading up the dryers while I was operating the steam press in the back. I could do that job with my eyes closed. Almost did — had to do it mostly by hand, like a blind person, because the room was so humid my glasses had a steam on them almost an inch thick.

"When that girl walked in, the air changed. All the moisture in the building seemed to be sucked upward and out the ceiling. Maybe she gathered it all into herself, but I know it was in one instant that my glasses cleared and the clouds of vapour pouring out of the sides of the steam press evaporated. *Poof!*"

I forgot about chopping the poles and focused on the glowing heater of Vi's cigarette.

"When I went out front to see what was happening, there they were, like any two teenagers, talking about school and athletics and going to the movies. But Sam had changed. He was under a spell from the moment he set eyes on her.

"She turned and flashed me a look so cold and dead that I stepped back. Then she smiled and came forward and said, 'Nice to meet you.' When she shook my hand, her palm was wet, maybe from all the moisture she'd extracted from the air. I felt like my hand could almost go through hers, it was so transparent, ethereal — did you know that word is derived from *ether*?"

I hugged my knees to my chest.

"Like in science? The one that disappears?"

"It means lighter than air, something supernatural, not from our earth. Maybe she wasn't even there. What do you think of that?"

In the dark, Vi was grinning. Her false teeth gave off a solid white glow.

Maybe my mother was a ghost. Maybe Sylvia had transformed herself and she wasn't really in the crazy hospital where she was supposed to be. This thought tormented me. If she wasn't in the hospital, where was she? I had difficulty getting back into the story, but I forced myself. That's where the clues were.

Vi proceeded, barely pausing to draw on her cigarette.

"She asked me if I would excuse Sam so she could take him to the movies, something unheard of at that time. Back then, in our part of the world, girls never asked boys out. But I said yes, feeling how lucky Sam was that she chose him. Sam felt it too. I was under a spell. After she left and the vapours descended, resting on my skin and in every nook and cranny of my body, I stood, my hands pulling the laundry out of the press and hanging it by rote, my eyes safe behind two misty lenses, and the lucky feeling left me. It left me abruptly, and I was filled with a tiredness and a sadness so profound, I had to leave that place, lock up for the night and go out to the hotel. From that moment on, Sam and Sylvia have been together."

Vi made the turn into Apple Ford.

"Until now, that is."

I pressed my back against the seat. That outpouring of words had sharpened my senses. I could hear the crickets, the tires rolling on the asphalt, a ticking in the engine. I could smell the roses in their gardens and someone's fresh-cut lawn. I could even tell who'd had barbecue for dinner.

Vi stared at me, one eye on the road. I looked out the window. Could Vi feel the change in the air as we pulled closer to my house?

Seeing the house made my stomach churn. If Sylvia was a ghost, maybe she was still at home, watching unseen, hanging around in the ceiling corners waiting for signs that her children didn't love her enough, the perfect way to get under their skin.

"Two more things," Vi said. "Sylvia is someone you can't understand, can't ever hope to know. But I do think it's important that you see for yourself and I'll tell that to your father."

She cut the engine and listened to the car's shakes and shudders. She reached across the seat and patted me on the knee.

"Well, Mercy. It's time to meet your maker."

"What's the second thing?"

"Oh, that. It's supposed to be a surprise, but you're better off being prepared. Your father is sending you to camp."

"Camp? What about Nicky?" I held my breath.

"Never mind that. You'll have to get your stuff out of the trunk. My veins are throbbing enough as it is."

I scrambled after her, home again.

II

5

Your Wooded Grace

On my way back from the Trout Club Saturday evening, I coast past our house to the arena to check on Larry's rig and it is gone. I park my bike and come in the back door. The sun on the pink insulation stuffed between the studs and the roof rafters gives the addition a rosy glow.

I find Sam lying on the couch watching the Jays. Vi sits in an armchair knitting the off-the-shoulder orange and turquoise batwing sweater-dress she's promised me will be all the rage when I go back to school. Vi has never been the sort of expert knitter who fashions delicate pastel baby outfits or large intricate ski sweaters. Instead she prefers to make up patterns as she goes along, using a cheap nylon wool that squeaks when she rubs it between her fingers. After she cut down her smoking earlier this year at her doctor's insistence, her knitting output surged. She started the sweater-dress when she moved in this spring, reminding me of the time I stayed with her after Sylvia left five years ago. Then Vi had knit me a floor-length poncho of white pompons centred on alternating mint green and black blobs.

Vi hoists herself up and beckons me into the kitchen.

"The barbecue's lit if you want to help me get some burgers ready."

Nicky joins us and we eat from paper plates set in green baskets and drink cola from Styrofoam cups. When Vi moved in, she brought boxes of disposable dishes pilfered from Effie's. The last time she stayed with us, just before Sylvia returned, she brought only a single suitcase.

"The addition looks good. Warm," I tell Sam.

"Thanks. Vapour barrier's next, then drywall. Looks like Nicky's wild vacation is over."

Nicky smiles, his cheeks lumpy. He swallows, takes a swig of pop, and says, "Too bad Uncle Larry isn't here for the drywall. You said it's difficult. It's probably better with three of us then, right?"

"If Larry didn't get home today, Nadette would have been on him."

"It's not like she likes him very much," I say.

"True, but she doesn't want him anywhere but home."

"She doesn't trust him," Vi says. "And who can blame her?"

Sam shoots her a look and the tip of her tongue appears between her front teeth. Her current wig is a shingled auburn, her horn-rims replaced by purple tortoiseshell frames that reach from halfway down her cheeks to above her eyebrows.

"Why doesn't Mercy just help us? I'm sure she wouldn't mind," Nicky says with a big smile.

I roll my eyes. "Hardly. I know I'm muscular, but I'm not strong like *you* are, Nicky. And I have to work tomorrow."

"Wouldn't hurt you, Mercy. It's getting the pieces propped in place that's hard about drywall — and the dust, of course — but there's nothing your brother can lift that you can't. And we do wear masks."

"Maybe when I'm done the boards."

"Maybe we'll have to help you with the boards when we're finished the drywall."

Vi tops up our cola. Sam adds rum to his from a bottle on the counter.

"Any money Larry didn't ask about me. He likely doesn't know about the operation. Four feet of intestine. If you tacked that length of gut against the wall it would be almost as tall as I am." Her Dr. Snow had talked Vi into having it out and now she feels released.

"I told Larry," Sam says into his drink.

Vi continues as if she hasn't heard. "Bet Larry doesn't know his own mother was eviscerated."

"What's that?" Nicky asks.

"It's a disembowelment," Vi says, easing her chair back from the table. "Where they slice you open and pull out your bowels. Remove your essential parts. Your viscera are your internal organs. Your innards. From the Latin."

Five years ago, Vi defined hysteria for me with a similar relish, pointing out the connection between the Greek word for womb and what was thought to be a woman's frenzy while I sipped a chocolate milkshake at her counter.

Sam gets up and stands under the horseshoe Sylvia had nailed over the doorway — with the round part at the bottom so the luck wouldn't run out. He swirls his rum and Coke in the Styrofoam.

"I'll show you, if you're so curious." She glances at Sam and lifts her flowered smock, revealing the bandage that stretches from under her bosom to well below the waistline of her pants. Sam takes off his wire-frame glasses and rubs his eyes.

"It looks like a giant Elastoplast," Nicky says.

Vi laughs as Sam edges himself out of the room. "One thing I've always liked about you, Nicky, is your spontaneity. You say what is natural to say, what makes a person feel good and human. Not like your father and sister, skulking around the fringes of things, grunting instead of conversing."

I open my mouth to respond as Nicky smiles but I decide against it. Why spoil her image of me?

Vi stuck with Effie's Diner in the years since that summer I sat twirling on the red vinyl and chrome stools, reading *Alice* and eating grilled cheese, but the combination of this operation and a new owner who's turned the BP station into a self-serve Texaco have forced her to give it up. She can't walk without pain, let alone bend over to get coffee cups and napkins from beneath the counter where Dan Smothers, the new owner, insists on keeping them. Dan is young and bull-ish, with a dark thatch of hair on his upper lip that matches what is on his head. Before the operation, when the gas was a thick rubber stopper rising like bread dough against her diaphragm, she would watch Dan outside at the pumps and imagine where else that hair appeared on his body. When she reached the thick fur that surely sprouted between his legs, her sex reminded her that the world did not sit inside this firm bubble of her stomach.

"Dan's pubes were on my mind as he was giving me the 'you're fired' speech," Vi says. "I pictured the hair taking terri-tory, shooting tendrils up his abdomen, sliding down around the curve of his thighs. Even as he talked about how my surgery stories were losing him customers, my mind was running my fingers through that luxuriant pile."

Nicky looks at me with his eyebrows raised. I bite my bottom lip and shrug. What does he expect when he encourages her with his questions and "spontaneous" comments?

Vi returns to her operation: "Four feet of intestine. How many things in this world are four feet long? Steamer trunks. Nine year old children. Dogs on their hind legs. The back seat of a Cutlass Supreme. I picture my guts as a living length of sausage-links, stretched out behind me wherever I walk, measuring themselves against the world. In terms of distance, four feet doesn't go far."

The summer I stayed with her, Vi told me a story about my grandfather, Earl. His father farmed pigs before the war. The first time he brought her home, Earl took Vi straight to the barn to show her off to his daddy. She wore a fashionable brown wool dress with patent leather pumps and a brown velvet hat holding her red hair in place. By the time they reached the barn, the black mud had ruined her pumps and stockings. She was in the middle of telling this to Earl when he opened the door — and there it was, strung up to the ceiling, legs laced together, a long, intimate slit bisecting it from throat to anus. The pig's mouth gaped and its forehooves arched toward a steaming bundle of lavender and red entrails. Earl's father approached Vi, rubber boots squelching, his hands coated with a pink soapy mixture. His grin was proud and she remembered his first words clear as day:

"What do you think of her?"

His teeth gleamed in the filtered barn light. He looked first at Earl, who nodded. Then he smiled down at Vi.

It was a long time before Vi realized he was talking about the swine.

Sam has given Vi his bedroom. He sleeps on a day bed on the front porch. We've always come in through the back door, even before the addition when a mud room was all that connected the kitchen to the outside. Before Vi's operation, Sam sold her house on the highway, gave away her budgies and put her furniture in storage, all the while insisting that when she got well she would rent an apartment and get a sit-down office job, maybe even at his company. Yet he was digging and pouring the foundation for the addition before Vi had even checked into the hospital. Sam swears the addition is for us and has nothing to do with his mother and to be fair it wasn't until after he first mentioned the addition that we heard about Vi being sick. She never contradicts him, but as far as she is concerned, Sam can talk office jobs all he wants; she is retired. She may never unpack again.

The afghan on Sam's bed is white like the one in my bedroom, only heavier. The pillows and sheets are white too, with embroidery around the scalloped edges. The headboard and four posts are black walnut like the bedside tables and two dressers. Aside from the driftwood lamp bases and pressed gypsy moth shades the room is free of Sylvia's crafts, unlike the rest of the house. Her dresser has a crocheted doily under a matching walnut jewellery box and hand mirror.

When Sylvia was well, I would sneak, frightened and sweaty, into this room in the middle of the night and climb deep into the bed's snug warm cave beside her. I was back in my own bed by morning and never sure whether I'd imagined the safe feeling or not. I figured since it took care of my fears so neatly, it had to be real.

I remember the powdery, milky smell of Sylvia under the covers and sniff the room, but it is filling up with Vi's scent of lavender, perspiration and menthols.

Nicky and I sat on Sam and Sylvia's bed. Vi had the same white luggage with red satin lining as before. Her caftans hung from the door in a garment bag. Vi opened the larger suitcase and took out a blue jogging suit.

"With my final cheque from the restaurant, I bought seven of these in seven different colours. I wear them with matching pompon socks and running shoes. They're smart and simple, just what I need."

She slid open the closet door. It was full of dresses — Sylvia's dresses. No more than one or two were missing.

"Look!" Vi exclaimed. "These clothes are ten years out of date and they're probably laced through with moth-eatings."

Nicky got up and examined the dresses with Vi. They pulled them out one at a time and held them up, against Vi first, then Nicky. Last time, when Sylvia was expected home, they'd left her dresses alone. I lay back on the bed and stared at the dusky ceiling. If Sam had lived all these years amid his wife's clothes, it was no wonder he'd never found anyone else.

Nicky dropped beside me, his face close to mine on the pillow.

"Remember when we used to crawl into bed with Mom? Dad wouldn't let us touch any part of him but Mom trapped us with her arms and her legs, sometimes both you and me at the same time."

I rolled on my side and gazed at Nicky, unblinking.

"Your father used to do that, creep into bed with me. He was the only one who did mind you, and I forbid him to touch me too," Vi said. "That likely explains a lot. I didn't believe in it but he got so frightened all alone when Earl brought people home after last call."

Sam learned early to hold himself in one position from the beginning to the end of sleep. He would lie beside Vi in his curl, knee to chin, and listen to the voices of his father and his friends in the kitchen — some high, some low, layering one over another like the smoke drifting through the half-open door. Vi tolerated Sam in her bed under two conditions, both designed so she could pretend he wasn't there: he didn't touch her and he left when his father came into the room. To his father, he was funny: Sam in his white vest and baggy drawers squeezing between his leg and the door frame never failed to bring forth Earl's laugh.

"That was a man with a laugh like a rutting moose."

I flipped onto my back again.

Nicky got up and pulled open a dresser drawer. I watched him through narrowed lids. Sylvia's clothes were there too. Vi emptied her two suitcases onto the bed then filled them with Sylvia's sweaters and nighties. Last time they'd left her drawers full too. Vi fastened the clasps and Nicky hoisted the suitcases onto the shelf above the dresses while Vi stacked her clothes in Sylvia's drawers. The process took an entire morning, even with Nicky's help.

"I have to be careful, in case I dislodge something." Vi told us. "The solid bubble in my stomach has dissolved since the operation, but I'm left with the sensation that my remaining internal organs are floating freely around my abdominal cavity. This bandage is tight and I don't bend easily with it."

"How long do you have to wear it?" Nicky asked.

I groaned. He was forever asking questions that encouraged people to talk about the most mundane aspects of their lives.

"In three days, Sam's going to drive me back to the hospital for an overnight so Dr. Snow can remove the bandage. You know what it feels like?"

"What?" said Nicky.

"Like duct tape on a bulging laundry bag, as if the bandage is all that's holding me together. When it comes off, I half expect my innards to tumble out. I hope Dr. Snow is prepared with a large scoop to put them back!" Vi leaned in close to Nicky and raised her eyebrows as if she were talking to a little boy. Nicky was sixteen, but he laughed.

Vi continued, encouraged: "I hope he hasn't forgotten anything in there. My magazines are full of stories about latex gloves and tie clips that got sewn up inside people who had surgery. The last thing I need is a remnant of Dr. Snow inside me."

Vi taking over my father's bedroom reminded me of the last summer Sylvia was home. Even though Vi's clothes now sat where Sylvia's had, expectation swelled in me, as if Sylvia was about to return, a new Sylvia, with new clothes, a Sylvia who would oust Vi once again and reclaim her room, her house, us, for good.

The drywall is mounted by the end of the long weekend. Nicky and Sam celebrate by hopping into the pickup — Nicky at the wheel — and driving up to the quarry. Uncle Larry's place up in Drag backs onto a similar quarry and Sam likes to swim there with his brothers the same way he likes to hunt with them and play euchre and hang drywall with them. He craves such encounters with the other males in the family; they soothe him and become a touchstone when he returns to his everyday life.

They go at night. I am reading a vampire novel on my bed, a rotating fan riffling a sheet over my legs. It doesn't matter that they don't ask me. As far as they know, I don't swim. I picture them at the quarry, the indigo sky standing over them with what feels like pride, the water spread smooth as pooled margarine on toast. Saying nothing, they look into each other's shadowed faces and strip down. The cool water runs over and through them as if they too are water. They swim for what seems like hours, back and forth across the square hole. Nicky's armpits ache, his body tingling as if all the water it contains has seethed into life. I am asleep when they return.

My day off that week coincides with the morning Vi has her medical checkup in town. Nicky goes along to practise driving on his learner's permit. Vi was adamant that Sam could sell whatever he wanted except her car, the green Impala she bought from us after Sylvia left, so Nicky gets to practise in that as well as the Ford pickup I learned on.

In the absence of Vi's snores I sleep until almost noon, the sun hot on my blankets. I take my time stretching my limbs and opening my eyes. The dreams, though short, seemed drawn out, repeating themselves in a loop so that by the time I wake up they feel lived.

3
I walk up three sets of dark winding stairs with
Mother at my heels. The steps are short and

my heels hang off the edges. I twist the key in the lock. There is only one bed. "There must be some mistake," Mother says. She edges around the bed, which fills most of the room, and stands at the lace-covered window. All the windows in France are dressed with lace. The curtain sags. Mother tugs it aside and stares down at the hard grey street. She pulls out a cigarette, lights it, sucks on it three times before she blows. She has always done this.

4

The relentless sun is straight over our heads. Mother is in shadow. She *is* a shadow. A slim-dressed silhouette. Ageless. No matter how I angle my neck, I cannot look into Mother's face.

All these visits to Paris are blissful. Yet the urge to see Mother's face goads me. I find myself staring at nothing, willing a head full of smooth black hair to turn around, turn around, turn around, like a mantra. Sylvia was Mother to me the summer she left too — at camp, after I'd seen her at the hospital and needed to separate her goodness from everything else she was becoming. I strain to recapture the sound of Mother's voice in the dream. Did she sound like Sylvia? Sylvia's voice was raspy in the weeks when she was breaking down. Did Mother's voice sound rough, or like Sylvia before she went crazy, like the Sylvia I named Mother at Camp Wanigamog? I am trying to hear three voices: Mother's from the dream, Sylvia's when she was crazy, and the real Sylvia, before she was anything but who she was, before she was anything but my mother. The trouble is, I can't remember any of the voices, not even the one I was dreaming minutes ago.

Nicky's body is changing, sculpting itself from the inside out. His arms are now hard above the elbows and his stomach long and smooth. One night, I catch him standing in front of the bathroom mirror with the door open.

"Look how brown I am," he says, holding out an arm. My skin is pallid by comparison even though I've been trying for weeks to get a tan.

"I think I'm going to be tall too," he says. "After all, you must be nearly six feet."

I withdraw my arm and glower.

"I'm not even close," I say, though I have no idea. I've refused to let Dr. McGarry measure my height since I was twelve in case he reveals that dreaded figure. "You have a long way to go."

"Check out these!" Nicky says, nudging my foot with his. He lines his instep up snug with my foot. "I bet we're not even the same shoe size."

I slip off my sandal. "Try this."

Nicky pushes his toes in but his feet won't squeeze any further. He reaches down and edges the leather up. His heel hangs over the back.

"Give me the other one."

He stuffs his other foot in and walks down the hall.

The straps of my sandals stretching across his toes make his gait change to the hip sway of a dancer. I remember Nicky twirling on the powdered floor in the nightgown I dropped over his head. He walks now as if he knows what he is doing, as if the sandals bring out a part of him that rarely appears.

Friday night Nicky announces that he is going to the ballpark after he is finished babysitting. At the beginning of the summer, Nicky took over my weekly babysitting job at the Jacksons'. He looks after the three children while their parents stay in town for a dinner date in a restaurant.

I watch the first half of *Dallas* with Vi, a tradition from when I stayed with her. It's a wedding episode. I tell Vi I've seen it already and go upstairs.

In Nicky's bedroom, I head straight for the Montreal Expos pennant on the wall. After unpinning one corner, I stop. If the photograph is still there, I do not want to see it. I do not want to turn the pennant over and find myself staring into *her* eyes. Sylvia's eyes. Mother's. It is funny that when faced with the opportunity, I can't bear to look at her. Or am I afraid?

No photographs of Sylvia exist in our house. In fact, we have no photos at all. Sylvia used a Polaroid on us when we were younger, sticking each photo onto a pre-glued page in a plaid-covered album and securing it with clear plastic. A few of the photos showed Sylvia but because she took them, most were of Nicky and me. After Sylvia left, I searched her bedroom closet, but the albums were gone. Either Sylvia took them with her or Sam destroyed or hid them. Maybe Vi had them in storage. It is difficult though endearing to picture Sylvia leaving with our photo albums, considering. That she left so much clothing encourages me that she expects to return. That she took our photo albums was insurance of another kind: the token reminders of a life she otherwise intended to discard.

I close my eyes then look up at the ceiling. His minor hockey trophy. That's where he stashed the pink shirt he stole out of Sylvia's closet. Surely that same shirt won't still be there.

The trophy isn't on his desk. I scan the room. When he got that trophy, he told me that everybody on the team got one for participating. Nicky now has a shelf full of trophies I have no recollection of him winning. I pay little attention to his life; I know only that he plays baseball and hockey and maybe a few other sports. I've never thought of him as trophy material.

I find the 1978 Tecumseth County Minor Hockey Atom Most Valuable Player trophy on the bottom shelf, at the back. The bowl is empty. Most of his trophies have an ornament on top shaped like a player of the highlighted sport. Only one other trophy, for Peewee Most Valuable Player 1979, is shaped like a cup. It is empty too.

The *Dallas* theme song drifts upstairs.

I scan Nicky's drawers, then lift his mattress and stick my whole arm underneath. My palm grazes several glossy pages, magazines I'll come back for another time. Then, right in the centre, my fingers land on a pile of fabric. I curl my hand up and pull the heap out.

Nicky has amassed a small stash of clothes, mostly Sylvia's. I sit on the bed with the pile on my lap and lift each camisole, bra and T-shirt one by one. I hold them with the tips of my fingers only, torn between repulsion at something she wore and tenderness for what she abandoned.

Near the bottom I find one of my bras, a soft Dici, the kind that moulds to the body's shape. The commercial even says, "Let it be Dici or nothing." It is much smaller than Sylvia's bras with the pointy cup inserts, and the elastic looks stretched right to the limit. It is strange picturing Nicky fitting into an item of mine, especially now. His hips are slim, but with each day he spends carrying lumber and hammering drywall his body expands. My body is firming up too but nothing is getting bigger. When I was twelve, my body shot straight up. The rest of me is still catching up. Nicky's body is taking its time to grow, filling itself in as it goes — an exercise in balance not extremes.

When I realize what I am thinking, my mind freezes, not wanting to acknowledge the possibility. But why else? Maybe the bras, slips and panties are for remembering her — for holding and looking at and touching but not necessarily for wearing. None of the elastic is stretched on Sylvia's bras. I squeeze the clothes together in a ball and stuff them back under the mattress.

If Nicky keeps growing at the rate he claims to be, he'll soon be wearing Vi's bras. I checked them out when she was unpacking, and Nicky must have too. Their size is startling; I imagine the heaviness of her chest and stoop forward to get a sense of its weight.

I'm in my bedroom when I hear him come back from the park. I knock, then open Nicky's door. He drops his hands from the bottom of his T-shirt which he seems about to take off.

"Hey," he says. His eyes look calm and shiny.

"How was the game?"

"What—"

"The game. Didn't you say you were going to the park?"

He sits on his bed and leans back against his pillows, one wrist behind his head. "Yeah, that. I didn't stay. Nobody was there."

I lean against the door frame and scrutinize his T-shirt. It is baggy and white, the kind that usually has an alligator on the pocket. I can't see anything underneath it. With his free hand, Nicky pulls the collar away from his throat.

"So?"

"So what?"

"Where have you been? It's really late. Vi could get worried, you know."

Nicky snorts. "Only if you unplugged the TV."

I laugh. Nicky never says a word against anyone, least of all Vi.

"As a matter of fact, I was visiting one of your friends. He said to say hello."

I stare at him.

"Rick. I was at Rick's."

I walk over to the trophy shelf and run my fingertips over the little brass plates.

"I heard you knew him. Apparently he gives you Baggies."

"Yeah. He tells me stories too. I think you'd be surprised at some of the stories he tells me."

I turn. Nicky's eyes are half-closed. He doesn't seem to be talking about me. I pick up a bowling trophy. Since when does Nicky bowl?

"Rick taught me how to roll a joint: how much pot to use and how to roll the paper so it has the right amount of pack. He lets me walk in to his place, go straight to the fridge and take out one of his Baggies. You know his whole fridge is stuffed now. He harvested his crop.

"He's just a horny old man," Nicky continues. "He's not as old as Sam but I'm sure he's over thirty. All he wants to talk about is his 'sex-capades.' He tries to make me talk about the girls my age in town, you know, like Kathy Jenson and Janine Taylor, and what I think is and isn't hot about them."

Nicky has a trophy for every sport I can think of. I find one for curling and one for lacrosse. No wonder he's never home.

"I told him I'd seen this new girl," Nicky is saying. "Rick said she must be pretty fresh because he's seen every sight there is to see in this town. 'This one's new,' I said. 'She's tall, not as tall as my sister, but with black hair and high cheekbones, like an Indian.' 'What's an Indian doing around here?' he said. 'I thought this was Waspville.' That's what he said. Waspville."

I put down the rugby cup I am holding and turn around, my arms folded against my belly. Nicky is staring at the ceiling now. Maybe he's looking at the spider webs I used to see. He shifts his head and looks at me for a long while then back at the ceiling.

"'It's weird,' I told him, 'but she looks like me kind of.'"

Nicky smiles as if he is getting away with something. I wonder if he might be talking about the Nicola who danced barefoot in my nightgown, but I dismiss the idea. Besides, it is too difficult to concentrate on Nicky's new girl; my mind keeps slipping off his story and picturing the reddish-blond hairs sprouting from Rick's shoulders.

"What did he say?"

"Hmm?"

"Rick. When you told him about this new girl."

"He laughed. He said, 'This I've got to see. She ought to be some girl.'"

Nicky falls silent. He takes a lighter from his pocket and twirls it between his knuckles.

"Actually, I didn't stay. I rolled a big soggy joint and when I lit it, Rick said he didn't want any because he was working."

Nicky puts the lighter back in his pocket and closes his eyes.

I leave Nicky's room and close the door. For some reason, I like Rick for doing that.

At home the next afternoon I carry a bowl of shredded wheat with a thick coat of brown sugar into the living room. I perch in a chair facing Vi, who sits on the couch in front of a folding table doing the *TV Guide* crossword puzzle. A game show is on where the contestants guess the letters of words based on obscure definitions that appear on a pixelboard.

The cereal is mushy, the way I like it. I scoop up a mouth-ful, glance over at Vi, then gaze into the bowl.

"Where is my mother, Granny?"

Since the summer she left, I haven't mentioned Sylvia out loud. Nicky's reference to crawling into bed with her is the first anyone has spoken of Sylvia to me. My wrists tremble and the spoon clatters against the bowl. Nicky isn't the only one who can ask questions.

Vi puts her pen down, eyes on the TV, and pulls a ball of orange yarn from a straw bag. Her shoulders stiffen as she casts a row of stitches onto knitting needles, but her face doesn't change.

"Dad won't talk about it. He—"

"Have you ever asked him?" A hole appears in the third row. Vi clicks her needles as if to make up for it.

"Not really. Because you can't. He won't. He hardly talks."

There were times I crawled into Sam and Sylvia's bed as a child and found her side bare, covers thrown back, save for Sam's hand, palm down, fingers splayed. After she left, Sam inhabited his double bed the same way, every part of him kept in a neat curl on his own side except for one hand reaching out, possessive, seeking, bereft. That taut hand against the sheets is the same to me as the voice behind the lines in Sam's cigar box notes: YOU ARE SOMEWHERE. I AM SEARCHING. WHEREVER YOU ARE. I understand Sam surrendering his double bed to Vi and retreating to the day bed on the porch. The day bed is a sanctuary: long enough for his legs but wide enough for only one body, a respite for his restless, questing hand, a place to sleep without the absence of his wife beside him.

I don't know whether what Nicky said about Sam is true — that Sam wouldn't let any part of us touch any part of him when we crept, scared, into our parents' bed. I don't know because I never tried. Whenever I saw that Sylvia wasn't in bed with Sam, I withdrew to the hall, my breath fogging the panes of the French door as I watched her where she lay on her back on the couch.

Asking Sam about Sylvia will hurt him, maybe even make him cry. That's the last thing I want.

"This is Sam's business. Not mine."

"But Granny, I have a right to know."

"Call me Vi. What right? Who says so? You young women and your rights. What about Sylvia's rights? A mother's rights to peace? Some things you have to let be."

"I'm her daughter."

"So?"

Vi has never spoken so sharply to me. There is no way to get angry at her. No one in my house ever gets angry; we just ignore each other or go out. But she is in my mother's room now. And then there is the odd Mother in the dreams. It matters what became of Sylvia.

"What if something bad happened to her?"

"What if it did?"

"Shouldn't somebody tell me? And what about Nicky? He deserves to know."

"What does it matter? Nothing would change." Vi pauses to light a menthol. She takes two deep drags then sets the cigarette in a ceramic ashtray.

"Everything would change. Every morning I wake up thinking this is the day she'll come home. I wouldn't have to be afraid of her return or planning my escape in case she does. Maybe if I knew what happened to her, or even if I knew why she was crazy, maybe I could prevent it from happening to me. I might as well be crazy at this rate. You and Dad will have to lock me up before *I* get away."

Vi knits manically. So many stitches drop it looks as if she is making a tangerine fisherman's net.

She lets the knitting fall on her lap, pushes a fist into her stomach, and mutters.

"What is it, Granny?"

"It's the bubble. That hard bubble is squeezing its way between my free-floating organs, filling in the gaps like plaster." She sinks back into the couch and tilts her face up.

When she speaks again, her voice is flat, none of her usual confidential tones: "Not one of my children has ever spoken back to me that way. The worst is Larry's Nadette, and even she's harmless. Sure my boys can be rude, but if I answer a certain way, they back down — every last one of them, even Nadette. You, my dear, are relentless."

"She's my mother."

"I'll tell you about mothers."

Vi's is a body of sharp pains, urgent pinching alarms. The night Sylvia disappeared, Vi was rocking in an easy chair made of a cracked burgundy vinyl that poked and scratched, snagging her pants, reminding her of the space she took up — the space she's always taken up.

After having four babies, three of which have grown into men, Vi's body fills even more space. Whatever space her surviving children — Sam, Reese, and Larry — are in is her space too; hers and Earl's. She's filled the world with their energy, their motion, and every action of theirs finds its way back into her.

It wasn't always so. For years when her boys were growing there were moments when their bodies receded from hers, when Earl pressed his wide and heavy chest onto her mouth, his sweat cool against her flushed skin, and her body was utterly her own. She thought it unusual that this should be so, that in the very act that should inspire surrender, she should find herself complete, intact, free of the limbs that stretched to wherever her children were. Those moments of wholeness were random, as random as Earl himself. Earl with his team of Belgians, tarpaper black with heads that angled down to look him in the eye. Earl who disappeared for days, even during the first years when she agreed to go into the bush and live in the lumber camp.

She had that whole feeling only with Earl. Making love is an amputation now, the limbs connecting her to her children strangled at the joints. She tolerates it, has even learned to lust for it. She never liked or disliked the whole feeling; rather, she experienced it as uncomfortable, foreign. In Vi's mind, this physical connection to her children is punishment for her failings as a mother.

Though ambiguous about motherhood on the surface, deep down Vi is iron hard. Her own father, Alfred Wise, was mean as piss, cold in his soul but full of spit and bile on the surface, a man whose highest achievement was an appointment as foreman at a tire plant, a position he lost within a matter of months for beating an employee in a fit of temper. What Mr. Owen the owner of the plant didn't know — what no one seemed to know — was that for her father it wasn't a fit. His entire being was in a state of constant anger. His mouth was open at all times — sputtering out string after string of curses, spewing what seemed an unlimited supply of liquid.

Her own boys are versions of this first man, creatures whose basic nature can be disguised by no amount of education so she faults herself nothing. Her boys are the chaos surrounding her calm nucleus. They grew despite her — in Reese's and Larry's cases, mostly without her — and she prefers it that way. Money is what has kept her in the centre, what has propelled her forward. As long as she's worked and money has come in, she's been able to silence the string of Alfred's curses that lies at the bottom of her mind, the festering stratum of black mud at the base of a swamp. Vi doesn't consider herself a strong woman, but she knows she is intelligent. Any knowledge she can gain from the words she underlines and savours from the dictionary under her bed is hers and hers alone. She has not released her knowledge to her sons, has protected it as dearly as she has money.

Vi was denied a mother, or so she tells herself. She thinks of her mother as a woman who lived in the house, a woman named Ern who, with her skin the colour of scum on water and her monumental distorted body, was a monster sitting dumb on an extra-wide bolted-down chair beside the kitchen cookstove. Ern wore cotton house dresses covered with a long apron sewn from leftover mattress ticking. Her socks were white and rolled down to her ankles, her feet stuffed into a pair of brown leather men's slippers that stayed new looking from year to year because she rarely walked. In the mornings, Vi cut up fish, pork or venison and potatoes and dumped them into a pot on the stove. She covered the food with water from the pump out back. Sometimes she threw in a carrot or onion from the wild grass on the southern side of the house. She'd hand Ern a wooden spoon and be rewarded with a gummy smile and a dutiful stirring that didn't stop until the noon hour when Vi and her father came in for lunch. That smile was Vi's greatest shame in life because she'd turned her face and grimaced nearly every time it was given.

"Sometimes you're better off," Vi says to me now.

She doesn't say better off how — and I don't ask — but it sounds as if she means better off without a mother. Sylvia is farther away than ever. I don't like it. All I want is to know.

"But my mother. You said something about the night she disappeared—"

Vi kneads her belly and lets out a gust of stale smoke breath. "There are some things I can't speak. Will not speak."

She softens her voice and adds, "Your father's the one, not me. I can't help you."

I place my cereal bowl on the windowsill under a pot of aloe vera cradled in a macramé holder. The spoon rattles against the china.

"You don't even know, do you?" My eyelids are sticky.

Vi picks up her cigarette.

"As far as I'm concerned then," I say, in what I hope is a normal voice, "she might as well be dead."

I kick a scuff on the drywall on my way out.

Our garage is built in every way like a small barn, complete with hay doors, loft, feeding pen and a single stall. The main part of the floor is a bumpy concrete; the rest is dirt. A hanging trouble lamp plugged into the house via an orange extension cord is the only source of light. Sam scatters his tools on the built-in shelves and I lean my bike on its kickstand just inside the great doors. Fourteen blue boards rest against a side beam. The rest, unfinished, are stacked in the middle of the floor.

When Sylvia wanted to raise rabbits and then chickens, Sam fenced in a feeding pen with chicken wire — accessible from the garage by a hinged flap — and fixed up a space heater to warm the eggs and any potential chicks. The animals were prone to escape and Sylvia would hustle us outside to flush them from the gooseberry bushes so she could swoop down and collect them in her shirt or coat and deliver them safely to their pen. Sam called her "Mama Bunny" or "Broody the Hen" when he got home. She chastised him for building holes in his fences.

I'd asked Sam to put a horse in the stall — or at least a pony — even before I'd been to camp and sat astride Clancy, my face against his hot neck. The stall was the right size but the town wouldn't permit it, he said, and it was expensive. I had to content myself with a brown rabbit named Beezus and a hen named Laverne who looked the same as Nicky's hen Rocky Balboa.

The loft's black broken hay hasn't changed since the days when Nicky and I climbed the wooden wall ladder to smoke cigarettes. Nails like pointed licorice twists spike down from the roof which slopes right to the floor and makes it necessary to crawl to reach the front corner — the place I was always most afraid to go because it meant risking a nail in my scalp if I got startled or jerked while crossing the unstable middle boards. I tuck my head in and sweep my fingers through the hay bits here. My hands are not disappointed and I have to force myself to keep my shoulders around my ears in my delight and relief at palming the smooth wood once again.

I get to the Trout Club after dark. The next-to-last stretch is a recently oiled dirt road and my eyes sting from the greasy dust roused by passing cars. I pass cattle-less fields shining in the moonlight before I turn onto the paved Ford Road where the rocks and cedars so tightly edge the shoulders I have to concentrate not to veer into the lane and almost miss the entrance. The sign, set back in the trees and lit by a single floodlight, is visible to cars but not pedestrians and cyclists. Trees throng even closer to the Club's driveway than to the Ford Road. Low-hanging stars and the occasional modestly placed floodlight help the moon brighten my way. I pedal hard and ephemeras whip my face. When one flies into my mouth, I spit it sideways. The trees end and I cycle past stables and red cedar Pan-Abodes. A fresh manure smell mingles with cedar and moss, not unlike the muck-and-pine scent of Camp Wanigamog. The trees thicken again then I emerge in front of a white clapboard lodge with green trim. I drop my bike against a bush. A steep hill rises in levels, with a set of stairs in the middle leading to a veranda that wraps around the front and both sides of the building. Floodlights beam from beneath trim flowering shrubs and warm lamps glow through screen windows. Pine Adirondack chairs painted forest green and white sit at evenly spaced intervals. On the third storey, various sized dormers jut out, flanking a hexagonal turret that buttresses a pointed green cap.

The package on my bike rack is intact. I discard the grocery bag and unroll my gabardine skirt, patting it flat in front of me like a prayer mat. I place the lightning man in the centre. He won't stand upright; never has. He doesn't really have any proper way to sit or stand, just rocks on his side like a log. Which he is. In our conversations at Camp Wanigamog the summer I made him, I teased him about his logginess and his branchy qualities, feeling like Dorothy addressing the Wizard and calling him "Your Wooded Grace" and "O Divine Bark." I took comfort from his power, holding him between my palms and folding around him in sleep. He was there to keep me from going crazy.

I lean my back against a tree trunk. Most of the numbers have fallen off and I shuck as many more as I can. I have nothing to say to him. He never answered me anyway and that is not why I brought him here. There is no reason really; I made him for protection and he didn't make me safe. But I didn't abandon him; I concealed him instead. What could he do for me now?

I shut my eyes and try to separate the sounds. June bugs flail against the screens as swing music drifts over their shells. Voices murmur and dishes smack and boards squeak under shoes. But that is over there. Here, there is near silence. Here, I am going deaf. The odd whine of a mosquito might penetrate, maybe. But when I listen closely, when I *strain*, not even the sound of my own breath, nor her voice — not even these are in me here.

6

Vanishing

My father tossed a hockey bag onto my feet. "Hurry up. We don't have much time." I folded back the blankets and sat up. The sun was all over the room and Sam hunkered down by my open dresser drawer, frowning at a typed list.

"Vi's bringing the rest of your clothes after breakfast, but you're going to need other things."

"Like what?"

"Like a flashlight and a rain poncho and a ground sheet. I've got a lot of that in the garage. Check this over and put in everything you can find that's on it."

"Where's Nicky?" I remembered my father and grandmother talking about camp before I had gone to bed. "Does he have to go, too?"

"He's making pancakes, and no, he's not going with you. It's a girls' camp. Don't worry about it. Going to the farm every day is like camp for Nicky," Sam said, closing the door behind him.

What I'd suspected at Vi's was right. There must be something wrong with me or else Sam wouldn't send me away and not Nicky. And so fast too.

When I had walked in last night behind Grandma Vi, dragging a garbage bag full of T-shirts, Sam was sitting up and patting the newspaper on the coffee table for his glasses. His eyelids were paler than the rest of his face. The TV was on but Nicky wasn't around. I wanted more than anything to cross the room and lean into Sam — the way I used to with Sylvia when she would comb my hair into braids: my face in his neck, my arms around his ropy shoulders. His tube socks were high on his calves, the way we pulled them when we wanted him to play with us on the floor. The newspaper lay folded open to the crossword puzzle, the boxes nearly filled with Sam's tilted capital letter printing. He sighed, his forearms on his knees. Vi pushed me forward and I stumbled.

"Tell him," she said.

I didn't want to speak. What if Vi was mad that I didn't want to stay with her? What if Sam was mad that I wasn't doing what he wanted me to? What did he want me to do?

"It's not working out," Vi said. "She wants to be with you." She said nothing about me running away though Sam might know already if Jack Sousa had called.

"Is that what you want, Mercy?" Sam asked.

I stared at the rust and gold hexagons on the carpet. What if I said yes and he told me I was wrong to want that? What if I didn't really want to be here? Nothing was different really: Sylvia's ceramic ashtrays sat on the end tables and her macramé planter hung in the window. But her cigarette package and lighter weren't on the sill and her knitted slippers weren't in front of the couch. There were no *Good Housekeeping* magazines on the coffee table and no craft projects on the sideboard: no half-wired driftwood lamps or unglazed flowerpots or cut-out pieces of coloured paper or glue or varnish or brushes. Nicky's socks and running shoes, sure, and Sam's moccasins, but nothing of Sylvia, nothing that said this woman, my mother, lives here and uses this room and will be back any minute to resume her life.

Sam said he'd been thinking about sending me to camp for a while. He and Sylvia had talked about it in the winter. When he said that in fact it was my mother's idea that I go, that she'd thought I'd like it, I gave in without protest. Vi nodded, so maybe she had known too. Sam hadn't been sure it was a good idea but he said he had made up his mind the moment I walked in that I needed the company of other girls my age.

"It's an opportunity," he said to Vi. "Wilt James' wife works for that camp, in the office, and she knows our situation and says they'll let Mercy in on short notice. You can even go tomorrow, Mercy, as long as we let her know."

He had seemed so eager, happy to have found a solution, a place to send me. Sam's way of dealing with his family members these days seemed to involve sending them away.

But Sam was wrong when he said being at the Sousas' was like camp. Nicky got to come home at night. Being at camp was like being in the hospital. It was *away*. Sam must believe that I could go crazy too. Maybe he thought I already was.

Mrs. Sousa had cleaned my room, but otherwise everything was as I'd left it. Except for the lightning man. I'd forgotten about him at Vi's, but the red-capped glue bottle sitting atop my ballerina jewellery box reminded me. I looked for the lightning man in my drawers, under my mattress, behind my books. I searched my bedroom closet and found the box of lightning wood scraps and the lace-edged remains of the paper circles I'd cut. The more I looked, the more clearly I pictured the lightning man and the stronger his power became.

I went into the hallway. The house smelled different without Sylvia, like fried onions and mouldy clothing and a citrus scent that must have come from Mrs. Sousa. I opened Nicky's door and spotted the half-made wooden figure stuck all over with paper numbers on the floor beside Nicky's bed. I squatted and stared at the idol without touching it. The figure was crude, but it did resemble a man. I was pleased; Nicky hadn't destroyed my lightning man.

I went into my bedroom and grabbed one of the T-shirts from the floor. Back in Nicky's room, I wrapped up the lightning man, folding the ends of the shirt over like a birthday present. I stuffed the package into the bottom of the hockey bag and covered it with clothes. Then I went downstairs to sample Nicky's pancakes.

The car was an oven. I was wearing corduroy cutoffs with strings hanging down and the backs of my thighs stuck to the vinyl seat. Sam had packed my North Stars so I'd pulled on white knee socks and crammed my feet into my two-tone Sunday school shoes while Sam idled the Impala. The shoes were tighter than the last time I'd worn them and my feet pulsed.

I unrolled my window and pointed my elbow up into the sunshine the way Sam did. The chrome on the door burned my skin but I said nothing. The car had the gasoline smell of a flooded engine along with dust and cigarettes and dried grass. The windows were filmed yellow from the smoke. Sam stretched his arm behind me on the seat as if I was his date. He faced the road and backed out of the driveway.

"By the way," he said, gaining speed. "I've got a bit of time, so I'm taking you to see your mother." He palmed the steering wheel with his left hand, swung the car out onto the road, faced forward and pushed the gearshift into Drive.

I tried to catch his eye but he remained intent. I watched the road with him. My throat threatened to close up with mucus. I stared at the thumb-sized silver knob on the lighter and tried to remember to breathe. Knowing the lightning man was going too made me feel better.

"Aren't I too young?" I asked eventually.

"You're about to turn twelve. That's close enough."

I couldn't think about seeing my mother. Thinking about it would make it too real, too scary. Instead, I called up Vi's story. I tried to picture my father in his flip-down Polaroids and his cap with a corncob badge as the Sam who had fallen under Sylvia's spell in the steamy dry cleaners. When he snapped his head from side to side, checking an intersection before a turn, I had a brief glimpse of the popular boy he'd been. But as hard as I tried, I couldn't see that fearful, almost sultry person who'd fallen under Sylvia's spell.

A pool of water appeared ahead on the highway, shimmering and cool, like a puddle you could swim in. I wished I could swim and imagined myself sliding into the water like a knife and slipping into another world, like Narnia. Sam was a good swimmer who liked to cut across a lake in an Australian crawl, his arms regular as wheels. Nicky was as happy in a pool as he was a lake or the quarry — or most especially, the river. Sylvia wouldn't go in.

Whenever Sylvia took us to the swimming hole, I wore sneakers and made sure I kept to the stony parts, avoiding the pasty mud where leeches lurked, never letting the river water wind any higher than my knees. Sylvia stayed right out of the water, scanning the shoreline for treasure instead. Nicky, meanwhile, was prone to climbing a tree and flinging himself into any part of the river deep enough to catch him.

When the car neared the puddle, the pool disappeared, folding in on itself until it was a shiny thin line. Another one sprang up so I stared at it. Each time, I missed the moment of vanishing. I resolved to pay more attention.

"Where do the pools go?" I asked.

Sam rubbed his chin. "They're called mirages. They aren't real. They appear in the desert to wanderers who are thirsty."

"But I'm not thirsty." Saying so made me crave a Coke.

"Mirages happen because of the sun and the heat. They've got nothing to do with you." He removed his cap, swiped his streaming head with a handkerchief, then plunked the cap back down.

I watched yet another mirage pool shrink up into nothing.

"Why is Mom in the hospital?"

Sam didn't hesitate.

"So she can rest and get better."

"Why can't she rest at home?"

"Because the hospital can take care of her."

"We could take care of her."

Sam raised his eyebrows. With the Polaroids, he looked like a fly.

"Obviously we can't."

He jammed an eight-track into the player and Roy Orbison came on. Sam sucked in air. I stared at him, missing more mirages.

"Besides, that's what hospitals are for. They'll make her better. Then she can come home and everything will be the same."

Sam's voice had an edge. I opened my mouth to ask another question and he slammed on the brakes and hit the horn with three sharp blasts.

"Jeez!"

I sank back in my seat and adjusted my arm out the window. The tape player clicked as it changed tracks and Roy's voice quavered out from the door speaker: *Down down down dowmbee doo-wah.*

The hospital was pink. It sat right across from Dr. McGarry's building and kitty-corner to a Dairy Queen.

"Can we go to Dairy Queen after?" I asked, but Sam grabbed my hand and pulled me toward the front doors. His head bobbed left and right as he strode through the parking lot traffic. My voice got lost amid the din of the cars and people shouting and the next thing I knew, I was in a large elevator, perspiration streaming down my back. I swallowed and tightened my grip on my father's soft yellow palm.

We went straight to the third floor where a nurse approached us from behind a big round desk. Everything was pale green and smelled closed up and musty, like Vi at night after she'd removed her teeth and wig. The nurse was squat with a moulded toque of brown hair. She wore half-glasses perched on her nose, which jutted out at an alarming angle from her face. Her shoes and hose were a light green that matched the hospital interior.

"You must be Mercy Brewer," she said, her voice sweet. I leaned into my father.

"What a pretty name. I'm Nurse Weaver. Your mother's told us all about you and your brother. I hear you're going to camp. What a lucky little lady!" Her smile was enormous and long-toothed, her eyes directed at Sam. Somehow she knew about camp when I myself had only found out that morning.

Nurse Weaver pivoted.

"This way dear," she said, giving a crisp wave. I stood my ground, hanging onto Sam's hand. He released his grip and still I hung on. Sam didn't budge either.

When I looked up at him, he shook my hand away and said, "Go on. It's only your mother." He turned and walked over to the three green chairs lined up against the far wall.

Nurse Weaver beckoned, her face frozen in the same smile. "Come along, dear."

I trudged after her.

Even though it was sunny outside, the hallway was dim and most of the rooms had their curtains drawn. Strange gurgling noises came from some. I held my shoulder blades stiff to catch the trickling sweat.

We stopped at the second-last room, which was slightly brighter than the others. A drawn curtain exposed a view of identical brown roofs. Nurse Weaver bustled in.

"Your daughter's here, Mrs. Brewer. Young Mercy is here. What a beautiful little lady she is too, if I may say so." Nurse Weaver moved to the corner of the room and fussed over a shadowy form bunched up in a metal bed with wheels.

She sounded so fake. How could my mother take it? I hung back in the hallway.

"*Come on,* Mercy, your mother wants to see you," the nurse said realizing I wasn't right behind her. Her voice echoed around the room which was empty except for two other beds with scrunched-up sheets. I couldn't remember any other person who had ever used my name so much.

I entered the room and Nurse Weaver moved down to the bottom of the bed. She busied herself with tucking sheets and blankets under the mattress. A figure emerged from the pile of covers with arms extended and I looked away. Nurse Weaver hissed and gave me a push.

Sylvia had shrunk. I walked over to the bed and let the arms embrace me. My mother was warm like before, but now her body was all angles and depressions. There were no more soft strong spots where I could bury myself.

Sylvia was wearing a pink quilted jacket tied in a little bow under her neck. Her arms looked the same except for a plastic bracelet on her wrist. From the neck down, however, she'd transformed into a shapeless lump without boundaries or edges — nothing to hold onto or get comfort from.

Her face was thin and a watery yellow. Her eyes were heavy and purple like before but also wet. A red lipsticked smile shook across her face. She looked older than Vi. I stepped back. Nurse Weaver was lining up the creases on the curtains.

"It's good to see you," Sylvia said. She reached over to a tray littered with movie magazines, tissues, headbands, nail polish bottles, emery boards and lipstick tubes. She rummaged until she found a small pack of Peter Jacksons with a lighter stuffed in the side.

Her hands steadied as she pulled out a cigarette, lit it and inhaled deeply. They trembled again as she set the box back down. Chipped red polish coated her nails. Clumps of mascara sat on her eyelashes, trailing tiny black combs below and above her eyes. The path of the loosely applied lipstick didn't match her actual lips.

Circles of smoke swirled.

"Do you want some pop or something?" Sylvia asked, as

if she was addressing an important friend, not her daughter. She exhaled.

I nodded, looking out the window at the tiny cars on the bright pavement below.

"Can we get some ginger ale for her?" Sylvia asked Nurse Weaver in a sweet wheedle that was more like Nicky's or my own when we wanted a cookie or to stay up late. The nurse left.

"How is Nicky?"

"Fine, I guess. I've been at Grandma's, so I only saw him this morning. I've hardly seen him since — well, for a long time." I didn't tell her about the pancakes that were chewier than her pork chops. I looked down at my feet. The part where the laces tied up across the bridge hurt.

Sylvia stared out the window and puffed on the cigarette. Ashes dropped into the folds of her blanket. She turned her head and a dirty pink ribbon flopped in her hair. When I was in kindergarten, Sylvia had stored my ribbons in her own bedroom in a round talcum powder box made of opaque plastic so I wouldn't ruin them. There was a colour for each dress I owned. The ribbons were an inch wide and velvet on one side. If they got dirty, Sylvia washed them by hand with a special soap. I hadn't worn those ribbons in years. It was odd to see Sylvia wearing one that wasn't perfect.

Sylvia leaned back in the pillows and the flesh from her face sagged. She really did look old.

"Why do I have to go to camp?" I asked, stroking the place where the green blanket folded over the edge of the mattress.

Sylvia sighed and smoke trailed out of her nose and mouth. Her face was the same drained mask I'd seen when I peeked in the bedroom door on that last day. My pupils twitched.

Love
Oject

"Because your father wants you to. It's too much for him to look after you in the summer."

"What's so hard about it? Why doesn't Nicky have to?" My voice looped higher. I clenched the blanket, pulling it away from the mattress.

"Because."

"Why?"

"Quit asking me questions, okay? I came in the hospital to get away from that nonsense. Leave me alone."

Sylvia raised a shaky hand like a traffic cop. I held my shoulders tight, even though the sweating had long since stopped. Sylvia reached over to the table beside the bed and jabbed her cigarette out in a frill-edged tin ashtray. Without lifting her eyelids, she shook out another cigarette, lit it and rolled over onto her side, facing the window. She dragged long and hard then let the cigarette hang from her lips as she stared out into the glaring sunlight.

I watched her for a while, then picked up a movie magazine and sat down on the chair beside her bed. I flipped through the black-and-white pictures of Liz Taylor and Ali MacGraw and swung my legs against the chair until Nurse Weaver returned with my ginger ale. She set the plastic cup down on the tray and furrowed her brow so she looked like she had four eyes: the normal pair that floated above the rims of her glasses and the wobbly magnified pair visible through the glass. The ginger ale didn't have any bubbles in it. I picked it up and sipped. It was warm.

Nurse Weaver approached Sylvia's bed and plumped up the two thin green pillows wedged behind her neck.

"Come on, Mrs. Brewer. Mercy came all the way here to see you. You can certainly be nice to your daughter while she's

121

here." Sylvia shrank even more at the plastic voice. Nurse Weaver put her hand on Sylvia's shoulder and pulled her over on her back again. Sylvia's body went limp, becoming a dead weight as Nurse Weaver adjusted her into an acceptable position. My mother's expression stayed fixed and defiant. She pulled her lips in and chewed at her lipstick.

I turned to the back page where the wigs were. Most were short and curly with names like the Madison and the Sassy. They were ugly, even though the faces wearing them were beautiful heart shapes with full, smiling lips. Vi wore wigs like these. I liked the long-haired ones better. When I'd tried on Vi's frosted shag, I'd paired it with her sleeveless gold turtleneck, white pants and mules and pretended I was a feminist or a comedienne like Carol Burnett or Phyllis Diller. There were only two long-haired wigs in the ad: the Rebecca and the Monaco. I pictured myself in one — a glamorous and famous movie star with a gorgeous, silent boyfriend like Ken, whose limbs were never as flexible as Barbie's and whose hair was uncombable. Without Sylvia's daily taming ritual, my own hair curled in all the wrong places. During my first week at her house, Vi had taken me to a beauty parlour and had my hair shorn into a pixie cut. I feared my hair would never grow long again. Sylvia didn't even notice.

"See, she doesn't want to talk to me," my mother was saying. "She'd rather read. They're all like that. Rather be doing something else all the time. Where's your father, Mercy? Why didn't he come to visit?"

I closed the magazine and replaced it on the pile. I straightened the pile, making sure the corners lined up. I pulled my shoes under the chair. My feet throbbed.

"Sam's in the waiting room, out there."

I swallowed the last of the ginger ale. I didn't know how to leave without annoying Sylvia even more. She was speaking to Nurse Weaver, who seemed ready to go as well. Sylvia was on her fourth cigarette.

"You see what I have to put up with? What is this business of calling your father 'Sam'? Where's your respect?" Sylvia's eyes grew moist again. Behind the tears, they were ice.

The ginger ale was corroding my chest. I couldn't swallow. I wanted to cry too. This wasn't my mom. This wasn't Sylvia either. This was more like the witch I used to imagine, only worse, much worse. This witch had no power. That was the scariest part of all.

"I'll go get *Daddy* for you," I said, and walked out of the room. My face muscles strained up and outward with the urge to cry but I closed my eyes and forced everything back in. The feeling in my toes was gone and each step felt like walking on marbles.

Sam was sitting in a vinyl chair with a cup of coffee and *Life* magazine open on his crossed leg.

"She wants to see you," I said, sitting down beside him. "Then can we go to the Dairy Queen?"

Sam raised his eyes, his forehead a network of lines.

"She okay?"

I shrugged and swung my leg, hitting my tight shoe against the chair leg. Out of habit I glanced around for a copy of the blue book with the story of The Boy with the Arm.

Sam sighed and stared at a spot on the floor about six feet away.

"Alright then," he said. "I won't be long. You sit right there and be good."

He heaved himself up, put his hands on his hips and strode off toward Sylvia's room. He was back in less than five minutes.

The sound of yelling followed him but he grabbed my hand, yanked me up and marched me toward the elevator. I kept my eyes on the floor numbers, concentrating on a chocolate-dipped cone from the Dairy Queen.

My shoes squeaked as we crossed the hospital lobby. Sam walked fast so I had to hop and leap to keep up, my armpits aching from the stretch, each step sending a shock through my numb feet. Outside, the prickly sunshine was blinding. I sneezed. Sam shoved on his cap which he'd removed in the waiting room, and flipped down the green plastic Polaroids.

The car was hotter than before and we both rolled the windows down all the way. After paying the parking lot attendant, Sam put on his turn signal in the opposite direction from the Dairy Queen. He glanced left and right, then squealed out of the parking lot. This manoeuvre caused several people on the sidewalk to whip their heads around and stare like placid cows observing a tractor. It also caused me to cry. I pushed my nose against the door so Sam wouldn't see. The tears streamed down. My head ached with the heat and I sniffled. Roy sang *I'll never be blue, my dreams come true.*

"What's the matter?" Sam asked, his low voice gentle as though he were talking to a baby.

My shoulders shook.

"Are you sad about your mother?" He sounded relieved not to be the only one upset.

"I wanted to go to Dairy Queen," I sobbed, fully crying now. I blubbered and wet bubbles emerged from my nose.

Sam glanced over at me, his eyes with the Polaroids big green holes like a fly's. When he looked back at the road, he swerved, jabbed the horn and cursed.

"Now see what you've made me do!"

I sniffed, unable to stop myself now though the time for crying was over.

Sam sighed. "I'm sorry. I'll take you to Dairy Queen, and then we have to get you to the camp bus."

I wiped my nose on the hem of my T-shirt.

"Sure, Dad," I said, crooking my elbow up so it was pointing out the window at the same angle as his. A pink triangle of sunburn was emerging there. I smiled a little bit with one corner of my mouth and hoped for the burn to deepen.

7

'Scuse Me While I Kiss the Sky

T he counsellors stood in a line and introduced themselves when we got off the bus. They were named after
animals or food: Moose, Chipper, Ducky, Pickles,
Salty. The camp director was a short redheaded woman called
Woody Woodpecker. Their yellow T-shirts bore a picture of a
grinning brown beaver and the words "Camp Wanigamog: A
Dam Fine Camp."

As the counsellors unloaded the bus, I approached a short
girl with big boobs and a rounded bum whose parents had cried
when they dropped her off. She had thick glasses and a shiny
forehead and wore a plaid blouse and stretchy jeans even
though it was hot. She looked easy to make friends with. I tried
to separate my toes, but my shoes crammed them together.

I sidled up and stood with my shoulder lightly touching the
round-bummed girl's. She was standing at the edge of a group
of taller girls. Two wore the same shirt as the counsellors.
Whether she knew them or was trying to attach herself to the

group, I couldn't tell. She looked at me through bottle-bottom lenses that suspended her huge grey eyes.

"I'm Mercy," I said.

The girl smiled with her lips closed. "I'm Cherry."

"What kind of names are those?" a thin girl with a whiny voice said, staring. She had a big nose and straight hair parted in the middle and was one of those wearing a camp shirt.

"I kind of like them. The names that is." A muscular girl with flat orange hair and bangs grinned at Cherry and me. Rabid freckles spilled over her face, arms and legs. She wore big sunglasses with a rhinestone heart on one of her tinted lenses.

"I'm Angie," she said. "This is Jo. You must be virgins."

Jo cackled and Cherry joined in. After a delay, I added my own laughter with no idea what was so funny. The other girls squinted at me. On cue from Angie, they laughed even harder.

Cherry, Angie and Jo were in my cabin, along with a set of short-haired twins, Lindy and Beth. Our counsellor was Chipper, so named for her cheeks and her disposition. My bunk was directly below Cherry's. Two small squares cut high up at each end of the room kept the light out, even in the afternoon, and my bed felt like a cavern. Above me were springs and the striped bottom of a mattress.

When it came time to go to campfire, the cabin became a scramble of motion. I tucked my jeans under my arm and walked outside toward the outhouse.

"What are you doing?" Jo called. "You're going to make us late."

"I really have to go. I'll just change in there."

"Sure."

The other girls laughed and I continued, confident they had accepted my quirk of not liking to change in front of people.

Cedar trees surrounded the outhouse so the air was cooler there. A triangle cut in the door for ventilation didn't stop the stink.

The others were standing in a line outside the cabin when I emerged.

Chipper blew her whistle and marched off in the direction of the amphitheatre.

My shorts were balled up in my hand. I turned to go into the cabin but Angie's arm stopped me.

"Drop them here. You can get them later."

"But I don't have my sweater."

Angie grinned but her eyes meant business.

"You really haven't been to camp before, have you?"

I shook my head.

"The most important thing is to act like one of the group. If you play the game they leave you alone and you can do what you want."

She prodded my lower back. My spirits were lifted but I felt chilly. I dropped the shorts on the steps.

"March," Angie said, following the line.

I was right behind her.

The days passed in a blur. From dawn until bedtime, Chipper rushed us from one activity to another. All the cabins ate together at picnic tables pushed into long rows in the Big House. Breakfast was oatmeal, Tang and pre-buttered toast with jam from a plastic square. Our cabin — we'd chosen our name, the Pink Ladies, ourselves — started with Canoe Paddling at 7:30, followed by Lake Swim. After that, Handy Krafts and Sports for Two, then a lunch of hot dogs or macaroni and cheese. Afternoons featured Nature Hikes followed by Group Games that pitted cabin against cabin in Capture the Flag or Red Rover, then Horseback Riding and Pool Swim. Dinner was fish sticks or sloppy joes with garden salad, milk and Rice Krispie squares. Evenings started with Quiet Time, to write letters home or play cards, and ended with Campfire.

We walked everywhere in a line and sang every chance we got. Since we were the Pink Ladies, we alternated as many of the songs from *Grease* as we could remember with traditional camp songs like "Old Hiram's Goat" and "Noah in the Arky Arky."

After Group Games, we returned to the cabin to put on blue jeans to go to the stable. Sam had packed my floppy rubbers with orange ridged soles instead of the knee-high black riding boots that the list had specified and that the other girls wore. Instead I put on my two-tone Sunday school shoes which, despite the painful fit, featured a raised heel. This choice did not go unnoticed.

At the stable, we met Aldo, who wore a grey ponytail and was so short and bowlegged Jo said he used to be a jockey. After a brief lesson on the parts of a horse's body, Aldo talked about how to approach a horse. He assigned us each a horse that would be ours for our entire stay. Mine was one of the bigger ones and was named Clancy, like a policeman's horse from an old movie. Aldo said he wasn't an appaloosa, but he had the colouring: grey splashed under white.

Cherry and the twins lived on farms, and Angie and Jo took regular riding lessons, so Aldo devoted more time to me. I learned to speak to Clancy before touching him and to always approach from the front. I had been around the horses in near-by fields but despite my pleas for Sam to let me keep a pony in our garage, I knew little more than to hold my hand flat when offering a carrot or apple. When I reached for Clancy's slimy black nose, Aldo cautioned me to place my hand on his shoulder or neck first, then scratch the bridge.

"Never dab the end of his nose," he said.

I stroked Clancy's forehead and met his liquid gaze.

"Make eye contact, that's right," Aldo said. "You're doing good. It's about communication. He can read you and you have to tell him what you're doing."

"What, talk to him?"

"Talk to him, sure, but stay close. Let him know with your hands and your movements and your confidence. He knows fear and takes it on. Get him to look at you and take your time and you'll be fine."

Around me the other girls tickled their horses' muzzles and throttles. Clancy snorted.

Aldo clasped his hands and helped me swing up over Clancy's broad back. I laid my palms on Clancy's neck and pushed my face close. The smell was as good as fresh bread or Sam after he'd been cutting wood. When I sat up again, I felt solid, real, in control. There was nothing like it.

Down at the lake, I'd disguised my inability to swim by staying near the shore and playing Marco Polo. That afternoon we had our first swimming lesson in the pool.

The swimming instructor was Moose.

"Listen up!" he shouted, first off. "Meet me at the deep end. Single file. That's an order!"

He lifted up the whistle that hung on a cord around his neck and gave it a shrill blast. He pressed his bare heels together and marched. Everybody at Camp Wanigamog marched.

All the girls scurried over to the deep end like obedient gazelles, dry bathing suits clinging to the rounded parts of their bodies. All except me; I remained stuck in place, my feet planted on the bumpy concrete near the wobbly blue shallow end.

Moose turned to me, his one eyebrow raised.

"You! Let's go. I said *deep end*."

I looked down at my feet, which suddenly seemed abnormally long and white.

"I don't swim," I said, chin tucked in.

"What was that?"

Moose's voice boomed from inside his chest.

I couldn't answer. Moose blew the whistle again. I shifted to one foot, rubbing the other behind my knee. He dropped the flutter board he was holding. A thrill of impatience shivered through the girls waiting at the deep end.

Moose advanced toward me, his great feet smacking the dry poolside. I looked over the fence to the paddock and searched for Clancy. I imagined Clancy and me cantering off into the fields, then farther into the woods, and eventually into the mountains that I was certain existed somewhere in this province. Even though Aldo had led Clancy and me around the paddock, I trusted Clancy to guide me.

A shadow fell.

"You are going to swim. You are going to swim in the deep end like everybody else. You will walk over there now. Understand?"

Moose's voice had that low roar that Sam's took on when he was giving us trouble. I only knew how to obey such a voice.

I followed Moose to the end of the line but a sick pink core of fear welled up inside me. I saw myself choking, filling up with that impossible water like blue Jell-O or the marble eye that Great Uncle Roof, Grandpa Earl's brother, once dropped right into the middle of his mashed potatoes at Christmas dinner. If I went in that deep end the way Moose wanted me to, I would sink twelve feet to the bottom and lie there, a bloated corpse pickled in chlorine.

When it came my turn, I grabbed a flutter board and jumped in, kicking my way right to the shallow end. The instruction was to use whichever stroke you knew to swim the pool — and that's what I did. When I reached the other side, I tossed the flutter board over the edge and refused to get out. Angie rolled her eyes and the rest of the group laughed then ignored me. Moose set his jaw and gave up. I stayed where I was. I had to prevent myself from drowning in that marble-eye-blue water.

By the end of the week, it was as if I'd never been anywhere else and would never leave. At dinner, before we returned our dirty trays and dishes to the mess table, Woody Woodpecker got our attention with a gong so she could read announcements, mostly concerning the Campfire agenda, and hand out mail. It hadn't occurred to me that anyone might write to me but when I saw Cherry get her daily letters from her mother, father and sisters — and Angie and Jo get letters from their boyfriends and best friends — I let myself hope that I might get one too. Since Woody read our names out alphabetically, I found out early that nothing had come for me, but I listened in case Woody found an overlooked or misfiled letter at the bottom of the pile. After a few days I gave up hoping and contented myself with hearing Cherry read her sisters' accounts of their squabbles and Angie's recitations of her boyfriend's rhyming lines of love.

One day Woody did call my name and I tripped over the bench, kicking Jo in my eagerness to get to the front. Woody greeted me with a gum-revealing smile and gave me not one but three envelopes. Two were large and stiff like cards but the third was small and creamy with ragged blue edges. On the back printed in raised navy script was *Mrs. Sylvia Brewer, Apple Ford, Ontario* and our postal code. If Sylvia was using stationery with our address, did that mean she was home? If she was then I didn't need to stay here. I tucked the cards into my shorts. I wanted to run back to the cabin but I had to sit back down and wait for Woody to distribute the remaining letters.

The cards were for my birthday, the arrival of which I'd lost track of as the days without Sylvia piled up. I didn't want anyone to know, so I took the letters with me to the outhouse during Quiet Time, tossing the envelopes down the hole after opening them. The first, a purple card with lilacs, had the greeting *To a Dear Granddaughter.* Inside was a verse and the signature *Grandma Vi* in green ink with a note: "I am knitting you a dress of afghan squares for back to school. You pick the colours." The second card said *For a Special Girl Who's 12!* A white wheel fixed to the card with a grommet had been turned to display the age through a cut-out window. The card had two pages in the centre like a book. Each side had a condensed fairy tale on it with bright pink and blue illustrations. Sam had printed "HOPE YOU'RE ENJOYING YOUR BIRTHDAY PRESENT (CAMP). MORE WHEN YOU COME HOME. LOVE DAD." Nicky had added, "I miss you, Sis!"

My face pressed forward as if I could cry. But I didn't cry. Was it possible I could go home now? They seemed to want me there.

I held the creamy envelope to my nose. Even amid the out-house's stench, I could detect the tang of ink and wood pulp. I eased my pinky under the blue-edged flap and carefully separated the glued paper. This one I would save.

Inside was a sheet folded like a card with writing on the first two pages and half of the third. The loopy script was familiar yet shaky.

Dear Mercy:
I wanted to write you a birthday letter instead of card. I bet the sun is shining. It always does on this day.

I am in hospital still but moving to a different place than where you saw me. A home, called a Rest Home. Your mother needs *rest*.

I certainly won't mind leaving this place, let me tell you. That nurse you met, I'm trying to have her fired. She's been wearing my clothes and sometimes (I told your father this but he thinks I'm cracked) I'll be thinking about getting up and pulling the curtains and she comes in and pulls them. Or I'm about to open up a magazine and start reading and she picks up the same magazine and reads it right in front of me. But only when she's in my clothes.

They put me in one of those jackets with the long sleeves that wrapped my arms around my body like a flag whipped around a pole so only my fingers could speak to me, tapping out patterns on my shoulder blades. I had my own language through my fingers in that jacket as I rolled against its waves.

You watch what happens to your body and don't let anybody near it. It's babies that does it. You wouldn't believe. It's funny giving birth. Ha! All those serious eyes peering over tightly bound mouths, mouths covered against germs. As if they had to worry about germs. Christ, a baby is being born into that mess and he didn't get to wear a mask. (I have assurance that it's alright to say Christ the way I just did — saying it doesn't affect the relationship of love with the Lord. It's just a word. Repeat it over and over, let it detach in your mind and you will see. Love, not church, is what I understand.)

Come to think of it, I didn't get to wear a mask either. It was okay for me to breathe my own germs. But what about *their* germs? Bet they never thought of that.

Lucky they gave me those needles so I was smiling when the baby came. What's so funny, Mrs. Brewer? they asked, but I was too polite then to tell them it was the sight of all those suspended, solemn eyes staring at my twat that was making me laugh. If that wasn't funny then what was? (Did I tell you that Jesus said *twat* is okay too? Well it is.)

Like I said, watch your body. Don't let them put anything in it. They put a coil inside me after my boy was born but my body tried to chew it up and spit it out. Instead it ate me first, enough so that I didn't need a coil anymore, didn't need anything because they took all the important parts out. Coils eat things. They take exactly what you give out and do it right back to you and then some. Just

like people. If my body hadn't tried to chew it first
— I hate my body but they did this to me. Don't let
it happen to you. Promise me.

Look at me rattling on like this. I hope you are
enjoying camp. You already know so much about
the outdoors but you will find it invigorating. Keep
an eye out for driftwood. I love you, Sunbeam.

Mom.

Parts of the letter sounded like Sylvia before she went away.
Like my mother. I couldn't remember her calling me Sunbeam but
she did used to say that Sunbeam was her baby nickname for me.

Other parts were like no Sylvia I knew. Talking about
birthing and bodies and saying swear words like Christ and
that other word. Was it possible someone else wrote the letter
for her? Maybe the nurse who wore her dress and opened her
curtains? But all the handwriting was the same. Maybe she dic-
tated the part she wanted to say and the nurse added the rest
without telling Sylvia.

Since the saying of the Lord's name in vain and the stuff
about coils made no sense, I could ignore them. But one fact I
couldn't overlook: Sylvia was leaving the Dairy Queen hospital
but not coming home. She was going to a different kind of home
than ours. The only homes I'd heard of were Old Folks' Homes
or Homes for the Incurable. I'd also heard of Mental Homes.

Cherry knocked on the outhouse door and asked if I was
okay. I jumped up and stuffed the cards back into my shorts.

"Fine," I said, flipping the bow-tie catch and hopping
down. "Everything's fine."

When I returned to the cabin it was still Quiet Time, so I lay on my bunk and daydreamed Sylvia gliding around a Rest Home in a long white gown, her hair trailing down her back. The Dairy Queen hospital was close by but the only reason I got to visit was because I was being sent away. Who knew how far the Rest Home was. Besides, Sylvia should be rested already after weeks in the hospital. In fact, all her time on the couch should have been enough rest. I couldn't even write her back. Sylvia had tricked me by using our Apple Ford address.

Angie got up and sat on Jo's bed, then Lindy's, then Beth's for about five minutes each, whispering and glancing over to me. I shut my eyes and remembered the soapy sweat smell of Clancy's neck.

When Angie climbed up to speak to Cherry, the edges of words drifted in and out of my hearing. Then I clearly heard Cherry say, "I don't want to. That's not fair."

Angie's voice cajoled up and down, smooth as baby's skin. I could almost feel Cherry shaking her head. Angie's voice got sharper. Eventually, Cherry must have given a grudging yes because Angie bounced down the side ladder and sat on my bunk with a smile.

Hope surged in me. Maybe I wasn't excluded from the secret. But Angie didn't say a word. Something was up.

Angie's smile stretched upward.

"What's happening?" I asked, sitting up and backing into the corner of the bunk.

"We're going on an overnight tomorrow. It's the first Friday."

"What happens on an overnight?"

Angie snorted. She took a deep breath then spoke in confidential tones.

"We take tents and go out to the woods and camp on the other side of the lake, just the Pink Ladies."

"What do we eat?"

Jo snickered from her bed. My head rang from Jo holding it under the water before we got out of the pool.

With exaggerated patience, Angie explained: "We bring it ourselves, make a campfire, and cook it. Simple."

"We carry it?"

"We all have a big backpack. Don't worry, it won't be too heavy."

I had a million other questions, but I held them in.

Angie edged closer. Her voice dropped. I wondered if this was the big secret.

"Tomorrow night, we're going to play Truth or Dare. Are you up for it? Everyone else is going to play."

I had never heard of Truth or Dare. I nodded.

"Good."

Angie returned to her own bed without another word.

Fifteen minutes before it was time to leave for campfire, I sat on the stoop and stared at the clothesline stretched between two cedars and laden with sagging bathing suits and slouching towels. The line was the same unnatural blue as the pool water. At one end hung Chipper's bag of personals, or as Angie pointed out, her brassieres. If I wore a bra, I would hang it on the line, not in a personals bag sewn from a J-Cloth. I wouldn't mind if any of the male counsellors saw it.

Chipper came to the door.

"Hey. You're the first for once."

"Yep."

Minutes later the other girls rushed out.

"First you're the last one out, now you're too early. What's your problem?" Jo's voice was sour. She was still pulling on her sweatshirt.

The Pink Ladies sang "Goin' on a Lion Hunt" and its companion piece, "Goin' on a Hippie Hunt," as we marched to the campfire. I mouthed the words — *Long Hair, Granny Glasses, Smelly Feet!* — and kept my eyes fixed above the others' heads on the horizon at the end of the fields. I took care to sit near the back of the circle so no one could look at me.

The songs and skits swirled around me. The more I concentrated, the more I was able to shut out the others' voices and think about the sky, the horse's neck, the hot vinyl of Sam's car seat. Sylvia before she left, before I had even invented the witch-mother. I conjured up Sylvia's smells: powder, flour, lemon, sugar. Her good smells. I could only think of this Sylvia as Mother. Memories flooded me: holding onto Mother's leg for safety around strangers, or even ladies at church; Mother's palm resting on my head and her nervous laugh, shared with the other mothers whose children ran off to play anywhere else; Mother's fingers in my hair, bathing Nicky and me with the bathroom window open to the cool night air, our bodies slippery slick, sticky almost, sliding around splashing the puddles on the green and black linoleum floor; Mother's hands in soap, her laugh, her anger, her red arms lifting us out; Mother holding her fat blonde baby girl to the sky and calling her Sunbeam.

I wanted to shout, sing, call these memories out. I slipped away from the group, crawling along the grass until I reached the nearest tree. I slunk behind its trunk then darted to the next tree and the next, a fugitive holding my secrets on the tip of my tongue. When I was out of sight of the group, I ran full throttle toward the cabin, hurling myself into my bunk and punching my face into the pillow.

There was a pause before everything rushed forward and I was in the middle of a torrent of Mother, of sadness hate anger, of powder water smoke tubes choking me until I couldn't hold it in and I spilt out everywhere.

I fell asleep, my throat and mouth tight as if full of swamp water. I dreamt of dryness, of rocking on a boat in the middle of a lake, of wheatfields with the sun beating down on me until I bled little pinprick drops of blood.

When voices came along the path, I almost heaved with sobs at the force of waking up. I managed not to move so they'd think I was asleep.

Cherry spoke from somewhere near my feet. My pillow was at the wrong end of the bed. "She's probably sick. We should take her to the nurse."

"She's not even asleep," Jo said, poking at my soles. I struggled to keep my eyelids from twitching.

"Figures," snarled Angie. She found my head and pushed her face close. "Whatsamatter? Baby dudn't wike campy poo?"

I considered pretending to wake up.

"Now we can't do anything because she'll be listening," Jo said.

"Why don't we go to sleep early? We probably won't sleep very much at the camp-out tomorrow," Cherry said. The springs above me creaked.

Lindy and Beth agreed. Angie had other ideas.

"You babies can go to sleep early if you want but me and Jo are going to stay up and play cards."

They seemed to forget me. I flopped over and faced the chipboard wall. Chipper came in and flipped off the light. As soon as she closed her bedroom door, Angie and Jo flicked on their flashlights and began a game of Crazy Eights.

When I finally slept, I plunged straight into a dream of my mother lying in the hospital with aqua clotheslines hanging from her veins. I fought my way through endless damp green sheets that clung to my face and stuck to my arms. The sheets got too thick so I followed my mother by her smell of unwashed hair and cigarette smoke. When I got close, I tried to cling to her thigh, but Sylvia turned to fumes and flew up to the ceiling.

Shortly afterward I woke up, choking. I raised my hands to my face and found a cool wet towel. I peeled it off, stumbling out of the bunk as fast as possible. My mattress was soaked. A musty odour rose from my skin.

"What did you do, wet your bed?" Jo sniggered, her flash-light beam an eye glowing through her sleeping bag stuffing.

"Losing control of your bladder is a sign of mental illness, you know," Angie hissed.

"Yes, I have heard that. Maybe she needs a straitjacket."

"Apparently Woody keeps one in the Big House."

I grabbed the hockey bag and lugged it outside, my throat filling. I ran to the safety of the outhouse. Inside burned a light matted with fly and moth cadavers. The girls wouldn't follow me here. The shit smell and even the possibility of snakes slithering up were suddenly okay.

I wasn't sure if I'd wet my bed or not. My jeans and sweat-shirt were sopping. I peeled them off and pulled my night-gown on over my clammy skin. I stuffed the clothes into a ball and opened the door. Some moonlight trickled through the pine needles and the dew was like tears on my feet. I tossed the wet ball into the trees and sat down, my back rest-ing against a wide pine.

Mental illness. They must have read Sylvia's letter. I groped around in the hockey bag and found the cards and the letter tucked inside a pant leg where I'd hidden them. There was no way of telling. Sylvia didn't say she was mentally ill. People went to hospitals and homes for many reasons. Maybe the straitjacket reference was a coincidence. I tore the letter in half then quarters, eighths, sixteenths and finally into confetti pieces that I dumped down the outhouse hole. I could remember the "I love you, Sunbeam" and forget the rest.

I rummaged around in the hockey bag for the lightning man. Many of the numbers had fallen off, but his body was intact. I placed him in front of me so the moon shone directly on him. I leaned back and squinted him into a tiny troll with features similar to Aldo's: a crunched-up brown face with crooked mouth and wise eyes. I knelt forward and slid my palms up and down the burnt wood, its smoothness soothing.

"My name is Mercy, so please Your Royal Timber-ness." I pictured Alice addressing the caterpillar, the Cheshire cat, the King and Queen of Hearts. I wanted the lightning man to know that though I honoured him, I was playing a game and I wasn't mad.

Nonetheless I stroked the knotted nub that twisted off at his top end, steering my fingers away from the scarred rim where he'd been severed. I was convinced that, no matter what, the lightning man would keep me from going crazy.

Back in the cabin, I checked my bed for dry spots. The inside of my sleeping bag was soaked. Angie and Jo must have squeezed the wet towel on me. I eased myself between the mattress and the wall, holding the lightning man tight against my body, my eyes open against the night.

The next morning, I was up and dressed before everybody else. I wrapped the lightning man and stuffed him into my bag.

I wanted to bring him out into the sunshine but I couldn't risk the others seeing him. So he remained hidden away.

My hair was plastered to my head. I hadn't washed it all week. Unwashed hair wouldn't normally bother me but Angie and Jo might make fun of it. They both took showers in the Big House stalls every day and used expensive salon shampoos. We didn't have a shower at our house and I liked showers even less than I liked baths.

I touched my fingertips to my part. Here my hair clung closest to my scalp and was warmer. I scratched then brought my fingers close to my nose. A moon of white flakes sat under my nails. It smelled the way the school janitor Mr. Van Droolen sometimes did if you stood too close to him. It also smelled like my mother and I kept my finger under my nose, drinking in the odour. Hair was supposed to smell this way. I liked my hair to smell this way.

Inside my hockey bag, I found the ridged opaque plastic box that contained a bar of soap so unused the word *Dove* was still visibly etched in its surface. I searched further and realized Sam hadn't packed shampoo. So the state of my hair wasn't my fault.

I grabbed a towel and headed outside, where a fog had crept so close to the cabin it obscured the trees fastening the obscenely drooping clothesline. The muted sun burned through the mist as it gained strength. Birds burped and chortled, making me forget the sadness that had filled me all night. I headed down the path.

A lacy mist danced over the lake's surface, which was flat and calm with grey lights swooping through its darkness. Occasionally a series of rings rippled out from the centre. Sam had told me that the ripples were fish putting their lips up to the surface to kiss the sky. I preferred his version to Nicky's insistence on the truth: "They're just eating bugs and *LAR-vay*," he would say in my ear when Sam wasn't looking.

I laid my towel on the clotted sand and pulled off my clothes, leaving them in a pile. I walked to the water's edge, the soap bar in my fist. My Speedo with the red, white and blue maple leaves hugged my body, but there were two teacup handles where small breasts were supposed to be. "Buds," Angie would say, laughing hysterically. "My mom calls them buds." Besides Cherry, Jo was the only one with anything resembling buds. Jo made a show of putting on and removing her bra, especially before swimming. She was also the only one who wore a bikini.

I dipped my toes in the water. It was warm. I bent down and put my fingertips in then traced wet trails up my calves. I waded in, my feet squashing in the mud. In the distance, the mist was rising and the sun billowing through.

Time was running out so I did what Sam did at Uncle Larry's quarry and ran splashing into the lake until the water reached the tops of my thighs. Then I cast myself into the lake with my nose plugged and my face scrunched up until I was all wet and sitting up to my neck in cool water.

I was fine in the water when my feet could touch and I could plug my nose. I rubbed a good lather up and applied it to my head with one hand. I scrubbed and scrubbed, working in the lather, picturing the oil rolling off my hair in bubbles. Then I leaned my head back and let the hair stream through the water. Thick soap suds lay on the surface and white filaments fluttered beneath. I slid the soap over my arms, legs and bum, pulling my bathing suit aside to reach all parts. The soap bar was slippery. The tighter I tried to hold on to it, the more it shot out from my hand.

When I was finished, I stood up, brushed the mud from my bottom and waded in to shore. Most of the mist had disappeared. I dried off, pulled on my clothes and walked back.

Cherry stuck close to me while we packed for the overnight. I wanted to know Cherry better, but I was suspicious of the way she got along with everyone even though she appeared to be a nerd. I couldn't understand why I was unable to do the same.

"Can you believe these clothes my mother forced me to bring?"

Cherry's smile was warm, almost a plea. She had a bagful of long-sleeved checkered blouses and stretchy jean shorts with two-inch hems and a seam down the front of each leg. Earlier in the week, Angie and Jo had each lent her a Camp Wanigamog T-shirt and she alternated between them. Today, however, she was snapping up one of the checkered shirts.

"If we're just hiking, it won't matter," she said. Her tone was mild and practical but eager for agreement.

As we packed, Cherry admired everything I owned, especially my embroidered flare jeans.

I whispered that both pairs were bought at the Salvation Army.

"What's the Salivating Army?" Cherry whispered back.

"Sal-vay-shun. That's a place where you buy second-hand clothes. It's all spread out on a big table in sizes and you walk around and pick out the ones you want. My mother took me there."

It was true, Sylvia had taken me to the Salvation Army many times to buy clothes — just not in the past year. The embroidered jeans came from a box Sam had brought home a few weeks before my mother went to the hospital. He said he got the clothes at a garage sale, but I wasn't sure. I didn't really care; the jeans were neat and nobody had to know. I was used to secondhand clothes. What was the difference? I folded the jeans then rolled them into a tight tube.

"Where do you try them on?"

"You don't, unless you try them on right there in front of everybody. Some people do that. My mom tries — tried to make me do that sometimes but I wouldn't let her." I crammed the jeans into the hockey bag. My knuckles brushed the smooth torso of the lightning man.

"My mom shops at Simpsons-Sears, through the catalogue. She doesn't like to take me to stores, because I'm awkward. Sometimes we have to send things back two or three times because the size is wrong."

"Weird," I mumbled. It occurred to me that my father would have to take me shopping now that my mother was gone. Unless he brought home more boxes, I'd probably be wearing the same clothes until I was twenty.

"Do — is your mom still around?" Cherry asked, absorbed in delicately picking pieces of dirt from the white rubber ridge on the perimeter of her shoe.

"Of course. Isn't yours?" I spoke louder. Hadn't she read the letter with Angie and Jo? Maybe she was pretending.

"Yes. You know that. I mean, what you said. And she didn't drop you off at the bus. It sounds like your mom's not around anymore."

"Well, she is. She has a dangerous job though and she goes away a lot. Sometimes she picks up strange diseases from other countries. She's pretty sick right now."

"What does she have?"

"Some kind of malaria, I think. She's a pilot. They have a special Rest Home for pilots who catch highly contagious diseases."

I jumped up, grabbed my bag and went outside. It didn't sound like Cherry was pretending not to know about Sylvia. I could tell Cherry wanted to ask more but I'd made up enough. I was surprised at myself — and vaguely ashamed — because the mother I did have wasn't like the one in my story and never would be. I didn't really want the pilot mother, but what was scarier was that I was beginning to wonder if I even wanted the mother I had. Of course I now had a picture in my mind of Sylvia as a malaria-stricken pilot. Yet, despite having invented most of it, I had told Cherry some truth. My mother *was* in a Rest Home. Although the Rest Home for Highly Contagious Pilots was somehow more acceptable to me, it was still a Rest Home and now Cherry knew something was wrong with my mother, that my mother wasn't normal.

Cherry made sure she was walking beside me when we left.

"I'm sorry," she whispered, before the group had even left the cabin area. She wore a white beach hat pulled down low on her forehead to meet her glasses.

"It's okay," I said loudly, "*Gilligan.*" The others giggled. The name was appropriate. It was good to be laughing with the group.

Cherry's eyebrows arched and her face crumpled. Then she regained composure, touched one hand to her hat brim and set her mouth in a patient, practical line. She seemed older and the name died out. I had lost my edge — and probably the only person who was likely to befriend me on this trip.

Much of the hike consisted of following a narrow path through a field of long grass as thick as unbrushed hair. The lake was below us on our left. Snatches of blue appeared from time to time through the tops of trees, but mostly we couldn't see the water.

Angie picked a bunch of grass and stuck the stem of one in her mouth, chewing it with her front teeth, Huck Finn style. Jo followed suit and soon the others did too. When I stooped to pull up some grass, I used too much strength and ended up with a dripping lump of earth hanging at the bottom. When Cherry laughed, the rest of the Pink Ladies turned around and groaned.

"Figures you'd try to copy me," sneered Angie, ignoring the stems of grass arcing like fishing rods from the mouths of Lindy, Jo, Beth and Cherry.

I broke the stem off at a node, discarding the clod. Lindy or Beth looked back occasionally, though Chipper insisted we keep a quick pace and they soon forgot. I stuck the grass between my teeth like Angie and savoured the bitter green juice that leaked onto my tongue and behind my gums. I allowed my lids to flutter halfway down. The rest of the walk became a performance, a rhythmic dance, like the side-to-side cadence of Clancy's walk.

After an eternity of grass-blowing and singing "Found a Peanut" and duets of "Summer Lovin'," we reached the edge of the woods. It rose straight out of the ground and joined the trees on our left. One minute we were walking in the field and the next we were beneath tall orderly trees and sun that trickled like a waterfall through the leaves. These were the same woods that outlined the lake, but a much thicker section. The path continued. Here it was solid dirt, clogged at the edges with a mulch of brown leaves.

Despite the repellent Chipper passed around, the mosquitoes still landed with airy precision on our arms and legs, unnoticed until that telltale prick. The mosquitoes flew out of reach when we tried to slap them, but if, as Angie pointed out, we waited until the mosquitoes had sucked enough blood that they were full, they exploded when hit and blood sprayed everywhere. By the time we reached the campsite, our arms and legs were covered with gory splotches and mosquito fragments.

We set the small "deluxe" tent for Chipper and a big tent for the Pink Ladies at opposite ends of a grassy clearing. After we'd pitched the tents, prepared dinner and cleaned up, it had been dark for almost an hour. Chipper said we'd have to wait until morning to swim. The lake was below, reached only by a steep, rocky path — which was one of the reasons Chipper didn't want us going down there at night.

All we could do was sit around the campfire. Chipper led us in a round of camp songs — as well as highlights from *Grease* and *Bat Out of Hell* — to wear us out, but after all that hiking, the more we did, the more energy we had. Chipper was the one getting worn out.

One by one we went into the trees with a roll of toilet paper. Then we ducked under the awning and slipped through the canvas and screen flaps of the big tent using flashlights to find our sleeping bags. I crawled in last and everyone screamed at me to close the screen so the mosquitoes wouldn't get in. It was too late. The air whined with the intensity of a dentist's drill, the mosquitoes dive-bombing our ears.

"It's time for Truth or Dare right, Angie?" reminded Jo, before I was all the way inside my sleeping bag. It was still slightly damp.

"We should wait fifteen minutes until Chipper is asleep. She might come and check on us," Angie said.

We stayed silent with our flashlights off as long as we could, inhaling the rancid insole warmth of the canvas and listening as a chorus of outside buzzes and cackles harmonized with the slapping of skin.

Eventually, Jo unzipped the screen and poked her head out the tent flap.

"Her light's off," she reported.

Angie switched on her flashlight and propped it under her chin so her face glowed red and yellow.

"It's time to play. Is everybody ready?"

We murmured in agreement.

"Lindy's already asleep," announced Jo, who had to climb over everybody to get back to her sleeping bag. She shook Lindy until she sputtered awake. Angie shone the light into Lindy's eyes and she looked as if she might cry. I knew better than to pretend I was asleep.

"Does everyone know how?" Angie asked. Her hair appeared pink in the glow of the flashlight. She stared at me.

"I don't," Beth said quietly before I had the chance to volunteer my own ignorance.

"Me either," I said.

"I'm not too clear on the rules. It's been a long time since I played," Cherry added.

Jo rolled her eyes, but Angie was happy to explain.

"First of all, we'll only use one flashlight, so Chipper won't get suspicious. We'll tell her one of us just got back from the washroom."

Cherry and Jo turned off their flashlights. The tent's canvas sides flapped as the wind picked up.

Angie continued: "I say, 'Truth Dare Double-Dare Promise to Repeat,' and then I choose someone, like Jo, and that person has to choose one, like Truth, or Double-Dare. Then I get to think up a question she has to answer truthfully or a dare she has to do. A Dare isn't as hard as a Double-Dare."

"What about Promise to Repeat?" asked Cherry. "I've never heard that one before."

"I don't like that one. That's when I say something and you repeat after me."

"Repeat something like what?" asked Lindy.

"Like, 'I ASK STUPID QUESTIONS.'"

Angie smiled.

"Oh."

"Everybody understand?"

When nobody answered, Angie began: "Truth Dare Double-Dare, Promise to Repeat, Jo."

"Truth," Jo said without hesitating.

"How does it feel to have a man's name?" asked Angie in her best interviewer's voice.

"I get teased about it at school sometimes, but I think it's obvious I'm not a guy."

It was obvious. Jo was the only one in the group — besides Cherry, who hid hers — who had grown-up breasts. Angie had her "buds," but Jo's were big enough that she needed to wear a bra at all times. She was proud of this fact and often walked through the cabin wearing just her bra and a pair of shorts. The bra was white and slightly see-through. Behind it, her breasts looked like two pieces of hard fruit. Jo's face was long and thin, with a prominent nose. The breasts didn't make her any more attractive, just enviable.

"There's another rule," Angie said, before Jo had a chance to choose her victim. "You can't choose the same one two times in a row. You can't always choose Dare or Truth."

She passed the flashlight to Jo. "Whoever asks the question gets the flashlight."

"Truth Dare Double-Dare Promise to Repeat, Mercy." Jo's voice was low. She shone the light in my face.

I wasn't sure if Angie meant I couldn't choose the same one as the person before me or the same one each time it was my turn.

"Dare, I guess."

Jo laughed wickedly, holding the flashlight between her knees and rubbing her palms together. The shadows around her nose made her seem sinister, hawk-like. Angie tilted her head and raised her blonde eyebrows.

"I dare you to kiss Angie."

"Eww," shouted Cherry and Lindy.

"That's gross. She's a girl," said Beth.

Angie smiled.

"Mercy won't mind that. Will you?"

Was Angie saying it was alright, it's a game and if you do it we could be friends, or did she mean that I secretly liked girls and not boys? Either way, I did not want to kiss her. I waited and eventually Cherry, Beth and Lindy were waiting too with a grossed-out fascination.

"C'mon, Mercy. You wanted to play, so you have to follow the rules. Just do the dare and we can keep going. No big deal."

Angie's expression was benevolent. She wouldn't ask me to do something she didn't mind doing herself. If I had to kiss her, she had to be kissed. Since Angie liked boys, talked about them all the time, kissing her must be a test. If I passed it, Angie and Jo would accept me.

I pushed back my sleeping bag and knee-walked to where Angie sat cross-legged. Angie closed her eyes demurely. I closed mine too. Imagining kissing Sylvia or Vi made it worse. So I thought about Pickles, the craft counsellor, who looked like John Denver and liked dill pickle potato chips. I balanced on my hands, leaned over and gave Angie a dry peck to the left of her lips. She smelled mentholated, like a chest cold salve. Angie lips didn't move but when I opened my eyes, she was staring right into them. I scrambled back to my bag. All eyes were on me.

"Your turn, Mercy," said Jo, softer now.

Everyone looked away.

I chose Lindy. When she said "Truth," I asked her what it was like to be a twin. After she answered, the questions and dares relaxed, with most of the dares involving running outside or making a loud noise. Cherry chose Promise to Repeat once and Jo got her to say, "I look like Gilligan." I eased into the game. Maybe the kiss had been the worst of it. Maybe I had finally proven myself.

After a while, most of us were lying on our sides. Our voices had taken on a stringy manic quality from lack of sleep. Lindy and Beth were drifting in and out, waking only when it was their turn. Without thinking, I chose Double-Dare when Angie asked me. Angie looked at Jo, who nodded. On the last Double-Dare, Angie had asked Jo to moon Chipper's tent.

"Take off Jo's shirt and kiss her boobs."

Angie had a flushed look of defiance. She sat on her knees and leaned forwards. Cherry propped herself up with an elbow. Jo remained lying down. Her face was slack.

"No." I clenched and unclenched my fists.

"Gimme a break, Mercy. It doesn't mean anything. Grow up. We all did our dares."

Angie was smiling as she spoke but her jaw jutted out.

"Your dares weren't like this."

"That's your fault, not mine."

Exasperated, I looked at Cherry. Cherry shrugged and gave a half-smile. I blew loudly through my nostrils and crawled over to Jo. My face burned and my heart pounded. I set my lips and rummaged around inside the sleeping bag for the bottom of Jo's T-shirt. I pulled it off. Jo still had the bra on underneath. I had never worn a bra and had no idea how to unhook one.

"Do I have to take this bra off?"

"Of course."

I gagged as I slipped my hand around Jo, repulsed at her bony back. Jo didn't move, looking bored while I steadied myself with my left hand.

"Quit trying to feel me up, Mercy," Jo said. "Everybody's watching."

I sat back.

"Why don't you take it off or sit up?"

Jo sat up and turned her back to me, clutching the sleeping bag modestly to her chest. I unclasped the hook. A red groove glared from Jo's back where the strap had dug in. She stayed there until I pulled the shoulder straps down. Cherry and Angie were so silent I couldn't hear them breathing.

Jo's torso was thin and angular, her shoulders two curved lumps. I didn't know what to pretend I was kissing. I shut my eyes tight, lowered my face and pecked Jo near the top, where it was hard beneath the skin.

"That wasn't her boob," said Angie.

"She's right," said Jo, wriggling around. Her face looked bored, but she couldn't keep still.

"And you have to open your mouth and really kiss her."

"That's not what you said."

"It's a Double-Dare. That's the double part."

I steeled myself. Eyes wide, I kissed the breast to the left of the nipple with my mouth open. It made a squelching sound. When I pulled away, I saw little bumps all over the nipples. Jo sat there with the same placid cow expression on her face.

"What do you think, Jo?"

"Definitely."

"Definitely what?" I asked, resisting the urge to wipe my mouth with the back of my hand. I slid backward on my feet and hips to my sleeping bag.

"Definitely a lezzie," said Angie. "Jo can tell by how much you enjoyed it. She's a lezzie too. Right Jo?"

Jo nodded. She made no move to put her bra or her T-shirt back on.

"Get out. She is not," said Cherry. "You talk about boys all the time."

"It's a cover." Jo raised her lips in a smile.

"I think you want to sleep with Jo tonight, don't you, Mercy?" Angie's eyes were intense.

I looked away.

"Of course not. I'm not a lezzie."

"Jo thinks you are."

"So what? I'm not."

"Leave her alone," Cherry ventured.

When Jo and Angie ignored her, she sank back, perhaps curious to see how far I would go, or how far they would make me.

"Are you sure, Mercy? Are you sure you didn't enjoy kissing me and kissing Jo? You know we liked it a lot."

"Yes."

"Yes, you enjoyed it?" Angie clapped her hands together.

"Yes, I'm sure I didn't. No, I didn't enjoy it."

"You know, she tried to feel me up too when she kissed me," Angie told Jo.

"Doesn't surprise me."

"That is not true, Angie, and you know it. Nobody saw that happen because it didn't." I zipped my sleeping bag up to my neck and turned my back.

"You know you want to, Mercy. Jo's going to come over there and slide into that sleeping bag with you. What do you think about that?"

While I couldn't stand Jo, the prospect of those breasts against my body, especially after having pressed my lips against them, was excruciating. I rejected this thought, disgusted. More than anything, I wanted to run away. But Chipper wouldn't believe me if I told and I didn't know how to get back to Camp Wanigamog. Not that it mattered. It no longer mattered if I never went back there again.

Angie turned the flashlight out and I lay still, not answering as Jo squirmed over into my sleeping bag. Jo took my hands and placed them on the breasts. Jo's cool palms calmed me. I didn't move, letting Jo's firm sponginess seep though my fingertips and into my pores, my own body taut.

"See, Angie," whispered Jo. "She's feeling me up. She's a lezzie alright." Her tone was affectionate but etched with malice. No one spoke and it seemed as if Jo and I were the only ones awake.

A shade descended over me, preventing me from halting my actions. All that existed was doing: my hands and skin and legs and feet. I rubbed and kneaded and stroked those breasts while Jo's harsh body wiggled around my own, elbows and knees jutting into me. Jo didn't respond to my body except to press her hipbone against my belly.

I moved around so that my pyjama top was up under my armpits and Jo's breasts could touch my flat chest. Jo shoved my head into the sleeping bag, guiding my mouth. I touched my lips to each nipple and kissed, tasting each pore, feeling each tiny bump.

Jo's voice above me said it was good to meet a lezzie once in a while. It wasn't the superiority in her tone but the complicity that made me stop. I pulled myself back as far away from Jo's body as possible in the sleeping bag and inched up to the top, holding my head away from Jo's although it was difficult to ignore her legs against my own.

"How about Angie? Wanna do this to Angie too, Lezzie?" Jo taunted.

I struggled out of the bag. My top was up around my armpits and I tugged it back down. It would be stupid to deny I was a lezzie after what I'd allowed myself to do. Jo's face wavered, greasy and repugnant in the dimming flashlight beam.

Both Jo and Angie stood up with me. Jo pulled her T-shirt back on but left her bra off.

"We're going for a walk now, Lezzie, and you're not gonna be a crybaby and call for Chipper — or else you know what?"

I looked at Cherry, who closed her eyes and turned away. Right now it was Cherry I hated most of all.

"Or else you know what?"

I didn't answer.

"We're gonna tell Chipper that you're a lezzie and about what you just did to Jo. That's practically rape, you know. They'll kick you out of camp and tell everyone what you are. They could

even send you to jail. Even if you plead insanity, they'll send you
to a mental home."

My mind stayed black.

"A what?"

"You heard me. I'm sure you have a good idea what that's
all about — '*Sunbeam.*' Let's go."

Like a robot, I allowed them to lead me down the path to
the lake where they removed my pyjamas, snickering. Angie
took off her own shorts and lay down on the three-foot-wide
strip of bark-flecked brown sand that was the shore.

"Kiss me there," she said pointing.

When I didn't move, Jo elbowed me and I obeyed, putting
my lips between Angie's legs. It was small and wet like a kit-
ten's mouth without the serrated tongue. It tasted like my own
fingers after I touched myself there. The between-my-legs
smell. I didn't enjoy it now, but for a long time both Jo and
Angie demanded that I stroke and kiss their bodies while they
writhed around on the sand. The lake sat beside us, grave and
brooding, the surface crinkled from the breeze, the water making a gentle *blop blop* against the shore. The sky pavement grey,
the palest of moons poking through threadbare clouds. No
smells but the cologne of mosquito repellent on skin and the
tree juice odour of what floats on the water and spreads on the
sand. An occasional owls' hoot like a blow into an empty Coke
bottle. The lupine yodel of a loon.

Angie and Jo never touched each other and they never
touched me. I shivered in the lake air. There seemed no reason
for removing my clothes.

Abruptly, Angie and Jo stood to dress. Jo put my pyjama
top on over her T-shirt and Angie pulled on my pants.

"What are you doing?"

"You're going to walk into that water until we say *stop*. Keep your back to us and count to a hundred so that no one sees us leaving with a lezzie."

"Who would see you? It's the middle of the night."

"Chipper might."

"But I can't swim."

"Tough. You only have to stand there anyway."

It didn't make sense to let them force me into the water but I didn't want them to tell about my shameful acts. It didn't occur to me that they'd participated in the disgrace as much, if not more, than I. Sylvia would stay crazy if she found out her daughter was a lezzie. The thought of my mother conjured up the dream images of wet whipping sheets and angry blue cords. Echoes of Sylvia's feral moans. Jo kicked at my legs and I stepped toward the lake.

As soon as my feet touched the wetness, my fear of the deep left. Maybe I would drown and the water would swim inside me and halt the wailing at the bottom of my mind. I would never have to see another naked body, never have to kiss one, never see my mother again. No one would know about me. I waded in deeper, the cool water lapping first up my calves then my thighs, buttocks, belly, armpits, neck.

"You can stop now," Angie called from a distance. "Count to a hundred and then you can come out."

I counted   *one, two, three*   and thought of orange fish, *four, five, six* — mermaids with ruby eyes and emerald hair; *seven, eight* — sneaky moss-water light; *nine, ten* — maybe Sylvia would be happy now that I was gone and Sam wouldn't have to worry about me; *eleven, twelve* — the animal shrieked louder and suddenly I was drinking the water, gulping it, clotheslines of blue pain in my nostrils, slimy green sheets knotting around me, tightening, yanking me under. It wasn't like sleep. It wasn't peaceful. I fought the sheets, pushed at the cords and burst like a fish reaching through the surface to kiss the sky. Jagged, irregular waves disturbed the oil-slick lake. No elegant round circles for me.

My head screamed with red pain but my arms were working, slicing through the water, my legs kicking, pulling me into shore like an expert, like a champion, like Sam. I was swimming.

When I could touch ground, I lowered my feet and ran through the grey sheets of water, thrashing my arms until I made the shore where I crouched — choking, then disgorging bile. I crushed my face into the sand, ground grit under my eyelids, stones into my tongue, one blue marble eye staring up at the sinking white moon, white like the necklace on the wolf's-howl loon, like the wailing animal's gown, the bones of the dead fish I was, washed on the beach. The water wearing me away, picking at me until I was a skeleton lacing the shore, waiting to be found.

When I came to, Cherry and Lindy were rubbing me with a towel. They had my clothes and told me to return to the tent before Chipper saw. My skin was purple, Cherry said. I put my clothes on by rote.

Cherry and Lindy were like strangers, extensions of Jo and Angie. On the walk back up the rocky path, I burst into tears and sobs as long as a train poured from me. It was hard to hold my weight for long on one leg and I kept slipping. Chipper couldn't help but notice my arrival. She took me into the deluxe tent, bundled me in a scratchy grey blanket and insisted that I lie there until it was time to go.

Through the tent flap, I watched an isosceles of pearled cement sky, and a memory dislodged. It is strong and preposterous, but I can't escape the certainty that it happened. In it, I am four and Nicky is three. I hold on to one of Sylvia's hands while Nicky holds the other. We are walking up the hill to our house, returning from playing in the park.

The frame around the memory is hazy. I don't remember the weather, only that it isn't winter. When Sylvia goes up the path to the front door, I separate from my body and stand on the sidewalk watching the happy mommy and boy and girl pass under the maple tree, climb the steps and shut the door behind them.

The little girl who is left behind is me — but not me. I am now free to do whatever I want, no matter what Mommy says. I wear boy clothes: a sweater and stretchy pants that feel good against my skin.

The memory isn't in full colour. Rather, it plays like a black-and-white negative, with hues of crimson, brown and navy showing through, washed over with grey.

I stare at the door. Something stops me from going inside; I am left behind. Eventually I turn and step off the sidewalk. I am conscious of a lighter weight but a heavier movement. I have more impact on the air as if the air has thickened its molecules and is now a web obstructing me, or perhaps I am now lighter than air and resistance meets each motion.

My heavy swimming steps take me into the street, which is no longer a road but a place where kids can play and cars slow down for them. I carefully lie myself down in the centre of the road. The asphalt is a solid bed, its surface rough and warm, but I am buoyant and it supports me.

A big truck comes over the hill to the north, slowing down. I stay put, unafraid, and let the truck run right over me.

If I hold my arms against my sides and keep my breath measured I will be fine, as long as the wheels don't touch me. Even then, I trust I would remain intact.

After the truck passes and turns at the church, I get up, brush off the small stones stuck to my pants and walk calmly into the house. Already I am uncertain about the correctness of telling my mother.

Inside, no time has passed. Even though the memory seems slow and deliberate, it is as if my mother and Nicky have just come inside too and I am only the slightest bit behind them.

I could never remember whether I'd told Sylvia and I was unsure about other parts of the memory: Did the truck keep going or did it vanish after it passed over my body? Did I make up the turn, fill in the detail so the picture was more complete? If so, what else did I invent?

But this memory was real, not a dream; it had the clear ring of experience, of events that fit. It confirmed my separateness. Part of that little girl had not returned to my body. And if I was not entirely joined to my body, if I wanted, I could do anything. I could let anything happen to me.

I lay without sobbing in the deluxe tent, listening to the wind whistle along the ridge pole and waiting for the others to carry me home.

Sam drove into the Camp Wanigamog parking lot in a black pickup with no tailgate. He hopped down and brushed at a streak of dirt that ran across the shoulder and down the back of one leg of his green Tecumseth Chiefs uniform. He took off his peaked cap, smoothed his palm over his skull, replaced the cap, then strode toward where I slouched next to Chipper and Woody Woodpecker. I hadn't told either of them what had happened, hadn't spoken any words besides the most obligatory yes's and no's. I couldn't tell anybody. Why would I?

I climbed onto the red seat and rolled up the window while Sam spoke to Woody and Chipper. I wondered if he called them Woody and Chipper or if they gave him their real names. I couldn't hear what they were saying and it wasn't worth the bother to try. The truck smelled clean, like pine needles and lemon and mothballs — not like smoke and not like Sam. The steering wheel had a column-shifter mounted to it, like the Impala, and the same eight-track player — with the same Roy Orbison tape punched in — hung from a bracket under the dash.

When Sam came back, I considered asking him about the homerun slide that had surely led to the stain on his pants but he didn't say anything and I found I didn't want to either. He didn't seem mad though, which was worth everything.

He started the truck and Roy came on: *There goes my baby, there goes my heart.*

I felt better already.

We were nearing Vi's place on the highway when Sam spoke.

"Would you be happier staying at home?"

"Really?"

"You're twelve now. I can trust you. Nicky will still go to the Sousas' but you can stay home as long as you keep the house tidy and don't get into any trouble. Can you handle that?"

"I can clean." I was glad he hadn't said "any more trouble."

"Can you cook? Because if you could make the odd meal we might not need Mrs. Sousa at all, though it wouldn't hurt to say yes to a casserole or two."

"I'll try."

"Let's stick with cleaning up and see how it goes. It won't be for long."

We coasted down the hill and turned. We crossed over the Tecumseth River. A ball game was in progress at the park.

"We're in a tournament. Do you want to come? Your brother's there."

"Unh unh."

"Do you mind if I go?"

I shook my head, not wanting to break the happiness between us and the mutual relief at having agreed upon a course of events without having to talk about why I was coming home early, but really I did mind, I minded very much. I did not want to be in the house alone. But that was how it was going to be. We had agreed that I would be in the house alone and if I was going to have to go there anyway it might as well be sooner rather than later.

Sam swung the hockey bag out of the back of the truck and heaved it into the house.

He stood in the mud room, scratching the back of his calf with his cleats.

"Can you lift that upstairs yourself?"

I nodded.

He checked his watch. "I should go. Do you mind?"

"Nope."

He put a hand on my shoulder and placed a thumb in the centre of my chin. "Are you sure?"

"I'm sure."

"You didn't say anything about the truck."

"Is it ours?"

"I brought it home yesterday. It smells new, though of course it's used. I got it from a lot so it's all spruced up. Just needs a gate but I can find one of those at Hoppy's or maybe through Larry. Your brother and I switched the eight-track over last night."

"It's great, Dad."

"We still have the Impala. I thought two cars would be better. For now."

His voice trailed off and I looked away. Sylvia used to have a car of her own, a Beetle, but it had died and Sam hadn't replaced it, promising to car pool to work on the days she needed to go anywhere, which had been fewer and fewer. Now that she was gone, he'd finally gotten a second vehicle.

"I have to go. We've got at least one more game tonight — maybe two, depending on whether we won this afternoon. Come down if you want. I think Jenny Taylor's even there."

III

Cowboy Joe Loves You

"I'm seeing a therapist," Duncan Matheson says, leaning his shoulder into mine as we stand at the Trout Club sinks, me washing and dipping in bleach rinse, him drying. He has a long, wiry body but I am taller, which with Duncan makes me feel good.

In high school, Duncan was the first guy I consciously tried to like. The first guy I truly liked was Vido Russo, who starred in a school production of *Godspell* at the end of Grade Nine. Vido Russo had glossy black curls and lips that turned up at the corners. When Vido's Jesus was sacrificed, I couldn't cry because Sam and Nicky were sitting beside me, but later in bed I ground my hips into the mattress at the image of a fiercely beautiful Vido-Jesus, his tongue swirling in my mouth, curls like shimmering ribbons against my neck.

When Vido Russo passed me in the hallway at school, I stopped, head leaning to one side, short gusts blowing from my nostrils, and stared, filled with goodness and tragedy and devotion. Vido himself hung with a group of Italians who lived in a new subdivision at the limits of the Tecumseth County High School zone. He left the next year to work in construction.

My like for Duncan was different. In Grade Ten someone taped a note to my locker that read, "Duncan likes you." That was all it took. Soon, Duncan stood in for the Vido-Jesus in my pre-sleep kissing scenarios, skinny, pointy-nosed Duncan who wore glasses and ran on the track team. We were in the same Sunday school class and sang in the choir together, staying late to lie side by side under the pews and at the count of three, launch our bodies feet-first toward the chancel to see who could shoot furthest. We played a similar game under the school bus seats back when our bodies were small enough to fit. But I quit choir and religion altogether when Duncan took confirmation classes to become a member of the United Church and I dis-covered Evolution. The rosy light behind the stained-glass Jesus no longer felt holy and while my arrested sob for Vido Russo's crucified stage-Jesus had held a passion of some purity, my desires were corporeal and there were better and more com-pelling reasons for most things than those given by God and for those things otherwise unexplainable, God was no help either.

Duncan liked me back, gave me birthday cards and song lyrics and I went to choir practice a few more times, but we were unable to speak more than two or three words to each other. I was bothered too by Duncan's intimacy with Reverend Green and Nanny Risenbrot, the organist, now that he was a sworn member of the United Church, as well as by the fact that his tenor was higher than my alto. Before long, Duncan's attentions embarrassed me and I no longer even wanted to unfold his unicorn poems and calligraphic renderings of "The Rose" when I found them stuffed in the door crack of my locker. I stared at his slack-lipped yearbook picture and found it was as easy to convince myself that he was ugly and hateful as it had been to insert Duncan into the bedtime kissing fantasy.

By the time I started at the Trout Club, I was indifferent about Duncan Matheson. Since the first day, though, we've talked like old friends. I am loathe to admit it, but Duncan makes the job fun, especially the way he compares the members to the fish they worship so much.

"Are you crazy?" I ask. I only half-believe that Duncan is seeing a therapist.

He hangs his head.

I hate when people hang their heads and decide Duncan is telling me this news because he likes me. If one of us is crazy it's me. Crazy is my birthright. Duncan's mother isn't crazy. Mrs. Matheson may be a church lady who thinks kids dressing as Smurfs on Hallowe'en constitutes devil worship, but she is sane — and more importantly, she is at home.

I don't tell Duncan that the possibility I may be crazy is more real than ever. It has been only a week since my first dreams of Mother and I've had two more:

5

Mother takes photographs of doorways and windows. The postcards she buys show rooftops and stoops. Always, the first thing she does is adjust the curtain.

6

We walk toward the *Tour Eiffel*. It slips in and out of view. Mother is fascinated by the river. We cross and re-cross bridges, stand on

the built-in stone benches and lean over to
watch boats float by. The wind lifts my hair.
Mother's doesn't move. Her face is a blur
caught in the wind, in movement, in despair.
I sway toward the water, but my hands hold
tight to the railing.

I prickle with the urge to be in that landscape. I savour
French words and linger over French lists of ingredients on
cereal boxes and chocolate bars. If I were there, really there,
could I make her turn and face me? If I were there maybe I
could look in her face for real.

I burn to ask more about Duncan's therapist. Duncan's
high, tight shoulders tell me he wants to say more. Silence irri-
tates Duncan. He likes to be involved in a constant stream of
conversation. I lower my lids and feel for the utensils in the
warm soapy water. When I started, I couldn't put my hands in
water that contained bits and pieces of other people's food, but
now I pretend I am blind and know only the shapes of fork
tines and spoon bowls. If I lean forward, a warm beam falls
across my cheeks. The sun is baking out there and the waitresses on the afternoon shift lie on military blankets, pinking
their skin before the supper rush.

How can Duncan have a psychiatrist? His mother would
only approve of counselling if it came from Reverend Green.

I would love to have a psychiatrist. I'd tell him about the
dreams and he'd tell me whether Sylvia is alive. Maybe
Duncan could be my psychiatrist, though I am used to listening to his problems, not the other way around. Telling him
means I'd have to hear his opinion. It also means talking about
Sylvia. I don't speak to Duncan about my mother any more

than I speak about her to anyone else, especially since Duncan lives in Apple Ford and knows the story.

If I did have a psychiatrist, I'd probably end up fucking him. That happens a lot. I glance at the weave of hairs where Duncan's forearms disappear into the red-and-white-checked tea towel and wonder if Duncan has fucked his therapist. *Fucking* is Rick's word. It would please Rick to know that when I think about therapists I think about fucking.

"Is it a woman or a man?"

"None of your business."

I tilt my head. After a few weeks of working together, Duncan tells me everything though there isn't much to tell. Now, when he has something worth talking about, he clams up.

Duncan pinches each utensil in the cotton cloth, sliding the fabric up then back down the stainless-steel length.

I have the sink drained and Javex-rinsed before he finishes.

"It makes a difference," I say.

Duncan tucks the end of the tea towel into the waistband of his pants.

"Let's go out for a break."

"Tell me."

He looks from side to side, then leans into my ear: "A big-bosomed woman, just like Mom."

He twirls away and strides to the patio doors.

"Your breath is like garlic. And besides, your mother's tits aren't that big." *Tits* is another Rick word.

"Garlic! Yours is the mildew on my feet."

We sit on a log several feet inside the woods. The trees here have long ridged trunks that come off in strops, revealing wood stained orange like flesh. I pick at one. It comes free with the ease of a clean-peeled scab. I say a silent apology to His Loggy

Lordship, whom I hid the other night in these very same woods. I can smell the blackened ashes from the staff campfires along with the malty sourness of spilled beer. I unbutton my blouse and slip it off. Underneath I wear a burgundy maillot with strings that gather in the centre of my chest and tie around my neck in a vee.

"Man, I wish we had some drugs. What happened to that artist guy in town who gives you guys pot?"

"Gives what guys pot?"

"You and your brother. Everybody knows about it."

"Maybe he gives Nicky pot, but what makes you think I'm getting any?"

"You spent enough time there in the winter and he's twice your age."

I keep my tone light. Duncan knows just enough about Rick. "Exactly. I bet he knows more than your big-breasted analyst."

Duncan picks up a handful of curly cedar needles and rubs them between his palms. Once he asked me if I thought the trees felt pain when I stripped off their bark. I snorted but didn't answer. I'm not sure if they feel pain but I keep peeling because I don't want to admit that they might.

"I don't even have smokes," he says.

I shrug.

"And she's not big-chested. He, I mean. He's someone I talk to once a week, that's all. Satisfied?"

Duncan shifts so he is sitting in the shade. I can feel my skin crisping.

"It's a good idea. I'd like one."

"So. Ask your dad."

"Right."

"Or your grandma."

"Sure. She'd tell me to knit one of those poodles that cover up toilet paper rolls to take my mind off things. What's the point?"

We laugh.

"You don't need a therapist to take your mind off things. Just cozy up to that artist guy."

"You know his name is Rick."

"Rick. And get him to give you a bag. I hear he's got a fridge full — and more. He's growing it in the swamps around here."

"Why don't you cozy up to Rick? Same difference. If I'm going to cozy up to anybody, I'd rather cozy up to your analyst. What do you tell him?"

I untie my straps and rest back on my hands.

Duncan looks at the tops of the trees. He picks up a stick and pokes it in the ruined fire.

"What would you tell him if you could meet with him?"

"I'd tell him all about my sex life."

"Why don't you tell me instead? I'm more reasonable."

"I would tell you, Duncan, if I had one. You sound like Rick."

I flick a strand of hair from my eyes.

"Come on. You know you have one."

"Rick is not a sex life. More like a lust life."

"You know he'd do it with you in a second, if you'd let him near you."

"I've let him near me."

"How near?"

"Near enough."

I blink a few times, feeling the weight of my lashes on my cheeks. I shade my eyes and wish I had sunglasses or a cap.

"Do you tell your therapist about your sex life?"

"I'm the one with no sex life."

We fall quiet. Outside, here, there is no noise, no wind. A chipmunk runs face-first down a tree, hangs for a moment, then darts back up.

"Well, Dunk, that therapist of yours has you fooled. You're just as crazy as ever. What do you want? To be normal, like the people who work here? Like the people in Apple Ford? Spare me."

"I tell Dave—"

"Dave?"

"I tell Dave things I could never tell anyone. Even you. For example, I tell him I think about cunts all the time." Duncan pauses and stares at me, eyebrows arched above his glasses. I stare back, determined not to react. I wish I had gum.

He continues. "The ladies in the choir, I see their cunts when I close my eyes."

"Even Nanny Risenbrot?"

Duncan rolls his eyes. "All the ladies in the choir. They look like teeth. The cunts, I mean." His face winces up in a smile. "Teeth. Sweaty teeth waiting to chomp me. I can't imagine kissing a girl even because I see those cunts like rabbit traps, clacking along, waiting to snap me."

Duncan focuses on the spot where the chipmunk disappeared.

"Cunts?"

I hold back my giggles. I've never heard Duncan swear before. Mrs. Matheson had more than washed his mouth out with soap when she caught him. I can barely say the word myself. I've never even heard Rick say it.

Duncan doesn't answer.

Maybe he wants to kiss me. His navy eyes flash; if I squint, he is cute. The cunts don't alarm me, but the prospect that at any moment he might lean over and place his lips on my skin makes my bones shrink back from my flesh. It is always like this. I am either flooded with attraction for someone or utterly repulsed — and sometimes both at the same time. Even with Jo and then Angie, shameful want lurked underneath my disgust. Duncan, with his sickle nose and pinchy lips and unbendable body, is someone I don't want near me. I cross my legs. Does he see a rabbit trap cunt when he looks at me? I picture smooth grey metal, with rivets and jagged teeth. The image is pleasing.

Based on only a few weeks, I've built a lifetime of fantasy around Rick. I've written both parts of a correspondence between us, leaving the letters in clear plastic bags in hollow trees down by the tracks and picking them up the next day.

It was winter when I met him, a weepy, fog-filled February with soggy grey snow clinging to the beige grass. The air was warmer than usual, which made me grateful, but it was an in-between-time, like a dream of cupboards and drawers between nightmares. I've never trusted melting in the middle of winter. It is borrowing time from the spring ahead. The more warmth we steal in February, the longer spring will take to arrive.

The false spring spurred Sam's addition plans. He and Nicky stayed up nights at the kitchen table making three-dimensional drawings, calculating dimensions, deciding on the location of doors and windows and estimating supplies.

I'd met Rick by chance. I was in the habit then of walking around town at night, a dream-time of my own, catching the scent of maple or cedar smoke from red-brick chimneys. Apple Ford was empty after dark, no cars even. I was heading for the park after babysitting to see how much the river had swollen. He was standing inside his screen door wearing shorts even though the temperature hovered around zero. Seeing him startled me so much I stopped and we spoke. He invited me in for tea and I went.

I was an inch taller than Rick so I sat on the floor while he filled a tin kettle from a tap over a concrete laundry sink in the back. I absorbed his apartment as a series of details: the crude two-by-fours holding up the loft bed; the clay, paint and plaster splatters on the floor; the roll of chicken wire; the crumpled balls of newspaper; the intricate pen-and-ink postcards of landscapes that on closer look revealed genitalia. Each item added to a roaring inside me. Soon I wouldn't be able to get his voice or his cedar-smoke, peppered-sweat scent out of my mind.

He heated the kettle on a hot plate and poured the boiling water over jasmine leaves in stained teacups. While the tea lasted, he faced me on a folding chair and talked about women: the women in town, girls my age, women in their twenties and thirties and beyond. It was hard to see women older than me as attractive.

Last summer he moved into this storefront in the same building that contains the once-a-week bank and an ever-shifting variety of stores selling specialized wares: riding tack, pine crafts, souvenir dolls, Christmas decorations, scented candles. Friends of his parents own the building. He'd taken a year off to hike Europe and before that had lived in a Pan-Abode on the edge of the river at the bottom of town—the same cottages where Sylvia had taken pottery, though I didn't mention this to him. The married ladies in town set him up on dates, he said, but it was the women arranging the dates who really wanted him. One woman grabbed his ass in the hallway at a party. He wouldn't tell me the name, but I knew everyone in town.

"You have a great laugh," he said, when I guessed.

I absorbed the comment, not thinking that one could be returned.

When he talked about other girls, I was aroused by what he observed: the globular breasts on one, the horse-riding thighs of another, the overlapping front teeth of a third. He found a redeeming feature in each one. His grin was cutting and I agreed with him on every account. I wanted him to talk about me that way but worried about whom he might tell. My feelings rose out of me, coating my skin with a film I couldn't shake off. I tried to convey how I felt through looks and pauses.

Sometimes Sam was sitting in the warm macramé light when I got home. He knew I was babysitting and never questioned the time. I'd pull up a chair across the table and let him explain to me how the squares he'd penned on graph paper were going to translate into an extra room by the end of the summer. In April — maybe March, at this rate — we could dig, he promised. I sipped at the rum and Coke he'd poured me and understood nothing. Geometry was one thing. Taking the lines sketched on paper and making a real room was another.

Every few days I found an excuse to visit Rick. He worked until four in the morning and said if his light was on and the inside door was open I could enter without knocking. If I didn't have a babysitting job, I waited for those nights when Sam was asleep by eleven and crept out the back door and down the now-frozen side yard. Some nights, before going home or even before my visit, I detoured past Mrs. Brant's water pipe and succumbed to a drink. Each visit, Rick talked to me the way he would a boy, about women he'd fucked and women he wanted to fuck.

I might as well have been a boy. The great length of my limbs makes my presence in the world unavoidable. My arms are as long as a man's, my legs longer. My breasts are small saucers overturned on my chest, my thin torso hipless. I grew so fast I've often felt like Alice learning how to twist her serpent neck to dive down into the trees. In my three years at Tecumseth County High School, no one has asked me out. Not even Duncan, despite the rhyming unicorn stanzas. It has to be because of my height. I can't allow myself to think otherwise.

Mostly, I sat on a folding chair and stared at Rick's back while he worked. I had his back mapped out in my memory. Once, without wiping the clay off his hands, he eased himself between my knees and asked me to massage his shoulders. I held cupped hands above him for a long time, then finally pinched a piece of skin between each thumb and forefinger and squeezed. Rick took one of my hands in each of his and moved them until my fingers were pushing his flesh around and the heels of my hands were digging into his muscles.

"You've made bread before."

"Once. In Grade Three."

"Treat me like a lump of dough. Knead me."

I liked the wordplay. I did need him. I moved my hands from the top to the bottom of his back, not daring to venture beneath the waistband of his shorts. Later I realized I could have if I'd wanted. I held my knees as far apart as possible, my hands circling, prodding his muscles, the soft indents above his hipbones. His own hands, streaked with the red clay Apple Ford was known for, lay face up on his knees. The smell of Plasticine and riverbanks. I couldn't see his face and took care just to massage, my fingers memorizing the bumps and scratches of his back.

Now backs are arousing, and repulsive. Everything I find erotic has the opposite claim on me. Some backs are thatched with hair, others clustered with angry oozing spots. Jo's back, with its chain of skinny bumps. Duncan's splatters of mahogany freckles. The sight, or even thought, of those backs alarms me, raises bile in my throat. But the perfect back, Rick's back — stretched over a worktable, muscles like beach sand shifting and rearranging themselves beneath the skin — has lodged in my mind.

The final time I saw Rick, it was he who touched me. A month had passed and Sam was amassing rectangular paper bags of concrete in the garage. He'd torn down the mud room and was hauling the scraps to the dump on Saturdays. I cancelled my Friday night babysitting without telling Sam and met Rick behind his building. He drove me in his blue Rabbit to a bar in the city and we danced in one spot through gravelly power-metal anthems, his hands roaming up and down inside my angora fisherman's sweater. Nothing real was touched, his fingers glancing off my skin in their haste. I felt red and bursting as I climbed into his car. He could have done anything then — even taken me up into his loft bed — and I wouldn't have protested.

On the drive home, he fiddled with the heat, turning it on full, wiping the steam off the window with his sleeve and leaning forward over the wheel.

I'd drunk three Mason jars of Kamikazes, and the lime-flavoured drink had loosened my tongue.

"The girls in school say they like to be surrounded by men's arms, they like to feel tiny, protected and safe." I tried to keep a neutral tone but feared I sounded mouthy.

Rick played with the radio.

"There's not a man on this earth large enough to surround me like that and even if there were, he would be a freak. These girls always say, 'I'm too fat.'"

I had no idea what I was talking about. When I imagined the impossibly small weights of most girls, I pictured a creased brown envelope stuffed full of bones unable to unfold.

There were only two teachers taller than me: Mr. Brown and Mr. Farkel. Both were freaks who hunched over at the waist and had loping gaits. Even Vi's tales that Sylvia was tall in her day make it worse. Look what happened to Sylvia.

Tall makes me conspicuous. Dancing with Rick, I became one of those hunched, skulking creatures I loathe. Before I could climb into Rick's loft, I had to be clear. I had to know that in his eyes, I was not a freak whose body would overwhelm him. That he didn't expect me to go mad at any time. Or at least that, if he saw the madness, it didn't matter.

Rick's silence convinced me. He'd given up on the radio and moved back to the heater. After a while, he dropped his hand onto my lap and kneaded my thigh. I steeled myself and felt only the pain of it.

There was no kiss, no hug, nothing as he dropped me off at the bottom of the hill. I must have done something wrong but there were no words to right it. I wanted my hands on that back while the rest of him wandered over me.

I eased the Rabbit's door shut behind me. I would never visit him again. He'd never get anyone else stupid enough to massage him. My skin was pressed and throbbing. Once, while we were dancing to AC/DC, his hand made it down the squished front of my jeans, between my lips, tugging at my hairs, but that was as far as he went.

My jeans smelled musky and between my legs was damp. Fortunately, no one was awake.

I shouldn't have let him touch me in the first place if this was all it was going to be. I don't know the language for asking my way into someone's bed. The language of absence, of pulling back and gathering desire in my imagination, is the only language in which I am fluent.

For several nights afterward, my dreams featured hands, backs, broken-handled teacups, wineglasses with the stems snapped off. I lay in bed trying to get back to the moment the glass separated, for that one slight pleasure, but my dreams offered up only the fractured pieces.

Duncan claims the staff holds campfires on Mondays after sundown. Though I usually give him little credit, I believe him because he is now living at the Club. That Monday after the morning shift, I ride home and strip down to my bathing suit without going into the house. The sun is planted mid-sky, the only clouds stretched so thin they are more of a haze. Nicky is nowhere to be seen. I've considered leaving my bathing suit behind one day, as bait. Would Nicky be tempted to add it to the stash under his mattress? Would he dare? Strands of desiccated grass lie scattered about the newly mown lawn. A broad swath arcs around the sawhorses' splayed legs embedded in the summer-hard dirt.

I grab a yellow-and-orange-flowered towel from the clothesline and spread it on the shorn grass as far as possible from the house. I lie on my stomach, bury my face in my arms and have another dream:

7

Mother says to call her Sylvia. She has another name, Anna. I have never heard it used. At Mother's christening, her grandmother offered

her mother money to name her Sara. When her
mother refused, her grandmother called her
Baby instead of Sylvia. Anna was a compromise.
This is the first story I have heard of any family
Mother might have.

I lift my head when I hear the truck drive up. My face is
hot and bunched, my skin soap-slick from sweat. I want to put
my head down and burrow back into the dream but can't
because Sam is walking toward me, bits of cut grass attaching
to the cuffs of his khakis. This dream feels real.

"How are those boards coming along?" I can't see his eyes
through his tinted prescription lenses.

"I wanted to wait until it wasn't so hot."

"If it's a tan you're concerned about, you said yourself it
was better to get one standing up working."

"I did."

"Or you could move these sawhorses inside the garage." He
pushes at the nosepiece of his glasses. A patch of wet spreads
in the pit of his shirt sleeve. "If you set up now, you can still get
some done after we eat."

"Dad—" I say as he turns to leave.

"Umm-hmmm." He looks back at me over his shoulder
with one hand shielding his brow.

I am about to ask him about Sylvia's other names when I
see the notepad sitting squarely in his left shirt pocket beside
two capped pens — one blue, one red.

"Nothing. I wanted to ask you where the extra sandpaper
was and then I remembered."

"There's a coffee can on the workbench with some
sheets in it."

"Yeah, thanks."

"No problem."

I wrap my arms around my knees and open my mouth against the salt-greased skin. As a child I rested against Sylvia on her bed as we read her Baby Name Book. We looked up my almost-names and the names I would call my babies and even the meaning for Sylvia — "from the forest" — but there was no mention of Anna or Sara or any alternative names for Sylvia. No mother, grandmother or christening either.

But she is Baby in his notes. LET ME CALL YOU BABY. I thought the line was about phoning her, but maybe it is about her name. A name withheld even from her husband. Are the dreams coming from life or are they something more? Could they be both?

After dinner, I tell Sam I forgot I have an extra shift. I put on jeans and a white polo shirt and strap my K-way pouch around my hips. I grab my bike and cycle back to the Club.

The staff quarters where Duncan said we should meet is a two-storey cottage, its forest green clapboard and brown roof of a similar style to the Big House at Camp Wanigamog. The main room tunnels into darkness when I enter from the bright end-of-day sunlight. My eyes flutter and soon shapes appear and I can focus on a senior waitress named Brenda Wilkins who sits wearing a slip at the end of a picnic table three times normal length like those at the Big House. Fan blades thwack the air near the ceiling and cluster flies buzz against screens.

"Where is everybody?" I ask. I've never talked to a Club waitress before. Maybe I am too early.

Brenda sucks a cigarette, her long cheeks dimpling. Smoke hangs above her like layers of a strudel. She rolls her eyes and twitches her head in the direction of a man sitting on the side of the table nearest to her, his head down. He riffles a deck of cards, his body coiled in readiness to play.

I try again: "Isn't there a party tonight?"

"What's it look like?" the man says, eyes on the cards.

Brenda smiles. "Have a seat," she says.

I scratch the back of my knee with the uncut nail on my big toe. I should have made Duncan meet me on the road.

"I won't bite," the man says, his eyes pointed at Brenda. He has pale fried hair and a compact body wound tight.

He lifts his haunches off the bench, rattles the table, and asks, "What are you waiting for?"

I come over, pull out the bench and slide in.

Two beers later I am in the middle of losing rummy to Levon Wilder who is up to see Brenda on her day off. Little is said. I've lost my Sam-taught urge to speed-add the points once a hand is laid. It is too hot to hold the cards up in a fan, let alone open my mouth and form words.

If the heat oppresses Brenda, it is not verbally. Since her turn is after mine, Brenda keeps a running commentary on my throwaway cards, acting like I am on her side and I'm going out of my way to throw exactly the cards Levon can't use.

It is strange having Brenda talk to me as if I am a normal person. The senior waitresses never talk to kitchen help. On our smoke breaks, Duncan and I cut up the waitresses, especially the older ones like Brenda. Duncan will find her slip funny because she is big, but Brenda looks more comfortable than I feel in jeans and a polo shirt.

Each time our beer bottles are empty, I grab new ones from a squat Frigidaire that smells like onions. After the third round, Brenda grips my wrist.

"It's no problem," I say, resisting the urge to pull away.

"It's Levon's turn. Right, honey?"

"I am the guest here — don't forget, Bren. I drove down from Wigton."

"She's a guest too."

Levon straightens the cards, flicks an elastic band off his wrist and wraps it crossways around the deck in one practised gesture. He grins, revealing fangs. His cheeks fold into deep creases, making his small plain face devilish.

Brenda lets go of my wrist and pats the back of my hand.

"Don't get too excited, hon, he's taken."

"I already have a boyfriend," I say, thinking automatically of Rick.

Brenda winks. "I know all about it. Everybody does."

My ears flare. No one but Duncan knows, and he doesn't know much. I haven't even seen Rick since March. He is a boyfriend of the mind: an invention, improvised on the body I knew only briefly. The word *boyfriend* is overdoing it; he is so much older and barely qualifies as a friend.

Levon stands. "Even *I* know about that big-nosed guy who hangs with you."

His laugh is scratchy. He dances his eyebrows at Brenda.

"How about that beer?" Brenda asks. It takes me a few seconds to realize who he is talking about. "Duncan? Duncan is *not* my boyfriend, thank you very much." My wrists shake, partly with relief that Levon and Brenda don't know about Rick.

Brenda laughs and meets Levon's eyes.

"Beer."

Levon eases himself out from the bench and I catch the smell of detergent from his shirt. When he stands, his knees point sideways, so his walk requires him to roll with his hips, a swaying step, like a dancer with no rhythm. I give in to my childhood need to look away from anything abnormal. I glance once more when he is back at the table.

His head quivers and he rests his amber marble eyes on me for the first time.

"It was an accident, alright?" he says, lips thin, mouth compressed.

I swallow and look away.

"Open the beer and stop bragging," Brenda says. She rubs her cleavage with the side of her thumb.

Levon unfastens his belt and pries the cap off each bottle with his buckle. His shirt rises up and exposes a stomach lightly covered with hair. His skin seems to sink into his bones.

"He does that so you'll look."

I do. I smile up at Brenda then remove the elastic from the cards and shuffle.

Levon thumps a bottle each down in front of me and Brenda.

"I'll tell you why I walk so funny."

"She's not interested, Levon."

"It's a good story," he says, folds piling up on his forehead.

"I'll tell you a good story." Brenda leans across the table and rests on her forearms. She takes Levon's chin in her hands and kisses him. He holds himself taut, beer bottle tilted on his knee. When she finishes he raises it to his lips, licking them first.

I cough.

"Maybe I should leave." I wonder where Duncan is. Where everybody is.

Brenda sits back down.

"Don't bother. It's too hot."

Levon grins again, reminding me of Rick. Something about carnivorous smiles. A tight shock shivers up and down the insides of my thighs. Then it is gone.

"It happened when I was waiting for the school bus. We lived on a highway and the kids from five other families waited at my stop. I slipped on the gravel in the lineup. None of the others noticed; even Mrs. Phelpston, the bus driver, didn't notice. Exactly then Mrs. Phelpston decided to drive off, and the bus ran right over my legs, turning them sideways. To this day, I hate those snaky yellow vehicles. If it weren't for the children inside them, I'd run every last one of them off the road."

Brenda raises her eyebrows.

A moth spins out against the screen. I imagine Levon lying under a bus. An older boy named Jeff Spragley let our bus run over his foot once. He climbed on right after, unharmed. My four-year-old body had lain straight, facing upward, arms folded across my belly as the wheels of a truck rolled slowly past on either side of my knees then my shoulders, the oily undercarriage so close I could have reached a nail up and scraped dirt. The greasy exhaust smell of Chipper's deluxe canvas tent.

"Tell her another one, Levon."

"I'll tell you one that'll make the hairs on your pussy stand up and march around the room."

Levon grins at Brenda, who lights another cigarette. I want one too, but they aren't offering and asking would feel strange. I don't mind these two telling stories as long as they don't ask me any questions.

"About four years ago — the year before you came here, Brenda — I worked at this club."

Brenda nods, smirking.

"My buddy Lewie and I were sitting at this very table drinking when all the colour drained from Lewie's face. 'Look,' he said, pointing behind my head, but I just kept playing. I wanted to cuff him, but I turned and we both saw it: a flash of light, quicker and brighter than a firecracker, somewhere up there near the ceiling fan.

"Come to think of it, he died not long after that."

Levon holds a cupped hand out to me. Our thumbs touch as I drop the cards into his palm. His skin feels like the buckskin suit Uncle Larry had made from two deer he shot out of season one year.

Brenda blows smoke at Levon.

"Get real," she says with obvious enjoyment. "You know that never happened. It's fake. Isn't it, Mercy? We can see right through it."

The door clacks open and Duncan bursts in, squinting. He sways, blinded.

"There you are," he says to me when he can focus. "Did you get any drugs?"

Levon clamps his lips. I gaze at the light grizzle on his chin, my mind on the detergent shirt and the buckskin hands.

A few nights after Rick took me to the city, I took acid for the first time. It was the March Break and Sam let me borrow the car to go shopping with Sara Bunnell. Sara had left school a semester early to go to college and lived in a rented room in a subdivision townhouse.

We drank a two-dollar bottle of wine bought at a mall wine shop that didn't ask for ID. Drunk, we sat on the carpet watching music videos and laughing at the haircuts until tears smeared our cheeks. The wine gave me the courage to take out my wallet and show Sara the two squares of white paper I'd bought from a guy in the school smoking area who had used black magic marker to write *To be a rock and not to roll* in runic letters on his jean jacket. Sara separated the tabs and placed one on her tongue and one on mine. By the time the woman who owned Sara's townhouse came in with her friends, Sara and I were lying on our backs on the brown carpet reading messages in the stippled ceiling:

> *Cowboy Joe loves you y'know.*
> *In Time you spin and flutter.*
> *What you make, you create.*

The rest of the evening comes to me in scenes.

SCENE ONE
I am naked and unable to remember how I got that way. The others are naked too though no one touches. While Sara dances to *Led Zeppelin IV*, I sit on the couch watching the spaces between me and the others.

SCENE TWO
I lie on a single bed with a wrinkled white sheet. The bed is in a corner and I have the wall side. Sara sleeps beside me. My eyelids are screens filled with full-colour 3-D animation. My hands explore Sara's back, pressing the bronze flesh until I know it by heart.

With each smooth inch I yearn for the bumps and hairs of Rick's back. As I conjure him into my mind, my exploration turns into a massage. This back will be the next in a long line of backs that had started reluctantly with Jo's. I am determined to know every back I can get my hands on. This one has a mole which my fingers come back to again and again.

I am happy to be here with Sara, whose droning account of her own hallucinations has faded quickly enough. My fingers won't stop. As the night progresses, my fingertips probe every inch of Sara's back, blotting her skin, pulling Sara's essence out through her pores. It isn't sexual as much as surgical, an information gathering. Sara's body is firm and round, her skin naturally brown. I close my eyes and let my fingertips feed my hallucinations.

SCENE THREE

A man and woman stand framed in a halo of light in the doorway.

"Don't stop," the woman says. It is the woman who writes poetry and has the long flat tits that had flapped earlier as she danced to "Misty Mountain Hop." She even has a teenage son.

The man says nothing. He is young, maybe in college. His name is Adam. The Zeppelin has stopped. I hold my position and wait. Soon the cartoons will come back and these people will be gone.

The woman places a thick, ridged object in my hand. Thinking it is attached to Adam, I drop it. Adam and Eve. Is the woman's name Eve? I check, and yes, they are naked. Good. I won't have to cover up. The woman steps halfway into the room, picks up the object and places it back in my hands, then retreats to the doorway.

"Use it," the woman says, her voice almost a song. "Use it on her. She'll like it. You know she will."

My fingers loosen and the object rolls onto the bed again. I am aware of what it is. Sara had told me about the vibrator: it belongs to the woman who owns the house and it is so loud that everyone can hear it downstairs — even with the TV on.

Ronda. The woman's name is Ronda.

"Use it yourselves," I say finally, my voice nasal, far away.

They stare at me, then Ronda says, "It's yours if you want it. I won't spoil your fun."

They shut the door and I place my head beside Sara's on the pillow. I try to sleep but my mind won't stop moving. I want to fold my arms around Sara, but the vibrator's presence makes me too aware. I kick it off the bed and roll on my side to face the wall.

Sara was gone in the morning and I haven't seen her since. That's fine. I refuse to let Sara build in my mind like Rick has. In hopes of dismantling Sara, of melting her down, I've replayed that night's scenes on the bus to school and later, while riding my bike to and from the Club. The same technique after Camp Wanigamog effectively tempered my memories of Jo.

A dream from the weeks following Rick and Sara, the first dream of Mother, and the most disturbing, comes to me now when I'm riding my bike:

> Mother's powdered-milk smell is imprinted on my body memory. She is shapeless, a sculpture of tubes, sockets, joint, pores, colours flashing in and out with jumbled words pouring out. The word human does not fit her. She is too large. Too much. I want to merge. My jaw stiffens and refuses to open enough to accept anything more than a straw. I must either bolt or press myself so close I can breathe Mother's air, and our fluids will flow together.

The dream prods me, hunts me until I don't know whose body I hold inside me, whether it is Rick's, Sara's or even Mother's flesh I am remembering.

Now there's Levon. In the days following the first campfire, thoughts of Levon flood me as I pedal to and from the Trout Club: Levon's improbable body crawling over me, the crooked legs, the grizzled rawhide skin. I have a substantial list of what is unappealing about him, but it is a relief not to think of Rick. It is Levon who comes to me in a dream that night, rises up in the closed green interior of a school bus and wraps

his arms around my shoulders, looming behind and above me,
that razor-lined smile nudging my scalp.

The Levon dream is a welcome break from the onslaught
of Mother dreams. I mash my face into my pillow, slip my hand
between my legs and try to re-enter but I can't get past Mother:

8

At night I share a bed with Mother. Mother —
I cannot call her Sylvia, nor Anna, nor Baby —
has lost her uneasiness. At night Mother settles
in early. I sit near the window, my fingers tangled in lace curtains, my flashlight held over a
book until my eyelids droop. In the bed, I position myself face down, breasts flattened against
the sagging mattress. Mother wheezes, whistles,
snores. I shove my head under the pillow, wishing for Wonder Woman's invisible dome.

9

I cannot think of any part of Mother's body
without repulsion. The hard yellowing nails
on her bulging red feet. Her rounded calves
and thighs. The flaking and ridged skin. The
long deflated breasts which she must lift into
her bra. I have never looked at them up close.
I suspect them of blemishes — pimples and
moles, like those on her back, on her flaccid
behind. My own long white feet are becoming
chapped and red around the heels. I am certain I will never have to lift my breasts.

Coming out of this dream is a struggle. Each time I think I am awake and try to stand I find myself locked in sleep. Finally I force my eyes open enough that slits of semi-darkness filter in. I jump up and pull on track pants to go to the Club. My clock says twenty past four.

I sunbathe while working on Sam's boards at home as often as I do at the Club. It is easy enough to stay out of Vi's way; I don't even need to go into the house if I wear my bathing suit to the Club. Vi spends her afternoons on the couch watching her plays. The parallel with Sylvia's last weeks at home has not escaped me, but at least Vi has the energy to follow a plot.

One afternoon, I stand sanding a knot with a piece of Number 00 sandpaper Sam has wrapped around a block of wood. A can of plastic wood and a rag to brush off dust sit on my milk-crate table. I've decided to prep all the boards and then paint instead of completing the boards one at a time. Sam approves.

Nicky squats near the peak of the addition roof, spreading tar and fitting in shingles. His tape recorder sits on the fence playing a mixed dance tape. He wears a baggy white tank top with a fluorescent orange logo and ripped jean shorts.

I've wrenched the sawhorses out of the dirt and moved them closer to the house and Nicky's music. The armholes on his shirt gape but his chest is shadowed. I can't tell what he wears underneath, if anything.

Vi shuts off her show — the same one she's been watching for thirty years as she keeps reminding us — and emerges in her blue bathing suit with white piping that looks as old as the soap opera. Weeks have passed since she had the bandage removed. Her body is like a land mass, measurable only in acres and miles. The bathing suit stretches over her like sod on a field, fitting whatever shape she happens to be.

With her caftan over her arm, she drags the orange canvas chaise longue about six feet away from Nicky's ladder and sits.

She closes her eyes against the sunlight.

"You'd better move farther back, Granny, because I might drop something or drip tar on you." Nicky straddles the roof's peak. White cotton peers through the ripped threads on the bum of his jeans.

Vi stands and hauls her chair back so one side of her is in the shade.

"You're old enough now to call me Vi," she says, running her fingertips across her belly. The panel is tight enough to hide her scar.

"Viiii." Nicky stretches out the *aiii* sound.

"Yes, dear. What do you think?"

Nicky breaks a shingle off a row and eases it into place.

"Cool," he says, even though the name clutters his tongue. Vi always makes this request and he always ignores it.

He shifts his weight onto his upward leg and reaches for the can of tar. He stirs the glue with a wooden stick then drops a dollop beside the tile he just applied.

Vi watches for a while.

"It would be much more practical if you spread enough glue for several tiles instead of just one at a time."

Nicky doesn't look up.

Vi leans back and crosses her ankles.

"What happened to your soap opera — your play?" I ask. I've decided to be more like Nicky and ask people questions about things they want to talk about. It doesn't hurt that Nicky is now acting miffed and silent.

Vi arches an eyebrow. Even if she might still be mad at me, she never misses an opportunity to talk.

"Now that it's summer, all my plays are full of teenage lust. As far as I'm concerned, teenagers are half-formed people. Lust oozes out of them in all directions but their bodies aren't bodies yet — they don't bear witness to the battles and triumphs of the life inside them. They've suffered no excavations, bear no scars, have nothing to show where growth and loss has occurred. Do you know the word *cicatrix*? Either of you?"

I shake my head and Nicky says, "No." He fiddles with the sleeve hole of his tank top.

"A cicatrix is a scar or seam made of the new tissue that is formed when a wound heals. It's also the mark left when a leaf falls from a tree."

"Nicky's body has scars from the stitches he had when he ripped his head open on a nail in the loft. He's a teenager. Does that count?" Even my attempts at light conversation come out sounding mean.

Vi shakes her head. "Take me for instance. My body is rough terrain: full of U-turns and rocky passes; it is no longer a love object but rather a coat that is ripping at the seams. It is only in this skin that someone's touch can reach me, not in that bright new flesh that you young people flaunt. Your bodies are hard and resistant, unable yet to absorb each touch, each growth, each inch of decay. Everything bounces off your young bodies: late nights, drinking binges, junk-food diets, and still they gleam, firm and shiny. If your bodies can withstand all that, surely they can withstand the scars of desire."

"You're saying you don't like teenagers?" I grin.

"Not quite. I'm telling you why I can't watch my afternoon plays any longer."

Nicky sits now, one hand under his shirt, on his belly, his feet in high-tops, resting on the top step of the ladder. He wears the slightest of smiles.

"There is no point to desire if the body is not going to wear its mark in the aftermath, if the body is not indeed transformed. It's the older actresses, the ones who reveal their ages in their thin bony hands and the desperate tendons of their necks, whose weary tumbles on hotel beds interest me, but we see them less and less as summer wears on and the TV tries to capture the idle teenage audience. In fact, you two are exactly the viewers they're aiming at."

Despite my affection for *Dallas*, I can't imagine anything more boring but I keep my mouth shut. It is nice to be talking with Vi again. I brush the dust away with a rag and turn the board over. There are no visible knots on this side so it won't need as much sanding.

"When I was young," Vi continues, "desire slipped on and off me like clouds on the sun. I married early and for a long time equated desire with Earl's feverish fumbles after a day of logging. It was only later, long after my children had marred me in their own ways, that desire began to make what was absent in me known."

It is strange to hear someone else talk about desire, even Vi. Is that what is going on in my mind, in my fantasies and dreams? I can see it with Rick and with Levon. Maybe even the tamped-down feelings for Jo and Sara. But what about the dreams of Mother? Is that desire? What is missing in me? Where are my scars? My cicatrix?

The day Sylvia came home, Vi had sat out here in the same bathing suit under the same pear tree and laid down her suspicions. To serve the truth, she said. To lower our expectations. I hadn't understood her then; her words served only to compel me toward this wayward mother nobody could pin down.

Vi's temples are perspiring. She scratches her forehead through the band of her wig, moving the perched chestnut curls of her Sensational Shag back and forth.

"Maybe my head is shrinking. That happens sometimes, I've heard. Perhaps I should grow my hair out, maybe get one of those perms. Grey hair would make me look older. But I *am* old. I have grandchildren who are teenagers, who can build houses and drive pickup trucks."

Nicky and I were still children that day we sat waiting for Sam to bring Sylvia home, but my clothes were already getting tight. Now Vi was shrinking and I loomed over her. Too bad we didn't have a mushroom we could nibble to even us out.

Nicky laugh and sticks another tile in place. "Why not?"

"Yeah," I say, "nobody wears wigs anymore."

"Except heavy metal singers," Nicky adds.

"I'll tell you, I'm only in my fifties, but this bathing suit in this lawn chair with this itching wig makes me feel old. I needed something or someone to throw me off track again, but who can I ask? I can't very well ask my teenage grandchildren to introduce me around. It was easier on the highway with the diner. This town is so goddamn small, all I probably have to do is walk up and down the streets a few times and I'd meet everyone in it."

My mind flashes on Rick. I wonder if Nicky is thinking the same thing.

Vi settles back, face to the sun. "Maybe for once they could come to me. But first I'll have to clear the path a little."

9

Underground

Underground

I t was August now and I was growing. My feet got big first, giving my body a look of groundedness. For weeks, I'd walked around on my new solid feet, a normal-sized girl impossible to topple.

I minded about my feet but they grew before I could stop them. The only shoes that fit me now were my runners and that was because the seams around the toes had given. After Camp Wanigamog I decided to forgo footwear. To toughen my soles I practised walking on our gravel driveway and the hot asphalt road. In the afternoons, I tested my leathery skin on the chunky stones by the railway tracks, walking bare heel to toe along the sizzling rails, arms held out like telephone poles. Indians wore moccasins made from tanned deerskin, but I couldn't get any unless I went up north to Uncle Larry's. A more heroic Indian wouldn't need moccasins at all in the summertime — and perhaps not even in the winter. If I could harden my feet into shoes I might enhance my own true stealth.

After my feet, I resisted growing. At night I curled my body into a ball and wedged myself between my mattress and the headboard. Some nights I slept in the closet, my shoulder rounded against one wall, my heels pushing into the other. The restriction, I hoped, might reverse the process which was altering my bones.

I lay awake in those odd fetal squeezes, hands pressing my flesh to hold everything in. In the quiet of the middle of the night, I listened for the faint crackling and shifting of the bone cells. I was sure that beneath my nightie, the bones were pushing closer to the surface, their growth greedy, their white liquid glowing under my skin.

After Sam left with Nicky in the mornings, I crouched in a tub of steaming water for over an hour, turning on the faucet with my toes when it got too cool, my skin crab red below the surface. I'd read in one of Vi's movie magazines that hot water had shrinking properties. I hated baths, particularly the part that involved spreading soap suds over my skin and rubbing it in with a facecloth. My forays into the tub were for the singular purpose of halting my growth. It disappointed me that my callused feet lost some of their crust in the water. When I emerged from the bath, I hated the humid air and the need to blot my skin to take the water away, so I wound towels around my body and head, arranged one over my shoulders like a cape and sat folded up in the space between the end of the tub and the wall until my body had dripped dry.

Mrs. Sousa came to clean at the end of the week. She sent lasagnas and shepherd's pies home with Nicky so we didn't need to cook. After my shrinking ritual I picked up whatever was lying around the house. I threw Nicky's and Sam's clothes in a basket in the mud room. Everything else I put in its proper place. I let Sylvia's voice direct me since I'd never tidied the house before, only my own room. I watched Mrs. Sousa spray polish on tables and wipe with a rag and scrub the toilet boil with powder and a wire brush. On days when she didn't come, I moved through the house imitating her routine, imagining Sylvia's voice finding fault with Mrs. Sousa's dusting and waxing — and praising my own cleaning prowess.

As I grew I resorted to wearing my smallest, oldest clothes, T-shirts and shorts from last summer and before that Sylvia had neglected to box up for the Sally Ann. Seams pulled taut at my crotch and underarms but I liked wearing clothing that Sylvia had seen me in.

I wasn't sure what I was getting away with, but people in town thought I was getting away with something. Nanny Risenbrot interrupted her conversation with Glad O'Connor at the general store to say hello to me, her eyes resting alternately on my chest and the brick of sponge toffee I was buying. Outside the post office, Mrs. Matheson looked down and up my long white legs and frowned. I curled my shoulders forward to loosen the fabric of my T-shirt.

One day, Jenny Taylor asked me on the street why I didn't wear a bra, as if it was my fault, as if I was asking for something by letting those two bumps go free. I wasn't supposed to be someone who should wear a bra. Girls who wore them fell into two categories: those who could fill them and those who were wishing. Girls like Cherry who were fully developed needed thick-strapped bras and had no choice. Girls like Jo needed bras too but what I had were soft disks that moved around under the skin and hurt when I touched them. They were more like Angie's buds. I didn't want to be the kind of girl who was wishing, but what Jenny said made me realize that going without might be as bad as wishing, like showing off.

Asking Sam for a bra was out of the question. We had a shaky peace in the house and I didn't want to tamper with our code of silence. He accepted my need not to talk about camp and I didn't ask any questions about Sylvia or anything else that might embarrass him. A bra fell into that category. That's why I decided to sneak one of my mother's. I hadn't been in my parents' bedroom since before Sylvia had left, hadn't even seen it: Sam closed the door after him in the morning. It was only open when Mrs. Sousa was cleaning it and I left it to her, omitting it from my own ritualistic sweeps through the house and averting my eyes when Mrs. Sousa was there as if Sylvia's room might reveal something unspeakable. Anything was possible when I opened the door in search of Sylvia's brassiere. What if I found some private, shameful remnant of Sylvia's final night — an item Sam had preserved, or been unwilling to remove? Maybe part of Sylvia lingered, preventing him. There was also the chance that all reminders of Sylvia were gone, that the room held no evidence of her ever having shared his bed. This possibility was the most eerie of all.

When I was younger, I had explored the drawers of my mother's dresser nearly every day, when my mother was there and other times on my own. I knew the drawers' contents by heart, and chose them based on my mood.

The long bottom drawer was for memory moods, when I didn't want to think about now. In a true memory mood I required my mother's memories for the world to pull away and leave me alone.

The bottom drawer held thick woollen sweaters zigzagged with Easter egg patterns. I had tried the sweaters on, but they scratched. What I was really after hid under the sweaters: a pale blue cigar box that held postcards of motels and buses and the occasional train. Some of the postcards had trees or hills in the background; a very few had people. Most were from towns in the north and eastern states, like Estevan or Maiden's Peak. Three were from Europe with captions written in another language, but not French.

Vi had postcards like these too. She kept them in a quilted pink plastic envelope with the word *Mementos* stitched in red script across the front. I didn't tell Vi I'd snooped and found her cards and I didn't ask her about them. It seemed like everybody had a stack of postcards from somewhere though I'd never received a single one myself.

Vi's postcards had stamps on them but no writing. Sylvia's had never been mailed. I'd sat on the bed beside Sylvia and as I looked through the cards one by one, she described the picture for me as well as what was going on outside the frame — what had just happened or was just about to. The cleaning lady about to open the last door on the left of the motel. The toque that had fallen out of the cable car. The bus driver who had walked off to get a coffee. She relayed these moments with a matter-of-factness that failed to reveal whether she had witnessed or was merely inventing them. Each time she told these stories they were the same and since the cards had no stamps, Sylvia must have visited each place herself or had a friend bring her the cards. I never asked. The postcards were small jewels. It didn't matter whether I was alone or sitting on the bed beside my mother. The cards themselves were important, not the stories that went with them. I didn't care about the convertible pulled away not one minute ago or the armadillo who showed up too late. I was like this about souvenirs — content to leaf through photo albums, even when their owners weren't there, but indifferent to the stories behind each picture.

The middle drawer, full of summer clothes, fit none of my moods. I was more interested in the top two smaller drawers. The top left drawer was for dress-up moods. Sylvia had opened this drawer herself, lifting out coloured glass beads strung with knotted gold thread, draping them around my neck and winding them through my hair. This drawer contained palm-sized pots of rouge, thick gold tubes of lipstick, flying-saucer compacts with powdery mirrors and puffs, a rainbow of pencils and more than ten bottles of nail polish. On nights when Sylvia went out, I was allowed to use the polish on my own nails, even to borrow a bottle selected by my mother and keep it in my room.

The little drawer on the top right was off-limits when Sylvia was in the room. I had once taken out a pair of large nylon panties while my mother was getting the photo albums down from the closet. I'd looked at the white cotton part between the leg holes the way I always did with my own underwear. It was stained a light yellow.

"Mine are like that," I'd said, pleased to have something the same as my mother's. "What is it? Why is it like that?" I repeated my questions until my mother came and sat on the bed without looking at me. When I fell quiet, my mother turned her head slowly and fixed her gaze on the panties.

"Put those away," she said, her face pulled back in a look that read, *I can't believe you're even touching those.* I got the same look when I made an obvious observation, or when I looked at my own underwear. I never dared to sniff mine when my mother was around — I did that only in the bathroom with the door locked. I rolled the panties in a ball, the way I'd been taught, placed them back and shut the drawer. Sylvia smiled again and went into the closet to get the Baby Name Book instead of the photos. I forgot about the panties at the prospect of imagining myself going through life with a different name. I settled against Sylvia on the bed and together we read the list of girls' names and their meanings. Sam had wanted to call me Mercedes she said, after the car, but she had compromised on Mercy, though her first choice along those lines would have been Charity, for reasons she wouldn't explain. She'd liked Sadie too.

Sometimes, I opened the top right drawer on my own. This drawer was for risky moods when the world receded around me and I focused in on one thing. I checked the white part of each of my mother's panties for the pale stain. Some had it. Some had nothing. Some had brown — I didn't want to touch those pairs. There was more too, under the panties: metal tubes filled with creams, like the tube of cream for cuts and burns, and pill bottles with solid black marker lines on the labels.

At the back were two paperback books, one called *Your Erroneous Zones* and another called *When I Say No I Feel Guilty*. I didn't want to touch that one. I stuffed it under the bras so I could look at the bottles of blue pills and tubes of cream instead.

On the day I decided to search Sylvia's drawers for a bra I was in a new mood. More dangerous than the risky mood, like jumping into deep water with my eyes closed. I chose a sunny evening when Sam and Nicky were at the ballpark. Sam's bedroom door had a hole where a doorknob should be. The door hung shut, not tight in the frame. At any time I could have brushed it with my shoulder or nudged it with a finger and it would have swayed open. It was amazing that, even with my body growing out of control, I had not hit it with a stray elbow

or a wandering foot. I bumped everything else, the purple sometimes as common as the freckles on my skin.

I hooked my finger in the doorknob hole and pushed, keeping my finger in the hole as I stepped into the room, the door a
security blanket. The only window was covered by a Venetian
blind, making the room almost perfectly dark. Furniture loomed.
There was no overhead light so I had to unhook my fingers and
feel my way around until I found a lamp. The room didn't really have a smell, rather a series of half-scents. Wood and cotton
that never saw light. The lemon of Mrs. Sousa's polish and the
sour man smell of Sam's dirty work shirts. Candle wax too and
peppermints and pennies. Much of Sylvia had fled: it was Sam's
domain now. The prickling at the back of my neck disappeared,
taking with it some of my enthusiasm.

With the fingers of my left hand still caught in the door
hole, I reached forward and swiped at the air with my right until
I found the corner of the bed. I wrapped my fingers around the
post then let the door float shut. What little light I'd had faded.

I was alone in my father and mother's bedroom with both
hands on the foot of their bed. Sam's room now. Not Sylvia's.
Not Sam and Sylvia's. The excitement returned, but it was more
like being shut in a closet. I wondered if Nicky had felt this way
when I locked him in his closet. Maybe that explained his fit. A
circle of light coming through the doorknob hole calmed me. I
moved hand over hand along the mattress until I was near the
bedside table. I sat on the bed. It was made. I inched my fingers
along the bottom of the table, over a book and what felt like
handkerchiefs until I was touching the lamp. It had a funny
ridged switch and I had to fumble with it a few times.

Even with the light on, the room was dusky. At first I
couldn't even see the bedpost or the lamp. Pictures flashed:

segments of the heap of white clothing that had been Sylvia breaking down on this very bed.

While my eyes adjusted I became aware of Sylvia's former presence in the room. When I was four and my body had split into two, I'd felt lighter, more free. This feeling was the opposite. It bore down on me, pushing my shoulders, invading my body, forcing it to share its domain with another, with Sylvia — or rather the contorted animal in white sheets I had witnessed the day Sylvia went away.

I was heavy now, my weight out of proportion with my height. If I stayed here much longer, the animal inside me would twist me up until it was I who lay bent and deformed, wailing at the end of the bed.

With rapid twitchy motions, I glanced around with hurt animal eyes. The chest of drawers loomed and the room's corners crept inward, the shadows squeezing me, sucking at me. Part of me resisted: if I concentrated I could see the room strictly as Sam's. I fixed my eyes on his polished shoes.

When I moved to open the brassiere drawer, the presence got denser, more desperate. I bore down on it, to shove the animal as low as possible in my gut. I switched my focus to my father's collection of peaked caps hanging behind the door and pushed myself up. It took all my energy to get to the door, hook my fingers into the circle and flee the room. I was in slow time, the same time I'd been in when I'd separated from my body. The animal presence tugged at me, clung to me, did not want me to leave the room. It filled me with a need to throw myself on the bed, to grip its sheets and pummel it with my head. If I fought, I could stop the darkness from crawling over me. An unbearable pounding in my head insisted I get inside the mattress, smother the very pain that prodded and compelled me.

But I would not. I wasn't the one who was crazy. I yanked the door open and pushed out into the hallway. The presence snapped away from me, as if it were held by a thick rubber band to the middle of Sam's bed and could not leave the room.

I was short of breath and damp all over. With the invader gone my body seemed vast: I no longer wanted it to shrink. Rather, I hoped it would grow and grow and I would never again have to share it. Was Sam aware of Sylvia's presence in his bedroom? Maybe every night when he went to sleep he had to lie beside that hurt animal — or maybe it entered him as well. I shook my head. How could he stand it?

To ask Sam these questions, I would have to tell him about being separate from my body as well as having shared it. If for one second Sam didn't believe me, I would have nothing left. Sam had to believe I wasn't crazy, that the invasion had happened to me, just like Truth or Dare and kissing Angie and Jo had. Sam didn't need to have a crazy daughter and a crazy wife. And I needed him to know I wasn't. If he doubted my part in what had happened, if he suspected even slightly that I was crazy too then the presence might as well come inside my body. I wouldn't be doing my body any good. There would be plenty of room.

One evening as I stepped into the hall I heard Nicky whispering behind his bedroom door.

"Hello, Mary."

I held my breath and heard it again, louder:

"Hello, Mary."

No answer came. I tiptoed down the hall and closed my hand around his doorknob.

"You are beautiful," he said. "I've always known you."

When I opened the door, Nicky hopped up from his bed then sat down again on a pile of clothes. His eyelids were lowered and his mouth twisted in a sneer.

"What are you doing?"

"Just sitting here." He was wearing his rocketship pyjamas with the navy cuffs.

"You can't just sit there. Who were you talking to? I thought you had a girl in here."

Nicky's eyes darted toward the wall. His Montreal Expos pennant drooped. Two tacks were missing.

"Maybe I did. Maybe she crawled out the window. Or she's hiding."

"We have screens."

He shrugged, the sneer now a tiny U of a smile.

I gave up and went back to my room.

Without layers of Sylvia's smoke everywhere, the house was flat and stale, too dull, lacking a muted quality of light only present when she'd been around. I craved not only the nip of smoke in my nostrils but the hazier view of the world its grey vapours afforded.

Nicky had taken up smoking while I'd been away and I quickly followed suit. There were older boys who played on Sam's baseball team who met Nicky after dark and sold him cigarettes from their packs. He stole singles from Mr. Sousa and lifted matchbooks from the general store when he was counting out pennies for blackballs.

We smoked our first cigarette alone together in the garage loft, careful to scratch hay over our butts and spent matches when we finished. We puffed squatting by the tracks in the blurry dawn as trains barrelled past, a soup of oil, mist and tobacco fumes scourging our throats. Nicky led me on hands and knees into a concrete drain behind the post office to the spot where the pipes converged beneath the intersection of Victoria and Front. The space fit four or five kids. A grate at the top for runoff let in enough light to see other faces. As long as the day was dry, the drainpipes were a great place to hide and smoke.

Nicky sat with his haunches resting on his heels, holding the cigarette between the tips of the first two fingers of his right hand, the way Sylvia did, watching the smoke flatten into layers and spiral up toward the grate. Nicky seemed more interested in being surrounded by smoke than taking it into his lungs. If he could, he would leave a burning cigarette in the kitchen ashtray at all times.

Though I brought the filter to my lips more often than Nicky, I didn't inhale either but not for the same reason. I worried about the films I'd seen in health class: the corroded black lung framed next to healthy pulsing pink tissue; the old man without enough air to blow out a match an inch from his mouth; the nose eaten away by cancer. If I held the smoke in my mouth with my cheeks loose it couldn't hurt me, or at least not as much.

I preferred to be alone with Nicky. When the other kids were there I stayed for the length of one cigarette then crouch-walked back out the cement cylinder.

One morning sharing a cigarette in the woods beside the tracks, we came across a fallen log. When Nicky kicked it, the wood gave.

"Rotten," he said.

"It wouldn't make very good driftwood," I said, fitting the arch of my bare foot against its bark ridges.

He glanced at me and picked up a stick which he poked into the log. We didn't usually talk while smoking.

"It's probably lightning wood," I said, joining him. "Maybe it's not so bad." The lightning man had been in Nicky's room when I came home from Vi's. I wanted to see what Nicky would say.

Smoke billowed from the cigarette dangling from his lip.

"Might be from that week," I added. "Remember those thunderstorms? You know. When Mother left. We had a whole week."

If Nicky could remember, if he told me the same things I remembered, then I could be certain that events had happened as I'd thought.

Yet Nicky pressed his lips together. He didn't like me calling her Mother.

"I don't know," he mumbled.

I tried Mommy instead and Mom but they didn't work. I tried insulting him, calling him a baby, and blaming Sylvia, calling her a witch. None of it made a difference. Nicky wouldn't budge.

He dropped the cigarette into the log without toeing it out.

Maybe Nicky didn't remember or maybe he knew something I didn't. I gave up and let my own memory slip a little bit away.

Another night after Nicky came home from the Sousas', I'd stepped into the hall, breath shallow, and was straining to hear Nicky speaking when a whistle came up the stairs. Nicky was out of his room before I could scramble back into mine and pretend to emerge into the hall. Nicky shut his door tight behind him then stepped back.

"Get down here. Both of you. I made some dinner and it's on the table." Sam's words were close together.

"Sure, Dad."

I snorted at Nicky and ran right down. Nicky didn't follow. I heard him close the door.

Sam whistled again.

"Don't make me come up there!"

"I'm coming!"

What was the big deal? The only time Sam ever cooked, he fried up burgers. If Nicky and I happened to be in the room, we got one. Otherwise, we'd been living on Mrs. Sousa's casseroles. Nicky and Sam ate a lot of hot dogs at the ballpark and I'd learned to heat up a tin of soup.

Nicky walked into the kitchen and asked, "What's the problem?"

Sam rolled his eyes. The kitchen table was set with a yellow and brown tablecloth and white china plates we hadn't used since Christmas. I sat hunched so far over the table it was impossible to tell I was almost as tall as Sam. Nicky never sat at the kitchen table. Usually he took his casserole and buttered slice of bread to the living room and ate on the couch in front of the television.

"I've cooked some dinner. I've got something to tell you and this is the only way to get you both together."

Sam's eyes glinted, but his forehead was lined with the wrinkles he got when we disappointed him.

"Move your big feet," Nicky said, pushing at me. "Why don't you take a bath sometime? They smell."

Nicky loved baths. He had one every morning and every night. He knew nothing of my morning shrinking ritual but that wasn't about getting clean.

I pulled my feet in but otherwise remained motionless. Sam filled each plate with blackened hamburgers and fried macaroni and cheese mixed with canned peas then sat down while we ate in silence. I ate my macaroni and most of my bun but I didn't touch the meat between.

"Aren't you going to make her eat the meat, Dad? She never eats the meat."

It bothered Nicky when I used my fingers to pick at food. He was delicate about his own eating. He liked his food to be separate on his plate, like borders of a country. If one type of food touched another, he considered it spoiled.

I turned to Nicky and opened my mouth, revealing a clotted mixture of noodles and bun.

"That's enough. To be honest, I don't care what she eats. Now. Let's get down to business. Your mother is coming home in a week. Your grandmother is going to stay with us, to get things in order. She's driving over tonight."

He looked first me — then Nicky — in the eye.

"Now. Put that in your pipe and smoke it," he said, cocking one eyebrow. Curve lines appeared around his lips. He took a bite from his burger and chewed the meat as if it were a cud.

I thought of Nicky saying "Hello, Mary" and being so careful to close his door behind him. I laid down my knife and fork. I couldn't eat another bite.

The next morning, I stayed in bed. The rain streaming through the maple leaves outside my screen seemed to drip right into me, making me dense, unwieldy. I stared at the ceiling where I used to see spider webs. I had begun waking up with thoughts of my mother's death. If the animal presence was in Sam's bedroom, then it wasn't with Sylvia. That meant that Sylvia was either dead or all better. Since camp, I had chosen to think of her as dead. Sylvia's death comforted me. Death was honourable and final, not like crazy. Sylvia was much less trouble if she was in the ground than out in the world somewhere.

If what Sam said was true and she was coming home, she must be better. I would have asked Sam but his pleasure at his surprise announcement stopped me. Behind that pleasure lurked secrets, secrets about what our mother might really be like, about what changes had taken place and whether she had changed at all.

I uncurled my legs and stretched them out to full length. The covers didn't quite reach my ankles. I regarded my feet. What would Sylvia think about having such a long daughter? I might even be taller than her. I pulled my feet back under the covers and tucked my head in. It was all too strange. It was a good thing Vi was coming to make sense of it all.

"With my veins, I hope you don't expect me to climb up there," Vi declared when Sam carried her bags to the bottom of the stairs.

Sam set the suitcase down and sighed. "You're going to have to climb them sometime, if you want to bathe."

"I have arthritis too. In my joints. I'll sleep downstairs. It's easy enough to take sponge baths and I don't need to keep too clean anyhow." She winked at me, then Nicky, who shuddered. "I'll just sleep in your room, Sam, until Sylvia comes. Then I'll take the couch. I don't mind. Not one bit."

Sam's cheeks flushed. He stayed silent. Vi pulled at the cuffs of her jacket and smiled. She was dressed for a journey even though her place on the highway was only a ten-minute drive away. Her wig was a frosted caramel shag and her travelling suit lilac. Sam picked up the white suitcase and the travel bag and carried them into his bedroom. I held my breath in case Sam had to do battle with the animal presence.

Sam turned the light on, then beckoned. Nothing happened.

"I'll have to come in here every night before you go to sleep and choose my clothes for the next day," he said.

Vi pushed past him. "Suit yourself. I like to stay up and watch my talk shows before I go to bed so you'll have plenty of time."

Sam emerged from the room with his lips pressed together. "One of you go in there and help your grandmother. Mercy. Go on."

I backed up and shook my head.

"I'll help Granny," Nicky said. He stepped into the bedroom and I was left in the hallway with my father.

"What's your problem?" he growled.

"Nothing." I rubbed my ear with my shoulder.

He turned and left the hallway. A minute later I heard the screen door open and close then the cough-whine of the truck's ignition.

I moved to a spot just beyond the light from Sam's bedroom. I watched Vi instruct Nicky to fetch ten hangers from the closet. She handed him one outfit at a time and showed him how to adjust the hanger so the dress hung the right way.

Nicky concentrated on the task, following our granny's directions to a T. I would have thrown the hangers across the room.

"Come on in, Mercy," Vi said from where she sat on the bed.

I smiled, hung my head, and stayed put.

Vi chuckled. Nicky was busy straightening a royal blue caftan covered with large orange and green palm fronds. He didn't seem to register whether I had come in or not. He liked clothing to hang in a perfect line. In his own closet, the few shirts and jackets he owned were evenly spaced, each placed in such a way on the hanger that it seemed flat. He didn't need Vi's instructions — wasn't listening in fact. Nicky was engrossed in the pleasure of the fabrics beneath his fingers and the ritual of hanging the clothes.

Sam's room was plain, like any other bedroom. The bed was not as large and consuming as it had seemed in the middle of the night or on the day I'd encountered the animal presence. It was not a giant cave waiting to rise up and engulf us. Rather it was a square four-poster neatly covered with a crocheted afghan.

Nicky averted his eyes and hung a blouse at the end of Sylvia's closet. He seemed to be struggling to hold his back straight. He glanced over his shoulder at Vi. She sat on Sam's side of the bed, holding one of her calves in both hands and squeezing it like a zucchini she was testing for ripeness. He seemed not to notice me in the doorway.

He grabbed a black-and-silver striped caftan from Vi's suitcase and adjusted it on a hanger. Then he stepped up to the closet, plunged his left hand into the rack of clothes, leaned forward and buried his face.

He stayed there for only a second, then stepped back and hung up the caftan. He studied the closet, his fingers twitching, then turned around and gazed at Vi's suitcase. A few items remained, mainly large greying brassieres and girdles as well as several unwrapped packages of hose.

"Do you want the rest in a drawer, Granny?"

Vi looked at the suitcase.

"Go right ahead, honey. Don't mind me though. I have to remove my nylons. Maybe when you're through you'll be a nice boy and get me something to soak my feet in."

"Sure, Granny."

Nicky looked like he didn't care what he had to do for her.

From the dresser, he watched from the corner of his eye as Vi hefted her bottom up off the mattress and, balancing on her tailbone, reached her hands under her skirt and pulled the nylons down over her hips. The borders of her underwear showed, stretching partway down her legs, tight adhesive bandages binding flesh that cushioned out like bread rising over the a loaf pan. Her breathing quickened and a pocket of skin opened up between her eyebrows.

She sat up, pointed the toes of her left foot and eased the left leg of her nylons down. She repeated the procedure for the right, pushing air through her lips with every few inches. The nylons released an antiseptic scent like the stuff Sam rubbed on his shoulders after baseball, mixed with a tinge of urine.

Her legs were marbled, laced with intricate streaks, green, blue and purple. She tilted forward, landing with her balance squarely on her buttocks again, and stretched for her left foot. The back of my neck prickled. I wanted to see her toes emerge from the sock of the hose, craved it in the same way I wanted to see what was under a scab as I was peeling it away.

Nicky turned back to the dresser.

He chose the second drawer down, the first long one. He moved briskly, not looking too closely at the contents.

In one arm, he hugged Vi's underclothes, a complicated mess of hooks and elastics, while with the other he pushed aside the clothes in the drawer. He dumped Vi's underthings into the drawer, patting them down with his left hand while the right reached into Sylvia's folded pile of summer clothing, separated an item and pulled it out. He kept his eyes on Vi's underthings. In one swift motion he lifted his T-shirt, pulled out the waistband of his shorts and the elastic of his briefs and pushed the article of clothing inside his underwear. I imagined it warming his skin, his belly turning scarlet as if it were blushing. Now all he had to do was close up the suitcase and get out of the room. Then the foot bath. If he was quick, he might have time to run up to his bedroom.

Nicky snapped the suitcase shut. He moved over to the door hoping Vi wouldn't notice his gravid shorts. By this point I had backed into a dark corner, ready to scoot down the hall as soon as he made for the door.

"Nicky."

He paused, arms folded across his stomach. Vi's toes were there in front of him. They were round with square tops. They all curved under, lying folded in supplication, and the little one of the left foot was black. It had no nail and seemed like a piece of stone — an ornament she had screwed on, like gold teeth, a showpiece. I pictured Nicky's hands washing her feet in milky water, his fingers unscrewing the decorative toe and pushing it into his pocket.

"I need some salts. For the foot water. Epsom salts will do. Calgon's good — I doubt Sam has any though. Just regular table salt is fine too. By the way, is your stomach giving you grief?"

"I'm fine, Granny," Nicky smiled. "I'm just glad you're here to take care of us."

Before I had a chance to retreat, Nicky had turned and raced past me and up to his bedroom. There was no turning back. He'd taken an article of Sylvia's clothing and stuffed it down his pants. Eventually he would have to take it out and do something with it.

The summer had turned cold. When it wasn't raining, clouds shouldered the sky.

Vi's routine in our house wasn't much different from what she did at home. Sam, wanting to change our home life for the better now that Sylvia was on her way, had asked Vi not to smoke indoors and she complied, leaning out the back door for her morning puff and lingering in the car for a last few drags before coming in at night. She was still on afternoons at Effie's, so I had the house to myself for a few hours before Sam and Nicky got home.

The day after she arrived I waited a good half-hour after her car pulled out in case she came back. Though I'd seen him go, I opened Nicky's door gingerly in case he sprang out at me. Leaves swished outside and brisk air rushed in through his screen. I left the light off and began my snoop.

The usual places — the backs of drawers, the crevices around mattresses, the tops of shelves — turned up nothing. I slid under the bed on my belly and found only a balled-up sock. I stood in the centre of the room and looked around. Nicky had covered his walls with pennants. He had three trophies on his dresser, along with an assortment of worksock monkeys and a stack of hockey cards. His bookshelves contained more cars and train parts than they did books.

I lifted his baseball mitt off a hockey trophy that had a cup, like the Stanley. Inside the bowl I found soft, thin fabric. I lifted it out and spread it on the floor, smoothing the wrin-

kles with the tips of my fingers. It was a flimsy T-shirt, sleeveless, that had a V-neck cut into the shapes of flowers and was
a light pink, a pink with orange in it like the webs between my
fingers when I'd held a flashlight to them at camp. I sat with
the backs of my hands on my thighs and thought about Nicky
alone with the shirt.

What had he felt when he'd plunged his face into Sylvia's
clothes? Was it like skin?

I glanced at his wall and noticed the Montreal Expos pennant was pinned back in place with strips of Scotch tape holding
it firm. A pennant is not an isosceles triangle, Sam would say.

I got up and ran my fingers over the pennant. It seemed I
could feel a ridge in the felt, a raised line that when traced,
formed exactly a rectangle.

With my thumb and forefinger nails, I pulled out the
tacks and set them on their heads on Nicky's dresser. I found
a wedge of untaped felt and picked at it with my fingernail
until I was able to ease the pennant away without ripping
either the wallpaper or the tape. When I got it free, I carried
the stiff triangle over to where I'd spread out the shirt and I
turned it over. On its back was taped a black-and-white photograph of a woman leaning on one elbow, looking slightly
over one shoulder at the camera, head tilted down. She had
hooded dark eyes and defined lips that curved at the tops
and curled at the edges. Her hair was dark and short with little bangs at the top of her forehead. Her hand draped down
out of the frame.

She was beautiful. More beautiful than the faces in the
wig ads. More beautiful than, well than anybody I'd seen. I
stroked my finger down one creamy cheek. The photo was a
shock to see not because of who she was but because of her

beauty. The woman in the story. The sloe-eyed Sylvia who'd
sucked the steam from Vi's laundromat and put my father and
every other man, including my uncles and Mr. Sousa, under
a spell of love for her.

Her expression was haughty and I understood at once why
Nicky had talked to her. She dared whoever was looking at her
to speak, perhaps so she could reveal how superior she was, perhaps only to connect.

I didn't look long, not because seeing Sylvia's image upset
me but because of the greed. I seethed with wanting her image
inside and on me.

I held the shirt like skin first to my lips then draped
over my face.

Here was a Sylvia from before Nicky and me, maybe even
before Sam. If I'd met her then, would she have liked me? I
wanted everything about her. I wanted to be her, to have those
sullen lids, those aloof lips. If I could absorb her as she was
before she'd even considered going crazy, perhaps I could
understand what had happened, find the place where it started and make it different.

I was precise when I returned the pennant to its place on
the wall. I got Scotch tape from my bedroom and pulled off
three fresh pieces to replace the fuzzy ones I'd removed. I fixed
a piece on each leg of the triangle then pushed the tacks in at
each corner, running my fingers once over the felt surface to
make sure the photograph didn't show.

I stuffed the shirt inside the bowl of the hockey trophy and
covered it with Nicky's ball glove. Nicky had had hooded eyelids and a sneer the night I caught him saying "Hello, Mary."
Sylvia's look in the photograph. A similar expression to the
one he'd worn another night, the night I'd dropped my night-

gown over his head. Nicky's conversation with the photograph he had named Mary hinted at what might happen if he tried my clothes again.

I left his room with a promise to catch him trying on the shirt. I had to see his face when it turned the way it had that night he danced in my nightgown across our bare wood floor.

Vi took it upon herself to speak to us about Sylvia. Sam sure wasn't about to do it. His announcement that she was coming home was the last he'd said about Sylvia.

She brought up the subject one night during the news. I was still up, but Nicky had gone to bed. All Sam could say was, "I've learned not to have any expectations, Mom, and you shouldn't either."

Whatever that meant.

When Vi protested, he interrupted: "I want my kids to experience her as she is. They're old enough to make their own judgments. We've been on our own for a while now. They don't need me, or you, telling them how it will be, or how it should be, or how we would like it to be. They're smart kids and I'm going to make sure they see how it is."

Vi rubbed her gums together, sucking on the inner lining of her cheeks. Most nights she waited until it was time for the news before she took her teeth out. Sam's shoulders tightened as she squelched.

"Children need their mothers, Samuel, plain and simple. Not telling them about her could be dangerous. They might have too many expectations of Sylvia, or worse, they might not think of her at all. Telling them about her could take care of that."

"I'm not keeping anything from them. Mercy knows. She was there and she saw her mother in the hospital the day I took her to camp."

Vi sucked harder on her cheeks.

"That's not what I mean. You have to talk to them, tell them about her. Maybe that business at the camp would have been different if you had."

Sam slapped his hands on his thighs and stood up. His body blocked a hanging lamp and the room dimmed.

"Suit yourself, Mom. You always do."

Vi had told me that disagreeing with Sam was pointless. He was stubborn, like his father, and she knew from experience he was even more so when it came to his kids. She had a victory of sorts — she could tell the story, her way — but Sam was not going to say any more than he planned, no matter what she argued.

"You have a good sleep now, son. You can consider the subject closed." Vi rubbed her cheeks between her gums. The dentist said it wasn't good for her but she couldn't help herself. She had showed me where her cheeks were lined with ridges from all the contact.

Sam raised an eyebrow at the sucking sound her S's made when her teeth were out. The Christmas after the last of her molars were pulled, she had chased Nicky and me around the house — cackling, cheeks sunken, lips curled in. We shrieked, running to our beds and burrowing under the covers to get as far away as possible.

She didn't frighten Sam, that was for sure. When he wanted to go to bed, he did, even if I hadn't. He took the cushions off the couch and pulled out the Hide-a-Bed. He disappeared into his bedroom, then reappeared carrying the next day's clothes and wearing his briefs. Now it was Vi's turn to flinch. She tried to keep her eyes on the television, but it was difficult not to notice Sam's wide back and the dark hair that trailed like an errant tail up his spine. Vi checked to see exactly how like his father Sam actually was, but it was hard to say with his briefs so loose. Where he got this shamelessness, she had no idea. And in front of his daughter *and* his mother, no less! She wouldn't even take her wig off until she was alone — even if, as it was most nights, the wig was hot and itchy and driving her crazy. Sometimes it shifted or slid forward but she left the company of others before she would adjust it. Her nylons were an exception. These she removed whenever she came indoors, preferring her piggies bare.

Vi saved her story for a night when Sam was staying overtime at work.

"Your mother had this best friend, a girl who had moved to town at the same time as Sylvia, only unlike your mother, everyone knew who her parents were. This girl's father was a good man, just had a lot of bad luck or maybe made some bad decisions. He was of that breed of man women should stay away from — though strangely enough, this kind of man usually has himself a girlfriend.

"Sylvia's little friend was named Wanda Kronin, and when I say little, I mean it sincerely. She was well under five feet. Today, you would call her a 'little person,' but she had more energy than two regular-sized adults put together. I have this theory that the bigger you are the less energy you have. Now I should have lots of energy because I'm not that tall. But I certainly am big, there's no denying that."

It was hard to tell how big Vi really was. I couldn't gauge her size beneath the caftans she wore around the house; she claimed her ankles, which swelled over the tops of her soft slippers, were that way because of circulation problems — *not* fat. In fact, according to Vi, none of her weight was due to fat per se but rather the cumulative effects on her body of her various operations. Her body was a bloated entity that billowed out of her control. Dieting wouldn't make a difference although Lord knew she had tried everything on the market, sticking mainly to diet shakes and boxes of Weight Watchers candy.

I pondered her greying underthings and the logistics of where they might be placed on her body. Vi's body didn't curve but rather presented itself in a series of tiers: breast, stomach, lap. Where might a bra fit in there?

Nicky seemed to have trouble following Vi's story. I, on the other hand, hung on her every word. I needed this story, this vantage point, this glimpse into the timeline of my mother's life. I experienced it like a novel or a movie, sinking in as if it were water and my body and head submerged. I was with Sylvia, in her skin, smoking her cigarettes. When Vi told about the time Wanda and Sylvia went away for a week in Wanda's father's snow plowing truck, that same week that all the snow melted down in the middle of January, small grey rivers snaking down the street and warm enough that you only needed a sweater, I imagined the motel room they must have rented, the men they'd met — tall, well-built road men like the construction workers who came into Effie's, men who bought them coffees and gave them Licorice Allsorts while telling them tales. I thought too of the postcards in Sylvia's bottom drawer. At least fifty, maybe a hundred different postcards of motels and buses across America and some in Europe. How much had my mother travelled?

Maybe that's what she'd been doing all summer, since I'd visited her at the hospital: visiting more motels and riding more trucks and buses. I couldn't think about the road men part though, not with my father due home from overtime any minute.

Though he hadn't paid much attention, Vi's stories got to Nicky. They were more real than the mother who was due home in a few days. When he stood to go to bed, Nicky had a hard time acting normal, but it was the only way. He knew I had a sharp eye for detail. Without even trying I could spot the slightest hair out of place, leaf wedged between teeth or crust around the rim of a nostril. Nicky was meticulous about his appearance. Whenever I took pains to point out yellow stuff in the corner of his eye or a smear of chocolate milk on his upper lip, Nicky was mortified. There was nothing he could do because I didn't care if I had ketchup on my sweater or tooth-paste in my hair. Nicky said good night to Vi, kissed her pow-dered cheek and left. He paused on each stair, listening as we kept talking about Sylvia. From the pull of his shoulders and the wideness of his goodnight smile, I knew something was up.

I waited through one more story then told Vi I had to go to the bathroom and crept upstairs, keeping to the left side where the stairs didn't creak. At the top I eased myself down. I could hear Nicky describing a huge walk-in closet filled with glam-orous sparkling gowns, feather boas, smart-fitted suits with net hats and several pairs of high heels. His words were clear, upbeat — giddy, perhaps — at the sight of the photograph's gleaming black hair and turned-up lips. He paused then said, "Mary," his tight whisper rising in a slight question on the sec-ond syllable. His voice sounded small now, without resonance.

Then he was quiet. Was he listening for her response? Did he get one, made up, or real? I stood up and waited for him to resume his conversation, preparing to sneak Indian-footed down the hall and catch him slow-waltzing, lamp-lit, in the stolen pink shirt under the impassive gaze of our storm-mother's very self.

But he didn't speak again, whether because I was not as stealthy as I thought or for other reasons unknown to me. Anyway, I couldn't bring myself to step further forward and so missed my chance to see the creature I'd dubbed Nicola on the bath night that seemed so long past — if indeed it was she who lurked behind my brother's closed door waiting for Sylvia's fabric to release her.

10

Rooting

Though I'd known him forever it wasn't until I was tall and it was summer that I had my first real conversation with Duncan Matheson. My Sunday school attendance had dwindled in the months leading up to Sylvia's leaving. Vi slept right through a Sunday morning so I hadn't started up again. Now it was August and the minister was on a break until after Labour Day.

Nobody was around and I was sitting by the river at the swimming hole looking from the shit-brown froth-edged water to the field across the park. It was the same field from the graveyard dream I'd had the day my mother went crazy. I squinted the sunlight into little purple bubbles and tried to fill them with headstones surrounded by wild lilacs. The effort gave me a headache.

At first I didn't recognize Duncan. I was used to him being fat. Even back in June, when school let out he'd been fat. Yet here he was wearing track shorts with slits up the sides. His body hung from strong knotted shoulders that stuck forward, his legs long twists of taffy. He had a face that couldn't decide whether to smile or not, with an upside-down coat hook of a nose, a face that seemed in the middle of melting.

"You should. Try running," he gasped, folding himself down beside me. He wasn't as tall as me but he acted as though his body was as much of a surprise.

"I can't do sports," I answered. It was easy to talk to Duncan here. I never talked to him otherwise, nobody did. In Sunday school he'd given up on trying to marry one of us and alternated allegiances between Jenny Taylor and Susan Baker. Both Jenny and Susan let Duncan talk with them at church as long as he understood that talking to them was not okay on the street, on the bus or at school. At least I was consistent. I ignored Duncan everywhere.

Duncan was acting as though talking to me was normal.

"You've got the legs for it. Because they're long."

I looked down. My legs grew straight out from my abdomen like the immense hopping appendages of a tiny-bodied insect.

"You'd be a great runner. Or any kind of athlete really. What about swimming? Are you going swimming?" He pointed at the hole.

"Yeah, right. In that sewer?" Ever since Camp Wanigamog, I had yearned to swim, dreamed of it, but if other people were around the water turned heavy, pushing against me so I swam as if through sap. Swimming was part of my secret life. I planned to find a place along the river where no one would catch me. Before that though, I had another mission more pressing.

I stood up.

Duncan stood too, jogging in place. His glasses slipped down his nose and he pushed at them with the back of his wrist. "I run every day. Why don't you come sometime?"

"Maybe," I said. "But I highly doubt it."

I walked away. Halfway across the park I heard a splash. I turned but couldn't see past the embankment. I headed back toward the Stevens' field.

Squinting made the graveyard seem possible. But when I opened my eyes normal it was still an empty lot, a field where nobody went, a place so open and unwanted it would be the perfect hiding spot. A pioneer graveyard could be hiding beneath its ugliness and no one would ever think to look there.

In search of evidence, I had taken the forest-green hand-stitched *A Small History of Apple Ford* out of the library. The book said nothing about graveyards in Apple Ford. The United Church, the most obvious contender as a graveyard locale, wasn't even standing in its original spot. The Apple Ford First Methodist Church had been built on the corner of a field ten miles north because that was where settlers had thought a town would form, but when the railroad came through, it became clear they'd miscalculated — the church was too far from the settlement. So they'd built a foundation on Front Street and lifted the original church, which had none, onto a heavy truck and carried it there. When my Uncle Larry told of a buddy who'd awakened one morning on his parents' farm and found a church in the yard, as if it had dropped out of the sky, I felt the urge to unravel his story, to undo the dream and pull up its roots. I insisted the church was meant to be somewhere else, that his friend's parents' yard was a mistake, an accident, a stroke of fate. Uncle Larry believed nothing of the sort. To him, the church was there, he had seen it, touched it even. Its presence was enough. And besides, it was his story.

The original Apple Ford First Methodist Church had stood up near where the highway was now. It made sense that a graveyard might exist there, but that didn't explain my dream. It was more than a dream, really, because I believed Apple Ford held a graveyard and it was important to find it before my mother came home. In the middle of the park with Duncan's splashes behind me I wanted to run into the Stevens' field and dig and dig until I unearthed the fragments of stone and wood and bones that taunted me. I held back even though I had no reason to be scared. The field was open, public. Someone would see.

I waited in the middle of the park, my forehead burning in the sun, until Duncan climbed up on the riverbank. Head down, I walked back over.

"Duncan, I lost my wallet in the Stevens' field and I need someone to help me find it."

Duncan's glasses peered up at me from inside his left shoe.

He wiped his face with his shirt then wrapped it around his head. He put on his glasses and nodded.

"By the way," I said as we neared the asphalt driveway that separated the park from the Stevens' field, "if you find any-thing else interesting, let me know, okay?"

"Like what?" Duncan's shorts dripped a wet trail on the hot pavement.

"Fossils. Indian artifacts. That kind of thing."

"Do you think we'll find anything? It's just the Stevens'. If you really want to look for artifacts, we should go where the old woollen mills used to be. Or behind the water tower. That'd be more interesting than the Stevens'."

"My wallet, remember?"

"Right."

Duncan held down the line of barbed wire while I stepped over it. With my legs I needed little help. The grass scratched my knees as I headed straight for the centre of the lot.

"Wait."

Duncan was still holding the fence wire down.

"What is it, Duncan? Are you scared or something?" I was no longer afraid. In my mind, the graveyard was clear as day, full of lilac bushes and crooked white stones.

"You aren't wearing any shoes." Duncan rubbed his hands on his thighs as if they were dirty. "You could step on glass or something."

I lifted my right leg and pointed the sole toward him. Its hard, blackened condition was obvious.

Duncan tilted his head. "You wouldn't want to hurt yourself. I could walk in front of you and make sure the way is clear." He let the wire go and came toward me. I rolled my eyes and waited.

"Come on, Duncan. This is going to take forever."

"You have to be thorough when searching for these things."

"What things?"

"Artifacts. Remnants. Evidence of the past. We need to be scientific about it. Exact."

"What about my wallet?"

Duncan raised one eyebrow. I didn't mention the wallet again.

For hours, we combed the Stevens' back lot, Duncan walking in front, his body almost doubled over as he parted the grass with his right arm to peer at the ground. I followed him, sometimes tiptoeing in his footsteps, other times forgetting and stomping ahead. We found garbage — plastic and foil wrappers, bottles, tins. Duncan hurled the beer bottles back by the fence.

"That's what's going to cut my feet you know. All that glass you're throwing," I said each time, yet none of the bottles shattered.

"I want them in the same spot so I can come back later with a bag and collect them for money." No matter what I said, Duncan answered with calm and reason, making even my notion that we might be stomping on the buried bones of past Apple Ford citizens seem normal.

Still, we could find no evidence of a graveyard. The longer we looked, the more I expected to find the corner of a headstone sticking out of the dirt. At the back of the field, where the fence held back the trees lining the river, Duncan found a broken vodka bottle.

"We'd better not go farther. A lot of people drink out here, near the river. You really could cut yourself."

I checked the ground behind me and sat.

"Give me that," I said, staring at the dirt — ugly brown dirt that looked like it didn't want anything to grow in it; mean dirt that refused to give up its secrets.

Duncan handed me the bottle.

I pushed the sharp end into the packed earth. It resisted. I pushed harder, but the bottle stuck as if it had hit a rock. I gripped it with both hands and pulled.

"Come on, Mercy. It'll break. Your wallet isn't under the ground, and whatever else you're looking for probably isn't here either."

"But it is, Duncan. It's got to be. I dreamed it."

"Dreamed what?" Duncan was serious.

I took a deep breath and told him: "A graveyard. I dreamed of a graveyard here. Over and over I've dreamed it, and once the dream felt so real, I swear it was like I got up and walked down here. I know it doesn't exist really, but part of me thinks it does. I shouldn't have told you, but you came all the way here."

Dirt streaked my bare skin. I looked like a little kid. I sat back on my shaking hands. It was easy telling Duncan, as long as I didn't reveal that up until a few days ago I thought my mother was dead and now that she was coming home it was more urgent than ever to find the graveyard I'd dreamed on the day she went crazy and left. The lightning man had lain untouched in his denim swaddle at the back of my closet where I'd thrown the hockey bag the day I came home from camp. Burying him in the graveyard I'd dreamed was supposed to protect me. I no longer saw how putting him to rest in this unyielding earth could accomplish that.

Duncan stared into the trees. "Maybe it did exist. You don't know that. Maybe they brought in a giant grader and covered it with earth. They can do that now. That's what they do in subdivisions. Maybe nobody wanted the graveyard, so they got rid of it. It could happen."

"Then why would I dream about it?"

"The people who are buried there might want to make sure nobody forgets. Maybe that's why it appears in your dreams. Because they know you'll come and search for it. Isn't it enough to know it could exist?"

I stood up with the weightlessness of my dreams. I brushed my palms on my shirt and headed back toward the park.

"Whether it's real or not doesn't matter. It's not here. You better hurry up if you want to protect me from broken glass."

Duncan jogged up in front of me and fell into step.

"You know, I wish I had dreams like yours." He watched me over his shoulder.

"Maybe you're lucky you don't," I said, my lips dry and slightly burnt. I wished I'd told Duncan about my mother, but it wouldn't make a difference. My mother wasn't dead, grave-yard or no graveyard, and she was coming home.

Sam went alone to fetch Sylvia. He and Nicky had spent the morning washing the truck with water from a green garter-snake hose, drying it with towels then buffing it to a gleam with Turtle Wax and a chamois. Vi stayed behind with us to finish cleaning the house. It was hard to know what Sylvia would expect: when we were younger, the house had been spotless. Near the end, dust and smoke had blurred the edges like snow about to turn to rain. Likely, spotlessness didn't matter to Sylvia, but Vi wasn't taking any chances.

The home where Sylvia was staying was two hours away. Vi suspected "The Home." She wouldn't have put it past her daughter-in-law to have made up the whole thing. For all we knew, said Vi, she'd shacked up with some man the entire time and not even told Sam. He was a fool for taking her back. Should've divorced her while he had the chance.

I was used to Vi saying what was on her mind but her sus-picions about Sylvia were shocking if only because they con-firmed some of what I'd been thinking myself. It both gratified and alarmed me to hear them spoken out loud.

Sam was supposed to be home around two but he was never one for promptness. At one, Vi brought sandwiches and iced tea outside and we sat in lawn chairs beside the pear tree.

It was a bright August day, all yellows and blues, but cool on the arms and legs, the way Vi liked it.

Nicky and I wanted to dress up for Sylvia. We sat in motley, too-hot assemblages of what we considered our best from the past winter. I wore a round-collared plaid dress in baby blue with a foot-wide shirred elasticized band around the waist. In the winter, the dress had grazed my ankles and I'd worn it with my Sunday school platforms. Now the cuffs strained against my forearms and the hem was closer to my knees than my feet. Tights bound my thighs about halfway between my knees and my crotch. The shoes were possible only if I curled my toes to a point and didn't lace up. Nicky's cords, shirt and sweater vest fit him fine.

"Now I don't know what you two are expecting to see," Vi said, sucking at the place where her false teeth joined her gums. "But your mother might be different from what you remember. She's been gone a long while."

"Have you seen her, Granny?" Nicky asked. I clicked my tongue then became absorbed in pinching my tights and edging the wool up my leg.

"Well, I've known your mother longer than you have. A circumstance like she's in can change a body. She should be here, with her family. That's all the cure she needs. She needs real life instead of lying cooped up in some 'Home.' Just don't expect her to play nice, that's all I'm saying."

Vi sipped at an iced tea, lips pursed. She wore her bathing suit, a crinkled blue affair with white buttons down the front and white elastic trim. She pulled a strap down and showed us the crimp marks it left on her breast. "All over my stomach and buttocks too," she assured us. The bust had cups, which no one wore anymore, but there was no way Vi was going anywhere without cups. Her robe sat within arms' reach.

"It's a shame, really," Vi said. "If Sam would give me some money, I'd be happy to outfit you kids properly."

"That's okay, Granny," Nicky said.

"We like what we're wearing," I added, tugging at the arm-hole seam.

Vi snorted. "No matter what I make you kids, you pooh-pooh it."

I opened my mouth, but she held up her hand.

"Don't try to butter me up. I know the truth. My sense of taste is not what it could be. I know how other women look at me for an extra half a second before looking away when I catch them staring. The pause is there for a reason, don't you mistake it: to show me my place."

Nicky got up. "Do you want anything else, Granny?"

"No, dear, it's alright."

He turned and went inside without saying anything to me. I glowered at his back.

"It doesn't matter what other women think though, Mercy. I hope you know that."

I shrugged.

Vi leaned over, her whisper nearly louder than her normal voice.

"Men come to me regular, no matter what I wear. They don't come to show me off like some peacock. They come for drinks and good conversation, but I don't fool myself. It isn't my conversation that keeps them returning to my door in the pearly hours at the beginnings and ends of their shifts. It's my body they wander into, returning again and again.

"It goes in cycles: a man will visit for several days in a row, then there'll be nothing for months. It's all the same to me. Someone always replaces them. I don't keep track, don't know if they do. You'll likely find the same thing, dear, once you start dating. Times have changed, though. They sure have."

I glanced back at the house to see if I could spot Nicky, but the windows were opaque in the sunlight's glare. I stared down at my white-tighted calves. It might be several years before I started dating. It surprised me that Vi thought it would even be a consideration.

"I didn't begin as this kind of woman, Mercy. I want you to realize that. When I was married to Earl, your grandfather, I was faithful as the day is long, putting my energy into my boys and the dry cleaning. I did laundry up in Drag, too — you know that — before I moved here.

"When I surfaced from the steam long enough to breathe, Earl was never anywhere to be found. For years my image of him was muted by steam. He was gone for days at a time — I heard rumours that he had a woman in the city — but the grind of the steam press, the endless sheets, shirts and uniforms, the boys wanting something every minute occupied so much of my vision that I often didn't give Earl a second thought.

"When Earl was around, he startled me. He was a big, soft man, with the handsome good looks of a Negro. He had some mix in him, I am sure of it. Of course, Earl would never hear of that talk. When we'd just married, in those gentle months before the first baby, I'd sit on his lap and tease him about the child being dark. At first he acted like he didn't understand, then he pushed me to the floor as if I had a disease. He wouldn't talk about it at all, just said I was never to mention such a thing again. Well, when Larry was born, our third boy, Earl sure got a good look at the genes he was carrying. There was no mistaking the features of that one."

"But by then it didn't matter. By then Earl was fading into the steam, and I pressed sheet after sheet, absorbing the moisture with every pore. It wasn't until it was too late, until Earl finally got up the guts to move out, that I wanted him back. But Earl, in his shambling way with his wide-lipped smile and round hairless head, had made his exit long before.

"Only after he died did I give up on him for good, even though he'd long since remarried. It was after he died that I got the itch and turned like him. I opened my doors, my arms and my legs and let men just like Earl come over for drinks and conversation."

I wondered if other grandmothers talked like this to their granddaughters. Vi talked faster and faster as the story went on, though she hardly moved in her chair. I wished I had a book with me.

"It bothers me to see you two so excited about your mother's return," Vi said. "Mothers are important, I'll be the first to admit that, but if there is one thing I know how to do well, it's spot a type. Your mother is just like Earl, only devious."

Devious? What did she mean? How was Sylvia like Earl?

Vi railed on: "I spotted Sylvia's type from the get-go; I've known it for years. Part of it was the shellacked bubble hair and the mini dresses hand-sewn and tailored to lift every angle and curve on her body. Sylvia knew quite well that women didn't dress that way in a small town, and she took advantage of it, strutting down the street in patent leather heels and matching purse while the rest of the women wore sandals and shapeless shorts.

"The motels were another matter. I can't prove it, but I suspect Sylvia didn't lose her affinity for motels after she married Sam. I know it from the postcards I got maybe once or twice a year from motels in places like Bright or Mento, unplaceable parts of the province unconnected to any cities. The backs of the cards were blank, save for my name and address — which were printed on War Amps address labels stuck below the stamp.

"At first, I thought the cards were from Earl, rubbing it in even after his remarriage or sharing with me some sick joke on his new wife. But those address labels took effort and planning — not Earl's strong points. After a while I pegged the sender as a capricious lover whose feelings for me had amounted to more than I realized. Now I am convinced it was Sylvia all those years, making daytime escapes to motels and throwing it in her husband's face via his mother.

"When I think of the postcards of Dew Drop Inns and Wagon Wheel Motels I've got sitting in the bottom drawer of my spare room desk — well, it doesn't matter. Sylvia certainly is a type alright, out for number one and number one only. Like I said, she is like Earl, only devious. In a woman, it's frightening. It'll be best for you and your brother if your mother stays crazy."

I couldn't take my eyes off Sam as he pulled up the driveway in his pickup, one arm lolling out the window, the other on the wheel, eyes straight ahead; I glanced at the dusky slunk-down figure beside him. My father pushed out of his door and walked around to the other side, one hand caressing the empty tailgate frame. This would be the first time Sylvia had seen the truck Sam bought while I was at camp. Sam bent slightly at the hips as he swung open the passenger door and extended an arm to help the dim figure down.

Images of Sylvia crowded in on me: the young woman with short hair from Vi's stories, my child mummy, the witch, and the crying animal from the bedroom. My mother stepped as if her bones were made of brass and it took all her effort to bend her limbs. She moved like a broken thing, sucking in shadows, folding them into herself, all the sunlight refracting onto Sam.

Sam stood out in fine detail. Golden sparks shone in the tendrils of hair that curled over his sunburnt neck. He wore a shy, almost distinguished smile beneath flipped-down Polaroids as he led Sylvia over to where Nicky and I stood beside Vi. When he reached us, the shyness disappeared and the smile puffed with pride. He might have looked that way on his wedding day.

Vi had told a story about when my mother and father were first married. They were over at Vi's place all the time then. Sylvia hardly had two words for Sam, looked like she wished she were somewhere else. Sam never noticed, and according to Vi, would trip over his toes to get her whatever she wanted. The problem was, she never wanted anything, never asked, just let him fall all over himself trying to please her.

That Sam was the one I imagined I was seeing escort my mother over to the lawn chairs. It would be the last time I would see him this way.

Sylvia approached with a smile. She leaned down and delivered watery kisses first to my lips, then Nicky's. She laughed and said, "Not too tight," when Nicky hugged her. Her laugh was a gurgle, as wet as her kisses, like a baby's, only tired.

Her hair fell straight to her shoulders and was cut in a bang. She wore pumps and a dress — a smart apple-green knit, sleeveless, with an A-line hem that fell far above her knees.

Thick bands of orange acted as trim and a thin green zipper bisected its front from hem to neck. I remembered the dress from when I was four. Then, the dress had covered my mother like paint on a new car but now it hung from her shoulders, her body shapeless bones beneath.

I resisted Sylvia's hug, shoulders high. What could I say? I wasn't like Nicky, who ran ahead and opened the door, asking Sylvia every few minutes if she wanted something — a glass of water, the *TV Guide* to read.

Instead, I stood in the kitchen door watching the others gathered around the table with the bucket of chicken Sam had picked up as a surprise. I wanted to speak and be noticed, but I was losing connection with my body. When I tried to speak to Vi, she didn't hear. Rather than try again, I let myself separate and drift to a high-up corner of the room. I checked around me. Maybe Sylvia was up here too and we could talk. Up here among the cobwebs and cooking oil splatters we wouldn't be mother and daughter, we would be two people in the same boat, looking down at the family below, laughing maybe.

But Sylvia was nowhere to be found. At least not in those regions. She sat in a red pressback chair, loose green dress riding up crossed legs, tapered fingers twitching for a cigarette. I searched her eyes for some sign of my mother, of where she had been and why she was back in our kitchen, now. Sylvia gazed beyond me, through a glaze so thick I couldn't figure out *what* was looking at me, let alone who.

Sylvia gnawed at the narrow end of a drumstick, watchful as Sam and Vi licked chicken grease off their fingers and Nicky unfolded a wet lemon-scented napkin and dabbed its corner on

245

his cheeks. Vi stood and emptied the plate of grey chicken bones back into the bucket but before she could take it away, Sylvia grabbed the bucket by the lip.

"There's plenty of chicken on those bones. Don't you have any manners? It's incredibly rude to leave meat on chicken bones," she said, more to Vi and Sam than Nicky, whose bones were flesh free and shiny, or me, who had eaten only the skin. Sylvia held on until Vi said, "Fine," and let go. Sylvia snatched the bucket and plunked it down on her plate. Bone by bone, she nibbled off every remaining scrap of chicken, eyes like pocks searing out at whoever dared take the bones away a second time.

No one spoke. Already we were unbearable to her. She dropped the last wing in the bucket and shoved it toward the centre of the table.

"There. Done." She seemed unable not to be sarcastic. Even though the sun hovered just above the treetops, her eyelids drifted down. She stood and circled her hands in a goodnight. Her arms swooped in grand arcs as if the kitchen were smaller than she remembered.

"I'm ready for bed," she said to Sam, a smile fluttering up like rain on a windshield. She slowly lowered her hands down to her sides, hem occupying her fingers.

Sam stood, fretful and proud behind her. Sylvia winced.

His voice low, careful as ever: "Mom's suitcase is in there, so she'll want to get out whatever she needs for later."

He shot a look at Vi. Unmistakable. Sylvia surged, straightened.

Vi, subdued, lumbered out of the room.

"Why don't you take it up to one of the kids' rooms?" Sam said after her, face lifting as if the new idea was a miracle.

Vi planted herself in the doorway. "You know how I feel about those stairs, my veins and all. I only go up there when I have to. I'm not going up twice a day just to change my clothes."

One look at Sam caught, willing to store the suitcase in the kitchen if need be, gave Sylvia the strength she needed.

"Not a problem. Simply not. You see, you aren't needed here now. This is my family and I'm home now to take care of them." She spoke gaily, her voice full of parades.

I sat straight, agreeing in that moment that Vi was indeed an interference, an intruder. I looked away as Vi's face closed up and she backed out of the room. I wanted to be as close to my mother as I could, she burned so. Her well-being hung on an anxious thread that threatened to break as long as Vi remained in the house. Until Vi pulled out of the driveway, I hung too.

With Sylvia home, the house was muffled. A twilight time, not quite night and thus never quite slumber, but never bright enough to be day. Sylvia was a bruise, the tender purple centre of a bruise, and Nicky and I the yellow tired edges, lured closer and closer to the heart.

The first morning, before dawn, Nicky was sneaking through the living room with me trailing behind when Sylvia snagged his shorts with her long, hooked forefinger. I hung back in the hall.

An orange polka-dotted scarf held Sylvia's hair off her face, sinking her eyes deeper behind her cheekbones. Her knees were tucked up under a colourless brushed-nylon housecoat that zipped up the front. She kneaded her temples with the thumb and third finger of her left hand and wrapped her right arm around Nicky, tugging him close. He watched her fingers rub a dry patch of skin beside her lips. Her cheek stretched up, then down. She knew he was frightened. Nicky forced himself to look everywhere but into her eyes. Did she know Nicky had taken her shirt? He held his shoulders stiff.

"Nicky. You understand that I'm not well, don't you?" Her voice like ice cubes in water.

"I thought you were going to be better. That you were coming home because you were better."

"I *am* better. In some ways. But I still need more rest than most people. Your daddy wants very much for me to be better."

Nicky nodded. The word *daddy* was like a hangnail catching on fabric. It made Sam seem younger, inexperienced, inept.

"All I need you to do, sweetie, is come in here and make sure to wake me up about an hour before he gets home. That way, I can be ready for him, so he'll see I'm better."

Despite himself, his eyes flicked onto hers as she gave him a squeeze. He jerked away and knelt to untie and tie his shoelace.

"I'll do whatever you want."

Sylvia laughed from her position on the couch, moving her arm so it languished on his shoulders. She looked thin, flattened, a sheet of paper under the blanket.

"What did you call me?" she asked.

Nicky twisted his body away at the hips.

"Did I hear you call me Mommy? Or was it Momma!" Her laugh harsher, gritty Ajax at the bottom of bathwater.

"I didn't —"

He stopped. It was better to keep quiet.

She held quiet too, her eyes intent.

"I didn't think so," she said finally. She blinked then shut her eyes.

Nicky looked like he didn't know whether to stay or leave, so I came in. Sylvia's arm had dropped and she exhaled the light breeze of a snore but Nicky remained close to the couch.

"Don't hold your breath, Nick," I said on my way through. "She's not waking up for a long time."

Sylvia slept on the couch. One night I came down to get some juice and there she was, in the same housecoat and blanket she wore every day. When Nicky didn't believe me, I woke him up the next night and made him go down and see for himself.

Her bedroom door stayed shut. I stood outside, one hand raised, but couldn't bring myself to peek. It was one thing to spy on Sylvia, but I couldn't do it to Sam. The house was silent in the morning without Vi's droning arias. Sam's snores had ceased upon Sylvia's return. Did he sleep or was he lying vigilant on that bed as I'd seen him before, arm extended so when his wife crawled back in he could gather her close?

Even in the day, Sylvia didn't ever seem to go into the bedroom. She changed her clothes in the upstairs bathroom, hauling her suitcase up to take a bath before Sam came home. It was the same cracked brown suitcase Sam had lifted out of the back of the pickup when Sylvia came back home. We watched her stuff it behind the couch when she was finished. Nicky wanted to see what was inside but was unable to bring himself to open it.

Nothing would stop me. One morning I waited until Sylvia was out on the couch before I dragged the suitcase into the kitchen and snapped open the peeling gold clasps. Afterward, I met Nicky in the back yard, where he sat in the pear tree; I hooked my left leg over the lowest branch and hoisted myself up.

"The stuff she's got in there, Nicky, it's strange. Not creepy or evil or anything like that, but strange."

Nicky eyed me.

"First of all, she has hardly any clothes. Just that housecoat she wears every day, and the dress she was wearing when she came home. The green one. That's why she's always wearing the same thing."

"That's not so weird," said Nicky. "I do that sometimes. So do you."

"But at least I have clothes. I have choices."

"She has clothes in her closet."

"True, but she doesn't go in there and she never wears them. I told you about the letter, didn't I?"

"No."

"She wrote me a letter at camp and said the nurse was stealing her clothes."

"Maybe that's what happened."

"There's more. She said the nurse was stealing her clothes and whenever she thought about doing something the nurse would do it first."

"That is weird."

"Maybe she thinks we'll steal her clothes."

"What else?" Nicky swung his legs, looking at the patch of lily of the valley leaves that circled the base of the tree.

"Cigarettes. Lots of them. You know how Dad said she wasn't supposed to smoke around you and me? Remember she didn't argue even? Not like she did about Granny. Well she must be smoking, maybe outside in the middle of the night when we're not watching.

"And pills. She's got pill bottles in there — more pills than Vi ever takes, maybe twice as many."

"But she just got out of the hospital. That's normal. Maybe that's why she sleeps so much."

"She's not sleeping. She's on drugs. She's passed out."

I hesitated. I hadn't touched anything in the suitcase, only looked, and I wanted to make sure I described it perfectly. I wouldn't tell Nicky about the sex books I'd seen. That was my secret, but the rest was important.

"There was a jar of oily stuff, like stuff for your hair. And some cream in a tube."

"That's all? That's stupid stuff, Mercy. That means nothing. Maybe she was poor in the hospital. Maybe they took all her clothes and made her wear hospital gowns. Dad probably wouldn't buy her any. You're always telling him he should buy you more clothes."

I dangled my legs and thought for a moment. The backs of my thighs itched where the bark was digging into them. I had forgotten about bugging Sam to buy me more clothes.

"Why does she have so many pills then? If she's better and she's okay to be out of the hospital, out in public, why does she need all those drugs?"

"I don't know. Maybe they help her."

We were both quiet. I wondered how the drugs connected with the Sylvia we were seeing now for the first time in months.

"How could they be helping her if she sleeps all day?"

"Maybe if she wasn't sleeping, she would be doing something bad."

Nicky scowled and raised himself into a squat on the branch. He didn't like me finding out things we weren't supposed to know and spoiling everything.

"All I know, Nicky, is that if she can't be okay without any drugs then she's not okay, and she shouldn't be at home pretending to be our mother."

I held his eyes for a second, then swung back, locking my knees on the branch and hanging so my fingers grazed the tops of the lily of the valley.

Nicky jumped, pushing away from the tree so he landed amid the unripe pears dotting the lawn.

"So what are you going to do? Steal them? That'd be really stupid. Or maybe you should steal the cigarettes. That would be smarter."

Nicky couldn't see my face but from the way he held still and changed the subject, I knew he regretted making the suggestion.

He didn't stand a chance. Grabbing a branch, I hauled myself upright, then dropped down into the middle of the lily of the valley. It angered Nicky to see plants crushed like that, but if he said a word, I would do more.

I loped off toward the house. Nicky stayed outside. He hated to be involved.

When Sam announced we were going north to see his brothers in Drag County, I was glad. Maybe when he was around her all day, Sam would see what Sylvia was really like. Maybe he needed to see how other people reacted to her — especially Uncle Larry, her favourite. On weekends at home, she could get away with lying on the couch because Sam went off to ball tournaments with the Tecumseth Chiefs. I was forever seizing Nicky's arm and hissing in his ear, not even trying to whisper as I urged him to let Sylvia sleep in the afternoon, reminding him that Sylvia was wearing the green dress every night, as if he couldn't see, as if it mattered. Sam was acting normal, even smiling and talking about his work at the office, but he continued to bring food home — Chinese, fried chicken, burgers — so Sylvia didn't have to cook. We would be staying at Uncle Larry and Aunt Nadette's over Labour Day weekend and driving up with Vi in her car — to save gas, Sam said. Sylvia didn't protest, just sat with her hands on her lap and demurely declined a fourth slice of pizza.

The morning after Sam's announcement, the house hummed as Sylvia zipped from room to room, picking up objects and replacing them, sliding like mercury from pool to pool. It was a new mood: she'd been home for two weeks and this was the first time we'd seen her this way. With Sylvia in this mood, everything was as though reflected from two inches away. All thoughts of underground activity were lost. This mood of Sylvia's made Nicky and me feel like we had a better mother; here was the mother we'd nurtured in our deepest dreams, the one who woke and fed us in the morning, asking questions designed to let us share our knowledge while she bustled around us.

That Sylvia was wearing the same dress she'd arrived home in — the dress she wore at nights when Sam was around — was the only sign that this mood was no better than the twilight days when she huddled under a blanket on the couch in her bathrobe and slippers. I told myself that this mood came because she stopped taking the pills but the opposite could have been true. Maybe it took more pills to make her into the mother we craved and persuaded ourselves we remembered. It didn't occur to me to count the pills and keep track. When she was in this mood, I let myself forget the pills and the contents of her suitcase and any other suspicious I'd had.

Even while Sylvia wore the green dress, I couldn't penetrate the glaze covering her eyes. Yet the rest of Sylvia was so convincing it was easy to believe she was the same mother from before, only better. In this mood, her smile was so wide and bright it throttled the rest of her face. When my mother turned that smile on me, I could dismiss those lifeless eyes.

That morning I woke to a pink light from the sun slanting across my pillow, just missing my eyes. Sylvia stood at the foot of my bed, back to the window, face pale in the shadows. The dress was grubby around the hem. I figured I'd better hurry. Sylvia's patience was low and her tongue quick when she had an idea.

When I got out of bed, Sylvia made a sound like wet skin on porcelain at the undersized red nightie I wore.

"I bought that for you when you were just a little girl!" Her look confirmed everything I'd worried she'd think: my body was freakish, an eyesore, certainly nothing of her own in that.

Despite my new long dimensions, I was drawn to small clothing, children's sizes. Whenever Sam took me into town to the Woolworths and gave me ten dollars to buy necessities, I headed for the children's section and bought panties and ankle socks with coloured bunnies and happy faces on them. It didn't matter that the garments were stretched to their limit across my hips and feet. I wouldn't buy a bra in case he checked my packages. Instead I had taken to wearing Sam's shirts over a little girl's undershirt

Under Sylvia's gaze the neck on the nightie became too high, the sleeves too tight, the hem too short. I did not want to change in front of my mother, so I hunched my shoulders forward to loosen the fabric across my chest and picked up a pair of Sam's cutoff jean shorts and a white T-shirt with a Tecumseth Chiefs crest. I didn't dare lift my feet.

"What happened to you?" Sylvia asked. She glanced at my curtain. Suddenly it was important to tweak and pinch the pleats into proper folds.

"What do you mean? I just woke up."

I opened my underwear drawer, took out a fresh pair and tucked it under my armful of clothing.

"You know what I mean." Sylvia smiled. "You're growing up. You can look me in the eye." She forgot the curtains and swivelled around. She ground her high heels into the floor, each step a pivot as she moved closer to me. She pushed my shoulders back, let her hands linger. Then she stepped away, still pivoting. She poked her forefinger against my chest.

"You're growing out too. You need to start dressing your age."

I backed up, clutching the clothes.

"Everyone dresses like me. I just wear T-shirts and jeans. What's the big deal?" I glanced at the door behind me. Meeting those eyes was like looking too long at a light bulb.

"Wearing your father's T-shirts or some small thing you've grown out of isn't good enough — you could present yourself much better than you do. And your hair — that cut is horrible. You need it shaped — it's out of control. If we're going on a trip, you need to look more presentable."

A trip. We were only going to our cousins', where we went every year. I wanted to tell her no way, but Sam had said it was important not to cross Sylvia. The broad smile cutting across Sylvia's face told me she would not be crossed on this. Not without a fight. My mother was back — a shiny, metallic version — but I couldn't act like a daughter. Besides, how would I know which strategies my mother used now, which weapons or tactics to expect? If Sylvia did anything crazy around me while we were alone, what would I do? Would I touch Sylvia?

Would I myself break too? The prospect was unthinkable, so I was determined to do whatever it took to keep Sylvia stable.

I sucked in my breath. "I have to get it trimmed for school."

Sylvia arched her eyebrows. "Hurry up then. Your father left me some money. We're going to the market. Nicky's downstairs."

She left the room grinning.

At the market, Sylvia had forgotten the haircut. She bought bushel baskets of peaches, raspberries, cucumbers, corn on the cob, beans, peppers, whatever they had. Nicky and I sat with the baskets on the pickup bed on the ride home.

Back at the house, Sylvia armed Nicky with a vegetable peeler and me with a knife. We sat out back on a wooden bench in the sunshine. The peaches were first. Nicky peeled the fuzz off each one then I sliced the pulp into lengths. Soon our feet were surrounded by long yellow peach curls and wet stones. A slime covered our hands. We had to rub it off with a tea towel so the peaches wouldn't slip away. Nicky was saving the stones to use with his slingshot once they dried in the sun.

As we worked, three different boys came around to see if Nicky wanted to play. Each time, Sylvia came to the door wearing a smile that was enough to make the friend look once at Nicky then leave around the side of the house. They weren't used to Nicky's mother being around, but they were certainly used to their own mothers.

When each bowl was full, I called Sylvia, who came and took the peach slices inside to dump them into a pot on the stove. Sylvia strode in and out of the house, bare heels lifting out of worn patent leather pumps, fragments of direction and advice coming from her lips: "What do you—", "It's important to save peppers—", "This time of day—".

Nicky cracked jokes and elbowed me to laugh. Sylvia seemed happy, if her smile and feverish eyes were any indication. At one point, she stood behind him and held his hands to show him how to peel the peaches. She had raspberries on the go as well.

The kitchen was chaos. Raspberries and peaches had been poured into the pot along with Certo and mounds of white sugar, which was scattered everywhere. Sylvia stood at the stove in her apple green dress. Her hair rose off her face in tufts. When she turned, her skin was puffed into a crisscross of red and white. The kitchen was so steamy I could have written my name on the window. I sat at the kitchen table. When Sylvia arched her eyebrow, I said, "I need a break — it's too hot out there."

"Your father likes this stuff. He'll be pleased."

"He likes marmalade best though," I said. I stood to get myself a glass of lemonade. I was about to tell about the mandarin and pear marmalade Mrs. Sousa had given Sam, but one look at Sylvia's back bent over the stove, shoulder blades quivering like flags in full wind told me it was better to keep my mouth shut.

I sat back down and stared at Sylvia's calves, a foot apart, well below the hem of her dress. They were purple and mottled with long green veins bulging out in knots, the way the ones on Vi's calves did. They reminded me of upside-down bowling pins, tapering off into feet that seemed too small for what they supported.

Sylvia turned and offered a ladleful of dripping red fruit, smile quaking like the shoulder blades.

I shook my head. Sylvia didn't insist. Instead, she sucked the orange sticky mess into her own mouth, licking around the outside of her lips like a dog cleaning the greasy remnants of its dinner from its bowl. Her lips retained a blotchy stain, still there when Sam got home from work.

The kitchen was turned over. Mason jars half full of the peach-and-raspberry mixture covered the table and counter. Sylvia had carried the mixture in a ladle from the pot over to each jar, so viscous puddles sat all over the counter and the floor, some of it dripping down the lower cupboards. Mostly it was dry, but when anyone stepped in it, it stuck.

Outside, Nicky cut the tips off beans while the rest of the vegetables languished in the early evening sunlight.

Sam's arrival was a signal: Sylvia plunked herself down in the middle of the floor, her smile aimed straight at him, and declared herself exhausted.

Sam looked around the kitchen, his forehead wrinkled and reddening as if he wanted to yell and shame someone into cleaning up. Instead, he bent down, tacit hands held out to Sylvia, who stretched her arms right from the sockets, wrists turned up. Through the jam stains peered a series of long railway track bumps, each building on the other in an urgent mess. The skin on the bumps was paler than the rest of her skin and was curiously unstained by the jam.

"Stop staring," Sylvia said, eyes flashing.

I looked up and got a glimpse of what lay behind the glaze. I didn't recognize it but whatever it was, it sure was angry.

I mumbled an apology and backed out of the room. That night, I couldn't get the close burnt-sugar smell of the jam out of my nose. The smell stuck like jelly between my fingers, the stuff spreading over my nostrils and cheeks and down my throat. I craved the gelatinous sugary mixture but knew it would shrivel into bitter chalk if I spooned it into my mouth. I was left with this tension, this wanting what isn't what it appears to be. It was this night I returned to an old childhood dream of a castle and a struggle with an old woman. I woke just as I was about to plunge into the water.

The next day Sylvia was on the couch and the green dress was nowhere to be seen. The kitchen stayed the same until the following morning, when Mrs. Sousa came and cleaned it up. The vegetables sat outside in their bushel baskets until the next rain. After that, Sam lugged them to the back of the yard and dumped them on the compost heap. I put lids on the jars with jam in them and stored them in the basement — but I didn't know about paraffin wax and later, when I opened them up, I found a covering of hissing green mould. I took the jars to a far corner of the basement and smashed them against the concrete, leaving them for mice.

IV

11

The Way to Go Crazy

Manny Vulpino lifts a few strands of hair from the crown of Vi's head.

"This is where your hair is thickest. Let this grow. It will complement the wisps." He cups her chin with one hand and swirls the other through the air to show where her hair will be when she grows it in.

"Stay brown, or maybe auburn. Wigs are passé. The dyes we have today look so natural."

Vi smiles, her cheeks bunching against his fingers.

Manny is the second hairdresser she's tried. The first yanked the wig off and rolled her hair into curlers without even washing it first. Vi said nothing of course but when he was busy answering the phone, she picked her wig up from the counter where he'd tossed it and folded it into her purse.

Manny is different: he primps and fluffs, fussing with her hair as if it is his own. He treats her wig with care, fixing it onto a black velvet head, even though he wants her to get rid of it.

I watch over the edge of a magazine as Vi settles into the armchair and closes her eyes. Sam has let me drive the truck because he doesn't like driving Vi if he can help it.

"I don't have to look old if I don't want to, Mercy," Vi says. "Maybe some men will come into my life; there's a whole new crop now that I am in town. Most are married, but in my experience you never know."

Nicky drives Vi to one of her Manny appointments and convinces Manny to bleach out a streak of his own shoulder-length hair and dye it chrome red. He hides it at home by pushing the streak behind his ear or tucking it into a painter's brimless cap, but then he shows up to dinner with his hair hanging loose, framing his face.

"Now, Nicky…" Sam begins.

Nicky's shoulders set but the rest of him remains open.

"These hair appointments are for your grandmother. She's the one who's supposed to be getting a makeover, not you."

"I like it," Vi says. "He looks like one of those young men in the videos."

"That he does. Next thing you know he'll be wearing make-up. Well, each to his own." He reaches over as if to touch Nicky's hair then lets his hand drop to the table. "In the sixties, there was a Mustang that colour that I would have killed for. Candy apple red."

Nicky blinks.

"Each to his own," Sam says. "What do I know?"

After three sessions, Manny has built Vi's hair into a choco-late-brown concoction with blond wisps that tease down over her forehead. The rest of the hair sweeps up and out.

She accuses Manny of making her look like a soap opera matron, but he just smiles his rosebud lips and tosses her hair more vigorously with his small groomed fingers. After the first appointment, she told me she was toying with the idea of mak-ing herself available to Manny. On several occasions she tried to meet his eyes in his large square mirror surrounded with fat yellow light bulbs. Each time, his eyes snuck past hers like min-nows. Besides, he is so short that when she stands to leave, she can look down into the flawless black runners his comb leaves in his hair — and she is no statuesque woman. When she pic-tures him naked, his body hair is likewise moulded. She half-suspects he gels his body hair and blows it into place. The thought of such a man with monuments of black hair on his tiny chest, neck and armpits, even on his buttocks and crotch, makes her squirm and chortle, but does not arouse her. I remind her of what Sam said when he found out who was doing her hair. He told us about Manny's companion Tom Rumson whose basement houses Manny's Golden Comb Salon and to whose cabin Manny retreats for fishing weekends.

Vi doesn't care. She has taken to drinking malted SlimFast shakes with Weight Watchers candy for dessert and has gone five days without a cigarette. The Sears van delivered the three cotton summer dresses she ordered from the catalogue, one in turquoise, one in purple and one in orange. With a tummy-panel girdle and an 18-Hour brassiere, the dresses don't look half bad.

Today she is wearing the turquoise. Her brown speckled skin and the silver eagle necklace she bought from the Sunday flea market up on the highway add the finishing touches. She also bought pots of makeup — blue, green and mauve eye shadow and pink lip cream, each liberally peppered with silver flecks. Her glasses are gone, replaced by hard contact lenses.

As a finishing touch, she sports a new pair of navy Dr. Scholl's clogs, the kind with wooden soles that rise up under her toes and send a little spring into her feet.

"It's his loss!" she declares about Manny as she gets into the truck. "I look good. Good enough to go for one of my walks." She winks and grins, her lips large and candy floss pink. She's been taking walks since she got the bandage off. She says it makes sense to walk in this town of only six streets (if you count the looping avenue of cottages at the end). At least she won't get tired because there is only so far she can walk before coming to the edge of town.

When we get home, she hops out of the truck, adjusts her white sunglasses and sets off carrying a straw clutch purse.

I find Nicky and Sam around the side of the addition. I finished painting all the wide boards last night though I have yet to sand and paint the narrow pieces for Sam to mount over the edges where the main planks join.

Nicky holds a blue board in place while Sam leans out from a ladder, bracing himself with one hand on the eavestrough, hammering a nail with the other.

"Summer's half over," Sam chided when I told him last night what I'd done. He and Nicky were sitting on lawn chairs in their Tecumseth Chiefs uniforms drinking beer and discussing the progress of the roof. "If you play your cards right, you'll have a cheque in time to buy your back-to-school clothes."

"I don't care about that," I said and I didn't.

"Why are you doing it then?" Nicky asked.

"To help. Why are you?"

Sam breathed in deep and flexed his eyebrows. "She's doing fine. I'll give you a cheque tomorrow, Mercy, and as long as you do those little guys by next weekend, we'll be even."

Sam pulls another nail from his mouth now and shifts back toward the ladder. I check the thermometer outside the kitchen window. It reads 96 degrees Fahrenheit — for all his math games, Sam refuses to get a centigrade thermometer — but it feels like a hundred. I go inside and change into my bathing suit.

I am in the back yard lying on a sleeping bag when I hear Vi's clogs chewing up the gravel. I've been snoozing so I'm not sure, but it seems like a long time since she left. Every part of me except my feet is in shadow.

Vi looks up at the roof, then around the yard. When she spots me, she comes over. Since the operation and her daily walks, she is moving much better than she has in a long time. She swings her arms and legs forward, seeming to lead with her tilted chin. She lowers herself and sits on the sleeping bag, both legs straight out in front of her.

"I did it."

"You what?" I say, rolling over and pulling my knees up to my chest.

"Maybe it was the hair. Maybe the dress. Maybe the whole package, but I did it." Her smile is halfway between shocked and proud.

"Manny? You went over to Manny's and seduced him?"

Vi chuckles. "No, dear. Not Manny. Let me start at the beginning — okay, sweetie?"

She is in a good mood. Maybe she's been drinking. I'm not close enough to smell her breath.

"You remember how hot it was when I left. So hot that a body shouldn't be walking. Somebody should have stopped me though I'm mighty glad nobody did. It was so hot, the air gave off a hazy white shimmer.

"Usually, I recognize some faces in town to say hello to, but today no one was about — not even those nasty church ladies who keep trying to get me to join. Not even children were stirring. So I stopped at the post office and sat on a bench. The wrought-iron armrests burned the underside of my arms, so I kept my elbows tucked in. My head was baking through the white straw. The makeup liquefied on my face and I wondered if the silver sparkles would melt and leave skinny mercury tracks across my cheeks. I closed my eyes and let the heat cook me like a brisket."

Vi's story reminds me of a diagram from my chemistry textbook showing an oven's hot rays: thick black lines with arrowheads assaulting the body of a round roast. Another diagram shows moving circles that represent the roast's heated-up molecules in shameless motion. I smile and picture a roasting Vi, her ravaged innards swinging and bopping inside her cavernous form.

"The next thing I knew, there was a sweaty leg pressing against my cotton-covered thigh. 'That's a wonderful smile,' he said. 'Glad to see someone enjoying the heat instead of complaining about it.' I had to blink a few times to unstick the mascara. I was sitting next to a young man, maybe the same age as Reese, or Lar — well, anyway, younger than me.

"He wore a pair of black shorts that looked like my girdle only tighter and shinier. I was languorous — my latest word — with heat, stupefied, and my eyes rested a lot longer than was proper on the arch where his legs met his trunk. I pictured him folded inside the glossy black material, his testicles bathed in cool saline fluid.

"A minute later, I remembered myself and looked up. My sex was lathered inside its own stretchy casement, but that liquid, far from cool, was near rolling. Soon the halves of my labia would be simmering, like butterflied chicken breasts on the broil."

Vi lies back and folds her arms across her stomach, both hands palms down. She tells me the entire story, without leaving out a detail. I don't say a word. By the time she is through, I can't.

Vi tuned in to what the young man was saying in time to hear, "You're not one of those people who's going to say 'Hot enough for ya,' I hope."

"Certainly not," Vi said, wishing for a menthol. "Heat like this is good for you. It opens up the pores. It's cleansing."

They talked in this vein for a while: light, sardonic chatter that established them as the only sane ones in this town, perhaps on this planet, able to appreciate the sustaining benefits of a heat so extreme it clapped its arms around your shoulders and squeezed you so tight you could only breathe it in.

Vi regained her composure as they chatted, aware now that this man had a bicycle which stood propped up against a pole with a flag so limp the red and white seemed painted on. She noticed too that he wore nothing else but a pair of sandals. She found sandals curious on a man, but didn't dwell on this detail. Instead her gaze rested on his nipples, huge hard nipples that looked to be made from a tough rubber. She longed to touch one and hoped he couldn't see her eyes through the dark plastic lenses of her sunglasses. She caught herself in this modesty and decided it didn't matter if he knew what she was thinking. He asked where she lived and she answered by pointing north and asking him if she could come to his place for a drink of water.

She surprised herself. In the past she'd stayed silent and smiled and let men make their way into her car or her bed. But she couldn't do that with this one. Her grandchildren were home and her bed belonged to her son and his absent wife. Vi wasn't interested in desecration. Besides, this man might be twenty years her junior. Maybe he thought she wanted the glass of water.

He rolled his bike beside him and led her to a storefront half a block away. She knew it from previous strolls. In the window reptiles emerging from eggs and clay wizards sat in a terrarium with rocks and bits of moss. Crumpled balls of newspaper surrounded the terrarium and the backdrop was a paint-spattered sheet. He held the screen door open and rolled his bike in behind her, leaning it against the wall.

He smiled, off-white teeth eating up his brown face. She was grateful to see wrinkles. His was a body that looked as though it had weathered a few rounds, a body to feel at home with.

"Make yourself comfortable, my dear. The sink's in the back — the water comes directly from an underground spring, naturally cold as ice. It'll make your teeth tingle." He offered this up for her approval, a delicacy in the middle of his scrap heap of an apartment. "Or if you prefer, I could make you something a little stronger."

She lifted her sunglasses so they perched on top of her sculpted chestnut waves, and met his eye. Sparkling green like mountain water.

"I'll have what you're having."

There was a pause, an appropriate space for name giving, for orienting themselves in the scheme of things. Each was aware of the pause, but they were unified in their choice not to pursue it. The moment passed.

A folding chair stood propped against the wall and a tall stool sat under the work bench, but otherwise there was nothing that invited sitting. Vi chose to lean against a makeshift plywood counter piled with newspapers, a hot plate and a few grimy teacups.

She arched her back and aimed her breasts out and up as much as she could. They were heavy, and in her current array of Playtex contraptions, they didn't move far. She was grateful for the long line of cleavage afforded by the turquoise dress. The scar on her stomach had healed, though it glared red after a few hours inside the Playtex panel. She wouldn't think about that. That she could cover.

He handed her a plastic cup of clear pop and what smelled like vodka, then stood facing her, his shoulder against a wall hung with curl-cornered posters.

They drank in silence. Vi's body, welcoming the sugar, cooled to the temperature of the room.

She turned polite. "Is this your workspace?"

"It is. And my living space. My bed's up there." He pointed to a vague area above his work table. His intention was clear. They understood each other. She finished her vodka and pop and smiled. The only thing to worry about now was getting her up the ladder.

By the time Vi is finished telling her story, I am lying on my stomach again, my face buried in my arms, even though by now the sun has fallen below the trees and bats swoop above us. I can't let Vi see, can barely even admit it to myself, but my eyes are full and my cheeks are wet. I am crying and I haven't done that since before my mother went away.

"I'm having these dreams. About my mother," I tell Duncan the next day. We are on our break by the fire pit, smoking. The sky is overcast but it glares and I keep my sunglasses on.

"So what else is new?" Duncan says. Lately he hasn't said much. I had thought it meant he was willing to listen. Now I'm not so sure.

"It is new. It's not like anything I've told you before."

"I dream about my mother all the time."

"You would." I am determined to convince him my dreams are different. My mother is gone. I have no access to her on a daily basis except through the dreams. And I am beginning to wonder if I even want that.

"Everybody does. It's normal."

It is good that he thinks I am normal though he is mistaken. The dreams are in and out of my vision even as I sit on a log across from him.

"They aren't really like dreams. It's like she's alive some-where trying to give me a message. Or even worse, like she wants to take me over."

"Like an alien."

"Yes. In a way. Like that."

"That's normal too."

I flex my jaw. I am saying it wrong. He doesn't want to know about my dreams. He isn't hearing a word and acts angry that I am telling him something personal. I try to meet his eye, but he keeps his gaze level with the tops of the trees where a hawk circles.

"In the newest dream, this morning, I was crawling through bushes on my belly, hunting her. My body was smeared with dirt, shit, gull feathers, fish bones, jellyfish. Branches and tin can lids scratched me.

"What was different was that the dream didn't end when I woke up. I can still feel the scratches, the oily garbage on my skin; I even smell the fish. I can't get the fish smell out of my nose."

Duncan lowers his head deliberately. I take this as sympathy.

"I'm changed. I don't feel like me. I feel more like her."

He continues to look at me. I am relieved to tell him. Maybe now he will help me figure it out, the same way he helped me look for the graveyard that time. He didn't doubt me then.

"In a way it's funny," I say and smile.

"You might be making it up. David says I do that to get attention. Maybe that's all you want." Duncan laces his fingers together and stretches his hands, palms facing out.

"I'm not. I don't. I told you, I'm in those dreams even now, the smells and everything. You're trying to put me into a category because it's easier to tell your problems than to listen to anyone else's. It's not like you're my therapist. Just because you go to one."

The mistake is mine for choosing the wrong person to tell.

Coasting through the night on my bike, I recall an *Alice in Wonderland* party Rick told me about where the guests had to slide down a makeshift rabbit hole into the basement. Rick went as the caterpillar, wearing a hooded sleeping bag and carrying a hookah bought from a downtown head shop.

I imagine my own analyst in the form of a large, blue, mushroom-perched caterpillar:

Caterpillar: How can I help you?
Me: I'm having bad dreams about my
                    mother.
Caterpillar: At least they're dreams and not
                    real life.

Me:	Well, the dreams are starting to happen when I'm awake.
Caterpillar:	Then you are lucky. You get more hours of sleep than most people. You must be well rested.
Me:	But I'm not. The mother in my dreams is scary.
Caterpillar:	You might not say that if you knew her in real life.
Me:	That's the problem. I don't know her in real life.
Caterpillar:	Then count yourself lucky if she's anything in real life like you say she is in your dreams.
Me:	I think I'm going crazy.
Caterpillar:	If you think it, it must be true.
Me:	But you're supposed to help me not to go crazy.
Caterpillar:	I've been known to show people the way to go crazy, steer them in the right direction as it were, but only you can decide whether or not to go.

I build the Caterpillar's words as a barrier against the Mother dreams. Unlike the lightning man, the Caterpillar answers me back. The conversations make me laugh but they can't wash Mother away. I walk around in a half-sleep now, part of me waiting for the opportunity to submerge, the rest of me resisting.

This morning, I wasn't able to get out of the house fast enough. The last vestiges of Sylvia's presence have snared my skin, lodging in my flesh. The house is reduced to a series of supports like those Nicky is spending his days assembling, no more, no less. The fact that the house grows out of the ground doesn't impress me. It is wood and paint and brick and glue and fibreglass. It is a box, a coffin, sinking inch by inch into the muck to be reclaimed by the earth now that the taunting presence of Sylvia has left it and taken up residence inside me.

The house is a structure, merely that. Structures collapse, implode; I don't know how I can enter it. At any moment, the ceiling could cave in, the supports splinter and give way, the insulation expand and press in, sweltering us to a pink, itchy death.

At the Club, I worked a double shift, following Brenda out of the corners of my eyes. Brenda in her waitress uniform: white blouse, black skirt, bare legs, black moccasin shoes with a fringe. The waitresses aren't supposed to wear bare legs but after three summers, Brenda breaks any rules she wants.

I didn't speak to Brenda, though our eyes met whenever Brenda passed by the sinks on her way out for a smoke. I was aware of Duncan beside me, smirking and whistling through his nose. Once I asked him how he did it, as if it were a party trick, and he informed me that his nose whistled on account of his deviated septum. If he wanted to have it fixed, he'd have to have a nose job and he didn't want to do that. I bit my tongue. A nose job wouldn't do him any harm.

Tomorrow is Monday, the day of the staff campfire. There is little chance that Levon will be there; after all, the weekend will be over. But it is the only place in my life that I feel something could happen. Everything else is closing off.

"Nicky told me about Rick."

I put down the book I am reading about a hitchhiker murderer and stare at Vi. She stands in my bedroom doorway, her body loose beneath her nightgown. It is after two in the morning.

"It doesn't matter, Vi."

It is the first time I've addressed her as anything but Granny. Vi gives a nod.

"I'm sure it does to you. Despite all my rantings against teenage lust, I certainly do remember what it was like to be your age. Only too well, I'm afraid. Sometimes I think my problem is that I never stopped feeling like a teenager and somewhere along the line I got stuck inside this old carcass."

She comes in and sits at my desk. I can't remember her ever having been upstairs, let alone in my room. She glances around then focuses on me.

"I've been giving this a lot of thought. We both know I'm an old blabbermouth. I've always told you anything and everything about myself, including information I'm sure you wish you hadn't heard."

It's true: she has alarmed me at times. All those men's bodies she described in lusty detail. But by now it is normal for me to think about bodies in this way.

"Yet here I've been withholding from you the story you really want to hear. I have my reasons. Mostly shame, if truth be told, and partly for the sake of your father. On occasion, if someone really finds it necessary, I can keep my counsel. As you can imagine, it's a challenge." When she smiles, her lips droop. Her teeth are out.

"You don't have to," I say, realizing what she is talking about. My limp voice betrays me.

"Well, no. I know I don't have to. I know too that it doesn't matter what I think happened to your mother and it doesn't matter what Sam or Nicky or anybody else thinks. What you need to know is that nobody knows. Larry doesn't even know. Nobody does. So you have to find an answer for yourself, one that you can live with. And you have to do whatever it takes to find that answer or you're not going to have any peace in this life.

"That's why I'm going to tell you what I think because it'll be another piece in the puzzle for you. Also, from the looks of it, you'll never get your father's story out of him — nor your uncle's, for that matter — so this will have to do."

Vi sucks her cheeks and settles herself into my chair. She stuttered when she said Larry. She doesn't like to say his name any more than my father likes saying Sylvia.

Then she tells me not about Sylvia's final night, as I expected, but about another day, long before even my father was born.

Being a mother happened to Vi the way being born a daughter of Alfred and Ern Wise happened. An accident. It was all an accident. She believes this if she believes anything. The problem is that she often believes nothing. She is afraid to probe into the dark place behind her thoughts, the place she passes through on the way to her dreamless sleeps. Her biggest fear is that behind her pains, behind her work, her lusts, her television plays, her budgies and the cats she owned every year or so, there is nothing: a stillness so absolute that, if she searches for and finds it, will wrap her in its dry breath and never let her go. It isn't even a fear of death, which makes more sense. Vi's is a fear of life, of finding that inside she holds emptiness, and of having to live with that discovery.

Accidents, she can believe in. Accidents make sense, help her stave off the void. If events from moment to moment are accidents, then life becomes more interesting. This non-belief, or rather suspension of belief, has served her well through many jobs and men, and even with her children. But it collapsed when she saw her third son's face on the long night that Sylvia ran away.

When Larry came back into his house with his hands that way, Vi would not look at him — not that he cared, not that these people mattered. She had two sets of eyes, a front pair and a back pair. The front pair stayed open, allowing in a minimum of light and shadow and the barest recognition of shapes. The back pair saw what was underneath, the stories behind each person in the room, where they came from and what they were all about. At that moment the back pair of eyes were blank. Larry's stained hands erased Vi from life, removed her so completely from her family, or rather had them removed from her, that she could almost smile. Almost. The shame settled like dust on her skin. Her son's crimes were the dust she would become.

It was Sam's boy, Nicky, sitting on her lap with his arms around her neck, who anchored her.

The sight of her Larry's bound wrists brought stars to Vi's eyes, her chest flaring as it had so often when, after working the mangle iron for a day and an evening, one of the boys did something that made her see them not as her own but more like chickens she had to strangle or a cat she needed to pitch across the room for scraping its nail down her cheek.

She could not condemn Larry, not with Sam's boy in her arms, and not, especially, because what he'd done, she'd done once too.

It was a Saturday morning in February, the eighth grey day in a row, when Vi's father had refused to eat his oatmeal and announced that they wouldn't see him until Monday at lunch. That was fine by Vi. His second announcement was less of a relief: Vi was to give her mother Ern a bath; she hadn't had one for weeks. She was to take the tin tub with the angled lip down from its hook behind the stove, heap it full of snow, then drag it inside to melt on the stove. Ern couldn't sit in the tub, so Vi would have to wash her standing up.

Ern hadn't been bathed since the day before Christmas. Once a week she stirred soap flakes into some leftover tea water and raked the mixture through her hair. Ern's body held secrets in its folds. Those folds clasped her body's smells tight so it was only when one stood close enough to touch that her aroma of mould and potato was apparent.

It wasn't giving the baths themselves that Vi minded so much — after all, in her largeness, even standing was uncomfortable for Ern, let alone all the bending and reaching involved with self-ablution. Vi would have made a good nurse: her mother's body with all its rolls disguising crevices and caverns had been her greatest challenge and she had met it with both efficiency and care. Not an inch of skin went unclean when Vi was through. Bodies didn't repulse her: to her they were no different than laundry, as her cleaning of them revealed.

What Vi minded about washing Ern was that endless gummy grin, stretched so wide it almost leaked. Ern's smile was indiscriminate, appalling in its dumbness, lewd. Whenever Alfred talked, the smile appeared; when he was on a tirade the grin spanned the width of Ern's round face. The smile had spread when Alfred mentioned the bath, Ern's brown eyes gleaming with dull anticipation as he made his preparations to leave: short ribbed scarf crossed on his chest; earflaps tugged out of hat and patted over ears; overcoat hefted on and peg buttons fastened into corded loops; extra socks, then felt linings, then overboots pulled on — everything tightened and patted as Ern's smile grew, prodding Vi, smothering her in its intensity.

Ern's only skill as a young woman had lain — surprisingly, considering her dimensions in the years Vi knew her — in her flesh. When she was thirteen she'd had bowl-shaped breasts with nipples that rested right on top, dark red like licked-out cherry skins. Her skin was a dull cream, nearly a beige, bearing no resemblance to the streaky colourless covering it would become. Her other best feature was her round brown eyes that had a way of resting on the surface of people with satisfaction rather than knowledge or understanding.

Ern's parents had rightly decided that school was unnecessary and had sent her to town, to a woman named Mrs. Daisy who contracted girls out to do labour for farmers and merchants. Nearly every day, whether Ern was picking raspberries or delivering bolts of cloth balanced on her hip, she was stopped by one male or another. Even in the beginning, none of them spoke much more than a hello. What they wanted was revealed in twitching lips and eyes that flicked all over her. She wore no undergarments, and after a while when men came around she took to lifting her skirt before they even had time to wink. Ern had an uncanny sense of whom she could lift her skirt for and whom she couldn't. Every time she flipped her skirt up and lowered herself to her knees, her hands braced in front of her on dirt or slatted floor, she was entered and the smile swam over her face. That was back when she had teeth. A man would feel better about taking the long route home past Mackenzie's farm where Ern was picking apples when he saw that smile because he could convince himself that the girl had wanted him inside her, not the other way around.

Alfred Wise was fifteen the first time he saw Ern in Vineton's Dry Goods, in the back, receiving instructions from Mrs. Vineton. His mother called her Mrs. Vinegar, which Alfred thought was the funniest thing he'd ever heard in his life though he wouldn't laugh in front of his mother. Sometimes he'd laugh out loud on his way to work at the memory of it.

Alfred was at the store to buy molasses for his mother who was in the last year of her life. His mother hadn't gone into Mrs. Vinegar's in years. She said Mrs. Vinegar was sweet as sugar to anyone's face, but notice, you just notice how she won't look you in the eye. You even try it. Shine your own eyes right into hers boy and I bet she won't miss a turn. Nothing can make that woman acknowledge that there's others in this town worthy of her respect, even though they might not have two storeys or a machine-made dress.

Later, Alfred would laugh but he tried looking into that Mrs. Vinegar's eyes and it was true. It was around this time that Alfred developed his pop-eyes, the kind of obstreperous stare that demanded response and made him seem vaguely unhealthy. By the time Vi knew him, Alfred had been in so many fights from his gawking eyes that his mouth had caught up with his look. Alfred's pop-eyes must have embedded themselves in his genes because they showed up again in Vi's third son, Larry.

Ern was a few years older than Alfred when she first lifted her skirts for him on the day after he'd seen her at Mrs. Vinegar's. She was hanging sheets at the minister's boarding house, a job she did on days when she wasn't needed elsewhere.

Ern fastened a wooden clothes peg over the folds where one sheet met another. She cradled the sheet in one arm while she stretched one corner over the line and pinned it. The folded corners were pig's ears, scrubbed clean for a fair. The damp sheet in her arm was a baby pig recently saved from a chilly drowning death. She stretched the baby pig along the line until he was flat as a pancake and pinned his other ear to the line so he could dry. Ern had seen a pig farm only once, but the farmer had permitted her to cradle a piglet and the image had stuck. Even when nursing her own child in those years when she'd still had the mobility and interest, she'd thought of her as a pig, a pig malformed from its time inside her belly, a stretched-out pig whose ears wouldn't point up. At nights, Ern would sneak into Vi's room and slip clothes pegs on her ears, securing them to the corners of her pillows so that her child's ears would grow pointy as a swine's.

Alfred had always imagined he would wed; his mother believed it too. Only a month after his mother died Mrs. Daisy bullied Alfred into marrying the pregnant Ern and taking her off her hands.

Vi hadn't witnessed Ern's premarital talents. The only Ern she knew was the immense creature growing out of the double-sized wooden chair Alfred had built from leftover privy lumber and anchored to the plywood floor beside the stove. Still, Vi held the conviction that she was not of these parents. How could two people with brains like suet, unable to enunciate a single word, let alone hold a well-founded opinion, have coupled and brought her forth?

Her patronage, as she found out from the mothers of other girls in town, was extremely negotiable, but there was no doubting that Ern was her mother. Which made the gummy smile all the more loathsome.

On that particular Saturday, Vi was yearning. She thought

perhaps her feeling was nostalgia. She'd looked the word up the day before in the school dictionary and found that it fit, though it puzzled her that she had nothing in her past whose memory should cause such pain and such want. The pain was seductive: she allowed herself to feel it in small doses so it wouldn't get used up and be replaced by the ever-present scratchiness of her shame.

The snow was thick and powdery, old snow flecked through with black dirt that had glared at her for months. She'd read that snow was brown or grey in the city. She wondered if there was such a thing as black snow.

While the snow melted in the tub, Vi undressed Ern, no easy task. It was all Ern could do to lift her bottom from the chair. Vi had to be quick or else Ern would come crashing down and pin her fingers to the seat. Once Ern was up, she was up, an event in itself. She only stood twice a day, at the beginning and the end; otherwise, she sat in her chair, stirring. Vi's timing was slightly off on this particular Saturday and the tips of two fingers got pinched between Ern's hip and the chair. Ern seemed unable to feel it, so Vi snatched her hand away and ended up with scraped knuckles.

Vi untied the ticking apron, took it off and threw it in front of the door. Then she lifted the great flowered dress over Ern's head, releasing as she did, a waft of potato scent. Underneath, Ern wore a T-shirt over her immense breasts which, even while sitting, seemed to rest in the nooks where her waist rolled into her hips.

Vi had no idea how old this woman was. Ern's hair was the same iron colour as the tin bathtub. She pinned it into curls then left the clips there for days in a row. She never talked; all exchanges of words took place between Vi and her father, his voice a steady boil of anger, words that she couldn't hang onto, let alone remember from one minute to the next. Sometimes she imagined that behind Alfred's anger hid an intelligent person put into the household to save her from the blob that was her mother. She tried out all her new words on Alfred, her voice as loud and vicious as his, and was only half-pleased when they sailed right past him.

Not a day passed that Vi didn't think about her problems. They were on her mind as she piled a heap of torn towels and underwear on the floor beside the stove, ten squares to wash and ten to dry, one for each part of Ern's body. Most were for the middle parts, with one for each arm and leg and one for her head. Alfred had stoked the stove full of split pallets from the dump. The rims of the four circles on the top of the cast-iron stove glowed red. One of the hole covers was cracked. Through the gap, Vi could see yellow, orange and even white coals.

Vi was thinking about how she wanted to stay in school. Everyone said she should be a teacher. The previous year, she'd had a male teacher who had stood behind her, hands on her ribs, and kissed her neck as she wiped off the board. Even though she was no longer in his class, he said he'd do anything he could to help her. But Alfred had made no bones about it: when this school year was over, she would be a clerk at the dump where he worked so she could give the money to him.

"Lord knows I deserve it," Alfred said, "with all I've done to pay for you all these years."

Vi poured a heap of soap flakes into her palm and swirled them into the bath water from which a creeping cover of steam was rising. She picked up the first rag and scrunched it into the warm water. If she could, she'd sit with her arms up to her elbows in warm water all day, it felt so soothing.

Behind her, Ern's smile glowed. Vi shook the water from her arms. She unpinned each curl first, dropping the clips on the floor and working her fingers through the hair like the greasy strings that held together cuts of pork and ham from the butcher's.

Vi ran through her plan: she had four months left at school, would take her exams and go north to work at a lodge for the summer. Alfred and Ern would never hear from her again. She considered tallying up how much they'd spent on her over the years, including room and board, and paying them back in full but it wasn't worth it. Any money she made working would be hers and hers alone. With the money she'd save, she'd go to one of the teacher's colleges. She'd heard there was one in the north where the standards were easier. She would show them her exam marks and ask them to let her in a year early because of her unfortunate situation. (She'd say she was an orphan. There was no reason why they wouldn't believe her.)

Pellets of icy rain splattered the windows and roof, sounding like handfuls of sand. Vi squeezed the towel over Ern's soapy head, eliciting a few fragmented moans and grunts. Vi wrapped the towel around her hand and worked her fingers in between the folds in Ern's neck. It was like washing an animal: if Ern was pleased, she made a little noise. Her smile quivering at the corners making Vi wince. That smile nearly crawled. She supposed she should be lucky Ern never got angry.

Sometimes she tried to interpret Ern's moans: did she have words hovering at the back of her throat and lack the equipment to utter them? What words would a woman like Ern, whose life was spent in her own company, in the company of a body large enough for the thoughts and feelings of two, have to say? Would she speak of bodies, of growth, of proportion? Vi herself had a trim, matter-of-fact body — nothing to match the splendour that had been Ern's body before her marriage but lacking the potential, on the other hand, to match her mother's current dimensions.

Vi never knew what triggered it. She was washing Ern's back — both hands spreading over the towel, pushing it upward and around in a circle — and imagining a dark-haired man with big hands moving across her own back. Ern was leaning forward, gums slurping in what Vi knew was an ear-to-ear grin. Vi pinched her eyes shut. She wished she'd thought to rip off two smaller strips of towel to stuff in her ears.

The rain pelted the windows. The kitchen was steamy from the water, where flat, lazy bubbles popped into broken ripples on the surface. All of a sudden, Ern's body was moving, heaving forward and up, arms thrashing. She squeaked and whined, almost-words that might be a language of her own. Vi jumped, grabbed the cloth and hit her hip against the corner of the hot stove, her elbow jarring the tub and splashing water onto Ern's leg. Ern strained to stand, arms windmilling.

Vi had never seen Ern move so much. She had said nothing to her mother for years — and there were no words for what was happening now. She couldn't take this rebellion seriously: to do so would be to admit that this woman was not a distorted creature but rather the flesh from which she had slipped forth.

Ern bent right forward, arms swinging, fingers grabbing air, feet planted on either side of the bolted-down chair. She gained momentum, her brown eyes narrowed and purposeful. Vi snatched another towel, dipped it in the water without getting her hand wet, and swirled it. She stood for a second, towel dripping, as Ern's hands slapped for her hips and thighs. Vi laughed and threw the boiled towel into Ern's face.

It was easy after that. None of it was for any reason so there was nothing wrong. Ern had been out of control in the first place. Ern squealed high and long, shaking off the cloth, her face shiny red and dripping.

Vi wrapped two towels around each hand. Ern swung her head from side to side like a cow having a difficult birth, smile pressed down into a grimace. She grabbed the sides of the chair and pushed up, possessed now of a solid energy.

Her own energy rushing through her, Vi grabbed the lip of the tub, using the towels as mitts, and heaved it off the stove in Ern's direction, the scalding water lashing across Ern's breasts and lap as she struggled finally to her feet. A sound flared as if thrust by bellows from deep within that enormous body. Ern teetered for a suspended moment but she couldn't stand without something to balance her hands on, and the stove was too hot. Vi stayed behind the stove, rubbing her prickly-hot neck with her palm. Ern fell back hard into the chair, stamping her feet and grunting syllables. She gasped and coughed but still no words came. Vi wanted words. At least one word, even an *Oh* of pain, but none came.

The thrashing and howling and that dumb smile, now a rubbery gash, were unbearable. Vi lifted the tub from where it had fallen beside the stove, hoisted it high and cracked the corner down on Ern's head. She dropped it there, covering her mother's face. She found some machine oil below the sink and poured it over the dry towels that remained at Ern's feet, stuck some kindling through the stove hole until it was good and lit, then left it to lie near the oily rags. Ern was silent when Vi left. Vi couldn't bring herself to lift the tub to check her face. She'd had years of practice in not looking at Ern. There was no reason to break the habit. That she was still was enough. Vi has to believe that the smile stopped.

Since then Vi has thought of Ern only two times: during her pregnancy with Sam when each moment of that day washed over her like unhinged dreams, and the night Sylvia disappeared. She remembers the easiness of killing, and its elusiveness. The night Sylvia disappeared Vi considered for the first time that maybe she hadn't taken Ern's life.

12

What Will Be, Will Be

Uncle Larry's house in Drag County was covered in grainy red tiles the size of a roof shingle. Shiplap edges the men called them. Our house had a similar siding in green. Most of Larry's tiles at ground level had peeled off, revealing black tarpaper covered with faint white stencilled letters, so the house was two-toned, like a station wagon. The tarpaper gave off a ropy, not unappealing smell and made the air seem hotter near the house, a two-storey with three small bedrooms and bathroom upstairs, kitchen and living room down. The property was surrounded by bush, but there were no other trees between the house and the woods. Our cousin Larry Jr. said this was because of the gravel pit out back.

Larry Jr. promised that if we left in the morning and walked down a road cut into the trees to the north of their place, we could go to the quarry and swim.

"The quarry is special," Larry Jr. said. "We're old enough

to go on our own this year, so we can do what we want, even skinny dip."

He eyeballed me then added that even his Aunt Carla had skinny-dipped there.

"Yeah, right," I said. Carla, Aunt Nadette's sister, lived in their spare room. She was fifteen and a snob.

Nicky snorted as if skinny-dipping was stupid. Larry Jr. would do anything he was told as long as he thought it was his idea.

Previous summers our fathers had driven us back to the quarry. Larry, Reese and Sam squeezed into the front of a pickup while my brother, cousin and I heaved and rolled around the bed as the truck lurched along the dirt road, the men holding their brown stubbies high to minimize spillage.

Nicky and Larry Jr. clamoured around the men, hanging from their shoulders, climbing on their hands and submitting to being flung out into the dust-clear water. When the men tired of roughhousing, they challenged one another to speed laps. Nicky could keep up well enough, but Larry Jr. often ended up on shore with me.

Once Nadette and Sylvia had shown up, hiking down after us holding a cooler of sandwiches between them. Nadette used to swim when she was a girl and after much coaxing and a few beers of her own, would strip down to her suit and dive in, crossing the water with even strokes.

Sylvia didn't even own a bathing suit she said — and it was true, as far as I knew. I had never seen one in her drawers. She would use the excursion to hunt for northern specimens of driftwood.

She was wandering along the limestone lip, poking at a felled spruce, when Uncle Larry and Uncle Reese snuck up. They'd cautioned us with a finger to the nose not to warn her.

Maybe she did hear or maybe she didn't, but her screaming appeared to start before they reached her. There was a suspended moment where both uncles seemed to reconsider their mischief then each grabbed one of Sylvia's ankles and one wrist and ran leaping for the water, setting her loose only when they were in past their knees.

Reese ran back to shore, but Larry stayed put and watched Sylvia. Her shrieks stopped when she hit water and went limp and sank. Larry tilted his head in a pause, then threw his body forward and pulled her up in his arms. Water streamed off them. Sylvia fluttered her lids and looped her arms around his neck.

"My hero," she said, just as Nadette was yelling, "That's not funny!"

Sam butterflied over and stood up beside them, eyes puckered without his glasses. Mutely, Larry handed Sylvia over. Sam carried her to shore and she hopped free. She shook herself off and hiked back to the house. After that, we only went to the quarry with the men.

Nicky and I sat with Larry Jr. behind one of the tarpaper outbuildings and talked more about Carla. A bristly red hound lay tied nearby. Occasionally she'd get the energy to run and hurl herself to the length of her chain, baying as her body twisted in a flip. After two or three of these efforts she'd fall back on her stomach, panting.

"She has a boyfriend who dropped out of high school," Larry Jr. said. He said "dropped out" as if we didn't know what it meant.

Nicky shrugged. I stood up.

"She thinks my mom and dad don't know."

Larry Jr. paused. When this piece of information wasn't exciting enough, he offered more: "I've seen them too. I seen them in her bedroom one night, through a hole in the closet, when Mom and Dad were at a dance and Carla made me go to bed early. I went in there and watched what they did." Pleased with himself, Larry wiggled against Nicky.

Carla had shiny black hair like Nicky's that hung in her almond eyes, and brown-gold skin like Nicky's too. Carla didn't talk to anyone younger than her, not even me, but she wasn't mean about it. It was understood that she had better things to do. She was more like a real girl than I was. Like a grown-up woman.

I pictured Carla on her pink gingham bedspread, squirming beneath the dropout boyfriend. Nicky shoved Larry who shoved back. Soon the two were rolling around in a wrestle.

I walked away and tried to imagine how Carla and The Dropout's bodies would fit together. In my fantasies, I was never able to get rid of clothes. Every time I imagined taking off a sweater or a T-shirt, there was always one to replace it.

It was the same with sex. I could never picture where different parts went. I had seen the beautiful long mauve and brown folds between the *Penthouse* models' legs, but they were no help. Where was the entry point in those intricate creases and curves? My mind flashed on Angie. I quickened my pace and tried to concentrate on Sylvia and what she was up to, but it was too late. My senses had filled with Angie and her white freckled skin.

I came into the kitchen through the living room and stood in the corner, where the fridge met the wall. The fridge was short enough that I could lean an arm on it. The watery tomato smell of Nadette's lasagna overrode even the cigarette smoke.

Sam and Sylvia sat with Vi and Aunt Shanelle on flowered vinyl chairs around an imitation woodgrain table with its extensions pulled out. Uncle Reese stood and Uncle Larry sat on the counter beside the gas range. Nadette bustled about, taking dishes out of cupboards and setting them amid the bottles and ashtrays on the table. Shanelle kept getting up to help but Nadette kept pushing her down because, she said, Shanelle was expecting a baby and Carla was supposed to help out. Dusk was settling outside and the kitchen had only one small window over the sink so it was dim.

Sam was holding forth about his truck purchase, describing the number of RPM's the engine idled at and comparing miles to the gallon with Larry, who'd inherited Earl's '65 Ford pickup. Shanelle made suggestions about ways she could help with the meal while Nadette talked over her about how her sister never helped around the house. Sylvia stayed quiet on the side of the table closest to the tiled wall. Both hands were on the table, the middle knuckles of her tapered fingers bouncing lightly off the ridged chrome trim. She threw vague smiles at whoever was talking so it might seem as if she were listening, but she wasn't. Her green dress lolled, looking more moss than apple, the orange trim a rusted hue not unlike the beer bottles in the sundown light.

Before long, Reese had his arm around my shoulders. I slouched to fit. He led me away from the fridge into the centre of the room.

"Looks like I caught myself a tall one," he said, looking right at Sam.

My cheeks burned. The uncles hadn't seen me since I'd grown.

"Not at all!" Reese laughed. "Get it, Sammy? There once was a woman from Tall — 'My woman got big feets,' 'Big-

Footed Woman Blues.'" Reese was an adult version of Larry Jr. and would go further and further if encouraged.

Nobody was paying attention to Reese. Nadette had plenty to say to Shanelle about childbirth.

Reese turned and stared into my eyes. With his wide forehead and thick curly hair, he reminded me of the Cowardly Lion.

"I bet you like parties," he said. His laugh rolled and spilled out of him as if he was the crazy bunny from the Trix commercial. "Eh, Sammy, what do you think? She'd make me a good partner at that dance tomorrow night! Baby save the last dance for me!"

I couldn't face my father. I curled up my toes and concentrated on making my feet look smaller than they were. Uncle Reese's arm around my shoulders was solid, containing me. I didn't want to move. I liked being in Uncle Reese's light. If he danced with me, everyone would notice. Up here, everyone went to the dances. Even Larry Jr. was going. They would notice me, but in a different way than because I was tall. I would be special because Uncle Reese had chosen me.

"Get this girl a drink. A tall, cool one!"

"Now, Reese," Sam said, "she's not even thirteen. She's too young."

He looked around the room for support, his own smile out of check. No one was listening. It was just Reese being Reese.

Reese blew smoke out of his mouth and said, "What would you like, honey?"

His eyes were beige like vanilla Kraft caramels. I cleared my throat and said, "Just a Coke." I glanced for a split second at my father, who nodded and winked. Reese's light extended to my father, too, opening him to a lexicon of shared winks and smiles.

Reese took his arm down. "I'll take care of it, Sammer. Don't you worry. She won't even know it's there. Remember, candy is dandy, but liquor is quicker."

He erupted in laughter. A piece of spit flew out of his mouth and landed on my cheek. I didn't want to raise my hand to wipe it off in case it embarrassed Uncle Reese. So it sat there, wet and cold, as Reese turned me around and pointed me toward a cooler on the floor. When he bent down to open the lid, I brushed my cheek with my forearm, my eyes meeting Nadette's. Nadette snorted. I quickly looked down again, rubbing the spit off on my shorts, but not before I noticed that Sylvia wasn't in the room.

My throat dried out. How long had Sylvia been gone? She'd been there when I walked in. The kitchen had another door, behind the table, that led outside through a back porch. She could have slipped out there or back through the living room. Either way I'd been so drawn into Reese's jokes I hadn't seen her get up.

"I'll pour you a Two-Fingered Surprise, honey. Hope you like it. Most do!" Reese roared.

I went into the living room. The most likely place to find Sylvia was the couch. She hadn't had any couch time yet today: Sam had taken the day off work, Vi had arrived in the morning, and by noon Sam had slammed the trunk on her Duster and we'd left. Sylvia was back in her dress for this visit and she'd insisted on bringing the cracked brown suitcase. Most certainly she would wear the unwashed dress to the dance. I planned to take the dress out of the suitcase when we got home and hide it so she'd have to wear something different unless she wanted to wear her housecoat everywhere.

The living room was empty, dark, the windows here little bigger than the one in the kitchen. I took the stairs two at a time, landing soft on the balls of my feet. I peered into each bedroom, but no Sylvia. I was surprised to find my hand shaking as I held the banister on the way down. My mother had only left our house once since she'd been home, when we'd gone to the market. Any absence now rang of permanence.

I went back into the kitchen and whispered the situation to my grandmother. As soon as Vi knew, everybody knew. Searching for Sylvia then became a game of adult hide-and-seek with Reese at the helm.

I hung back, searching the shadowy places — the corners and the spaces behind and under furniture. Like a mouse, Sylvia might have flattened herself and slid into one of the crevices where wall met floor or snaked through a split in the plaster.

It took Reese a while to lead the procession upstairs. He had to look behind every picture and lift every rug. Sam stood at the bottom of the stairs with Vi. "Whatever you do, Reese, is your business," was what he said, what he always said.

"I don't see what all the fuss is about," Nadette said. "She's probably curled up on one of the beds. It's dark, she's thin. Mercy must have missed her."

"Que sera sera," Sam said to my grandmother. "I'm a fatalist — you know that — and proud to say it. Whatever happens, happens. Nothing we do can stop it or change it. If my wife doesn't want to be here, I won't force her. But I'll be waiting at the door when she decides to waltz back in."

Vi looked up the stairs and rubbed her calf.

We arrived at Larry Jr.'s bedroom first. Reese turned on the light, stuck his head in and declared, "Nope." As the group continued down the hall, I went into Larry Jr.'s room and slid the closet door open. There they were, as I had suspected:

Nicky, piling shoes on his body, huddled beside Larry Jr., who snivelled under a pair of pants. Nicky thumped Larry in the chest. On the floor lay a hammer, a chisel and a flashlight. They had been working on making another hole.

"She's gone, Nicky," I said, pushing at him with my foot. He stared up at me, eyes as blank as that day when he'd flopped out of the closet.

"You'd better go and look for her. Nobody knows what they're doing here and if you don't get outside and start looking, she's going to be gone for good."

"What's she talking about?" Larry Jr. asked.

Nicky didn't answer. He knew.

The others had gone straight down the hall to the bathroom where light shone out from under the closed door. Reese was bringing up the rear now. All the doors in Larry and Nadette's house hung crooked, with diagonal wedges at the bottom. When he was younger, Larry would lie on his side and peer at my ankles through the bathroom door crack any time I was in there. He always wanted to know what was going on in the rooms he wasn't in. No matter where he was, he had the sense that he was missing important events somewhere else.

As the group stood outside the bathroom, knocking, Larry Jr. and Nicky crept downstairs. Uncle Reese pushed his way to the door, his voice rising above the rest, a singsong calling Sylvia out.

Vi stood at the top of the stairs, one hand on the rickety banister, the other on her chest. "It's like thick rubber bands are wound around my legs, squeezing the life out of them," she said to no one in particular. "I don't think I'll be going back down there any time soon." She added that she was breathing heavily and her heart was pounding but since her kids didn't care about her legs, why should they care about her heart? They were all too busy watching Reese, who knew how to give a show if ever anyone did.

The search was a waste of time. I'd checked everywhere upstairs. Even if Sylvia were in the washroom, everyone would feel stupid when she came out and saw them in the hall. Not an hour earlier, they had drunk and talked around her as if she was normal, and here they were now, waiting for her outside the washroom. It was appalling. Did they think she couldn't hear them? It was enough to drive anyone crazy who wasn't already there.

Reese got down on his knees and peered under the door.

"White sneakers. I definitely see white sneakers," he said. "Do you remember what shoes she was wearing, Sammer?"

"Haven't got a clue," Sam said from behind Vi, who hadn't moved from her position at the top of the stairs.

I could have told them she was wearing her same patent-leather pumps with the back seams pressed under her heels like mules, but no one asked me.

A shadow appeared. Before Reese could move out of the way, the door swung open, hitting Reese's knee and revealing Carla in one of Larry's undershirts.

"Where's the party?" she asked, making everyone laugh except Nadette and Larry.

Reese was wise enough not to make a comeback. He stood and edged toward the stairs. Nadette had a mean streak, especially when it came to her sister.

Nadette slid a finger under the elastic of Carla's panties, pulled it out and snapped it back hard. Carla folded her arms over her chest and smirked, eyes boring into the ceiling.

Larry Sr. backed off, following Reese toward the stairs. He tended to let his wife handle things, even though whenever he did nothing, Vi had words for him later.

"Sylvia ain't here," he said, his head down but his eyes fixed on Sam's.

"No. She's probably not even in the house. Wouldn't be surprised if she's sneaking a smoke. I'm not letting her smoke these days." Sam smiled at what might be perceived as an unnecessary cruelty. "Maybe she's with the boys."

Sam's calm relaxed the others though no one would meet his eyes. As the oldest they looked to him for how to behave. His bringing Sylvia home from the hospital to live — and up north to Drag to visit — embarrassed them though they would all agree it was the right thing to do. They seemed nervous imagining Sylvia not with them inside the house. After all she'd gone crazy. Could still be. The less Sam reacted the better. Then they'd think everything was normal and he could find her without any fuss.

Sam pressed past Vi and went downstairs, his brothers trailing behind.

"How about some euchre?" Sam said over his shoulder.

Larry laughed, loud and thin. "You must have read my mind, Sammer. I'll get the decks."

Vi tried to make eye contact with Carla, show her she was on her side, but Larry Jr.'s aunt was as fierce as her sister was shrewish. Carla lowered her eyes and held Nadette's. Then she strode over to the sink and leaned toward the mirror.

"Leave her alone," Vi said.

Nadette whipped around. "You keep out of it. What do you

know about girls, especially this type right here? You know, she wouldn't be wearing this if there hadn't been men here.

"And you, young lady. I don't care what you do. You hear that? I don't give a shit. All I'm saying is if you're planning on sleeping here tonight, you'll be sharing your bed with Larry Jr.'s cousin, because I already told Mercy she's sleeping in there. And you'd better be nice to this family, or you can go back to wherever it was you came from."

Carla squeezed her face up in a smirk and slammed the door with her foot.

"Somebody ought to talk to her," Vi said.

"I don't need your advice, nor your opinions, nor your words of wisdom. I'm not like Larry who has to have his mama to boss him around. You keep your words for your son — or better yet, for someone else. This is *my* sister. She's *my* responsibility and this is the way things go in my house."

Nadette whirled around and slapped the heel of her hand on the bathroom door.

"Let me in, or I'll get in some other way. This is not over, young lady."

Vi shook her head and started downstairs. She paused on each step to knead her calves. I came right behind her.

"The impudence of that woman!" Vi whispered. "I could probably say 'impudence' to her face and she wouldn't know what it meant. I have a lot of other choice words, let me tell you, but it isn't worth my time. That woman has a tongue so sharp it slices your ear off before you have chance or inclination to respond.

"But I know when to keep my peace. If Nadette wants her sister to hate her, that's her problem, not mine. It's not Carla she needs to worry about. Larry Jr.'s the one. If he's witnessing this, what's he going to grow up thinking about women?"

No one else seemed to hear Vi, or maybe they were used to tuning her out.

"I can't understand what it is with my sons and women," Vi muttered. "None of them chose well. Sam married a crazy, and Larry married a shrew." She sighed at Shanelle, who was setting cork coasters on the card table. "You're okay so far, Shanelle, but you just wait until you have that baby. Then your true colours will show."

From the window I could see Nicky and Larry Jr.'s shady bodies slinking across the driveway; I came out and sat on the stoop, dazed. No thoughts were coming into my mind and I stared at my hands and knees as though I'd never seen them before. The sky had cleared and was crowded with stars sunk into a deep blue-black. The sky here hung like a cloak that had been lifted up momentarily to expose Uncle Larry's piece of land cut into the pines and his crowded peeling red tile and tarpaper house. Too much sky.

Nicky and Larry Jr.'s voices washed over me above the silence. They were heading past the outbuildings. I followed at a distance. All this time spent wishing to have a mother home, and it was simpler the moment she left. With Sylvia gone, I breathed easier.

I dropped my head, opened my mouth and dug my chin into my clavicle. No wonder my mother wanted to leave if this was how I felt. Yet the truth was, no matter where she went, Sylvia was both there and not there.

I bit the insides of my cheeks to the limit of pain.

Even though she was home, had been less than three feet away the entire ride up, Sylvia held herself out of reach.

The animal presence was more real than the Sylvia who covered her head with pillows and slept in her bathrobe all day. It wasn't that she kept a piece of herself away. Rather, she teased us with her image while refusing to give up what lay behind it.

I rubbed my brow with the back of my hand.

What did it matter if Sylvia disappeared? Nobody minded — it was all a big joke. It wasn't like she made a difference. I was so used to having her gone that having her around was harder.

Larry Jr. was busy spilling secrets, telling Nicky how last winter Carla had gotten pregnant and her parents took her out of school and sent her to the city. She was away for months but when she came back she had no baby. She'd been kicked out of the house so she came to live with Larry, Nadette and Larry Jr. Larry Jr. wasn't supposed to know Carla was pregnant but she'd told him on the day she left. She wanted him to tell his parents he knew, said it would really piss them off, but he never had. Now she wouldn't talk to any of them. She came home to sleep when she got tired of The Dropout. Things were going to change, Larry Jr.'s father said, when school started.

"What's a hoar?" Larry Jr. asked after he finished this story. They were sitting on the hood of a caved-in sixties Galaxie that sat decaying amid a variety of decrepit machinery behind the outbuildings. Uncle Larry worked in a wrecking yard farther out of town and his own place was what he called an automobile graveyard. A path cut into the trees was the final resting place for auto bodies progressively more and more stripped down. Near the top of a hill cars were reduced to gritty rusted frames with the occasional axle or faded door panel visible through the ground cover. The hood on this Galaxie didn't spring like the ones on most cars. This car had no tires and was partially embedded in the earth. In daylight, it looked as if the ground was trying to eat the chassis, as if someday the soil would loosen the pressure a bit and suck the entire thing in. I imagined a big pair of dirt lips smacking afterward.

I lowered myself down in the long grass where they could see me if they wanted.

"A hoar? Why don't you look it up in the dictionary?" Nicky said.

The word sent a thrill through me, especially hearing it spoken. I wasn't sure of its exact meaning either but knew it had to do with sex and badness.

"I did look it up. It said something about grey hair or whiskers. It was dumb because Carla doesn't have grey hair."

"What does it matter?"

"'Hoar' is what my dad calls her when she's not there. Why would he call her that?"

"It means she's bad."

They were silent. I fixed my gaze on one small patch of sky in case a shooting star passed.

"You know, Nicky. Carla's not bad. She doesn't mean to do it."

Larry Jr. sounded as if he might cry. Nicky leaped up. He hated anything emotional or personal and would desert his cousin if he cried.

"Don't think about it, Larry. It's not worth it. She's only your aunt."

He kicked the bumper. The car didn't move.

Larry Jr. sniffled and jumped off too. "Let's check out inside the car. Maybe we can camp here tonight. Especially if my aunt comes back. Then no one will notice we're gone so we won't have to ask."

I stood up then and said, "Hey."

"What are you doing here?" Larry said, his voice sullen.

"I don't know. Just looking for you guys, looking for Sylvia. Your aunt is back, by the way, Larry."

"We haven't found her," Nicky said.

"I noticed."

We walked around to the back of the car where the rear windshield was punched in. There were balls of glass on the trunk so we had to be careful. With his hand on the window frame, Nicky climbed up first so he was squatting. Larry Jr. followed, pressing in close to Nicky as he peered in. I dropped back down on the wet grass, hands back, eyes on the stars.

"I can't see anything."

"What's to see?" Nicky sat back.

"There could be something in there," Larry Jr. said, putting on his superior voice. "'Coons might nest in there or squirrels. Maybe even a skunk. You have to be careful."

"That's stupid. It sounds like something your dad would say. Just turn on the flashlight."

"No. We can't. We might scare something and cause it to attack us."

Larry Jr.'s voice was shrill. He was back to his normal self.

"What happens when you're driving and you shine the headlights on a raccoon or a rabbit? What does it do? Does it attack?"

"No."

"Well. What does it do?" Nicky was enjoying himself.

"It freezes. Everybody knows that. Then it gets hit — BAM!" He smacked the palms of his hands together.

"Right. So don't you think the same thing'll happen if we shine the light in there?"

Larry Jr. looked into the car. A corner of the back seat was illuminated by the quarter-moon. None of us could see the floor though, or the front.

"I guess."

"And besides, Junior. If you haven't woken whatever it is up with your whining, there's probably nothing there to wake up." Nicky reserved the name Junior for times when he had our cousin neatly under his thumb.

"So, what do you want to do?" Larry Jr. asked.

"You can start by giving me that flashlight," Nicky said.

"I don't got it." Larry Jr. held out his hands. When Nicky lurched at him, he said, "It's at the front, where we were on the hood."

As Nicky jogged to the front of the car, I heard it — a moan mixed with a creak. I hopped up into a crouch and paused to listen the way Sam had taught me — like an Indian brave. I forgot about Larry Jr. until I felt the hot breath on my ear.

"Did you hear that? See, I was right. There is something."

"Shh," I said, standing. "We don't want it to know we're here."

Larry Jr. of all people should have known better. He was the one who lived near the bush. He must have seen deer and moose all the time. He and Uncle Larry went to the dump at night to watch bears rip open garbage bags. Nicky and I had gone with them once and were impressed by how small the bear was.

The sound came again, only softer this time. Nicky came back and stood with us. I wasn't sure I'd even heard it but Larry Jr.'s quick gasp assured me I had. I couldn't tell if the sound was right next to us or across the property. It was that kind of sound and that kind of night.

Nicky wrapped his arm around Larry Jr.'s neck and clamped his hand over his mouth. Together they moved step by step to the front of the car. I followed close behind. The noise came once more and Nicky put his face in so close to Larry Jr.'s the bridges of their noses were nearly touching. With his eyes, he warned Larry Jr. not to move or say anything.

I motioned them to stay put and pointed at myself.

I felt the hood for the flashlight. Larry Jr. squirmed. When he wasn't being an authority, Larry Jr. had a million questions. Bear was my first choice. Bears growled but who knew what kind of noise cornered mama bears made. Or sick ones. Then again, maybe it was a killer or a UFO. I stretched my neck and scanned the sky for red or green lights.

On my hands and knees, I patted the ground. It was rough here, and I couldn't see at all, not even outlines.

The noise erupted, full force. My head shot forward and cracked against the grille of the car. Tears sprang to my eyes as I struggled not to yell. I backed up, my hand pressed to my brow. It was wet, but no bump yet.

Because my injury had so absorbed me, it took me a moment to realize that Nicky and Larry Jr. were no longer at the front of the car. They weren't around the back either. I swallowed. My instinct was to follow them, but the brave thing would be to stick it out and discover what was making those sounds. Besides, it would serve them right if it was a bear and I got mangled all because my brother and cousin deserted me and took the flashlight.

The moaning didn't stop. It came from inside the car. Without giving myself time to think or swallow, I moved closer to the front door. I licked my palm and swiped a clean circle in the dirt. Then with both hands cupped around my eyes I peered in. It took a moment to adjust, but what I saw took the air right out of me. A face looked back at me — or rather, the eyes of a face. It saw me too and let out a scream so eerie I couldn't tell if it was animal, human or something else.

I jumped back and tried to run, but my legs had the rubbery feeling they got in dreams. I wished I had the flashlight or the chisel to defend myself. I took a few steps, tripped, took a few more, then sat, panting, in a patch of long grass. It was quiet long enough for my body to switch off the alarm. Surely someone in the house had heard the scream.

Maybe what I'd seen was dead. But I knew better. I'd seen an animal, or maybe even a murderer, but it was definitely not dead. I wished Larry Jr. and Nicky were still here to lead me back to the house.

When I caught my breath, I crawled through the wet grass in the direction of the lights, patting my hands in front of me in case of wayward metal as I went. Whatever it was, it would not get me, that was for sure.

13

Groupie Types

Groupie Types

Monday I go home after the morning shift and sit in the back yard and watch Nicky attach eavestrough to the new roof. Vi comes out once and sits beside me drinking iced tea. She asks if I am feeling okay and I say no, I am nauseous and need fresh air. Would she mind getting me some Aspirin and a sweatshirt? I let her take care of me but I don't talk and neither does she. When it rains, the three of us bring lawn chairs into the addition and watch water stream through the dirt on the new picture window.

After dinner, Nicky comes into the kitchen in jeans and a mint green polo shirt that bunches in the centre of his chest. He's landed an extra night babysitting the Jackson children. Of the three, the oldest is ten and the youngest, the girl, is seven. Vi and Sam watch a game show in the living room. I sit at the kitchen table fingering the knots on the lampshade.

"Want some dessert?" Nicky asks.

"Sure."

As he reaches up to grab the powdered donuts from the tall cupboard, his shirt stretches, revealing a horizontal seam across the middle of his back.

"What do you remember about Mom?" Nicky asks. He digs out three donuts and stuffs them in his mouth.

I lower my hand into my lap. He has powder on his lips and some flecks in his dark hair.

"Do you remember what she wore?"

It is strange to have Nicky asking me about Sylvia. He's talked about Sylvia when she was healthy but never about that summer.

"I remember her dress," I venture.

He crams in two more donuts and stands up. "Is that all? You don't remember anything else?"

"She had a pink shirt. I do remember that. A nice silky one." Though I don't remember Sylvia wearing that shirt, I have seen it in Nicky's trophy cup.

"Hmmm. Do you think her clothes are some kind of connection? I mean, it wouldn't be odd, say, if you wanted to wear something of hers. It would make sense, right?"

"Sure. I guess. Though the clothes are pretty old."

Nicky arches his back and fingers his waistband.

"Right." The volume in the living room goes up as a commercial comes on. Nicky holds the donut box out to me. "You didn't have any."

"I'm fine."

He bends the edges together and winds the box in a bag. He pushes his hair behind one ear.

"See you, then."

"Nicky, what about that girl?"

"What girl?" His hand hovers near his collar, a gesture not his.

"That girl you told Rick about. Did you make her up? Did Rick ever—" Though she had dark hair and mine is light brown, I can't bring myself to ask Nicky if the girl he told Rick about is me.

Nicky crosses his arms over his chest.

"I do remember the dress, the one you were talking about. It was green and orange. It's not there now."

"No, I guess it's not."

"And I did make her up. That girl. I do that sometimes — make girls up. I have to go."

He leaves, swinging the donut bag.

"Have fun."

At dusk I ride back to the Club under a thick sky. Wet dirt from the front tire sprays my ankles, but the rain has stopped. I drop my bike and wait on the stoop outside the staff quarters. No one is around. Most of the afternoon shift doesn't finish until ten. A medley of Beatles tunes with a disco backbeat drifts from the main lodge. The back of the staff quarters is bordered by a forest of tall pines in whose midst lies the lightning man. I can hear a light wind in the needles, the way I can with our maples.

The dreams are eating me up. My skin is turning white, pasty, old, no matter how many hours I spend sitting in the sun. Everything smells like powdered milk, with an underlayer of fish. My hair is thicker, greasier, and wind sounds whip my mind into a churlish frenzy. My world is confined to a series of movements, feet on pedals, thumbs on bike brakes, hands in wet rubber gloves, fork to mouth, brush to teeth, comb snagging hair, sandpaper grating wood. My identity is wiped clean. Even my potential for madness stripped away.

It is that simple and yet I reject it. I've grown up with a huge gaping hole behind me; one wrong step and I plunge. Now here I am in that hole, falling, with no idea why. I fall like Alice, at a calm pace, slow enough that I could reach out, take a jar off a shelf, read its label and put it back on another shelf. Only there are no shelves and nothing to grab onto as bit by bit I descend.

I hear the crush of feet on sand and feel furtive, panicky. Mother feelings. The image of a red belly ridged with crisscrossing white lines. I try not to look anywhere in particular. The night has become black. Then, before I realize who it is, Brenda is upon me.

"Hey there," Brenda says, all smiles. She sits down, one step above me.

"Hi," I say, eased.

Brenda chats about the shift, referring to a Mr. Scott and the Cowans as if I know them too. I can talk to Brenda, if only for Levon. Because of the story of the ghost light, Levon is a token. He is the only one who has shown himself to me during sleep since the Mother dreams began. I could love him for that.

"And Mrs. Kraut. She was such a bitch, I almost called her Mrs. Trout. She would've deserved it, too, and I wouldn't be too far off, but that would be it for my job. Ruby wouldn't put up with that."

"My mother died," I say. The words are easier than they should be, yet they astonish me. Though I take no responsibility for them, they give an unforeseen sense of peace.

Brenda lays a hand on my knee.

"Oh my God, I'm so sorry." Her words are rushed. The corners of her lips move up, then down. "I never know what to say."

"I wouldn't either."

"What are you doing here? They should give you some time off. Ruby's a bitch, but she's not that mean. What about the funeral, all that?"

I haven't thought details: funeral, coffin, flowers. The words I spoke are truthful. I feel awful, messy, my nose full of mucus, my throat smoky raw, the skin on my stomach loose and flopping onto my lap.

"I don't know where she is. Just that she's dead."

"How do you know?"

"I do. I just do. Wouldn't you?"

Brenda takes my hand and squeezes it. "I've never known anyone who died. Levon's known plenty. But you're right. I think I would know if Levon died."

The wind picks up and I listen for a voice underneath it, a voice that will tell me where my mother is. Not this sickly thing crawling through my dreams and under my skin, but my real mother. Sylvia. The lightning man rests in the woods where I left him. Where is his voice? I listen until my ears must be red and trembling but the shivering pine needles offer up no names.

Levon is on his third story.

"He was a giant man, bigger than you even," he says, indicating a waiter named Glen who is as wide as he is tall. "But his head was gone. Instead he had this thick neck with flapping veins and hanging guts. You could even see the white tip of the vertebrae, wiggling. The whole neck moved and a low laugh echoed along the road."

Duncan sits on a log across from us, eyes wide. "What did you do?"

"I stayed for a look then I turned tail and ran for my life. Funnily enough, right after that, the trees ended and I ran past a small cemetery, with the grass growing over the stones, and some of the stones falling over. That's where he must have come from."

Levon leans back. The fire crackles and those nearby fall into the same hushed, suspicious awe the Pink Ladies had after Chipper had tricked us into screaming at the end of her tale of an armless hitchhiker. Levon hasn't spoken to me once though he sits close enough to make my arms prickle. His face, from my dreams, is as intimate to me as a lover's. I don't want to speak for fear I'll be too familiar. I hope Brenda isn't the only reason he is here. Brenda sits on the other side, away from the fire with a guy I've never seen, ignoring Levon.

As everyone begins to chat, Duncan gets up and strolls over to my side, hands in pockets.

"Let's go up to the house. I've got something to show you."

If Duncan and I have anything resembling a code, this is it. We haven't smoked up together often, but when either one has something, we use this line. Maybe this is why people think there's something between us. I follow him up the path and wonder if he is indeed invoking the code or whether he has something else to show me.

"What do you think of Levon?" Duncan says, once we are inside.

"I like him."

"Like?"

"The way I like *you*. He tells a lot of stories."

"Can you believe they all happened to one guy?"

"They didn't. They couldn't."

"They did. He's not the kind of guy who would lie."

We stand inside the door.

"Did we just come up here to talk about Levon, or was there some ulterior motive?" I shove my fingers into my pockets.

Duncan cocks his head. "You turned out very pretty."

"You mean I wasn't before?"

I head for the fridge. Duncan follows.

"Of course. But everybody thinks so now."

"Not just you."

"No."

"Duncan. Why are you telling me this? Is this some exercise your therapist told you to do?"

I open the fridge door and push my face into the frosty air. Duncan is right behind me but I refuse to turn or to run away. I run my fingers along the wet sides of a beer bottle and picture his long sarcastic mouth closing over mine, his body tensing, his penis hard and twisted inside his baggy jeans. The faint smell of rotting vegetable matter washes over me. I take out two bottles and bump them into Duncan's chest. He grabs them, his hands full now. This is good.

"It's not what you think, Mercy."

Duncan's blue eyes probe mine. He sits at the table.

"What do I think?"

I take out four more bottles and close the door with my foot.

"I don't know, but I'm not making a pass at you, if that's what you think."

Only Duncan would say "making a pass," and only Duncan would have to clarify that he wasn't. My fingers are numb. A light rain rattles the leaves.

Duncan's eyes follow the fan blades.

"Do you think about death a lot?"

Brenda is the only person I told my mother is dead. I haven't had time to tell Duncan, and there is no reason why I should. Still, the coincidence is eerie.

I choose my words with care. "I think about other people's deaths, but not my own, if that's what you mean."

"I guess Levon's stories got me thinking. You know. About dying."

"They sure did."

My throat is thick. We are alone in this cavernous room with shadowed corners that seem to be creeping inward. Levon's ghost light could flash through and one of us might end up dead before the night is over. Duncan has never talked this way before. Maybe it is not him talking. If he keeps it up, I will be convinced that Mother's words are coming through his lips. That must be what Mother wants with me, to take me down, to suck me into death, to pull her daughter through every soul-wasting experience she endured.

"Duncan."

"What? For some reason, whenever I try to talk to you, Mercy, you listen, but you don't give anything back. You don't even tell me your problems, so why should I tell you mine?"

Smudges rim Duncan's eyes.

This word of Duncan's, *problems*, jabs me the most. It is a word I do not apply to myself. Problems have solutions. My life is not divided into neat little boxes I can call problems. There is too much to tell, and nothing.

"Maybe," I say, "I don't have any, 'problems.'" I force my lips up. He's forgotten about the dreams.

Duncan twists off the bench, his knee catching the corner of the table.

"Right. Everyone knows your mother got shipped off to a nut farm."

He glares at me, his eyes nearly popping out. Even his hair is shaking, from the roots.

A string of comebacks rushes through my mind. I turn and leave, giving him what will hurt him most.

Back at the bonfire, Brenda is gone. The logs are damp, but the sky is clearing and the fire blazes. I sit beside Levon. He stares at me. We are far enough out of the firelight that I can pretend no one else is there.

I hand him a beer and ask him to walk with me.

"Walking's not exactly my specialty," he says, but he doesn't pull his eyes away.

I return his gaze. The longer I look, the more daring I get. The rest of the world falls away.

Finally, Levon shrugs.

"What the hey."

He flicks his head. His eyes shift on and off mine, but my gaze never wavers. He flicks again, then asks for his stick, his words tight and rushed. I draw my eyes from his and get him his varnished wooden stick from where it is lying off to the side on the grass.

I follow Levon to a clearing where his truck is parked. A rush of noise fills my ears, as if conch shells held on either side of my head reflect the tidal roar of my mind. The truck is caked with mud. Levon leans his stick against it, reaches into the cab and pulls out a tarp, the oily amber of Wanigamog sand. He hands it to me, then yanks down the tailgate with a croak.

I climb in and wrestle the tarp down. It is bigger than the area of the truck box. I push it into the corners and kneel near the front. Levon hops up and perches on the tailgate. Then he swings his legs in and edges back with his buttocks so he is sitting beside me. The moon, shining through a cloud, illuminates his face.

I try to fix my eyes on his, but he rolls them up toward the stars. I balance my weight on one arm until my shoulder aches and watch the clouds drift apart. My ears clamour yet all around us is silent. There is nothing to say to Levon. I don't know him beyond his stories. Talking will only make us more aware of why we shouldn't be where we are.

When I look at Levon again, he is staring. I stare back and within seconds I am falling, only this is a fast fall, a willy-nilly fall, a fall where it doesn't matter what I do — any connection will be enough to stop my progress, if only for a moment. I lean into him, my gaze steady, and touch my lips against his. I am firm but I hold my tongue behind my teeth until he reveals his. It is like drinking water and I float.

His lips are soft, softer than between my legs, stretching back, the skins of drums I beat against, a song of release. The swishing birch leaves and moon-soaked sky carry not Rick, but Angie back to me in a rush. My falling mind grabs at anything it can and fills me with Angie's lips, Angie's thighs, Angie between-the-legs, twelve-year-old skin not yet stretched.

Levon presses hard against me, a crazy loose pattern of hip and rib bones, a skeleton man I fished up from the bottom of a trout pond, a ghost from one of his stories, and it is Jo now who I push back with my belly. Faint whiffs of smoke trail over us, mingling on my skin with the curved bones of Levon's fingers, clicking as they explore my skin. I ease Levon's jeans down, rubbing my thighs on his like a cricket squeaking out a song, his slim bones clattering against mine. I put my palm in the arch of his back and hold him hard to me. Cricket songs intersect with the rubbling and peeping of the frogs, lines of sound crossing, webbing us in. My voice, as I rock against him, is one of many in this forest. I don't hear it myself.

10

> I am submerged. My nose is filled with salt, with slime, with fish parts, my feet, behind my knees, every crevice coated with moss. Like a tractor, my mouth scoops and scoops, yowling. My teeth crunch on bones, motherbones. I suck to get every last bit of nourishment.

"I almost died in a swamp."

Levon's mouth is against my ear, another wet fish. It mutes the tidal roar.

"I was eleven. My buddy Evan and I were following the river and we crossed over on this log that snapped off right when I pushed off the shore and floated away."

My body is sodden, a log suspended in quicksand.

"The farther into the swamp we got, the more surrounded by water we were. It was loud: the rain, the water, it all made noise. At one point, after it was dark, the swamp spread out into a fast, deep area of the river. We had to swim. I jumped first and put my life against that current. That was before my legs."

My hair makes a scratchy sound as I nod, my ear against his head.

"I led the way. I didn't check back to see if Ev was okay. I figured if something went wrong, I'd know. I'd know if he wasn't there. But it didn't work that way. I crossed that broad brown stream and scrambled up the bank. When I looked he was gone. Just like that."

I am sinking back into the dream. Water fills my ears, my nose, my mouth. I am running, branches snagging my sweater, snapping against my arms, whipping my face. I run with no idea whether I am running toward something or away from it. I run like I am falling. The dream releases me and I rub my hand on Levon's chest. His hair is sparse here. I rub until his nipple hardens into a seed.

"I swam right back across the stream, but of course with the current and all, I don't think I ended up where I started. I zigzagged through the woods, calling Ev's name."

A branch crashes.

"Then it hit me. The smell. The swamp smelt bad enough, but this, this was sour rotting food, vegetables, and flesh too, the way a paper mill smells. I said *Evan* again in a normal voice, but got no answer."

11

Mother crawls in front of me. Mother's bones are thick, her legs long and smeared with mud. She is fast, faster than I am. Her smell is like bark now, Chinese tea, sparking my nostrils. Mother's breasts hang, swaying side to side, but her purpose is clear. She will escape. I must let her go, or get down on all fours and join her.

Levon's voice dies. Now he is only a breath in my ear, a bog wind, the rattle of gleeful, fished-up bones. I open my mouth to tell him, but my jaw has seized, just as in the dreams. It won't accept even a finger to pry it open. But I have to speak. Levon's friend went missing in the swamp, in the dark, rainy, howling swamp. I need to add my words on top of his, to shout down the swamp, to unbind my jaw, our joints, the voices.

With the tips of my teeth resting together, I tell of my own swamp, the thunderstorms that rolled and cracked and burned and smoothed away everything that wasn't rooted down. The thunderstorms that delivered my mother and took her away.

"It's the same rotting smell," I say. "That sourness that grows into your taste buds so that even the sweetest things have a taint from then on."

I hear my voice now, taking on Levon's cadence. The dreams press in fast and furious, but each word stays them, prodding them back.

Then I tell of Sylvia's final night up at Larry's sorry excuse for a house. I tell of Sylvia's fingers rapping on the tarpaper, and of walking every inch of ground through the long grass on bare Indian soles, divining her body, shut eyed.

There is more to say, much more, but my words are knocked away by a body that crashes onto the bed of the pickup, falling over me with thrashing arms and legs to get at Levon.

"I didn't go to the Trout Club to watch a bunch of half-blind people grapple in the back of a pickup," Nicky says.

"I didn't know you were there."

"Your voice brought tears to my eyes," Nicky drops a handful of dirt into the purling river below. "It was *her* voice. *Mary's* voice — the woman in the photograph. A witch voice.

Minutes before, the voice was alive and full of magic, but then it was someone else's, a crazy voice. Even though it no longer spoke words, I understood it better."

"Mary. I heard you call her that."

Nicky doesn't answer, just tosses more dirt off Copper Bridge where we sit shoulder to shoulder, legs dangling from the creosote-coated ties. It's too early for the train but the dark is easing and we're close to the bank just in case.

It was Rick he wanted to talk about when we first hooked onto these tracks across the road from the Trout Club, but we'd fallen into a peaceable silence worth not breaking as the pre-dawn sky and the sleepers led us forward. Now it was something else. Something more.

"I was always afraid you knew," he says.

"I did know."

"The whole time? But you didn't say."

"What could I say? I wanted to see you."

No one told Nicky where Mom went after the week of thunderstorms. Since I was gone, too, he knew Mom was fine. The odds of something being wrong with both of us were too great. He figured we were on a trip together. Mom crying was all he remembered from the night she left. Most of the time he tried to think about the air going in and out of his nose to make the thoughts of Mom go away.

While I was at camp Nicky had found a portrait in Dad's dresser when he couldn't find another photograph in the house. The woman he called Mary. Our mother.

He kept the photo in his bedroom where he held it on his lap and talked with her. He didn't find his behaviour odd, not then, not now. Who else was he going to talk to like a mother? I didn't say Vi, which should have been obvious.

He didn't know why he called her Mary. The name popped into his head. An old-fashioned movie actress name. His talks took place in his mind at first, but one day he found himself saying, "Hello, Mary."

It was a risk, the saying aloud of the name he'd given her — not her real name — as if he were taking away some of her power. What if she rejected the name? He had a lot to tell her about the part of him that occasionally came out in a fluttering hand gesture or a heavy eyelid, but the words weren't there. That element was emerging regardless and insisting on being recognized. It sat inside his chest making its breaths his own; it would show itself to Mary whether Nicky liked it or not.

He set the photograph on his dresser, propping it in front of a class photo inside a cardboard frame. She stared impassively at him. She had her own concerns and was not interested in the personality changes of a young boy. Her indifference only spurred Nicky on — her approval, if given, all the more meaningful because it was not easily won. He stepped back and gazed at her, his hands hovering, perching like restless birds — first on his shoulders then his hips then his chest. He needed different clothes. His Apple Ford Fishing Derby T-shirt and denim shorts felt harsh and awkward, the seams scratching his skin, constricting him, concealing him. He needed something more suited to the fluid hands and sly eyes now emerging.

The pink shirt he'd taken from Mom's drawer when he unpacked Vi's suitcase still hid in the bowl of his hockey trophy. He hadn't looked at it once. It was always there though, waving like a banner at the edges of his dreams, deepening his desire.

Now was the time. He took the baseball glove off his trophy and removed the shirt, handling it with the tips of his fingers only. He lingered for a moment before the photograph then laid the shirt on the bed.

Nicky unbuttoned his shorts and stepped out of them. He removed his T-shirt as well and threw them both in a pile in front of the heating grate. He approached the pink shirt then halted. Something irrevocable would happen once he put the shirt on. He forced himself forward regardless. He wanted it so much he could taste its taste of no air, of holding his breath and allowing the self that crept on the sidelines to fill him. His mouth sweetened, his breath quickened and his eyelids lowered. He was aware of the weight of his hair and the lightness of his voice. Mary's eyes rested on him as he reached forward and picked up the pink shirt. He slipped it on as easily as he might slide his body into bath water and he was there. Or rather, *she* was. In that moment, he was *Nicola*, the Nicola who'd glimpsed out that evening after the bath with me, the Nicola who'd recognized part of herself in the photograph, the Nicola who was waiting, always waiting to fill his body, the way it was meant to be filled.

Before Mom came back from the Rest Home, Nicky had to get rid of her pink shirt. The first time he took it off, it felt crude to stuff it back in the trophy so he'd folded the shirt in half and slid it under his mattress. Mrs. Sousa never cleaned there, but when Mom came home, the mattress wouldn't be good enough. There would be no aspect of his life — his drawers, his closet, his bedding — that he could be sure Mom wouldn't lay her hands on.

When Nicky was learning to read, she'd lean against his dresser, a Dr. Seuss book in hand, her long fingers behind her absently pulling open his drawers and rifling through his socks and briefs. Each day while he was at school his room shifted. He came to memorize the exact position of every object: the pillow, the rag rug, the balled-up sock pairs, the hockey cards, the robe on the hook behind his door, the blinds, the rock collection, the poster of Han Solo at the controls of the *Millennium Falcon*. In the evening, he ran his fingers over each object, adjusting it back into place before he could climb into bed and fall asleep. Every day one item had moved: a pennant taken down and retacked, games stacked differently, his clock radio set at a different station. The prospect of having her in the house made him remember. What might she shift when he left his room? Returning the shirt to her drawer was dangerous with Vi around and besides, part of him wouldn't permit it. He would have to hide the shirt away from the house — beyond her reach yet close enough to touch if need be.

The day Sylvia was due back from the Rest Home, Nicky got up before light and stuck his arm between the mattress and boxspring, thrilling when his fingertips found the shirt's fabric. As he dropped the shirt over his head, the transformation once again gripped him between the shoulder blades and each cell shifted as if given new shape.

Saying he had become Nicola was no exaggeration. Inside that silken shirt, Nicky's identity changed. He would be twelve the following year, an age when anything can happen, when genitals take root and assert themselves like flowers, where curves and lines, hardness and softness, tones, shapes, scents, tastes all start to matter. The world is shaded in and all is defined. Nicky hovered on blurred borders, and inside that pink shirt the lines being demarcated were not his. They were what he desired but not what he wanted to be. Inside that pink shirt, a girl was emerging, a female being shaping him in ways more frightening than even the expected changes. He didn't want to be a girl, wasn't supposed to be one, but how could he ignore what had so clearly always been? Even with her there, he was still Nicky. He thought the same way, wanted the same things only with the volume turned up; when she came out, he was himself, intensified. The danger was the lure of wearing the pink shirt, or even his mother's other clothes, all the time. His heart shimmied.

Inside that shirt the morning of Sylvia's homecoming, Nicky's penis was so firm it curved up and nearly touched his flat brown stomach. He stood in the middle of his room, trans-fixed. Everyone was asleep, so he was safe. The erection seemed not to belong to him although the feeling was certain-ly his. The folds of rosy fabric over his taut mauve skin stiff-ened him further. He wrapped his hand around himself, unsure whether it was the flesh on his palm or what it was holding that trembled. His breath gusted, his teeth clicked and noth-ing existed outside what he was.

He faced his mirror. It was warped with scratched patches but if he stood to its left he could get an idea. With his hands on his waist he rolled his hips but the erection stayed upright. He grabbed it again and moved it in an arc as if he were pee-ing his name in the snow. He shuffled up close to the mirror and stroked the hem of the shirt with his thumb.

He tried out different names: "My cock. My dick. My dink. My wiener. My wee-wee. My pee-nus." This one made him laugh out loud, his own hushed laugh rising like a girl's — Nicola's laugh. When Nicky first learned the word *penis*, he would slip out of the bathtub holding it in one hand yelling, "I have a penis! I have a penis!" with me right behind him, yelling, "Penispenispenis!" both of us laughing so hard we fell rolling on Nicky's bed, Mom angry at our wetness on the covers, at any mess or mention of body parts, her face so red we laughed even more. Of course I didn't have a penis. He wasn't quite sure what I had. He remembered a round plumpness between my legs with a straight line splitting me in half. Boys at school used the word *pussy*, a word that sobered him.

He sat on his bed on this morning, before the sun was anything but a pale promise on the horizon, and fell on his back, his hand in place. *Cock* had a precise, slicing quality. He preferred it.

The first time he put on the pink shirt, the erection wasn't a consideration. Nicola was emerging then, so it was the pleasure of the fabric on his skin, of the skin itself that had involved him so utterly. The fingers stroking his hair, his lips, his shoulders stroked Nicola's hair, lips, shoulders. That had been enough. That, and knowing Mary had witnessed.

This time Nicola was there, oh yes, along with all her sensations: the hair, the sneer, the eyelashes lacing his vision. She was there even more in the aching behind his nipples, a nudge like a tooth about to break through the gums. But the cock changed everything. It invaded the experience, grabbing it all to itself, defining it, so this moment seemed impossible without this cock in the centre. It was outside him and he couldn't possess it. He drew the cock up and squeezed it against his belly. He rubbed its underside with both palms, enjoying its ripe pear skin against this tight hollow and the way its tip stretched up toward the belly-button nub. The cock was his and not his. When it pressed against him, it pressed against

Nicola, sending shock waves up into those tender almost-breasts. But when he rubbed harder, pulling the pink shirt down so it fell across his knuckles, the release was distinctly his — raw, mellow, with a smell like turned-up earth.

After the cock returned to its crouch between his legs, Nicola was still there. His head cleared, he had more control though his heart raced. With the end of his flannel sheet, he wiped his belly, grateful the shirt was unstained.

He lay unmoving, picturing dark points pushing against the silky fabric, two bumps like mine. Longing rushed him — for my breasts, Mary's sneer, Nicola, Vi's underwear, cigarette smoke — and the cock was back. He was swift this time, wrapping it in the corner of his sheet. After, he pulled on his normal clothes over the pink shirt and made his way downstairs.

About three miles out of town stood an abandoned barn that looked as if it had given up on itself. The roof sagged and the sides billowed like a cow's full belly. Inside, chinks of light shone through long slivers of missing wood on the walls and roof. The hay smelled rank from mould and decay. Nicky had been there with his buddies (though never with me) to smoke, but they had to be careful the owner wasn't around.

Walking as Nicola was new. The pink shirt caressed him as if the wind held it in place. He caught himself rolling with the shirt, moving into it and easing back, playing it to keep his balance. The sun, not yet high, bathed one side of him in a light as blush as the shirt.

He left the road and entered a field which thankfully held corn, already ripe. He walked the towering rows and thought of other clothing. For a few seconds, he pictured himself in one of Vi's wide-strapped bras with the grey girdle underneath charcoal nylons but he rejected that thought — the shirt was quite enough. Besides, once he hid it in the barn, he was going home to concentrate on being a boy. He wouldn't even look at the photograph. He would work on forgetting.

He snuck in through the old cattle stalls. Though no cattle had used them in years, the smells of urine and manure past its time clung to the walls. He climbed to the upper loft and went straight to a corner he'd hollowed out behind the hay. Before he could lift the board that covered the hiding spot, Nicola was on him, all over and through him, rasping in his ear, wheezing through his lips and nostrils, squeezing sweat from his pores. She wanted him to stay in the shirt. He yielded and smoothed the fabric, soothing her and earning himself the twinges of an erection. Then he remembered the time. He had to be back to help Dad wash the truck. Mom was coming home. He pulled both shirts over his head and separated them, folding the pink one and tucking it under a floorboard. He put his own shirt back on and climbed back over the hay, alone in his body.

Under his mattress now, Nicky tells me, he has three pairs of my panties and two of Sylvia's. Since there is no way to safely throw Sylvia's in the wash, he wears them only in his bedroom so they won't get dirty. It hasn't occurred to him to wash them by hand. My underwear he can rotate, tossing them into my hamper after I go downstairs in the morning.

He wears something every day: my panties or a bra beneath his sweat shirt. When he stretches to hammer in a wall plug or squats to measure and saw a piece of wood, the fabric moves with him. He is always aware of it: this underwear makes him feel secure while putting him in danger, on the verge of being discovered.

Earlier tonight, before having donuts with me, he hooked himself into Sylvia's bra and a pair of high-waisted panties, both a celery green, and pulled a T-shirt and jeans over top. While the Jackson children lay on their stomachs on the floor watching TV, Nicky sat on the couch behind them and let a strap peek out of the collar of his T-shirt, the way some of the girls at school did. Yet when the oldest boy turned away from the TV to look at him, he panicked and adjusted the shirt.

At bedtime, the youngest boy and the girl insisted on sleeping in the same bed. He remembered me saying something about this when I babysat them, but he couldn't remember if I'd said it was good or bad.

Nicky lay down beside the youngest boy to read *Horton Hears a Who*. The oldest brother was reading comics in his own bed. The boy shoved up against Nicky's arm, his breathing hot and audible. The girl pressed against her brother. Occasionally, Nicky hunched his shoulder up, trying to dislodge the bra strap so it would slide down and reveal itself, but it stayed stuck.

When the boy insisted on another story, Nicky said, "No, it's time to sleep."

He turned off the light and slid down beside the boy. There was little room in the single bed, so he let one leg hang off. As the boy and girl wiggled around, Nicky stared at the ceiling imagining a way to take off his T-shirt and shorts. If they'd fall asleep he could, but they stayed awake. They giggled and poked him, their breaths sweet like boiled corn.

He got up and left the room. He couldn't convince himself that they would want him to wear only the underwear. He paused in the doorway, watching. Other than the times we crawled in with Mom, he can't remember ever sleeping in the same bed as me.

He went to the oldest boy's room and told him to turn off his light.

"Are they in the same bed?" the boy asked.

"Yes."

"You're not supposed to let them do that. They'll have sex."

"Yeah right. They're only little kids."

Nicky hasn't even had sex yet himself. How would these children know what to do? Was it even possible?

"Check for yourself. I bet they're doing it right now." The boy turned a page in his comic book, bored.

"Turn out your light."

"I will, as soon as I finish." He raised his thick eyebrows in a plea.

Nicky shut the door. He listened. Giggles were coming from the girl's bedroom. That could mean anything.

He tiptoed down the hall and stood in the doorway of her room. All he could see were two squirming bodies under the covers. He thought of the little girl. How could she let her brother do that? Did she like it? They were so young — whose idea was it? Did they just discover it? Were they even having sex?

He wished he were the boy, eight years old, in bed with his sister, body on body, rolling and wiggling around each other, breathing each other's breath, his penis inside her.

Nicky stepped backward, his cock pushing against the green nylon. He stumbled into the bathroom, took his pants down and looked at the thin fabric tenting his pelvis. He was so hard, the elastic pulled away from his stomach. He closed his eyes and floated. He came as soon as he touched his cock. When he opened his eyes, the underwear was stuck to him, gummy and cold. He moved quietly, removing the panties, rinsing them in cold water and patting them with a towel until they were merely damp. He put them back on beneath his jeans. When he passed the girl's bedroom, the children were asleep.

Nicky slipped the folded money from Mrs. Jackson into the pocket of one of the kids' coats hanging in the entrance hallway. He nodded and smiled as she droned on about how much her kids loved me. He wanted to be gone before Mrs. Jackson discovered the two youngest in the same bed. He hoped the coat belonged to the sister.

Rain melted down, but the drops were warm so he didn't bother to cover up. The Jacksons' property backed onto the railway tracks. The train passed, its clanging hissy energy shaking the rain off the trees. It was after eleven. After all the cars had gone by, Nicky crossed the tracks and headed up the hill to Rick's storefront.

From the folding chair, he watched Rick pinch clay into dinosaur noses and pointy wizard caps. Rick glanced around once to see who he was, then returned to his work.

Nicky thought back to the feeling of Nicola draping him like a stage curtain when his skin touched nylon. He had no more sense of an alter ego, of sliding from one self to another. It was all him now. Perhaps if he covered himself with enough clothes, makeup, and maybe a wig, he could bring her back. He'd felt more comfortable with the split; that way, when he was himself, not "her," he could feel safe and whole, not amputated. Now there was no her. There was just him, in a bra and panties sitting in an apartment with an older man.

There was nothing magic.

He sank deeper inside himself and didn't hear when Rick turned around and spoke to him.

It took a flick of clay landing on his neck before he noticed. Even though he hadn't come to get stoned, it was easier to get the pot from the fridge and make up a joint. Nicky slipped cross-legged to the floor, his head tucked down, fingers shaking.

Rick squatted beside him, put a hand on his shoulder and twisted the bra strap up.

Nicky trembled, spilling leaves.

Rick let go of the strap. It snapped.

Nicky waited for him to speak, waited so hard he didn't blink, his face so tight and dry, he couldn't cry if he wanted to.

"Here. Let me."

Rick took the Baggie and papers, his fingers deft. Tiny bits of clay crumbled into the joint.

Nicky wondered if clay caused cancer. He'd never been more aware of the bra. It held him like fingers, his own fingers as they might pinch another, his body the stranger.

Rick raised the paper full of leaves to his lips, licked the edge, sealed it with his thumb, twisted up the ends and handed it to Nicky. He lit a match while Nicky stuck the joint in his mouth, his eyes focused on a bicycle propped near the door.

"I've done that before," Rick said.

Nicky held the smoke in his lungs, swallowing to push it down further. He handed Rick the joint.

"It was fun. Kinky. Women love it." He kept his eyes open as he puffed. "You'll have an advantage there. A definite advantage."

Rick was holding the joint too long, more than half was gone. Nicky held his shoulders stiff and tried not to mind.

Rick didn't understand that it wasn't about women. He said he did, but he didn't. But what Nicky hadn't understood until now was that it certainly could be about women. He

335

wanted to take his shirt off for Rick but was suddenly shy. It was crazy. Rick was just a guy. If he'd done it before, it should-n't make any difference.

"Do you ever, you know, on your own?" Nicky's voice croaked.

Rick took one last long puff then passed the joint back.

"Not really. I'm too public. People come in and out of here all the time."

Nicky thought on this. "If you did it, they'd think it was okay."

"Not true. They'd run me out of this town in a minute. They already think I'm corrupting minors, sleeping with their pubescent daughters, all that."

He winked as Nicky handed him the stub end.

Nicky liked the dirty sound of *pubescent*. He flared his nostrils. After smoking, his reactions sometimes happened despite him.

"Don't be naïve. I get those groupie types in here quite a bit. You're all groupies in a way. You want to be around a per-missive adult, to see how much I'll allow you to do. Your sister was into that trip for a little while there. How is she anyway? Are those her knickers you're wearing? Even I'd wear a pair of her panties if I could get my hands on them."

Nicky couldn't follow. He didn't like what Rick was saying, was offended even, especially when he remembered that Vi had visited here too. But in the thick early stages after smok-ing, his mouth was parched and it was difficult to find words.

His own sister. Had I been there like him just to hang out? Or was I another of the little groupies Rick liked to talk about? The little groupies must be the girls Nicky had seen in here who were younger than him even — fourteen, thirteen.

"Now your mother on the other hand, she's something else." Rick whistled through his front teeth. "There's a talented woman."

Nicky's head snapped up. "You don't know her. You haven't been here that long."

"Here, no. But in Apple Ford, sure. I had a river cottage — a Pan-Abode. Your mom came to my place for pottery lessons. Now that woman was wasted on this town. Anyone would say so. Like she landed into the wrong life. Though she got herself out of here remarkably well, considering. Crafty."

Rick scratched the back of his neck. "You look like her. Is that what all this is about?"

Nicky pushed himself up, the elastic of the panties digging into his skin. Without looking at Rick, he moved through heavy air to the door and burst outside.

"Been nice knowing you," Nicky said.

The rain had stopped and the air was dense out here too. He trudged up the hill but when he reached our house, he didn't go in. He placed one foot in front of the other and walked north toward the Trout Club.

"I have to say something else," Nicky says leaning back with his elbows on the steel rail. I can see his face in the textured-grey morning light.

"About what?"

"About her clothes. Tonight when you said about the pink shirt, before I went babysitting, I was afraid you knew. But when you said about the dress too it didn't matter."

"What didn't?"

"If you knew or didn't know."

"Because of the green dress?"

"Because of that. The pink shirt made me worry about what I was doing and what you thought, but the dress —"

"The dress what?"

"It reminded me of her."

"Because that's what she was wearing."

"Because that's what she was wearing the last time we saw her."

14

What Went Down

My hipbone ached where I leaned against the counter and the bump on my head throbbed. Nadette was talking to me — really talking to me, as if I were an adult — pushing in closer, cigarette tweaked between the first two fingers of her left hand. After every sentence she jerked the cigarette up to her mouth, squeezing the filter with her lips as if she were sucking a chickpea through a straw. Lines appeared above her lips, lines like pointed stubble that broke up the monotony of her large flat cheeks and heavy jaw.

I was learning all about the sins of Nadette's sister Carla and about my Uncle Larry's failings as a parent. We weren't far from where Larry sat playing euchre, but Nadette kept her voice low enough so just I could hear. Whenever someone entered the kitchen to refresh a drink, Nadette's voice trailed down to nothing; she stepped back from me and craned her neck around the room like a chicken with a silly smile. Unless it was Larry. Then she told him he was cut off.

In those pauses, I plotted my escape, measuring out the number of yellow linoleum tiles between my feet and the door, calculating the exact angle I needed to turn myself so I could slip away from my aunt and escape hearing about the soft mouldy core of Nadette's disappointment.

"Maybe I'd be better off if I was like her," Nadette said, flicking her hand and dismissing the outdoors. "At least your mother doesn't have to deal with all this." Her eyes prodded mine, accusing me, insisting I reveal the truth about my mother and where she was hiding. Like her face, Nadette's body was flat and wide — thick, but not heavy. She had Carla's black hair except hers was cut short and pushed off her face. I sank into the counter; whatever I answered, Nadette wouldn't believe me. Nadette had found me out. She knew I was secretive, knew I reserved my knowledge for myself.

When I had come inside earlier after hearing the scream, I went straight to the washroom and found a dark red syrup between my legs. It was as if the blood had been waiting, lying dormant until the scream and my discovery, because as soon as I found it, I jackknifed forward, my organs twisting and pulling and shooting pain up through my chest, neck and head.

I'd bled once before, at school in the spring, so I knew what to do. In hopes that it wouldn't come, I'd refused to carry the pads around with me in a paper bag as the school nurse suggested. She said we should mark it on our calendars but I couldn't bring myself to do this either. Marking it was like admitting it. Besides, if I marked the days, I was sure it would come more often.

When the pain subsided, I leaned over and opened Aunt Nadette's sink cabinet where I found a big box illustrated with a field of golden rod. I took out a maxi pad, removed the paper strip and fixed the pad to my stained gusset. The panties were tight to begin with, and when I pulled them up the bulge was noticeable, front and back. I turned and stared at the mess of blood, urine and paper for a long time, pressing my fists between my legs to flatten the pad.

I did up my jeans and checked the mirror, front and back, bending at the hips and looking through my knees to be sure the pad didn't show. It did and there was no way around it. If anyone noticed, if Uncle Reese made a joke about it, I would die. I pushed at the pad one more time and left the bathroom.

That was how I'd been found out. Aunt Shanelle had been to the bathroom right after me and had seen the evidence I'd neglected to flush. She reported it right to Nadette who, after several complaints about mothers taking responsibility, had cornered me to set me straight. Nadette started with the joys of womanhood and details of her every cramp, moved to Carla's first period and how *she* hadn't felt the need to hide it from anybody and she was only eleven when hers started, and finally latched onto the sad failure of her marriage and family.

Through it all, I couldn't erase the image of the gaping toilet bowl filled with my blood and urine and left open for anyone to see. What if one of my uncles had found it, or Nicky, or my father? Besides, while Nadette nattered on, something or someone was out there and nobody had found my mother. Sam and Reese had gone out to search the quarry but they came back drunker than they'd started, wet hair hand-slicked back. Soon afterward, Sam went out again, a fresh mickey in hand, but everyone else was in the living room listening to records and playing euchre at a folding card table. I propped my arm on the lip of the sink and wished for someone, anyone, to come into the kitchen.

Larry Sr. played the left bower and took a trick. He was going alone with an all-red hand and had a chance of controlling the entire court. His only obstacle was the ace of trump Vi was holding. Reese sat across from him, his hand covering the remaining deck.

Larry had stacked some Charley Pride and George Jones albums on the record player but the last one had died out before this deal. The talk was about cards, making trump, taking tricks. Often the room fell into silence, Nadette's voice in the kitchen smoothing out the background, rising and falling in oily confidential tones, immaculate words like scissortips that snipped, piece by piece, at every good thing anyone had ever seen in her husband, blades shaving away curl after curl until what was left was a stony pith that reminded everyone of what Nadette had been a fool to marry.

Larry led the right bower and sat back as Vi followed up with the queen and Shanelle played a throwaway ten. Larry considered his hand. There was no way of escaping Vi's ace. He folded the cards into his palm and picked up his glass, swishing the melted ice. Since she'd come downstairs, Nadette had been keeping close watch on his rum intake, so he hadn't refilled his glass for almost an hour.

"I'm not playing another card until I get some al-kee-hole in my system. I don't care what she says." He set down the glass.

"No you don't," Shanelle said. "At least wait until the end of this game. Two minutes from now, it'll be over."

"This is my house, and I'll drink when I want and play cards when I want. Do you want a beer? I've got some stashed where Nadette doesn't know."

Shanelle shrugged and Reese laughed as Larry stood up from the table. Vi lit up a cigarette and Shanelle went to change the records.

Larry passed behind Nadette into the back porch and stuck his arm into the top of the closet. He rummaged around tossing scarves and mitts over his shoulder and muttering about light. Nadette droned on.

Behind Larry came a familiar sound, like the riffling of cards. Larry ignored it, got down on his haunches and shoved through the boots. The sound came again, a contemplative scratching. This time, Larry turned, supporting himself on one knee. From where I stood, I could see a shadow settle over the screen door. A hand rose and fingers strummed the length of the screen; a faint crackle as the nails snicked over each tiny square.

It was her. She stood with one arm on her hip, the rest of her curled in as if she were trying to press herself through the mesh. Larry grabbed his flannel hunting cap, stuck it on his head and tiptoed over. He had found her. Not Sam. Not Reese. Him.

I was careful not to move so Nadette would have no indication of what was up. I willed Larry not to turn on the lights. She was an insect, a praying mantis folded up on his door; lights might scare her away.

He grasped the door latch and winced at Nadette's vinegar-laced voice behind him.

"Look at him. He thinks he's going to be a hero, or some such thing. He's just as crazy as she is. Believe me, I know. What a pair. They deserve each other."

She stood in the kitchen doorway, arms folded. Nadette may have thought she was speaking to me, but as soon as she turned I was out of the kitchen behind her back.

I walked through the living room on swift Indian feet. Luckily, Reese was leaning back in his seat, smoking with his eyes closed, or I would have had to endure more commentary. Charley Pride's warm tones drifted after me as I slipped out the front door: *Love her like the Devil when you get back home.*

By the time I got around the side of the house, the figure was gone. A smell lingered, like engine oil. Sweat and chrome and iron. Before I could take a step forward, Larry opened the door. One minute he was inside, body resounding with Nadette's jeers, and the next he was out in the air, wrapped in the machine scent of the shadowy figure.

I followed Larry around the back of the house where there were no windows and the light didn't reach. The ground here was hard under my thickened soles. The figure stood halfway along the back of the house, holding her straight-razor body near the wall. He stopped beside her.

Was it her? My mind leapt to the eyes of the creature screaming in the back of the hollowed-out Galaxie. Whoever this was was small, huddled. Sylvia was tall. Even at her worst, when she was all skin and bones, her posture was as upright as they came. "Imagine a cross on your back," she'd told me. Maybe this was someone else, someone local whom Larry knew. Possibly even The Dropout. Or Carla.

I edged along the house, the tarpaper smell, the odour of this whole sorry situation, coating my nostrils. I drew near enough to the figure to hear her shallow panting — whether it was brought on by excitement or crying, I couldn't tell. Her eyes looked off who knew where. Even with the all the stars and the quarter moon, her gaze evaded me. I wanted to cry. It was her, I was sure of it. Larry lifted his arm and picked at the edges of the tile on the side of the house.

She stayed motionless, elbow and hip jutting out. I could smell Larry's armpits.

I expected Nadette and the others to burst from the screen door but no one came. Though I knew I should say something or run back inside, I needed to witness this. Here was the closest I'd been to Sylvia's craziness, and I had to crawl right inside and see it from there.

Sylvia carried herself as if Larry wasn't there. As if she was alone. Larry forgot the tiles and peered closer, reaching for her shoulders and tugging at her bare arms. He had rough palms, I remembered, from working at the wrecking yard, one of Nadette's complaints that he could never get the black grime arcs out from under his fingernails. He grated his palms against the bare arm as if he were trying to shave away small parings of skin, like cheese or inch worms. Her hot grease smell filled the air, mingled with Larry's own sour scent. Then she lifted her other hand, the unnoticed one, the screen-scratching hand, and placed it on his forearm as if to steady him.

There was something wrong with the hand. It hung askew, as if pulled away from her arm, and even in the dark I could see it was discoloured. Her dress too had stains. When she moved again, I saw that the liquid ran down her arm like blood.

Larry opened his mouth as if to speak but no words came. Sylvia's fingertips tapped out patterns on the wall, the way they'd tapped on the table earlier. Larry responded by humming. Her fingers drummed faster, moving to his shoulders as he put his arms around her.

He shuffled closer. The rhythm was all over Larry and it wouldn't leave me either. Their smell sat on the back of my tongue like film. Sylvia didn't move, her eyes fixed on the shapeless dark beyond. With her arm folded up like a wing, her drumming fingers picked up the tempo, striking sixteenth notes now. A tune lively and without purpose.

Larry's humming died off. And I watched her let him wind his body around hers. Let him pin her arms. Wrap her around herself. Thrust her up against the wall so only her fingers could move. Her tale rolled fiercely from her fingers, her language at its most intense when her body was contained. A tiny moan came out, then a choke. Her fingers beat furiously to silence her throat.

Larry crammed her against the building, surrounding her. He mashed his face against her hair, his unshaven cheek rasping like sandpaper against the soft wall of the house. He stepped back, stretched up his arms and, with his palms braced, inhaled. His shirt lifted away from his pants and he slapped his belly against her. His right hand, the one farthest from me, fumbled between them.

His breath quickened and my mind blackened.

He rubbed himself against her belly. He wrapped his free arm around her shoulder and tried to rock with her, pushing at her with his desperate cold sweat energy. She was pliable, unresisting.

With the hunting cap cocked on the back of his head, he looped his far hand behind her neck and pulled her head forward, crushing her face against his neck. She succumbed, moving into each push, even anticipating him. Her compliancy frustrated him. He used stomach, chest and shoulders to pin her against the house. With both hands, he pulled her dress above her ribs. Her body shrank behind loose stretched panties. It looked like the blood was there too, streaked across her belly. The dryness in the air, in my throat, was unbearable.

For a long time nothing happened. Larry's hand stayed between them. He grimaced and banged against her, hard. He enveloped her once more, cradling her so tight, her fingertips were heavy with the effort of language.

He shoved her against the building. Again. And again. His arms bore most of the brunt. The rest, he absorbed through her body. Over and over they hit the tarpaper frame until his arms were pulped. It wasn't until Larry finally sank to the ground, releasing her, that I caught her singing, the low clear tones of a clarinet. Even without his clutching arms, she stayed attached to him. Curled into him. Suctioned on.

And then they were gone. Both of them. Disappeared into the trees beyond the house. I didn't see them go, and it was as if they had never been there. Even the smell of the air changed.

I was hollow now. As barren as she. There was no longer need. And nothing left to be done.

Stalling. Stalling. When small-engined aircraft stall, the pilot cuts the engine and lets the plane drop several hundred feet. Sometimes she lets the plane roll over, or sink into a nosedive, or spin. Whichever she decides, there are a few moments when she is seemingly out of control, where the plane is moving through the air of its own accord, spinning, looping, twisting toward the earth, gravity coaxing it down. Even though the pilot knows that at any time she can turn the engine back on and swing the nose upward, and that at some point she will have to do just this, there are those moments of falling, of blissful, uncontrolled falling, that are unlike any others. And of course there is the possibility that the engine won't start again.

Outside time had spun by, like blue sugar in a steel candy floss vat. Then I was indoors and Larry was back too. He swaggered into the living room, steps deliberate, thumbs slung through the belt loops of his work pants. He halted before the card table and scanned the room, fixing his open right eye first on his mother in the far corner, then Shanelle on the couch looking at album covers, Reese at the card table straightening and restraightening the deck, and finally Nadette across from him talking, still talking. Larry's cheeks hung loose with his lips pulled up in a purse string. It was a comical face, a face he often made drunk. But no one laughed.

He crossed and uncrossed his eyes, rolling them up then down, retracting his eyelids so the whites bugged out.

He tucked his top lip in and sputtered, "Wheresh muh dwink?"

Still, no one laughed.

Then they noticed his hands. Charley Pride sang about marbles standing stately in the hall. Larry's hands hung from his pants like the casual victors of a barroom brawl. His hands and most of his forearms were coated in blood. Thick, pulpy blood — not streaks — that looked shiny and undried.

I probed the bump where my head had hit the grille, digging it with a thumb. The hands could have only one meaning. They forced us to see past the possibility of accidents and into the certainty of flesh. Those hands were connected to us, were of our flesh, and what they were covered in was not due to chance.

Nadette shrieked, an angry squawk that sent Larry reeling, his eyes those of a deer under the gun.

Nadette soon reverted to words: "Goddamn you, Larry, what's wrong with you?" As though until then she'd reserved some measure of hope that nothing was.

Larry turned in an almost-run, his lower jaw hanging like a panting dog's. His bridgework had fallen out, leaving a gaping hole behind his front teeth.

The screen door slammed and Sam filled up the living room doorway; Nicky came down the stairs, followed by Larry Jr. and Carla.

One look at Sam caused Nadette's eyes to widen and her mouth to shut.

Larry froze. There was nowhere to go.

Sam was as drunk as Larry, possibly even more so. He entered the house smiling, confident that someone had found Sylvia or she was about to arrive. He looked at Larry in a glow of brotherhood, might have been about to embrace him, when he spotted Larry's hands jauntily hanging from his belt loops. Later I remembered what I expected from the moment more than the moment itself: I expected Sam to get angry, to take Larry outside and beat him into a paste, bashing his head with a rock clawed from that hard resistant dirt.

I never figured out why he hadn't done that. Though I was glad he hadn't, it felt like it would have been the right thing for him to do.

Instead, Sam had collapsed, head in hands, into a folding chair, nearly toppling it backward. He squeezed his eyes as if against probing razor blades, and howled.

I stepped back and knocked into Nicky. My mind went back to Sam's golden red head the day a few weeks ago when he'd brought Sylvia home. His head still carried the burn of summer, the red jerky-blackened, an anger in the bare skin on top that was safe. As long as that anger was there, as long as the skin on my father's head shone red, I was protected. I could watch my Uncle Larry's bloody hands with coolness even though those hands made me want to sink to the floor and scream too, scream until my guts poured forth from my throat. My father's head, bent over his lap, vulnerable in its rage, was my talisman. Looking at it, I could believe that the blood had been there before Larry had even come near her, that Larry hadn't caused the blood, that the blood was an accident.

Nicky went straight to Vi and dropped in her lap. I hung against the wall between the stairs and the kitchen, not knowing whether to stand or sit. I told myself it was because no one had asked that I hadn't offered up what I'd seen, behind the house or even earlier in the car but even if they did ask I didn't trust that I could tell.

Everyone talked at once. Larry held still in the middle of the room, his eyes rolling from exit to exit, waiting for someone to move out of the way.

Nadette's voice rose above the rest: "We don't know what happened. The bastard could have — well, it doesn't have to be as serious as it looks." She sidled up to Larry, her hips just in front of his hands, her gaze a sneer. "Tell us, Larry. Tell us what happened. And don't you damn well lie because you know I can tell when you're lying. Don't you spare us one detail."

The others pressed in behind her, demanding to know what happened.

What happened. What happened. Like lines of memorized poetry from Advanced English, these words revolved in my brain. *The evil that men do.* Larry rolled his eyes over to Sam, then swept his gaze around the room, taking in the drooping ceiling tiles with their brown teacup stains; the unlit corners; the cracked, duct-taped, vinyl furniture; the grimy linoleum; the mould on the baseboard.

Larry laughed. At first a low choking gurgle in the back of his throat. Then it escalated, high and out of control, an idiot's bawl, or a rabbit's scream.

He took in what he had always called "this sorry excuse for a house" and laughed at it, at all of it. His mother with her rotting stomach and all the caved-in, horrified faces of his relatives turned toward him. As if it mattered. We were all so concerned about a crazy woman: where she had gone and what had happened to her, but that was just it: she was crazy. Didn't that say it all? There was no bringing her back. She wasn't who we thought she was, who we expected her to be. Yet, everyone's face stayed pinched and frowning. There was nothing to do but laugh.

Nadette's hand cracked solidly against his cheekbone, the sting a thrill, knocking his vocal cords into action.

"You want to know what happened?" he shrieked, his falsetto voice higher than a woman's even. "I'll tell you what goddamn well happened. Nothing. She's gone. She's gone where you'll never find her — and it doesn't matter, Sam, because she was no good for you. She didn't want you and you didn't want her. I know how that feels. And if I had my way I'd have gone too. I wouldn't be stuck in this sorry excuse for a house with *her*." He pointed at Nadette.

I'd never heard him say this many words before. There were more, pushing at his throat, more words for Nadette, his mother — hell, even his wife's sister sitting there on the stairs. He'd finally opened his mouth and what he had to say — what he'd been holding inside for all these years — really was so loathsome it stopped everyone in their tracks. But he wasn't a terrible man. Maybe what was coming out seemed so nasty because it had stayed inside him so long.

The words seemed wrong even though they were against Nadette whom he hated, it was clear now, hated with more energy than he'd devoted to anything in years, his hate a never-ending, narrow stream of piss hitting the dirt.

"Is she okay? That's all we want to know." Shanelle in Larry's left ear, her voice soft butter, her eyes trying to catch Larry's own, which wouldn't stop rolling, scanning this room over and over, jerking obsessively from object to object, from the lampshade so thin he could see the light bulb through it, to Nadette's ceramic horse beside the record player.

"That's right. We're not going to hurt you. Just tell us the truth." Reese on his right side — not laughing now, not even with him, his voice scary serious. One arm slipped around Larry's back, the other pushing at Nadette, his eyes stern, insisting she back off.

This look of Reese's calmed Larry down. Reese, the brother closest to him in age, knew to get Nadette away from him.

Nadette took the look further and went to the kitchen telephone.

"Lester," she said into the receiver, "you'd better get over here right away. We got a disturbance." Her voice dropped. "Possibly murder."

I couldn't hold on to the thought of my mother's death. *Murder.* I sat on the floor in a state of remembering I had something important to address, something momentous to absorb, some enormous emotion to express. I skated across possibility and skidded into Plexiglas walls that held me for brief broken-hearted moments then flung me out, spinning back into the confusing thick of things. *She's dead, her death, gone away, dust.* I formulated catch phrases to hang onto and got closer and closer. *Murder. Victim. Body. Corpse.* The true-crimes I'd read at Vi's pulled me through. The details. Millions of tiny details, like dots in a newspaper photograph, there for me to hold.

Sam raised his head and peered through the lattice of his fingers.

Larry sat on the cockled red and black couch, Shanelle on one side and Reese on the other, arms crossed, hands cupping elbows, the way Sylvia would stand, her hands inside a sweater if she was wearing one.

I held myself in this thought. Such tenderness in Sylvia's elbows, dry with eraser-pink ridges like the scars ribbing her wrists. But I felt no sadness. Or rather my sadness held no difference. The sadness that was already there, the longing I'd been carrying despite myself all summer and longer and calling love, was so great and so complete that the death of my mother could not deepen it.

I tested the sadness, allowed myself to picture Sylvia's hands, their wide hard knuckles spread with round comfortable grooves, then her oblong calves and triangle-hat ankles. I found my sadness would not topple, would not make room for grief.

Sam slapped his palms on his knees and shook himself out of the chair. He looked right at Larry whose eyes finally stopped rolling and met his.

This small triumph made Sam almost cheerful, as cheerful as one could be. He was making contact. My father would push right through this bloodied mess and get to the crux of what his brother had done. The details were important but grief unnecessary. Sylvia was damaged before she'd come here. Nothing Larry could have done was worse than that.

Murdered. Nadette said he was a murderer, carried his trespass in the grains of his skin. So much blood. The Shakespeare we'd studied had a line in it about blood, blood that would not wash off even though layers and layers of skin had peeled away. *Who would have thought the old man to have had so much blood in him.* I didn't want to believe Nadette when she said murder. But who could deny those hands, those wrinkles finely threaded with blood? *Is she dead? Did you kill her?* What few courtesies the members of my family had built up among themselves over the years were stripped away now that the police were about to arrive and one of our own sat on his sagging rectangular couch with vivid red hands.

Two policeman came in through the back porch. I'd seen both before at dances. They'd gone to Drag High with Sam and Larry; one of them, the taller, had been in Sam's class. His name was Lester Frank. The other was Russ Newman. They sat at the kitchen table and drank coffee while Nadette gave a statement.

"We'll take him in," Lester Frank, the more talkative one, said. "But we've got no murder charge without a body."

Sam nodded and rapped Lester's shoulder.

"Don't know what we can charge him with at all, really, but we'll take him in, if that's what you want." Lester slurped the last of his coffee.

"That's what I want," Nadette declared.

The officers had no fight as they escorted Larry to the car. His hands glared, palms puckered as they'd been since he was a boy. Vi told me how at night she used to smear Larry's hands with petroleum jelly and force him to wear cotton gloves to bed. Four times a year, when she helped the church sort clothing for their white elephant and rummage sales, Vi would pull out the women's dress gloves — yellow, blue, green — for Larry before she gave the sorted bags back. Most pairs were small enough to fit a child. Each morning she rinsed the gloves and laid them in the sunshine or beside the stove.

Those hands. Those hands on Sylvia's neck, fingers scraping her ribs, ripping the skinny flesh from her bones, digging through her like a child's hands in mud. Those hands trapped in steel circles and led away.

It was easy to slip out of the house with everyone so weird about Uncle Larry. Even Carla was subdued, if only because she was witnessing what she'd long desired: the spectacle of Nadette's ruin. The burnt-beef skin on the top of my father's head — its outrage at the family — propelled me.

As long as he could remember, Sam had been trying to walk like an Indian, to step through life without noise, leaving no trail, no clue of where he'd come from or where he was going. But he *had* left traces: Nicky and I were trace enough. And Sylvia. Her absences, her craziness — Sam's inescapable desire for her sounded all over him like firecracker explosions. She was the one without history, without future. We couldn't even latch onto her in the present.

My uncle's brain was obviously mush; getting his story was a waste of time. The story was already there in his bloodied hands and stupid revolving eyes. And I knew what I'd seen. Sylvia had been murdered. The simplicity of this fact calmed me. The real story was Sylvia's body. I could not fully believe in her death until I could touch the body. And the police — they needed a body too.

It was cooler now, the moon farther along its arcing path. The silence had an almost-hum, the mayhem from the house receding.

I tried it now — walking like an Indian. It came naturally to me to step this way, heel then toe, my body light, the air lifting me in a million tiny places. Doing the walk consoled me. I closed my eyes. It was important that I not see my mother's body first, that its mess not be able to imprint on my mind's eye before our flesh touched. Only through contact could I pull Sylvia's loss of life inside my own skin.

I wandered this way for a long time, convincing myself that my eyes were open and I was walking around in a place so utterly dark as to not reveal shadows or shapes. I didn't stumble, my path purposeful. My eyelids fluttered open once, then stayed that way, and I went back over the yard and combed every inch, from the house outward, eyes so wide they blinked frantically shut every minute or so. I strayed farther, certain my uncle must have dragged my mother's body to a hiding place, or even committed a final act in secrecy, perhaps in the woods.

The sky behind the trees lightened as I entered long grass, the blades leaving wet trails on my calves. Grasshoppers smashed under my feet, the lucky ones clicking sideways into the weeds. Moths landed with soft thuds on my cheeks and the front of my sweatshirt. I was disturbing a world of insects, a world that would not permit silent passage. I doubted that even Indians could be out here noiselessly: mosquitoes whining around my ears, my foot splashing into an old puddle, the grass. How to part the knee-length grass and pass through it without a sound.

I was ready to go to the outer edges of Larry's property if need be, and beyond. I would not rest until I had laid my hands on Sylvia's murdered skin.

VI

15

The One I Desired

Though I never did find her body, what I did find was significant. My feet led me right back to the hollowed-out Galaxie that cradled the wild-eyed creature whose scream got the whole night's events under way. I crawled through the window into the back seat, where I'd seen the eyes. It didn't matter whether the wretch was still there. I had to check every square inch of space on Larry's property, even if that meant creeping through every gutted wreck there was.

And what I found was blood: a great pool of sticky blood all over the back seat. The vinyl was ripped and a spring jutted out. The spring too: coated in blood.

I knew whose blood it was. The wild-eyed screamer was her. She had been bleeding before she even came up to the house and scratched on the door.

My cheeks burn. In the addition, Vi, Nicky and I are sitting on lawn chairs around a milk-crate table eating French pancakes — crêpes with melted butter, brown sugar and lemon rolled up inside. A Sylvia special. Mugs of cold tea rest beside our plates. Sam has left for work but it is early yet, though neither Nicky nor I has slept.

Vi hugs herself inside her caftan and I rub my fingertips into the unfinished floor. A roll of burgundy carpet and another of speckled underpad lean against the closet wall. Sam is letting Nicky and me decorate the new room. After breakfast, we're driving Vi's Impala into town to buy sage-green paint for the walls and dusty rose cotton so Vi can sew balloon blinds. Sam will show us how to lay the carpet.

The off-and-on rain has ended and the morning drips in the sun. *The sun always shines on this day.* Except my birthday was yesterday. My seventeenth. It rained and we missed it. All of us. Sam has promised to bring home cherry cheesecake and a bucket of chicken tonight.

I forgot about the ripped car seat and the blood-covered coil. Most likely Sylvia stabbed herself, possibly on purpose. Maybe Sylvia was already dead by the time she came back to scratch the screen at Larry's house. Maybe she was a ghost. Maybe the blood on Larry's hands was Sylvia's blood from before and had nothing to do with what he'd done. But what *had* he done? Sylvia hadn't resisted any of his moves, her only voice her fingers' entreating tattoo. Had I read her wrong? Had her song been one of desire?

"Why didn't you tell?" Vi asks and I have no answer for her. If I didn't tell, I could keep Sylvia alive to chance. Saying the story sets it into a truth. Yet nobody but Sylvia will ever know the truth. My telling might have made a difference to

Larry, but it changes nothing for Sylvia and nothing for me. Sylvia is gone, dead, one way or another.

Larry was held overnight but never charged. The police treated the situation as the familiar kind of domestic disturbance and returned Larry to Nadette and everybody went on. They even went to the dance though Sam didn't and I loved him for that. I loved him too for letting us stay in Drag County to look for her. The official search began on the Sunday but Sylvia's trail was cold and we went home, then back to school a week late, without her.

"I'm telling now," I say finally. Vi nods. Nicky's lips ease up wide in a smile and he lets his hair fall forward. He stretches his legs out and arches his feet. His own caftan falls loose across his middle. It has to be enough.

Nicky watched as Duncan jumped on the bed of a pickup and threw himself on me and another guy. Nicky wanted no part of Duncan's attack. He knew Duncan well enough to know he didn't usually fight. Besides, if Nicky fought, someone might discover what he was wearing.

"My clothes were a totem, protecting me," Nicky said this morning, balancing sure-footed in the auroral light as we tight-roped the smooth rails single file toward home. "But I would have stripped them off if I'd thought it would make a difference." He wanted my eyes and nobody else's to rest on him without his regular clothes. We'd shared everything, even Rick.

At first, Nicky thought it was Rick in the back of the pick-up with me. He could have driven up to the Trout Club on a different sideroad than the one Nicky had walked along. Now Nicky wasn't so sure. Even if it was Rick, Nicky would wait. He was used to waiting. He'd waited for our mother all these years — he could certainly wait out a lovers' tiff for me. He scratched at the waistband of the underwear and hoped the fight would end soon.

"Get her out of here or I'll kill her." Duncan's eyes drilled into Levon's. Levon propped his sprawled body up with his elbows, his legs oddly straight.

Duncan's knee was shoved against my ribs, but otherwise he took no notice of me tugging on my jeans. He was angrier than I'd ever seen him, but I understood. I would feel the same if I caught Rick in bed another woman, even now. I expected Levon to tell Duncan to fuck off, but Levon was riveted in place.

I jabbed Duncan's knee, then flipped my head back and thrust my jaw open with a loud crack. My face rang with pain.

"Duncan. Nothing's going to happen with you and me. I already told you. You even said that's not what you wanted. So what are you doing here? There's no reason to fight."

"Shut up. You're wrong."

"I'm wrong? You come here to beat us up and yell shut up and you think I'm the one who's wrong?"

Duncan glanced at me then back at Levon, who hadn't moved.

"Duncan! What is your problem?"

I edged back, my teeth parted in case I had to use them.

"Levon, get rid of her. I mean it." Duncan spoke in a growl.

Levon stayed still. I glared at him too, willing him to action. He had pulled back into a corner, his arms around his knees. I touched his wrist and he shrank further. Duncan slapped me away and took Levon's hand. Levon held on.

"Mercy, some things happen that are beyond your reach. We were just fooling around," Levon said.

"We?" I asked, suddenly unsure whether he meant he and I, or he and Duncan.

"We were just having fun. You had a story to tell and I helped you say it. It felt good but it's better if you let this alone." His hands rotated his kneecaps.

I tucked in my polo shirt and buckled my belt then crawled out of the truck bed without another word. One thing was evident: I was not wanted here. The Levon whose stories had run through my hands, glittering, smooth and elusive, was gone.

My mind was clear. Either the dreams had subsided or I was having a new dream. A new forest, new scratches, new mud to smear on my skin. I had no sense of direction and turned my back on Levon and Duncan as if they had never existed, as if minutes earlier I hadn't clamped my thighs around Levon's waist and clutched him inside me, trying to draw his stories from him.

My thoughts were on escape only, on the crackle of leaves under foot, on ducking beneath branches that threatened to slap. When I was halted and wrapped into arms, I did not startle. My embracer was merely a tree that had reached out to enfold me, long stick arms, thin solid trunk. Everyone was squeezing me, Duncan, Levon, Rick. My mother. I writhed at the thought of Mother.

I hoped Duncan was the one holding me. I wanted him not to be unpredictable and fighting, spilling over with pushed-down emotion. I wanted him back in the place where he told me his problems and I could say anything and think anything without having to change myself. Duncan was the only person who hadn't grabbed hold of my mind, urging me into fantasies,

pulling me into obsession. As much as I'd insisted on my line-
age, on my right to go crazy, it was more important than I had
realized that Duncan think I was okay. Duncan was not supposed to have feelings for someone else, to fall in love, if what
Levon said was true. Duncan was the person who dried the
dishes beside me and told me his problems, just as Levon told
me his stories. Nothing else. Duncan's steel-trap cunts seemed
part of the landscape of the Mother dreams now. I should kill
Duncan, hollow out his eyes. It was Duncan's flesh I should
bite and scoop, bite and scoop.

I twisted and strained, then gave up and sank into the
embrace. I was clasped so close, I could not see who it was.
My knees were bent and my face mashed against the chest
and shoulder of the one holding me. It might be a woman,
and I flashed back to the dream of lying flat on a hotel bed
next to Mother. I clung, my torso limp, and sobs wrenched
forth. I did not want my body, for all its desires, to be near
another's. I was giving up, giving in. I could have all the bodies and all the dreams I wanted. This embrace would never be
the one I desired.

My tears were the big kind that rolled free. The tears fell
and fell. I was liquid, but the arms held me, like the pear
branches I'd lain in as a child. I hadn't climbed a tree since
then, and would have liked nothing better than to be cradled
by branches, by wood flowing with life, with sap, with songs.

These arms holding me were flesh as strong as branches.
When my crying subsided, I was hearing a song — sobs and
tears not my own. Sorrow. The grip on me released and I was
loose enough now to stand up straight and see who it was.

When I saw my mother's black shining eyes in Nicky's
gaze, I squeezed him as hard as I could then stepped back. We

were close, inches apart. Our eyes were level, our hearts beat in tandem, our breaths mingled in the air before being inhaled again as one.

Nicky was the one who should hear about the dreams; now was the time. But the memory of locking Nicky in the closet and filling him with the witch-mother stopped me. The dead mother who baffled me in dreams was more frightening than any smelly, parsnip-nosed evil spirit I'd made up as a child. Nicky looked about to kiss me — not as Levon had, but in a way that would clear the air, unite us forever, create magic and bring our mother back into our circle so our lives wouldn't have to be this world of dreams and obsessions, this coming together in the woods.

He stepped back and lifted his T-shirt. When he was done, his clothes lay in a heap on the forest floor. His thick jet hair traced with crimson flowed over his ears and into the corners where his neck met his shoulders. The underwear stretched across him, the way leaves reach out from a branch.

He was beautiful and I said so.

Acknowledgements

I would like to acknowledge the Toronto Arts Council and the Vermont Studio Center for their generous financial and artistic support and say thank you to the Humber School for Writers and everyone at Dundurn for their energy and vision.

My warmest gratitude goes out to my friends, whose faith and guidance, editorial and otherwise, has sustained me.

— *Sally Cooper*